THE LiTTLe
DRAGONS

Amy McDonald

THE LiTTLe DRAGONS

Rowan Starsmith

With illustrations by Amy McDonald

Tigh na Cailleach
Falmouth NS

Published by Tigh na Cailleach
R.R.#1, Falmouth NS
B0P 1L0 Canada

Comments on *The Little Dragons:*

I was thoroughly enchanted and delighted by the best book I have listened to in a very long time. It is a well-crafted world of fantasy; man-eating dragons, little dragons, unfaithful kings, banished queens and princesses, Earth people, King's men, witch healers, and Little Dragon Keepers all trying to survive in a very believable world. As a well-written story should, it got under my skin. I laughed, gasped in surprise, cheered on and cried. It will be in my mind for a very long time.
Arlene Radasky, author of The Fox.

This is an awesome book! I love the author's boldness, writing outside the box, giving me twists and turns and unexpected plots. This is a nice long story where you get character development in the first ten or so chapters, then get the rest of the book to continue traveling along with people you now know and love (or hate).
Cynikat, Podiobooks subscriber.

Absolutely marvelous! PLEASE give me more! A wonderfully fresh take on an old theme. When the secret of the Little Dragons was revealed it was a shocker to me. It never entered my mind that would even be possible. Thank you.
Jonel Thomas, Smashwords edition reader

I absolutely loved this book. The only disappointing thing about it - it ended too soon. Which is not due to the story being short, but due to the fact I just couldn't put it down. I hope additional fantasy works (whether connected to this realm or not) by this author are planned for the future.
Deneene Curry, Smashwords edition reader.

Have just finished your wonderful book!! Absolutely amazing, totally draws you in and have been unable to put it down. You can imagine then my dismay to find out there is no sequel? Please, please, please, let me know when you write another.
Nikki Anderson, Smashwords Edition reader.

This is the most delightful book I've read in a long time, and believe me, as a disabled retiree, I read a LOT. Nothing in the plot seemed too far fetched nor ridiculous as can sometimes happen even in a fantasy story. I truly hope Ms. Starsmith continues the storyline since there are still problems to solve in the realm.

Kathleen Swinney, Smashwords edition reader.

PROLOGUE: THE DRAGONS

Old as the Night
Shimmering rivers of scales
Woven into ancient roots of our mountains
Creatures of Water and Earth
We sleep.

Touched by Sun we burst forth
Glittering creatures of Fire and Air
We hunt.

Hungry
Always hungry
Our Keepers dead by the sword
Their herds of cattle stolen
Now we hunt
Hungry

Listen
Someone approaching
An Old One
One-Who-Remembers
They, too, almost gone

MOTHER PEG

Crazy old woman! Mother Peg grumbled to herself. She used her walking stick to slash at a branch that had fallen across the path. Her small travel lantern shook and rattled, turning the trees around her into wildly dancing shadow-creatures. You're too old for this. What if you fall and can't get up? It's not like the main path, where someone might come along and find you.

While she caught her breath, she lifted her lantern to study the woods. This trail was as old as the memory of the People. How far had she come? Should she not have reached it by now? "I'm not lost," she announced to the trees. Her voice disappeared instantly, absorbed by the creaking forest night.

She pushed on. Another thorny bush grabbed at her skirt, another stone caught at her foot. Then a sharp turn, a tiny clearing, and there it was. "Well," she said aloud. "Well then."

Her lantern lit a stone surface eaten away by centuries of lichen and weather. The sharp details of the carving were gone, but still the Dragon curled around his tree, sinuous and terrible, his eyes filled with power, wisdom and pain. This was one of only three Dragonstones remaining in the Eastlands. There were others, particularly in the Northlands. Because of their isolated locations, the Kings had missed these few in their obsession to destroy the Dragon Priestesses and every mark they had ever left on the landscape, along with their precious knowledge.

Mother Peg's narrow chest filled with longing to the point of pain. The Dragon Priestesses and their Familiars, the Little Dragons, channels between the Great Dragons and the People, had made it possible to live well in the Land, in the light of day.

Once Mother Peg would have fallen to her knees before the Dragonstone. If she did that now, she might never get up again. She bowed her head, leaning heavily on her walking stick, and reached into a pocket of her skirt for some of the Sacred Herbs she carried there.

"Please, Great Dragons, Little Dragons, wherever you have gone, there is so little time left. All I want is to find clues to what the Dragon Priestesses knew. I have Healed many People in my time, taught many Apprentices, but all I ever truly wanted to leave behind is a key, or even part of a key, to the secrets of the Dragon Priestesses."

A flake of snow danced with lazy grace through the light of Mother Peg's travel lantern, then another. They were the fluffy, isolated snowflakes of Spring, but they shook Mother Peg out of her prayer. She was cold, and there were all those hurdles to cross again on her way back to the main path. She scattered the Sacred Herbs at the foot of the Dragonstone and, turning awkwardly, began to hobble back the way she had come.

JESSA

Between themselves, Ev and Jessa called the scullery "The Dungeon," not only because it was a windowless stone room, but because this was where they were sent every time they were caught breaking the rules. The kitchen, just outside the door, bustled with activity, warmed by its open hearth, brick bake-oven and the many lanterns hanging from hooks high on the walls. The scullery was cool, quiet and damp. Its single lantern cast angular shadows from cans of milk and cream standing in a shallow stone trough along one side of the room. An array of pots and buckets sat upside-down on racks along the opposite wall. Shelves held cheeses and eggs, meats and vegetables, anything that needed chilling. The cool dampness came from a small spring bubbling through a pipe in the wall at one end of the trough and draining out the other end.

Their assignment was usually peeling potatoes, and this was exactly what they were doing, seated on low wooden stools on either side of a large wooden bucket. Their elbows rested on its rim and their small knives sent long brown curls of peel into its depths. At least, Ev made long brown curls of peel. Jessa watched her friend's slender, brown hands working quickly and carefully at the same time, the way Ev did everything. Jessa's potatoes tended to shed their skins in ragged chunks. This was the third and final day of their latest exile. Jessa grinned.

"What?" Ev asked her.

"The look on Sister Mattia's face when she caught me in that dress!" Both girls giggled quietly. It wouldn't be a good idea to be heard by the other servants in the kitchen.

"Oh, but Jessa," Ev said, "It's a beautiful dress!"

A new Widow had arrived four days before. The Widows were high-born women whose husbands were dead and children grown. No longer useful to their families, they often chose, or were forced, to retire to the Women's Retreat House. They had rooms on the upper floor, poor compared to the mansions and castles they came from, but comfortable by the standards of this place. They prayed with the Sisters and most of them worked in the embroidery room making robes and hangings for castles and churches. They wore the same grey dress as the Sisters, although their veils were black.

The new Widow had brought two silk dresses for her journey to the Retreat House. Ev and Jessa were given the job of cleaning and pressing them for sale in the market. Jessa just couldn't help herself. She had to try one on.

"Oh! You're so beautiful! It matches your eyes!" Ev had exclaimed, raising her work-worn hands to her mouth while her friend danced around the room, swirling the brilliant blue skirt around her ankles. Jessa had pulled off the grey scarf that covered her hair and tossed away the pins that imprisoned it in a tight bun. It billowed in a thick golden curtain around her happy face. Sister Mattia had chosen that moment to walk in.

Ev went back to peeling potatoes while Jessa sighed and looked down at her rough grey dress, the standard uniform of a servant in the Women's Retreat House. "I wonder what jewels she wore with that dress. Do you think she had sapphires that same shade of blue? Set in worked silver? Around her neck and hanging from her ears?" she asked.

"Oh Jessa …" Ev began, but stopped and turned toward the door. There was music somewhere, just faintly audible, not the singing they did in the Women's Retreat House, but pipes and horns and drums. The kitchen was quiet. Jessa leaped from her stool and ran to the door. She peeked out carefully. Lanterns shone on rows of pots hanging on hooks, dishes stacked on shelves, long worktables strewn with cutting boards and tools. The fire crackled in the hearth, but no one was there. It must be midnight prayer time, when all the servants joined the Sisters and Widows in the chapel. The kitchen servants had forgotten the two disgraced young women in the scullery.

Delighted, Jessa ran across the kitchen to a window looking out across the Cathedral Square. The music was much louder now. The Square was lit with many lanterns, and bobbing torches entered from a street to the right of the Women's Retreat House. "It's a procession!" Jessa said to Ev, who had joined her. "Come!" She grabbed Ev's sleeve and pulled her across the kitchen. Ev resisted for a second, a frown crossing her face, then broke into a grin and ran after her friend.

A stone passageway on the far side of the kitchen led past wooden storeroom doors to an arch framing the bottom step of a circular stair. Jessa in the lead, the two young women gathered their skirts and ran up the dark steps, their dirty bare feet slapping on the stones.

Although they wore identical grey dresses and scarves, and were both medium-tall, they could have been from opposing sides of a set of playing-pieces. Jessa's pale colouring contrasted with Ev's dark complexion, her shining black hair and eyes. Ev was slender and wiry, while Jessa was built, as Sister Fidelity, the Cook, loved to say, like a brick house.

The Women's Retreat House leaned against the long side of the Cathedral and the tower stood at its outside corner. When they arrived, gasping, at the top, they ran across an open stone floor to a parapet. From here they could look down over the Square, across the wide front steps of the Cathedral to the Men's Retreat House, built against its other side. A tower matching their own marked its farthest corner. Over there a lantern faintly outlined a large group of men watching from their parapet. The Brothers in the Men's Retreat House were allowed out in public much more than the residents of the Women's House. In fact, many of their assigned tasks took them out for days at a time. Jessa cast a little spark of envy in their direction, but in a moment her attention was drawn to the scene unfolding below.

The procession passed in front of the Women's Retreat House and stopped in front of the Cathedral. Well-dressed men with torches and musical instruments, soldiers on horseback and glittering carriages stood in a line beneath them. The largest carriage, pulled by four horses, stood right in front of the Cathedral steps.

As they watched, four men stepped down from the carriage behind the large one and walked forward. Their colourful cloaks swirled around their feet and feathers swayed on their broad-brimmed hats.

"Look," Jessa whispered. "Princes. Or Noblemen of the Realm."

As she spoke the men placed themselves in a line between the large carriage and the Cathedral steps. In dramatic unison, they swept off their hats and held them at their sides. Jessa leaned forward to study them, tall and short, fair and brown, all with neatly trimmed hair and beards.

"Look at the tall one with the curly brown hair," Jessa squealed. "Isn't he handsome?" Ev nodded vaguely, but looked instead at the dreamy, delighted expression on Jessa's face.

A servant opened the door of the large carriage, and one of the men stepped forward and offered his hand. A woman stepped out and Jessa held her breath. Torchlight reflected softly from yards of brilliant while silk. Jewels glittered from neckline, bodice and hem. More shone from the woman's wrists, hands and ears. Her skirt was so large, a maid had to help her free it from the carriage and then walked behind her, holding it up so it wouldn't drag on the dirty cobblestones.

"A wedding," Ev whispered. "I wonder who she is."

"A princess!" Jessa breathed the words. "Or at least a noblewoman, probably marrying a prince or a powerful Man of the Realm." They watched as the woman and her retinue disappeared inside the Cathedral. "Oh Ev! Why wasn't I born to that?"

"Maybe you were."

Some orphans raised in the Women's Retreat House knew where they came from. Ev was one of these. Her mother, a servant in a wealthy household, died when she was eight years old. Her mother's employers had given her to the Retreat House, but she had occasional visits from her mother's relatives. Others came as babies, many simply abandoned on the front steps, with no idea of their origin. Jessa was one of these. Whether their past was known or not, however, once adopted by the Women's Retreat House their future was all the same. They would live and die as servants, taking care of Sisters and Widows under the rule of the Head Mother.

"Jessa," Ev turned to her friend, her brow creased in concern. "I started to say this downstairs. Please don't torment yourself with what you can't have. It makes you unhappy …"

Jessa did not hear. She wrapped her arms around herself. "What would it be like?" she said, "To dance in the arms of your husband? Your own Prince?" She began to move back and forth, humming a tune she imagined would be played on the glittering dance floor of a Royal reception. Suddenly she unwrapped her arms from herself and threw them around Ev, pulling her into a swaying imitation of a couple sliding across the polished wood of a ballroom floor. Ev tensed, then surrendered herself to the motion, giggling.

Just then a voice came from the stairs. "Is someone up here?" Sister Tibelda emerged, lantern in hand. They were caught again. Another three days in The Dungeon.

MOTHER PEG

Mother Peg stood at the edge of the woods. She leaned heavily on her walking stick and frowned at the sky. Dawn was approaching, painting faint peach streaks across the eastern horizon. The path at her feet was clearly visible now, winding out across the Barrens. Peg abruptly lifted the chimney of her small travelling lantern, useless now, and blew out the flame. No one could make it across the Barrens in daylight, let alone an old woman with a walking stick. As if to remind her of the danger, an ominous shadow appeared, outlined by the brightening sky. A sinuous, reptilian body beat huge translucent wings in effortless flight. The hairs stood up on the back of Peg's neck, although the Dragon was miles away. Using her stick for support, she turned and hobbled slowly back into the sheltering trees.

A few hundred feet back, a wooden cabin stood beside the path. The Order of Healers kept it for eastward travellers caught by daylight at the Barren's edge. Peg stepped inside. It was tiny, holding just a bed, table and bench, a cupboard and a small woodstove. Peg slid her light pack awkwardly from her shoulders to the bench, setting her lantern beside it. She hobbled to the cupboard and looked inside. As she knew it would be, it was stocked with a few fresh provisions. She had probably just missed the Healers who brought them. In the days leading up to Spring Equinox, Healers patrolled the roads welcoming members of the Order travelling from every corner of the Realm to the most important Gathering of the year.

Peg turned to face the east, where the sun would now be rising above the horizon, and said the shortest form of the Morning Prayer. Then she unwrapped bread and cheese from a square of oiled linen cloth, cut herself a few pieces and ate sitting on the side of the bed. She wrestled with the ties on her laced bodice, growling at her stiff old fingers. With the ties finally loosened, she gathered the neatly folded comforter to her shoulders and lowered herself clumsily to the soft mattress. Despite her exhaustion and the clean straw beneath her, however, the wooden frame of the bed ground against her old bones and kept her awake well into the day.

Peg started awake. She had heard a voice. Then she remembered where she was, the Healers' cabin on the west side of the Barrens. These were surely Healers, coming to see if a traveller had been stranded here at dawn. It was dark, so she must have slept after all. The voice came again and Peg recognized it. In a few minutes, her memory produced a name, Sister Martha.

"Hello? Is someone here?" Lantern light touched the wall over the bed. Peg tried to speak but her voice, unused for several days, came out as a croak. Martha opened the door and shone her lantern inside. "Mother Peg! Are you all right?" Martha stepped over to the side of the bed. There was a young man with her.

"Yes, yes, I'm all right. Just help me up."

Peg had to admit they were efficient. In minutes they had gently lifted her to a sitting position, straightened her blouse and re-tied her bodice. Martha even took out Peg's braid, brushed her hair, tangled from days of travel, and neatly braided it again. Well, they should be efficient, Peg thought. They're Healers, after all.

"Mother Peg," said Martha, indicating the young man, "This is Katten, my new Apprentice." Katten bobbed his head politely. He was cutting slices from the loaf Peg had left on the bench the night before. Martha continued. "Are you travelling alone? Where is Maida?"

"Someone has to take care of those noisy chickens and goats." Martha raised her eyebrows, took a breath as if to say something, but Mother Peg cut her off. "Also, we have a young man living with us, one of the King's People. I could hardly bring him here."

"Living with you?" Martha looked startled.

"He's very young, and ..." Peg tapped the side of her head.

Martha understood immediately. "Oh. They tied him out for the Dragons." Peg nodded and Martha grimaced. "However did he escape?"

"I don't know. A pair of shepherds found him, near collapse from exhaustion, and brought him to us. He had some Dragon scratches on him, but not very deep."

"A young man, you said?" Peg nodded. "I wonder how he lived long enough to grow up."

"Hidden, I suppose. He can speak a few one-syllable words, but he is silent most of the time, and he is used to going about his work in the dark with no lantern. At first sight or sound of a stranger approaching, he disappears, hides until they leave. Maida and I think it must have been his mother who hid him, and two other people. At first he kept looking around and asking after 'Ma,' 'Kee' and 'Ric.'" Peg paused to accept a plate of bread and cheese from Katten. "We're stuck with him for now. It's annoying, but what else can we do? I guess he's a help to Maida, with the goats and garden and all. Always hungry, though."

"Good thing you have the goats and garden then," Martha said.

"All a bother," Mother Peg sniffed.

Martha wrinkled her brow. There was a pause before she spoke again. "I worry about you travelling alone, Mother Peg." Peg sniffed again, handed her plate to the waiting Katten.

Katten tidied up while Martha helped Mother Peg to her feet. Voices outside announced the arrival of more Healers coming along the trail. Sister Edda and Brother Klaus, a married couple of Healers from the boundary between the Westlands and the Northlands, travelling with Father Mallory's Apprentice, Gleve. He came from even farther north, in the foothills of the Mountains.

Everyone greeted and kissed everyone else, in the fashion of the People of the Land. "Mother Peg," said Brother Klaus, "I wish you had waited another day. We stopped and spent the day with Maida. You could have travelled with us."

When Peg greeted Gleve, he caught her glance over his shoulder. "No, Father Mallory is not here. He is well, but getting stiffer and slower. He didn't feel he could walk so far."

How many of her generation would not make it to this gathering? Peg wondered. Would she ever make the trip again? She brightened with her next thought. For years, every time Peg proposed that the Healers spend more time interviewing Elders, or searching the older Healing Journals stored in their vast library, it was Father Mallory's voice raised in opposition. "Why spend time on that? We know all we will ever know about the Dragon Priestesses, and we put ourselves in danger if the Kings find out we are asking questions. We are Healers; we should spend our time Healing and learning more about Healing." This time Father Mallory was not here and she was. Maybe this was her chance.

The whole party started off across the Barrens together. Mother Peg refused their offered arms, insisting on hobbling along on her stick.

Katten walked beside her carrying her pack and holding her lantern so that its light fell just in front of their feet. After a little while, he spoke. "Mother Peg, people are saying that King Anglewart has captured a Dragon. Is it true?"

"Just because I live in the Westlands doesn't mean I take tea with the King," Peg snapped.

Katten looked chastened and shrank further when Martha rebuked him as well. "We'll ask Peg to tell us anything she knows when she's settled in front of the Hearth at the School."

The others were happy to travel at Peg's slow pace. They had much news to share with one another. Just past midnight, Peg began to hear the calming swish, swish of the sea caressing stoney beach. An hour later, they emerged from the forest and decended into the cliff-top clearing that held the Healers' School. Brightly lit windows welcomed them, outlining a cosy circle of buildings – dormitories, the Teaching Hall, Clinic, Dining Hall and Library – all surrounding the heart of the School, its circular stone Gathering Hall. Lanterns bounced along pathways, each held by a Healer walking between buildings or working in the pastures, gardens and barns.

Peg longed for the small bed she would occupy in the Women's Dormitory, but the group headed first to the Dining Hall. When they entered, a group of Apprentices were setting the long tables that filled the centre of the room. The clatter of meal preparation echoed from the Kitchen at the far end of the building. Many greetings came her way. Katten guided her to a circle of chairs in front of the Hearth where several other Old Ones were already settled. He offered to take her pack and lantern to her room.

Mothers Nell and Tess, along with Father Rob, rose to take her hand and kiss her on both cheeks. Mother Sarah moved to rise but made it no further than the edge of her chair. She reached out for Peg's hand instead. Sarah was now the oldest of the Old Ones, Peg realized, with a shock, because she herself was only six years younger.

They began to share news. Father Donnell had died three months before, leaving Rob and Mallory as the only males among the Old Ones. Mother Janua was too ill to travel. She had retired from her Healing practice a year earlier and was living with her son and daughter-in-law. Like Mallory, Lea and Orsa did not attempt the trip from their cottages far off in the Northland but sent their Apprentices. Both had asked for the School to assign younger Healers to replace them. Lea would move in with a neighbour, a widow who would care for her. Orsa would come back to the School to live out her days, as Sarah had when she retired two years ago. There were Senior Healers now who were twenty-five years younger than they were, Peg mused.

As word of Peg's arrival spread, Healers of all ages arrived in the Dining Hall to greet her. Many asked the same question Katten had asked on the path.

"I know little more than the rumours," Peg told them.

"Tell us what you do know, then," said Mother Nell.

Peg harumphed. "Just what everyone knows: Anglewart sent some soldiers into the mountains to search for Little Dragons. Most of them became Dragons' breakfast, as everyone knew they would. The few that made it back brought a Dragon's egg with them, stolen from a nest, although how they did that, I don't know.

"Anglewart had his servants keep it warm, and it hatched. He tried to keep the baby Dragon in a courtyard, with a collar and chain like a dog, silly man. Apparently they even let the palace children play with it, if you can imagine!" Several of the Healers groaned and shook their heads. "Of course," Peg continued, "It became wilder and wilder as it grew. I gather it finally flew into some kind of rage, killed a couple of the children, including the King's own daughter, broke its chain and flew away"

"I can't believe they let children anywhere near the thing," said Mother Tess.

"Well, I guess it was pretty small and harmless at first."

"So they didn't see any Little Dragons, I gather," said Sheil, an Apprentice of Sister Kendra's.

Peg shrugged, "Would they tell us if they had?"

The group fell silent, each wrapped in his or her own thoughts, sadness written on their faces. No one alive could remember living safely and happily, in the open, in the daylight. The Kings had come in the Old Ones' Grandparents' time, and the Terror began in their Parents' day. She knew there were Brothers and Sisters memorizing the Story, but could they tell it like the Old Ones could? What knowledge was disappearing, not only Healers' knowledge, but that of the People? Was there information out there somewhere – something said to a child long ago, something written and hidden in a wall, something coded into a song that someone still sang – something that would lead to the precious lost secrets of the Dragon Priestesses?

Mother Peg stretched her back, wincing as pain ran through her. She saw one of the Librarians notice. The woman rose quietly to her feet and began to glide in Peg's direction. What was her name? Holly, yes. Sister Holly.

Part of the Sacred Trust of the Healing Order was the collection and preservation of Knowledge. All Healers kept journals, recording what they learned throughout their lives. These precious leather-bound books were made in the Bindery, a building attached to the Library. They were issued to Healers and later returned to the Library, where they were kept and read, compared and discussed, analyzed and summarized. Peg sat at a small table, one of several grouped in the open centre of the room. The rest of the space was taken up with shelves, row upon row, from floor to ceiling, filled with generations of Healers' Journals. The room smelled of old paper and leather.

Holly sat down across the table. She did everything silently, from long habit, even through there was no one besides the two of them in the room. "Mother Peg? Are you all right?"

"Of course I'm all right. Just a little stiff. Sat here longer than I intended to."

Holly paused a moment at Peg's tone, but then continued on, in her professional way. "Is there anything special you're looking for? Anything I can help you find?" She glanced down at the Journals Peg had spread out on the table.

"Mother Calla," Peg prompted. "She was a friend of my Grandmother's."

"Really?"

Don't be so surprised, girl, thought Peg. It may be the ancient past to you, but some of us go back that far.

"She had her Healing Practice in the Westlands, didn't she?" Sister Holly said.

Well then, Peg thought. You know your Journals. She began to regret her sharpness with the younger woman. She barked at people too often nowadays. It was not the soft, patient tone that Healers learned for the practice of their craft.

"Several people have gone through that material," Holly continued. "In fact, haven't you read it before, last year at Gathering, or the year before?"

"I know, I know." Peg could hear her voice getting sharp again, but couldn't stop herself. "I just can't help hoping that there may be something we've missed, something that could be a clue."

Holly nodded, ignoring the impatience. "There are lots of stories, as you know."

Peg knew, of course. Holly was talking about the old rumours that some of the fleeing Dragon Priestesses, knowing they were doomed sooner or later, dictated their secret knowledge to the Healers who sheltered them. Mother Calla's name was associated with these rumours, as was Sister Liotra and Sister Terra. All were killed in the early days of the Kings, their possessions burned.

"So much lost," Holly said. A moment later, she turned her head toward the main door, clearly expecting someone to appear there. Peg silently cursed her failing hearing, but in a few moments, she too could hear slow footsteps on the broad wooden planks of the hallway floor, syncopated by a lighter click which must surely be a cane. One of the Old Ones. Then the steps halted.

MOTHER TESS

Mother Tess leaned heavily on her stick in the hallway outside the Library. What am I doing here? she thought. I should be going in the other direction, toward my bed. She had slept little the day before, troubled by a dream.

Ah yes, the dream. That was why she had started out toward the Library in the first place, to check the Dream Journals, see if she could get help interpreting this spectre that was troubling her rest. The dream had come to her five times now, or was it six? That made it important, a Command Dream of some sort. But what was it asking her to do?

It always began with a young woman, standing in front of Tess, her back turned. She was dressed in the purple cloak of a Dragon Priestess, never seen now, but who would need a purple cloak to recognize a Dragon Priestess? In the dream Tess's eyes were held irresistibly by the Little Dragon on the girl's shoulder. It was looking back, studying Tess intently, and it was beautiful. Its scales picked up the light and reflected it back in glimmering shades of blue. Its eyes were filled with rainbow colours, whirling slowly in a spiral. It had glowing, thick whisker-like things curling back from its head and the middle of its back. No, thicker than whiskers, more like the antennae of an insect, only elegant, moving lazily in the sun.

Sun! Yes, the dream took place in the daylight. They stood fully lit and unafraid on a path somewhere, outside. And then came another shock. The girl turned and she was not a Woman of the Earth. She was round faced, not tall, her skin white and pink, a Woman of the King's People. How could that be?

There was no time to wonder, though, because as soon as the young woman saw Tess, she stepped forward, saying something. With an effort, Tess pulled her eyes from the Dragon and focused on the girl's face. She was trying hard to communicate but there was no sound, just her mouth moving, repeating something over and over again, urgency in her large brown eyes.

Tess found her heart pounding, just as it did each time she awoke from the dream. Surely it was almost echoing down the hallway outside the library. Tired or not, she must see if she could find any references in the Dream Journals.

As she entered the library, Tess squinted her eyes in the light of many lanterns. As they adjusted, she started. Mother Peg and one of the Librarians sat at a table staring at her. Had they heard her heart beating in the hallway? No, no, of course not, surely just her footsteps.

The Librarian rose. "Mother Tess, please take a seat." She pulled out the chair she had been sitting in. Now Tess wished she had headed to her bed for a nap. She didn't want to talk about anything to do with the Dragon Priestesses in front of Peg. The woman was obsessed. But what could she do? Here she was.

She sat and scanned the open journals on the table. "Mother Calla," she said, and smiled at Peg. "Surely if you comb these pages any finer they'll start falling out of their bindings." Peg scowled back. Tess could feel her smile fading. "I have a family connection to her, you know."

Peg's eyebrows folded together."I'd forgotten that. What exactly was the relationship?"

Oh dear, not where Tess wanted the conversation to go. Peg had become so sharp in her old age, not like when they were young and Peg had made her reputation as the best midwife in all the Realms. Surely she would never speak to a labouring woman in this tone? Tess sighed. "My uncle, my father's brother he was, married one of Calla's daughters. She had several daughters, you know."

"Five," Peg snapped.

"Yes, five, and many, many descendents from there."

"I know there is a line of Healers from her daughter Yolande into the present. I've spoken to them all. They have no clue as to what might have happened to Calla's knowledge from the Dragon Priestesses, if it ever existed. But I haven't given much thought to the other daughters. What happened to those lines? There must be Healing Gifts there."

"I suppose there are, but her other daughters were scattered in the time of Terror. We're into her granddaughters and great-granddaughters now. I'm sure there are Healing Gifts among them, but none have found a way to return and receive training."

"Could you find out who and where they are?"

"Oh Peg," Tess said. "You're relentless."

"Of course I'm relentless!"

"I would have to do some research," Tess tried to avoid the intensity in Peg's eyes.

"And will you?"

"Some of them may be lost into the world of the King's People, you know. Most of them became servants in wealthy households. I know at least one line of Calla's daughters went to your King Anglewart's capital city."

"Hardly my King Anglewart!"

"They may well have taken the Kings' world into their heads by now, become just like them."

Peg snorted. "Pretty hard to become just like them when your skin is dark."

"Skin colour doesn't stop the Kings' ways from getting inside our heads."

"True," Peg admitted, her voice softening a little.

Tess relented as well. "For all my teasing, my dear, I know how important this quest is. I will do what I can."

"Well," said Peg. "Well then."

MOTHER PEG

The circular Gathering Hall, heart of the School, was dug into the ground and walled with stone. Inside, tiers of benches circled a central Hearth. Huge wooden beams held up the roof, framing a round hole where the smoke could escape. During each night of the retreat, this space was filled with teaching, learning, decisions and plans.

As always, Mother Peg put her name on the list of Proposers. When her turn came, she once again suggested that the Healers organize a project, a systematic search for clues among the oldest living People of the Land, in the Journals they already had, in any place a Journal might have been hidden during the years of Conquest and Terror. This time she added a new argument: King Anglewart had sent an expedition to the Mountains to search for Little Dragons. This could mean that the Kings regretted their destruction of the Dragon Priestesses and were now openly searching for their secrets. People would soon get the message that anything they might know about the Dragon Priestesses could earn them a reward. The Kings would use what they learned to increase their own power for their own war-like ends. It was crucial that the Healers find any new information first, and use it for the well being of the People.

With the new argument and without Father Mallory to lead opposition to the idea, the Healer's Council considered it. Peg watched Father Mallory's Apprentice, wondering if he would voice his Teacher's well-known opinion on the old man's behalf, but Gleve did not rise to speak. By the end of the discussion it had been agreed that a Librarian would be freed to systematically investigate some of the lesser-known Journals in the Library and all Healers would be issued an extra Journal and encouraged to interview everyone they Healed, especially Elders, searching for any new information about the Dragon Priestesses. Mother Peg was delighted with this decision. "Well then," she said, glancing at Tess, who nodded back, confirmation. Tess would use her new Journal to track down the descendents of Mother Calla.

GLEVE

Fifteen new Healers stood in a line near the edge of the cliff. They held hands and chanted with the semi-circle of Healers and Apprentices standing behind them, a gentle salt breeze blowing into their faces. Above them stars glittered in a clear, black sky. Far below they could hear the rumble of the tide coming in on the rock beach.

Once this Ritual would have reached its climax as the Sun broke the horizon, bathing the participants in her life-giving rays. They still walked in procession to the cliffs, raising their linked hands in prayer to the Rising Sun, but by the time the Sun herself peeked over the horizon, they had long since returned to the Gathering Space to complete their Ritual safe from hunting Dragons.

This was the Ceremony of Receiving, when the Apprentices who were deemed by their teachers to be ready for their own Healing practice were consecrated and received into the Order. The ancient words echoed in Gleve's very heart. This was his Calling come to fruition. His lifetime of dreaming and planning, his seven years of study, brought him to this moment. He felt satisfaction, awe, and also sadness.

There were two large empty spaces in this Ceremony for Gleve, two people who should be here. First, Maida. She was his friend, had been ever since she had turned up at the Healer's School seven years ago, frightened and shy, but insisting she had a Calling to the Order. They had gone through the examinations for Apprenticeship as part of the same group.

Gleve had never questioned that he would be a Healer. There were many in his family. His uncle had sponsored his Apprenticeship application. Maida, on the other hand, had run away from her family with no idea of how far away the School was or how to get there. She had wandered, asked directions, begged rides and food, driven by that strong sense of Calling. Mother Sarah herself had examined Maida and couldn't say enough about how her difficult journey to the School had already answered the question of her motivation. She was also clear that Maida had the Healing gift. Sometimes it pops up in families with no known Healers' line, she had said, and when it does, it tends to be strong.

The first day they met, Gleve had felt protective of Maida and she comfortable with him. They had quickly become confidants. She had been sent out to Mother Peg at the same time as he was sent to Father Mallory. They had traveled together as far as Mother Peg's cabin.

Their hopes had been so high, and now he had achieved his. He was a Healer. She was miles away, tending her goats. On the way to the Gathering, Edda, Klaus and Gleve had stopped for the day at Mother Peg's cabin. Gleve was puzzled; Mother Peg had left for the Gathering and Maida was still there. The pain in her eyes had shocked him. When she went out to do her morning chores, he had gone with her to the stable. She had shown him her bitterness. "She refused me as an Apprentice, Gleve. She considers me a servant."

"But Maida, Mother Sarah herself said you have the Healing gift, and she went on and on about your determination."

"Tell her," Maida had begged. "Please ask Mother Sarah to send me to another Healer as Apprentice."

He had promised her he would, but he had not done it yet. There was still a night left of the Gathering. He would find a way to tell Mother Sarah without being disrespectful to Mother Peg, although now he could not think of Maida's mistress, who should have been her Teacher, without anger.

The other missing person was Gleve's Teacher, Father Mallory. He felt so lucky to have been assigned as Apprentice to that gentle old man. He had been taught well and they had come to love each other deeply. His Teacher should have been here to share in his Receiving.

He closed his eyes, breathed in the chanting and drumming that surrounded him and projected it to Father Mallory. He conjured the image of the old man, here among the crowd of Healers behind him on the cliff, his smoky eyes wreathed with the fine wrinkles of his smile, his wispy white hair a disorderly halo around his head in the sea air.

What would happen to Father Mallory now? He was fragile and needed care in order to live daily life in his isolated Northlands cabin, let alone carry out his Healing practice. Gleve had put in a request to co-practice with his former Teacher or, if not that, at least be placed nearby. Sister Kendra, who chaired this year's assignment committee, had frowned. "We will take Father Mallory's well being into account when we select a new Apprentice for him," she had argued. "The need is not there in the forests and mountains of the Northlands; it's in the other three Realms, where the People are."

It was not good to be Received with first anger and then sadness in his heart. Gleve tried to focus on the stars, on the drums and the chanting. He sought the peace that should usher him into his new place in the Healing Order.

After the last chant of the Receiving Ceremony faded into the rafters of the Gathering Hall, Sister Kendra rose to read out the new Healers' assignments. Gleve held his breath as she called the names of each newly Received Healer, sending him or her out into the Kingdoms, some to take up Healing practices from Old Ones who had retired or passed on, some to build cabins in areas where People had to travel too far to receive care.

Finally her eyes focused on him and, amazingly, she smiled. "Brother Gleve," she said. "You will return to Father Mallory's cabin in the Northlands and practice jointly with him. Together you will teach the new Apprentice Lynna when she has finished her studies here at the School."

Gleve felt an explosion of delight and relief. It was not hard to pick out Lynna from the back seats across the Hall where the new Apprentices sat in a row together. She was the one that leaped to her feet with joy. Gleve stared at her in surprise. He had never noticed her before—why would he?—but now he saw that unmistakable fire in her eyes. She had a crush on him.

7 MOTHER PEG

After the morning ritual the Old Ones liked to gather in front of the hearth in the Dining Hall, talk a little and drink a cup of sleeping tea before going to bed. On the morning of the Receiving Ceremony, only Sarah and Peg were present. "So, my friend," Sarah said, looking sharply at Peg. "When are you going to bring Maida to be Received?"

"Stop that." Peg clattered her cup into her saucer. "You know I don't like to be teased."

"And you know I'm not teasing. That girl is as gifted as any Apprentice I've ever examined."

"Excuse me for saying it, old friend, but you're losing it. That girl has no Healers in her lineage and will never be one, no matter what exceptions were made to give her an Examination."

"Excuse me for saying it, old friend." Sarah managed to put acid into her words. "It is you who is losing it. Many exceptional Healers have no Healing lineage and besides, so much genealogical information was lost during the times of Terror, who knows who has Healer in them and who doesn't?"

"She's from a long line of cheesemakers." Peg pounded the arm of her chair for emphasis. "She's hauled I don't know how many stones up from the creek to make a sink and cool room and a channel from the spring on the hillside into my kitchen. When she's not making cheese, she's packing half her garden into crocks. I live with a dripping mess most of the time."

"Stop complaining." Sarah barked the words so loudly some of the Healers nearby turned to look. "You eat better than anyone I know living away from the School. She feeds you, takes care of you, all to learn some Healing on the side. We should take that girl away from you, assign her to someone who will appreciate her and teach her."

"The girl makes good cheese. She's a good gardener and cook and servant. SHE IS NOT A HEALER." Now the whole Dining Hall fell silent. Kendra's Apprentice, Sheil, rose to her feet and studied the two Old Ones for a moment. She took a step in their direction, then another.

"Now we've created a commotion," Sarah said.

Peg rose to her feet, glared at Sheil. "Well I don't know about you, but it's past time I went to bed." She left the hearth, thumping her cane loudly on the wooden floor.

The ancient Rites celebrated each morning built up the Healing Power of those present. On the final morning, Spring Equinox itself, the climax of the Sunrise Prayer released the Healing Power out to the suffering Land, a Prayer for peace, well being , and a return to happier times.

Long before the procession to the cliffs to release the Healing, however, the Spring Equinox Ritual began with the Remembering, when the Old Ones recited, once again, the Story.

The room was dim, the beams high above fading into darkness. Sparks rose from the Fire on the Hearth to the hole in the centre of the roof where a star or two peeked in. The benches were filled with Healers, women and men of all ages. They all knew the Story, but listened intently. This Ritual was the centre of their year, and the Story was the heart of the Ritual.

The Oldest One present always began the recitation of the Story. Sarah was approaching her ninetieth year, but her voice was still strong and her memory flawless.

"Once, before the time of our Grandmothers, the People lived peacefully and joyfully in this rich Land. People could go about their business during the day, work in the fields able to see what they were cutting, work in the gardens able to tell plant from weed, prune the fruit trees able to see clearly the final shape. The livestock could graze and the children could play in the sun. They say the People tanned dark brown and had rosy cheeks. They could build their homes in the open, handy to their fields and orchards.

According to the stories, when a Dragon flew over, the People would shade their eyes and look up to see what colour it was, blue, green, red, bronze or gold, and admire the sparkle of sunlight on its scales.

"There were three Orders to watch over the People: the Healers, the Leaders and the Dragon Priestesses.

"The Healers cared for their bodies and spirits, discovering and sharing the knowledge the People needed to be strong and well.

"The Leaders kept the Common Order, bringing the People together to discuss problems, resolve conflicts, make decisions and hold one another accountable for the Common Good.

"The Dragon Priestesses cared for their Familiars, the Little Dragons. Through the Little Dragons, they could speak with the Great Dragons, and so they made and kept the Agreement.

"According to the Agreement, the Dragon Priestesses kept large herds of fine cattle. Hungry Dragons could request one of these animals through the Little Dragons. The Dragon Priestesses would select the Sacrifice, and with great Ceremony lead it to a Feeding Place, respectfully take its Life, and leave it there for the Dragons' meal.

"Then, in our Grandparents' time, the Kings came. The Kings do not understand the Common Order and the Common Good. They do what they like and take what they want. Lacking Respect for All Life, they kill whatever stands in their way.

"The Kings follow the way of the sword. They thought they could protect their subjects from the Dragons by killing them. This they set out to do, and many Kings' men died in the attempt. They also killed many of the People and took their lands and livestock. Above all, they killed the Dragon Priestesses and the Little Dragons. They coveted the power of the Priestesses without understanding it. They wanted their cattle and land, and to them, Little Dragons were Dragons all the same, to be killed for the safety of the People."

Sarah's voice was fading. She nodded to Rob, who look up the story. "The Kings killed many Healers and Leaders as well, seeing all members of the Orders as rivals for the power they felt they must have over the People.

"The Healers were saved by Sheena, may her name be remembered for all generations. A young Sister at the time, Sheena heard that the eldest son of mighty King Gallward was dying of a sword wound. Although she knew he might kill her on sight, and would certainly kill her if she failed, she went to Gallward and offered to heal his son. Desperate to save his heir, the King let her try. She called for any Healer in the district who would help her. Several came to her side—her teacher, Mother Nessa; Nessa's teacher, Mother Jen, Sister Cath, Brother Gelas, and Apprentice Violet. May the names of these brave and skilled Healers be remembered for all generations.

"They went to Gallward's stronghold and worked day and night to heal the Prince. They bathed him and drew the sword-poison from his body with poultices. They trickled teas down his throat. At all times three of them kept vigil in Prayer Circle around him, holding his Spirit within his Body, feeding it with Earth Energy, until it began to respond.

"With his son restored to him, Gallward decreed that no one would kill a Healer again. And so, our Order was saved. Many Leaders were saved as well, because they looked like Healers as far as the Kings' People could tell. We took them in and sheltered them in our Order. Eventually the two Orders became one.

"This was not possible, however, for the Dragon Priestesses, for how do you hide when you have a glittering blue, green, red, bronze or gold Little Dragon riding on your shoulder? Though the Healers pleaded with the Kings, they would not bend. They killed all the Dragon Priestesses, every one. To our eternal sorrow, their secrets went with them.

"The Great Dragons loved the Little Dragons, for they are all kin despite the difference in size, and through them their mistresses, the Dragon Priestesses. The Great Dragons were angry, and came to hate all humans. They also had no one to feed them when they were hungry. If humans would not feed them in one way, they would feed them in another. And so began the Terror."

Rob turned and raised his eyebrows at Nell, who cleared her throat and picked up the tale. "Child and adult, man and woman, Kings' People or People of the Land, cow, horse, goat, duck, dog, cat, chicken – nothing was safe from the Dragons. Any creature caught in the open in daylight, in field or yard, on boat or road, could suddenly find themselves in the shadow of a hunting Dragon and moments later, impaled by its cruel claws. People and animals alike screamed in fear and pain as they were carried away to be eaten in a Dragon-lair in the Mountains.

"The People moved into the Forest for the safety of its leaves. Everyone learned to work and travel at night when the Dragons sleep in their craggy fasts. A land of plenty became a land of famine. The Kings' bond-farmers were city people moved by force on to the Kings' lands. They did not know much about farming in the first place and now had to learn to farm by night when the horse stumbles in front of the plough, wolves take the sheep from the pastures and foxes the chickens from the yard.

"The People of the Land who survived the greed of the Kings farmed the rocky soil in the hills. They could now foray into their fields only in darkness to plant and weed by the faint light of their lanterns. No more livestock could be kept than could be sheltered in barns by day.

People even kept their cows and goats in the kitchens of their cabins.

As people learned to hide themselves and their animals from the Dragons, the terrible creatures vented their hunger and rage. They would descend and roar with their fire-breath, burning acres of crops and orchards into a charred desert. Many starved, especially among the People of the Land, because the Kings hunted out and hoarded what food there was.

"We, the Remnant, have learned to survive. We grow what we can, hide what we can, and share all we have to stay alive. The Healers are sometimes given gifts of food for Healing the Kings' People, and this we share as well. The Common Good is still honoured among us."

Nell paused for breath. She looked to Peg. The young Healer beside Peg offered her arm. She took it, struggling to her feet and forcing her old knees to hold her. There was only a paragraph of the Story left, she grumbled to herself. Why did Nell decide to pass it on now? But she picked up the familiar narrative. "And so we remember. We remember the People and the Members of the Orders who died. We remember those brave Healers who allowed at least part of our Order and that of the Leaders to continue on. We remember the Little Dragons and pray to relearn the secrets of the Dragon Priestesses. If the Little Dragons still exist somewhere deep in the Mountains, we pray to find them and learn to speak with them and live with them again as Familiars.

"We remember, and we pray."

With the young Healer's help, Peg sat down, as all around her a soft chant began: "We remember, we remember, we remember, and we pray."

After greeting the first signs of pre-dawn, releasing their Healing Energy to the Land, and closing the Ritual back in the Gathering Space, the Healers returned to the Dining Hall where large pots of grain and vegetable stew sat on the warm Hearth. It was still called the Feast, although it was a thin shell of the Feasts of old.

The Old Ones sat together, Sarah and Peg as far apart as possible, waiting to be served. Tess looked around at the remnant of her generation. "I have to ask," she said. "Do you think the Little Dragons still exist?"

"According to my Mother's stories, the Little Dragons were exquisitely beautiful, and only three or four feet long, even when they were full-grown," said Father Rob.

"Oh for heaven's sake, Rob," Mother Peg snapped. "We all know that."

There was a minute of tense silence. Nell broke it, glancing at Peg. "When I heard that old Anglewart sent men into the Mountains, I hoped so much that we would hear that they at least caught sight of a Little Dragon." A young women listening to conversation giggled, probably shocked by Nell calling the powerful King "old Anglewart."

Peg shot her a silencing glance. "Well, who knows?" she said. "Even if they did see something like that, do you think Anglewart would not keep the information to himself? I'm sure he would kill the poor brave man who made it back and told him just to be sure such a powerful possibility remained only in his hands."

Tess sighed. "And maybe the man with the message would know enough not to say anything in the first place." The other Old Ones nodded.

"I think you are right, Peg. This search must mean the Kings are sorry they destroyed the Little Dragons, and the Dragon Priestesses with their knowledge," Tess said. "Or at least Anglewart must be having second thoughts."

"The problem is that they can only think in terms of war and power over people. I think they want to find the Little Dragons for that, as weapons, or maybe to communicate to the Great Dragons, to use them as weapons."

"Oh Peg!" said Tess. "Sometimes you are the ultimate cynic!"

"Well, you know they're offering rewards for anyone who can come up with a weapon that will kill Dragons," Peg snapped back. "Maybe they want Dragons to kill Dragons."

Nell broke in. "Where do you think they came from, the Little Dragons?" she asked, a question that was almost a Ritual itself among the Healers.

Sarah spoke. "I sometimes wonder if the Dragon Priestesses didn't share their knowledge before they were all killed because they thought they could communicate with us from the Spirit World."

"They used to be able to do that, didn't they?' said Joelle.

"My Teacher said so," Sarah responded, "But that skill too had something to do with the Little Dragons, and died with them."

GLEVE

Gleve's stomach was tied tightly in a knot. All he wanted was to unleash his long legs and stride toward home. He couldn't wait to see Father Mallory's face when his beloved Teacher found out Gleve would be staying with him. He also worried about Father Mallory. He had left prepared meals and buckets of water drawn and set in a row under the kitchen cupboard. But had it been enough? Was Father Mallory having to struggle back from the pump with heavy pails or climb up and down the treacherous ladder to the cool room under the kitchen? What if he became ill while Gleve was away? The neighbours had promised to check every day, but would they?

And now he had to travel with this grouchy old woman who was treating Maida so badly, and he had to see her all the way home. That meant facing Maida, although he knew he would have to sooner or later, and probably better to do it sooner. He rehearsed the words over and over again, trying to find a way to say it: he had broken his word to her; he had not spoken to Mother Sarah. Maida knew, of course, how intimidating the Old Ones could be. Surely she would understand. Wouldn't she?

It was all Gleve could do to follow Mother Peg's snail-like pace. He held the lantern up to light their way and reminded himself to keep his impatience out of his face. Of course he never questioned that he would accompany her home. What young, strong Healer would leave an Old One to travel for days through the woods alone? But he spoke with her as little as possible, and now she wanted to take him off of the main road, out of their way, travelling an almost-invisible little path to show him something.

Mother Peg glanced at him with those sharp, raisin eyes of hers. "We'll be back on the main road before you know it." How do the Old Ones read your mind like that? he wondered. She took the lantern from him and went ahead on the narrow way, in her maddeningly slow hobble. He had no choice but to follow, placing his feet carefully in her shadow.

The old woman stopped so suddenly that Gleve nearly ran into her. She looked around, creasing her brow. Oh no, he thought. On top of everything else, she's lost. But a moment later her brow cleared. "Here," she said, as she pushed through some bushes.

Gleve came behind her, stepping in front from time to time to remove fallen branches from the path, returning to trail the old woman. He almost ran into her again when she stopped. Then he took in his breath, impatience suddenly forgotten. Before him the lantern cast its light into a tiny, overgrown clearing.

Although there were many stories about these ancient wayside shrines of the Dragon Priestesses, he had never seen a Dragonstone before. It was badly weathered, but the skillfully-carved Dragon still twisted gracefully around his stone tree trunk. The eyes immediately captured him. Pitted as they were by time, and shadowed in the dim light of the lantern, they still looked at him, through him, considering his very heart, his every possible secret. He would have expected an image of a Dragon, come upon by surprise in the dark forest like this, to fill him with fear. But it didn't. Instead, he was flooded with peace and strength. Some kind of loving power radiated from the stone and filled him with warmth.

He became aware that Mother Peg was watching him. Now she quietly shifted her cane and reached out a bony hand. She was pressing a small pouch of Sacred Herbs into his palm. He loosened the string and shook some free. They closed their eyes and prayed, taking in the calm radiating from the stone Dragon.

"Bless you, young Gleve," Mother Peg whispered, "And bless your new Healing practice. May it be your generation that rediscovers the knowledge of the Dragon Priestesses and brings our People and the People of Kings back into the light of day."

She handed him the lantern again and hobbled slowly forward to scatter the herbs at the feet of the Dragon. As soon as she stepped back, Gleve went forward to place his gift as well. When she finally turned to go, he was surprised to find himself reluctant to leave.

"Has Father Mallory not shown you the way to any of the surviving Dragonstones in the Northlands?"

"He has often said that he would, but we just never got around to it. You know what he thinks of putting effort into the memory of the Dragon Priestesses."

"Would he still be able to do it?"

"It would be difficult, but maybe, with help."

"You must make him take you—soon!" Mother Peg looked Gleve straight in the eye. "When the Kings destroyed them, more survived in the Northlands than anywhere else. There were more there in the first place, because it is so close to the mountains where the Dragon Priestesses had their School, and the King's men had more trouble finding them because the country is wilder, and closer to the Dragon's dens." She paused, studied him. "It is important, Gleve, that you find out where they are. Father Mallory knows and we can't afford to lose any more of the little knowledge we have. Tell me you understand how important it is. Promise me you'll find them!"

He held her eyes. "I understand how important it is, Mother Peg. I will ask Father Mallory to show me the way as soon as I get home."

"Well then." She nodded and turned back to the road, satisfied. He let out a held-in breath. On their way again, finally.

 **MAiDA**

Maida was trying to resist looking out the window. Every time she did, Rafe clambered up from his favourite stool by the hearth to look as well. Sometimes he managed to set down his dish. More often it hit the floor and scattered food all over the room. From experience, Maida knew better than to give him pottery dishes or serve him much at one time. Rafe ate out of a shallow metal bowl. It made more noise hitting the flagstones, but at least it did not have to be picked up in pieces. The small servings meant she had to refill the bowl over and over again, because the big lad had a huge appetite, but that meant she could remind him each time that she wanted him to sit up straight, eat one bite at a time, use the spoon. In spite of this, by the time the food was half-consumed, he would forget and slouch over the bowl pushing the last of the meal into his mouth with his hand. If it were soup or stew, he would sometimes tip the bowl up and drink from it.

Maida had to restrain herself from laughing more often than she lost patience with him, mostly because he was always so delighted with the food, with his precious metal bowl, with everything. It was rare to see Rafe's round face wear any expression but a happy grin.

Tonight, however, he was grating on her nerves. It was difficult not to look out the window. She had been expecting Mother Peg to return last night, or even the night before. Sister Edda, Brother Klaus and Apprentice Gleve had come through just a day after Mother Peg left for the Gathering. They would see her safely home, but Maida worried anyway. Mother Peg was her responsibility to care for, and, despite the Healer's denials, her elderly body was getting very fragile. Always a tiny woman, now she was bent over and walked slowly, using her stick for support. What if she became ill or was injured along the way? What if they couldn't get her to shelter quickly enough when daylight came? However, there was nothing to do but wait.

In the meantime, Maida had precious little time left for learning. She had one of Mother Peg's Healing Journals open on the table, memorizing the herbs for coughs. Stimulating expectorants for a wet cough: elecampane, squill, cowslip, bittersweet, heartsease, white horehound, balm of Gilead, asafetida, blood root, mouse ear, queen's delight, rue, thyme, bryony, caraway, snake root, violet. For a dry, nervous cough, calm it with relaxing expectorants: coltsfoot, marshmallow, comfrey, plantain, ribwort, linseed, licorice, aniseed, lungwort, hyssop, ephedra, sundew, skunk cabbage, Irish moss, euphorbia.

She resisted looking out the window again. Rafe, finally finished eating, was watching Maida intently, his big round face echoing her worried expression. "It's all right, Rafe. Mother Peg will be home soon." She turned back to the Journal in front of her. Some cough remedies have a broad range of effects and should be used when there are complex symptoms: lobelia, garlic, ginger, mullein flowers, red clover, lovage, elderflowers.

Rafe stood up and stared out into the night. He turned to her, his habitual grin restored, and said, "M'Peg." Maida looked. There was a little twinkle of light bobbing among the trees. Her heart beating hard, she closed the thick Journal and carried it to the shelf in Mother Peg's room. She had left a pebble to mark exactly where it stood, a millimeter in front of the volume on one side, two millimeters back of the one of the other side. She placed the book, pocketed the pebble, and gave Rafe a guilty look as she returned to the kitchen. Thank goodness he couldn't speak, not that Mother Peg would listen to anything he had to say anyway.

"Mother Peg?" Maida called in the direction of the approaching light, her own lantern held high.

"Yes, yes, it's me," came back the response.

Maida hurried along the path to meet the Healer, Rafe bumbling along at her heels. "We were beginning to worry about you." Did her voice sound normal after her quick, guilty trip to the Old One's room? Sometimes she thought the old woman could read her mind, let alone her voice. At least this time there was important news to provide an excuse for breathlessness, disturbing news.

"No need," Mother Peg snapped. "I have company." She turned to indicate the tall young man behind her. "Meet Father Mallory's new co-Healer."

"Oh Gleve, you can stay with Father Mallory then?" Gleve nodded. Maida looked up at him, searching for his eyes, but he looked away. She bit her lip. He had not kept his promise. "Hi Rafe," he greeted the large man trying to be invisible in the shadows.

But what did she expect? It would take huge courage for an Apprentice, or even newly Received Healer, to carry a complaint to the oldest of the Old Ones about the second-oldest. It's just that he seemed so angry on her behalf, she thought maybe …

"So will you stay for the day, rest and have something to eat? Mother Peg asked Gleve.

"Thank you," he told her, "But there is still some travelling time left this night. I think I'll go on to Tummel."

"Well now you're free of this slow old baggage you can run ahead on those long legs of yours."

"Mother Peg! Don't say that. I always learn something new when I'm with you."

"Now, off with you," she said. "And greetings to that old curmudgeon you work with. And make him show you the Dragonstones."

"I will."

Gleve did not even glance at Maida as he handed her Mother Peg's travelling pack and lantern. He turned briefly to wave as he left the clearing, striding so quickly he was almost running. As she watched him go, Maida's bitterness sat on her tongue waiting to be swallowed again.

Maida turned to hand the pack to Rafe, but he would have none of it. He did not give Peg the choice the Healers gave her on the Barrens. He just picked her up and started walking toward the cabin, an even larger than usual smile lighting up his face. "Stop that, you big oaf," she squawked. "Put me down." Rafe ignored her, as usual. Maida bent to pick up Peg's walking stick, dropped as she was lifted off of her feet, and followed.

"Not right through the door," Peg demanded. "Put me down here."

Rafe obeyed, setting her down as gently as he could in front of the cabin door. Peg impatiently tugged her bodice and blouse back into place. "Oaf," she said. "At least let me walk into my own home on my own feet." Rafe simply smiled back.

The door was open, pouring light out onto the hard-packed earth at their feet. Maida and Rafe stood respectfully behind her, but behind them, the chickens began to gather, noisy in their welcome, or was it just interest in being fed?

Mother Peg raised her hands and gave the Blessing of the Threshold: "Ancient Mother, bless this house. May it always have warmth for sharing, food for eating, and peace for healing."

After a brief pause, Mother Peg lowered her hands. Maida came up and held out the walking stick. The Old One took it, hobbled inside and stopped to make a critical examination of the room.

Maida, too, looked around the cabin, seeing it through Mother Peg's eyes. Maida was proud of her housekeeping. The fire crackled on the hearth. Its resinous perfume mingled with the sweet scents of herbs hanging in neat rows from the beams above. Pots of vegetable stew and herb tea sat warm by the fire. The stone floor was swept, the table, shelves and counters scrubbed clean. The supper dishes waited for attention, but they were neatly piled. Maida watched the old woman's eyes fall on Rafe's dirty bowl and spoon still sitting on the hearth, bits of his meal scattered around it. She stared just long enough to communicate her disapproval.

Maida carried Peg's travelling pack to the Old One's room off the kitchen, resiting one more check for signs of her risky forays into the Journals. When she returned, she set a chair by the fire and helped Peg sit before carrying Rafe's utensils to the kitchen and returning with a damp rag to clean up the mess. On the second trip she brought a spoon and a bowl, which she filled from the warm pot of stew.

Rafe sat down on his low stool at his beloved mistress's feet, beaming joyfully at her. A little drop of spit travelled down his chin, as often happened when he was tired or emotional. "Don't stare at me, Rafe," Peg told him, "I feel like a carnival act in the town square."

He looked down at his huge hands, but couldn't maintain it for long. In minutes he was staring worshipfully at her again. Maida glanced out the window where the darkness was thinner than it had been. She turned to Rafe. "I think it's time for chores, my friend." After setting a full cup of hot lemon balm tea beside Mother Peg's chair, she fetched the milk bucket from the storeroom and led Rafe out to gather the goats and chickens into their safe stable for the day.

Maida returned to the cabin with the bulge of an egg in her apron pocket and a full bucket of milk in her hand, alone. Rafe slept on a cot in the hayloft over the stable. "He wanted to come back and sit with you again, but I told him you were too tired and would soon be going to bed yourself," Maida told Peg.

"And that's true, so put that milk in the cool room and come and tell me what's on your mind."

Of course the old Healer, as usual, read her like letters on a page. Maida put the milk away and returned with a cup. She pulled a second chair up to the hearth. "I was trying to hide my worry until you'd had a day's rest."

"You know better than that."

Maida filled her own cup with tea and topped up Peg's before she spoke. "We had a visit from one of the King's Men while you were gone."

"Well then. And what would bring some clanking man-at-arms to this humble cottage? Some sickness the King's Healers can't figure out?" Peg snorted.

"He is more than 'some clanking man-at-arms.' He's one of King Anglewart's Bailiffs. He said one of the King's daughters has got herself in trouble."

"As in, indiscretion-with-a-man trouble?"

"Exactly. Because she is the King's daughter, and engaged to the son of another King, her father doesn't want to feed her to the Dragons. Instead, they want to send her away, before anyone catches on. They want her to grow large and have her baby out of sight while they spread a story about a visit to relatives in the East."

"And they want us to find someone to take her in?"

"They know you are the one with the skills to take care of her, see her through her labour and delivery and return her unharmed. He even hinted that they think you can disguise the fact that she's no longer a virgin."

"They want me to take her in?"

Maida nodded miserably. "I suppose having lost one daughter in the incident with the captive Dragon, they want even more to protect this one."

"More likely the coming marriage is an important alliance for King Anglewart." Peg sighed. "And what about the baby?"

"They want us to find a foster home for it."

"And no one is to know about the royal blood."

Maida nodded. "Well, at least we may learn more about the captive Dragon," she said.

Peg groaned. "The timing couldn't be worse for entertaining a resident spy."

"Why?"

"The Healers at the Gathering finally gave their blessing to my project of searching for missing bits of Dragon Priestess lore. I have a list

of people I want to talk to. It will be almost impossible with a member of
the King's household here."

"Can you say no?"

"You know better than that, my girl. It could well mean death to say
no to him, although it might eventually mean death to say yes."

"You mean, if something goes wrong?"

"Even if he expects more than I can give, like restoring his
daughter's virginity." Peg held her walking stick up to the firelight.
"Thank goodness I can still hobble along the paths on my stick. The
King's daughter can't hear what is said in other People's cottages."

"But I thought you wanted to do less traveling. You said you might
start asking the People to come to you when it's possible for the ill person
to travel at all."

Peg laughed. "Good thing I'm not that far gone yet. And now
it's the only way. I will visit as many People of the Land as I can,
especially Elders, whether they need Healing or not, to search for the lost
knowledge. You will come with me and we will let our resident Princess
think we are called away to Heal."

"Which will often be true."

"Of course."

"We will have to be so, so careful what we say in front of her," said
Maida.

"Of course."

"When you need to talk to me, perhaps you can come to the barn
with me when I milk the goats."

"Goddess forbid." Peg looked glum at this prospect. "But at this
point, I guess it can't be helped." She brightened. "And meanwhile, we'll
learn what we can from her. There might be important clues there too."

Between the lemon balm tea and the comfort of her own bed, Peg slept
soundly and woke refreshed. The cabin smelled of fresh-baked bread.
Rafe scurried across from the barn as soon as the light faded, searching
the sky in all directions as he ran. "You should wait until it's darker,"
Maida scolded him. He mimed looking up and shook his head. "I know,"
she said. "There were no Dragons in the sky. But you must always be
very, very careful." She frowned at him to reinforce the message. Rafe
nodded seriously.

Maida allowed him to serve Mother Peg a meal of soup, cheese and
the warm bread at the table by the window. He pulled up his stool and sat

at her feet watching her, his long arms and legs sticking out at awkward angles, an expression of delight on his big round face. "Stop staring at me!" Peg barked at him. Chastened, he retreated to the hearth, carrying his stool, then took up exactly the same position. "Well, at least you're a bit easier to ignore a few feet away," Peg said.

In a minute he was distracted by the metal bowl Maida handed him. Ignoring the spoon Maida set beside him on the hearth, he lifted the bowl and drank. "I'll give you more if you use your spoon," Maida told him. He eagerly held out the bowl. The spoon slowed him down enough that Maida could serve a bowl for herself and bring it to the table opposite Mother Peg.

"Now you'll have to clean up the hearth," Peg remarked.

"I know." Maida glanced over her shoulder at the mess Rafe was making as he struggled to use the spoon. "But he has to learn these things."

"One thing I'll say, you have patience," Peg said. Maida looked up at her, startled by the praise. Peg's eyes stayed on her meal. "So, when can we expect our princess to arrive?"

"'Cess?" Rafe said, momentarily pausing to respond to a word he obviously knew.

"Yes, Rafe, we'll be having a princess come to stay with us for awhile," Maida said. To Peg, under her breath, she muttered, "Shouldn't have told him that." Peg rolled her eyes.

"'Cess!" exclaimed Rafe, yet another delighted grin breaking out across his face.

"You must not stare at her or bother her," Maida told him sternly.

Rafe nodded. "'Cess!" he repeated, then returned to his messy work with the spoon.

"Oh dear," Maida said quietly to Peg. "I'd forgotten about our 'condemned criminal.' What if the princess tells the King's Men we have a man escaped from the execution grounds hidden here?"

"Can we hide him? Tell him to stay in the barn?"

"All the time? Perhaps we can hide his background, tell her he was abandoned here when he was a baby. The King's People don't like the fact that we keep people like Rafe in our homes, but they know we do."

Rafe was by now looking at the two women with a worried expression, hearing his name repeated. Maida reassured him. "It's all right Rafe. You're safe here."

He returned to his food and Maida turned back to Peg. "You asked when the princess will come. I don't know exactly, but soon, I gather. They're anxious to get her out of sight."

"Perhaps we can do a little searching for information before she comes."

Maida's eyebrows went up. "But surely you need more rest from your trip."

Peg waved her hand dismissively. "I'm fine. I rested very well."

"What do you have in mind then?"

"I'd like to pay a visit to old Peyoter. His mother's line was full of Members of the Orders, including two great-aunts who were Dragon Priestesses. If anyone has any information passed down through family, it will be him."

"Well, if you think you're up to it," Maida said. "Peyoter will probably be running low on that salve for his arthritis anyway."

10 MOTHER TESS

Mother Tess woke, gasping for breath. Where was she? She peered around her at the scant furnishings of an unfamiliar cabin, lit by sunlight falling through cracks in rough shutters. The Apprentice traveling with her was curled up under the blanket beside her and, on a pallet on the floor, a double bump.

Oh yes. That young woodcutter and his wife, so nervous in the presence of one of the Old Ones. Tess relaxed, smiled to herself. They offered the best food they had in the house. Tess had insisted that they all share it.

They had also given up their bed. This Tess had accepted, her bones too achy now for a hard pallet on the floor unless there was no choice, which sometimes on this endless journey, there wasn't.

Then Tess remembered what had awakened her – the dream, again. She closed her eyes, tried to drift back into the dream state. If only she could figure out what the young King's People Dragon Priestess was trying to say. She had not had time to return to the Library and search the Dream Journals. She would have to figure out what it meant on her own.

Tess worried about the dream until the light faded toward dusk and the young couple on the pallet on the floor began to stir.

GLEVE

Gleve grieved over Maida. He had promised her. Bad enough that when the time came to ask Mother Sarah for a word, he had lost his nerve. It was even worse that he had been a coward about telling Maida, too ashamed to even look at her. Their friendship was surely broken now. She would never forgive him. He would not expect her to.

As he journeyed, though, the image of Maida's hurt eyes faded. He began to look forward rather than back. During the previous night's journey, as he had begun the climb into the foothills, it had been as if his spirits were rising with the land.

Finally he spotted the glimmer of lantern-light through the trees. He began to run, calling out Father Mallory's name. As he broke into the clearing in front of the small cabin, the old man opened the door and carefully stepped out onto the front stoop, peering into the darkness with his half-blind eyes. The light behind him shone through a wild halo of wispy white hair around his head. No one to brush it and tie it back, thought Gleve as he threw his arms around his beloved Teacher.

"My lad, my lad," Father Mallory laughed, kissing Gleve's cheek, tickling him with a white beard as skimpy and wild as the hair on his head.

"Father, I'm home! Home to stay!"

"What is that?" the old man asked, holding Gleve away far enough to peer into his face.

"I'm going to stay here. They have assigned me to co-practice with you."

Father Mallory pulled his former Apprentice to his chest once more. When he held him away again, his eyes were wet.

Gleve suddenly noticed how drawn and tired his Teacher looked. "Father, are you all right? Did the food I prepared last the whole time I've been away?"

"Yes, yes, it did and I am well—just tired."

"Then I will prepare a feast to celebrate our practice as co-Healers."

Gleve took a step toward the door, but stopped when Father Mallory put a fragile hand on his chest. "Yes, but quietly. We have a patient."

A young man, one of the King's people, lay unconscious on a pallet near the hearth. He was covered with a blanket, carefully tucked under his chin. The face above it was grotesquely swollen, the pale skin coloured red and purple, the eyes barely visible slits in the puffy flesh. Father Mallory had cleaned the wounds and stitched the cuts. He had had to shave off some of the young man's curly dark hair to stitch cuts on his scalp.

"Is the rest of him beaten like that?" Gleve whispered, glancing down the length of what was obviously a very tall body. The patient's feet hung over the end of the pallet.

"Unfortunately, yes."

"What happened to him?"

"I don't know. A couple of drovers stopped at the Foothills Spring. They heard someone groaning in the woods behind the meadow where they camp. They found him there, unconscious and nearly naked. He couldn't have been there long, probably since just the night before, or he would have frozen to death. Their wagon was empty, so they loaded him on and brought him here."

"They had no idea who he is?"

"No. The bits of clothing left on him and scattered about where they found him told them he wore the uniform of King Anglewart's service."

"It's not a Dragon attack, is it?"

"No." Father Mallory's eyes were sad. "More like a human attack."

12   MAIDA

By the time Peg, Maida and Rafe returned from Peyoter's cabin, dawn was approaching behind a thick layer of clouds. A light rain had begun to fall. In order to speed their pace for the last few miles, Peg had allowed herself to be carried piggy-back, like a child, on Rafe's strong back. He put every effort he could into carrying her carefully, and Mother Peg said that the ride was acceptably comfortable, to her surprise.

Rafe went immediately to put the goats and chickens in for the day. Maida gathered up the milking pail and a bowl of food. This she would leave with Rafe, knowing it would be too light for him to return and eat at the cabin.

Peg was anxious to write down what she had learned from Peyoter. She took her new leather-bound Journal carefully from the shelf above the writing table in her room, frowning at the other books on the shelf. Disorderly. She straightened them, then carried the new one to the kitchen and began to write. A little later Maida returned, eggs in her pockets, full milk pail in hand. While Maida poured the milk into pans in the cool room and skimmed the cream from the milk placed there the night before, Peg studied her notes, trying to remember if there was anything more.

"I should make cheese tomorrow night, or the next night at the latest," Maida said, returning to the kitchen and wiping her hands on her apron. "There's quite a bit of milk there." When Mother Peg did not respond, she revived the fire from coals banked on the hearth before they left the evening before. She filled the kettle and swung it on its metal arm over the growing flame. "Peyoter knows a lot," she remarked.

"He certainly does. I just filled seven pages with notes."

"Did you know that part about the Dragon Priestesses' apprenticeships, that they had to go off into the Mountains and have no contact with anyone outside their Order for the first seven years?"

"I knew it was a good long time, and very secretive." Peg continued to scan her notes. "You know, though, when I look this over, there is a lot of interesting detail, but not anything really new."

"Well, be patient," Maida said. "As you collect more notes, maybe some of the details will prove to be clues, pointing to something bigger, something new."

Peg went back to writing in her Journal and didn't stop until Maida brought her supper. After supper Mother Peg went to bed but Maida worked into the day, sweeping and scrubbing the small loft where she slept.

The next night, after darkness fell and the chores were done, Mother Peg and Maida sat at the table, Peg with one of her Healing Journals open in front of her, Maida reading the one book she was allowed to take down, Brother Findlay's Folk Tales of the Westlands. Despite refusing her as Apprentice, Mother Peg had insisted that she learn to read. "I'll have no servant that can't read a set of instructions or a recipe," the Old One had said, and Maida had been delighted. Brother Findlay's Folk Tales had become her textbook. She had been through it many times now, but never tired of reading it again. Part of it was just the sheer joy of reading.

Suddenly the peace of the little farmstead was broken by heavy boots and men's voices. Maida rose and went to the door. Lanterns approached from the west. Rafe paused near the stable, a shovel in his hand, then disappeared with a speed and silence that belied his size and usual clumsiness.

A large man in King Anglewart's livery came into the clearing, holding his lantern high. Maida recognized him as the Bailiff who had come before. The other men stopped in the shadows at the edge of the forest, their eyes wide with fear of the "witch." "Is Mother Peg here?" the Bailiff asked, approaching Maida.

"I am she," responded Peg, as Maida stepped aside to let the old woman come through the door.

"I am Aden, Bailiff to King Anglewart. I bring the Princess Liandra, eldest daughter of the King, to assign into your care."

"I am expecting her," said Peg.

Aden turned and signaled the others to come forward. Eight large men, dressed identically to Aden, struggled into the yard. Two bore a curtained sedan chair. Two more followed, carrying a large wooden chest. Behind them another pair carrying a decorated trunk. Lanterns bobbed on the corners of the sedan chair and the two chests, erratically lighting the path beneath the men's feet. They glanced around, wary and unhappy.

Normally they would take a member of the Royal Family wherever he or she needed to go by horse-drawn carriage, but the path to Mother Peg's cabin was too narrow and rough for that. One of the men stumbled and a sharp voice called out from behind the velvet curtains. "Ouch. Did you never learn to walk? Bumbling idiots!"

As soon as the chair stopped in the yard, a curtain twitched open and a pale young face glared at Aden and the two women on the step. It was topped with piles of carefully arranged blond hair and a sparkling tiara. "I present to you Princess Liandra," announced Aden, a touch of irony in his voice, Maida thought. Or was it relief?

Before Aden could continue the introductions, the Princess cried "No!" and tugged the curtain shut again. Aden nodded at the men carrying the chest and the trunk. "The box contains food supplies for the Princess," he told Peg. "The King is aware that it would be a hardship for you to feed the Princess. He will send food supplies every month while she is here."

"Thank you," muttered Peg. "My servant will show you where to put it." She stepped aside to allow the two men to maneuver the large wooden box through the door. Once inside, they followed Maida through the hearth room and into the cool room behind the kitchen where Maida quickly made room for it among the jugs and crocks that held their food.

She arrived back in the yard in time to hear Aden tell Mother Peg that the decorated trunk contained the Princess's clothing and other personal items she wished to bring with her. A brief smile flitted across Aden's face and just as quickly disappeared. Maida led the pair of men carrying the trunk to the bottom of the steps leading to the loft and left them to struggle upstairs with it.

At first Aden coaxed the Princess to leave the sedan chair. "No!" she insisted. "I'll not set foot in this mud-hole! It will ruin the hem of my dress!"

"I hope she brought something other than court dresses," Maida whispered to Peg.

"What else would the silly thing own?" Peg muttered back.

"You tell my father that he can't send me away like this!" Liandra wheedled Aden. "He always listens to you."

"Not this time," Aden said. "If you won't step down on your own, I'll have to ask my men to carry you into the house."

"Don't you let any of them lay a dirty hand on me!" shrieked the Princess.

"Then you must step down on your own," Aden told her.

Finally, Aden looked at the sky. "Your Highness," he addressed the Princess, "The stars are moving toward morning. We cannot afford to be caught by dawn and it is a distance back to Tummel. I'm afraid this is your last chance to step down on your own."

Greeted by silence from behind the closed curtain, Aden nodded at the men waiting beside the sedan chair. One pulled back the curtains and another hoisted the reluctant Princess over his shoulder. She was not tall, but very large and round.

Maida gasped. Peg looked at her sharply. "Ah yes," she whispered. "You've never seen anyone who is not half-starved, have you?"

The Princess shrieked and kicked every step of the way into the house. When the man deposited her in a chair beside the hearth, she leaped at him, clawing at his face. He easily grabbed her small, plump hands in his large ones and held her in place. "I'll tell my father," she sputtered at Aden. "I'll have you hung from the Castle walls. I'll, I'll … "

"I'm sorry to have to do it this way, Your Highness," Aden told her, calmly. "There is no choice. These are your Father's orders." With that, he nodded respectfully to Peg, then gave a signal to the man holding the Princess. He released her and both men left quickly. Liandra ran to the door after them. "Don't you dare go!" she shouted. "Don't leave me here!" She gathered up her skirts to run out into the yard, but a glance at the packed dirt in front of the door changed her mind. She shouted at the men until their lanterns disappeared down the path, then turned, her face scarlet, and scowled at Peg and Maida.

"Where is my room?" the Princess demanded.

"You will be sleeping in my bed in the loft. It will take me a few minutes to make it up. Why don't you sit down and …"

"Loft? Your bed? I want a room of my own, a proper guest room!" The Princess's voice rose into the register it had occupied when she was shouting at the departing men.

"I'm sorry, but it's all we have."

The Princess looked around her, taking in the whole cabin in one glance. "Well, make it up then," she said. She scorned the chairs by the hearth, preferring to cross her arms and stand in the middle of the room.

Maida resisted the urge to run up the stairs. She calmly ascended and began to change the bedding. Mother Peg pointedly returned her attention to the Journal on the table.

A few minutes later, Maida came back down the stairs, her own extra skirt and blouse over one arm and a bundle of sheets for the laundry under the other. "Your loft is ready, Princess Liandra."

The plump young woman gathered her skirts and stormed up the stairs. "Welcome to our home," Peg said as her silk slippers disappeared. There was a soft thump as she landed on the bed and Maida heard nothing more. Mother Peg turned a page in the Journal, her face set. Maida quietly returned to her Folk Tales.

Maida began to think about supper. She opened the wooden box in the storeroom and marvelled at the array of foods it contained – sausages, dried meats and fish, corked earthenware bottles of mead and wine, fruits and vegetables. Some she had seen only a few times in her life, some not at all. "Mother Peg," she called out to the Hearth Room, "I've barely seen most of these foods before. I don't know how to prepare them."

"They're not for you." A peevish voice came from the bottom of the stairs. Liandra stood there, straight-backed and regal despite her short stature, red eyes and dishevelled hair. She still wore her court dress, but the tiara had been put away.

"Our way is to share whatever we have," Peg told her.

"Not when King Anglewart's daughter is in the house," replied the Princess.

Peg's face darkened and she opened her mouth to respond, but thought better of it. She clamped her jaw shut and glared at the Princess. Maida had a sudden urge to laugh. Two equally iron wills in one small cabin. Had Mother Peg finally met her match? Then she remembered Mother Peg's remark about saying yes to the King also, perhaps, meriting death at his hands. Now she began to worry about Mother Peg's famous temper.

"Where is the bathroom?" Liandra demanded.

"Bathroom?" said Maida, who had never heard of such a thing.

"We have an outdoor toilet," Peg told the Princess, pointing to the door that led to a woven withy passageway protecting the path between the cabin and the outhouse.

"Disgusting!" The Princess hesitated, but clearly there was no choice. She disappeared down the passage, returning with her nose almost curled up. "Disgusting!" she repeated. "And obviously you have no idea how to cook," she added when she saw Maida's attempt to prepare foods she had never seen before. "I'll have to have lots of wine. Serve me!" she demanded. Maida, flustered, took time from preparing a separate meal for the rest of the household to pour the Princess a goblet of wine.

Once the Princess began talking, she didn't stop. "The pottery in this goblet is an inch thick! I'm supposed to drink from that? At the Palace we have crystal glasses for wine. And that's a filthy little room." She pointed toward the loft with her nose. "It smells."

Maida thought of the pallet she would sleep on today, on the floor in front of the hearth, and the soap and water she had stayed up late to wield the day before, and the work involved in washing bedding in the brook. She said nothing.

"If there's no bathroom, where do you take baths?" Liandra asked.

"There is a bathing place nearby, above a dam in the brook. Or, if it's too cold for that, we warm water over the fire and wash in that big tub, there on the wall," Maida pointed.

"Disgusting." This was fast becoming Princess Liandra's favourite word.

Dawn drew near. Maida made up a packet of food for Rafe and placed it in her empty milking pail. She looked meaningfully at Mother Peg. "One of the goats is limping. Could you come and take a look at her?" Without a word, Peg picked up her stick and hobbled behind Maida to the barn.

Rafe looked up from bedding a pen, delighted to see his beloved Mother Peg in the stable, which he considered more his home than the cottage.

"She's driving me mad!" Peg said to Maida as she settled on a stool. "I was hoping to go to Old Marya's cottage tonight."

Maida led the first of the goats to the milking stand. "Well, we shall go. We'll tell the Princess there is need of Healing in Marya's household. In fact, you should check Lib, see how her pregnancy is coming along." The rhythmic swish swish swish of milk hitting the bucket filled the small stable.

"Marya's mother was a Healer."

Maida stopped milking and looked up. "She was? Then why didn't Marya become a Healer herself?"

"There are always some from Healing lines that don't have the gift."

And those from other lines that have it, thought Maida.

"So we'll travel to Marya's cottage tonight and leave the Princess here on her own. She doesn't want to talk to us anyway, except to complain, and she won't run away. Where would she go? She might get her slippers dirty!" Peg snorted. "Can Rafe care for the animals, since we would probably be gone for most of two nights and the day in between?"

"Oh. I was thinking Rafe might come with us. You said it was passably comfortable riding piggy-back on the way home from Peyoter's cabin, and then we could travel fast enough to be there and back before morning. Your weight is nothing to him."

After thinking about it for a few minutes, Peg turned to Rafe. "What do you think, lad? Can you carry me around to People's cabins?"

He grunted happily.

When the household roused from sleep that evening, Maida told the Princess that they had been called away to Heal. "No!" Liandra shouted. Peg and Maida both stopped what they were doing, shocked. The Princess jumped to her feet, her face reddening. "You can't both go! And leave me here? All alone in the middle of the woods!"

"But you'll be all right here," Maida told her.

"No, no, I won't!" Suddenly Liandra burst into tears. Maida went to her and reached out to touch her arm. The Princess jerked it away. "Don't touch me!" she struggled to control her sobs. "Just don't leave me alone!"

"All right, all right." Maida soothed her. She gave Mother Peg a meaningful look. Shortly, both Teacher and Apprentice crossed the yard to the stable.

Maida urged Mother Peg to travel without her. "Rafe can carry the lantern and pack with you on his back, and he will protect you should that ever be necessary, won't you Rafe?" Maida turned to the large man standing beside Mother Peg. She thought his big, round face might break apart if he grinned any harder.

Maida sat by the fire mending one of Mother Peg's shifts and trying to ignore the Princess's continuous litany of complaints – the coarse pottery, the primitive utensils, the small Hearth Room, the tiny sleeping loft, the outdoor toilet. "I can't believe all you have is that tin tub for bathing," the Princess whined. "I must have a bath. I've been wearing this dress since yesterday evening. You'll just have to bathe me as best you can."

"Can you not bathe yourself?" Maida was polite, but could hear the edge in her own voice. She must be careful. Her own temper was already beginning to wear thin.

"A Princess does not bathe herself!" Liandra insisted. So, taking a deep breath, Maida heated water and prepared a bath in the tin tub.

"Now you will help me off with my dress, and you will not say anything about what you see."

Maida paused, surprised, but then began the lengthy task of unhooking the tiny metal hooks that held the bodice of the dress together. As she parted the fabric to expose the Princess's back, she saw what it was she was not supposed to mention.

"There are terrible scars all over her back," Maida told Peg in the stable the next night.

"Do you think Anglewart beats her? Or someone else at court?"

"Maybe," Maida frowned, "But they are in rows of four, like huge scratches. I wonder if it has something to do with the captive Dragon."

"Or a large dog, perhaps?"

"It would have to be a very, very large dog!"

Peg looked thoughtful. "They said a daughter of the King was killed by the Dragon, and other court children were injured. Maybe Liandra was one of them?"

"Well, she doesn't want me to ask about them, but we'll see. Maybe she'll trust me more as time goes on."

Peg snorted. "I'm not sure I can stand her that long."

"I think it would best for you to be on the road as much as you can, working on the Healers' project."

GLEVE

Through the kitchen window Gleve could see the stars fading and the distant mountains emerging as a jagged line, dark blue against the still-black sky. He covered his pans of bread dough with a clean cloth and left them to rise. A fire crackled in the grate. The patient was tossing and turning on his pallet. Every now and then he would mumble something. Father Mallory watched from the table, where he had several Journals spread out before him. "It's a good sign," he told Gleve. "He's struggling toward consciousness."

Suddenly the patient began speaking urgently, although most of it was unintelligible. The words that did jump out clearly were "Dragon" and "mountains." Father Mallory and Gleve looked at one another in surprise.

14 MELISANDE

The Queen sat at an open window, tears running freely down her plump cheeks. Her gaze remained fixed on the front gate, across the courtyard below, although it had been the day before when the carriage bearing her eldest daughter had clattered through it, lanterns bouncing as it jolted down the street toward the town, taking Liandra away – far, far away, just when she needed her mother the most.

"Queen Melisande!" A harsh young voice startled the Queen and she turned without taking the time to wipe her tears or compose her expression. The willowy young Thalasa stood before her, hands on hips and frowning. "What kind of Queen are you? Whimpering and crying like a beaten dog! Have some pride!"

Before the Queen could respond, an older, deeper voice cut in. "How dare you, a junior waiting-woman, speak to your Queen like that!" It was Imelda, Head Waiting-Woman, coming to rescue the Queen, as she had again and again, ever since Melisande was born. "A Queen is also a woman, and a mother, but you would not know how that feels." Imelda rose to her full height, which was considerable for a woman. Combined with her subdued but rich silk dress, she looked more Queenly than the Queen at this moment.

The younger woman scowled insolently at her superior. Although she was a junior lady-in-waiting, she was a Rodolph, one of the most powerful families in the Realm. Her classic patrician face made it clear that, although Imelda was chief of the waiting-women and Melisande was Queen, she looked down on them for their roots in the minor nobility.

"Leave us," Imelda commanded her.

Waiting just long enough, and moving just slowly enough, to reinforce her scorn, Thalassa picked up her skirts and left the room. The upper hinge squeaked, and the heavy wooden door thumped closed.

Imelda released the breath she had been holding and sat down beside the Queen, gathering Melisande into her arms. "There, there, lambie," she crooned, just as she had when Melisande was a tiny child. Melisande gratefully leaned into the older woman's breasts and released the sobs that remained trapped in her hurting heart.

"All my beautiful children, and now I've lost my last one," Melisande moaned into the wet patch on the front of Imelda's dress.

"Don't forget Farrell," the waiting-woman reminded her.

"I know, I still have Farrell, but he's nine years old and thinks of nothing but swords. In another year his father will take him too, and put him into soldier's training."

"At least your sons come to visit you from time to time. Few mothers can say that."

"Yes, and I love to see them, but they are changed. Torrie's heart is totally invested in his role as Heir. Eldrin nearly has to be pried off his horse at the end of every night's training. Once they become soldiers, there's little time in their lives for their mother."

" I know, I know," Imelda rocked her charge gently back and forth as a new burst of sobbing overtook the Queen.

The sobs faded into sniffles again, and the voice that came through them was suddenly angry. "They change when they become King too. Who would have imagined when I married that handsome, fun, passionate young man that he would become King, and start sending his children away for, for, the politics of it! And then that mad idea of raising that Dragon …" She broke off again.

Now Imelda held her tighter, and a tear or two trickled down her own cheeks, falling into the Queen's hair. They wept together for Ortrude, the Queen's sweet, cheerful second daughter.

The night passed quickly as the two women alternately talked and wept. Their tears had run dry when Imelda disentangled herself and went to fetch a basin of warm water. "Don't forget the feast for that Ambassador from the Southlands," she reminded her mistress. "Let's get you ready."

Although Queen Melisande was short, and round of face and figure, she had always had the gift of looking regal. Straight-backed, expensively dressed, displaying her husband's wealth in her jewelry, she was the ultimate gracious hostess. She could quickly find a spark of real interest in a guest and fan it into a lively conversation. The Secretary to the Southlands Ambassador was sitting beside her and she had discovered that he loved music. In fact, he played the harp when he had time away from his duties, mostly those lively dances that the Southlands people loved so much. Yes, he was enjoying the King's musicians who were providing accompaniment for the feast; he thought they were very impressive. Melisande tensed a little when he looked fully into her face. Imelda had called in Raissa, a waiting-woman gifted with skill at cosmetics. Obviously, she had succeeded in covering the ravages of the night's grieving, because Melisande sensed no response when the Ambassador's Secretary looked at her.

On the Queen's other side, King Anglewart was talking with the Ambassador. Melisande caught little scraps of their conversation during pauses in her own. They were talking about trade, horses, armies. Her back was turned to him, but she knew he would be engaging and cheerful, his handsome bearded face relaxed and laughing, while at the same time he would be watching the Ambassador like one of his own hunting falcons scanning the ground, waiting for a slip, a hint, an opportunity to pounce on an unguarded word. He would also be watching the Ambassador's cup, signaling the servant behind him to top it up every time the wine dropped by half an inch. It was, as always, exceptionally good wine, and exceptionally alcoholic. Queen Melisande had long ago learned to take no more than the occasional tiny sip for appearance's sake.

The musicians were taking a short break and the Secretary excused himself to go and have a word with them. There was no conversation behind her. Melisande turned toward her husband and caught him looking toward the lower tables with a hunger written on his face that she had not seen in many years. It was the look that was once hers, the projected longing that used to make a noisy scene disappear and link the two of them in exquisite, tingling anticipation of passion – a passion so powerful that he had defied his father and gone into hiding just to marry her.

She followed his eyes. They led to Thalassa. Her attention was, in turn, all on the King. Her eyes were slightly hooded but avid. Her face shone above the deep V of her bodice, tightly laced to display her creamy young bust. Melisande's stomach tightened.

"He's sleeping with her," Melisande whispered to Imelda, "Or if he isn't yet, he soon will be."

The Queen sat against her pillows dressed in her nightgown, silk sheets and an embroidered coverlet pulled up around her waist. Imelda sat close to her, on the edge of the bed. Thick curtains designed to keep the growing light of morning from disturbing the Queen's sleep held them in a private space. It was one of the few places where they could talk without fear of spying ears.

"But my dear, he has slept with one woman after another ever since Farrell's birth. You know that."

"But this is different. He looks at her like … like he wants to eat her up, like … like he used to look at me."

Imelda reached for the Queen's hand, squeezed it comfortingly, but her face began to register alarm. "And a Rodolph." Both women knew, too well, how important the alliance with the Rodolphs was to King Anglewart. Besides their old lineage and immense wealth, their estates were the key to the borderlands between the Westlands and the Southlands, a territory Anglewart's father had won at great cost and the current King struggled to hold. For that very reason the bride Anglewart's father had chosen for him all those years ago, the one he had spurned for Melisande, was a Rodolph, Thalassa's aunt.

"Imelda, I'm afraid. I'm no use to him any more. He wants me out of the way. Would he …?" She put her hands over her face. "If only he would set me aside! I thought he would send me to the Women's Retreat House years ago, divorce me, replace me with a higher-born wife. Then it was a terrifying thought to me. Now it's what I long for. I'm just so … tired!"

A moment later a small squeak in the door hinge gave warning. "Excuse me, your Highness." The voice of one of the kitchen servants came from behind the curtain. "I've brought your warm milk. I'll leave it here on the table."

The hinge squeaked again. Both women released the breath they had been holding. For years Imelda had been dripping salt water into that hinge. Every time the Bailiff responsible for repairs had it oiled, Imelda restored its squeak.

Imelda pulled the curtain aside and went to bring Melisande her cup of warm milk. She then kissed her on the cheek. "Goodnight dear Mel. Be careful. I'll not leave the anteroom. Call if you need me."

Several days later, Melisande did call. Frantic, the Queen had pulled the chamber pot out from under the bed and fallen to her knees, clutching her belly and throwing up, over and over again. Imelda, helpless, held her beloved charge as the younger woman writhed in pain. She would not send for the King's Healers.

MAiDA

"Each Dragon Priestess had a lifetime bond with only one Little Dragon." Peg sat on her stool and consulted the notes she had made that night. "If the Priestess died, her Dragon would join the Great Dragons or refuse food and drink and follow its mistress into the Spirit World. If a Little Dragon died, its Priestess became a Senior Teacher in the Order, but was never paired with another Little Dragon." Walking by with an armload of hay, Maida had never seen the old Healer as excited about anything as she was about this project.

"Remember old Thomas? Grimson's father?" Peg asked. "His aunt was a Dragon Priestess. She used to come and visit Thomas's mother with her gold Little Dragon. Of course, the Dragon Priestesses were never separated from their Dragons. They went everywhere with them."

"I wonder what it was like having a Dragon in your house?" Maida shivered a little at the thought.

"I asked Thomas that," Peg said. "He said the Little Dragons were frightening, especially to children, because they sat quietly on the Dragon Priestess's shoulder or the back of her chair and stared at the other people in the room."

"Oh my!" Maida exclaimed, trying to imagine a Dragon's, even a Little Dragon's, eyes on you. With no idea what a Dragon's eyes looked like, she pictured them as a larger version of goats' eyes.

When Mother Peg had scanned all of her notes for that night, she closed the precious Journal and set it carefully on a shelf Rafe had built for her behind one of the beams in the stable. She had decided to keep her current Healing Journal as well as the Project Journal well away from the Princess's eyes and came to the stable when she wanted to work on them.

The chickens had settled on their roosts and Maida was milking the last of the goats. Rafe had finished his work and eaten the supper Maida had brought to the barn for him. He yawned.

"Ah Rafe, my lad," said Peg. "You are a good beast of burden. Now

I think you should be seeking out your bed."

Rafe glowed with pride at what he took to be words of praise and, in this context, they were. Carrying Mother Peg on her rounds taxed even his strength. He yawned again and climbed the ladder into the loft.

Peg addressed Maida. "And how are you surviving with our self-centred royal guest?"

Surprised by her mistress's concern, Maida paused for a moment. Then, suddenly, her face crumpled and she was weeping. "I don't know how much longer I can stand her!" she sniffed. Peg used her cane to struggle to her feet and put her hand on Maida's arm. This further demonstration of caring released a flood of tears from Maida. She put her hands over her face and sobbed. Peg awkwardly patted her arm.

Then Maida started. "Look at the light! We must hurry back to the house!" She picked up the pails of milk and paused at the door, looking up into the grey dawn sky. Suddenly she gasped and stepped back, slopping milk and nearly running into Peg. The air around them filled with the slow flap flap flap of wings. Unmistakable – a Dragon. The creature's long shadow passed through the farmyard, black on grey. It hadn't seen them, because it didn't double back for a better look. The flap flap of its wings slowly disappeared into the distance. Maida's heart was pounding. "That was close," she said.

Mother Peg let out a long breath behind her. "Make sure there's not another one hunting with it."

Maida carefully searched the sky in all directions. "I don't see anything. Let's go!" She led the way with her buckets of milk. Peg came after, crossing the farmyard as quickly as she could.

Princess Liandra was sitting in a chair beside the hearth, bent forward and very pale. "Are you alright?" Maida set down the milk pails and moved toward Liandra.

The Princess immediately took control of her face and straightened up. "I'm fine!" she said, emphatically, then turned her attention to her skirt. She still wore the dress she had come in, dingy and a little tattered now, but in moments she had re-arranged it regally around her pudgy feet in their equally battered satin slippers. That done, the Princess started whining, "Where were you? I'm bored. I don't want to go to bed yet. Talk to me. Or better, yet, read to me." Liandra was intrigued with Maida's ability to read and often requested another Folk Tale from Brother Findlay's book.

"Perhaps you would find it entertaining to help me strain the milk and put it in the cool cellar," Maida suggested.

"Princesses don't work with milk."

"Well then," Maida said, her voice rising a bit, "Princesses will just have to accept their boredom." She turned away and set the milk buckets on the wooden shelf beneath the kitchen window.

Mother Peg settled herself in the chair on the other side of the hearth, her keen gaze fixed on the Princess. Liandra squirmed in her seat. "If you want to talk," Mother Peg said to her, "Then perhaps it's time we talked about your pregnancy."

The Princess drew herself up straight in the chair, her face reddening. "I am not pregnant!" she declared. Maida stopped and turned around. Mother Peg's jaw dropped open. Liandra looked defiantly from one to the other. "Stop gaping at me! I am not pregnant!"

"Then why are you here?" Peg asked her.

"Because my Mother thinks I'm pregnant. But what does she know? She went all hysterical, on and on, about 'lying down' with a boy, or a man. She tried to make me tell her who I'd 'slept with.' I have never lain down with any boy or man, or slept with one. When I could get a word in, I asked her if I could get pregnant if I never lay down with a man. She said no. Therefore, I am not pregnant!"

"Hmmmm." Peg looked thoughtful for a moment. "It's late this morning, and we all need sleep. But come evening, will you let me examine you?"

The Princess turned even redder and jumped to her feet. "No, no. no. It always hurts when Healers … You are not putting your dirty claws on me, you old crone!"

Peg's face darkened as well and she opened her mouth to speak, but before she could, Maida stepped in. "It's all right, Princess Liandra. Your body is your own here. No one will do anything you don't want." She cast a sideways glance at Mother Peg who scowled but said nothing. "Mother Peg is just offering to try and see if there is something wrong and that is why your moon bleeding doesn't come."

That morning, Maida helped Liandra take off her dress. What a silly design, she thought, impossible for the wearer to unhook by herself. No choice but to have a servant. She hung it carefully, although it was starting to look more like a rag than a dress. She picked up Liandra's silk nightdress, shook it out and gathered it to place over the Princess's head.

"You won't let that old witch touch me, will you?"

Maida stayed gentle as she pulled the folds of silk carefully down over the Princess's body, helped her into bed and pulled up the covers, but her vision had narrowed to a tiny, red dot. She had reached the limit of her patience and she knew it.

She spoke slowly, in a clear, hard voice. "Mother Peg is one of the most Senior and best Healers in the whole Realm! You are lucky to have her caring for you. We didn't ask for your company any more than you asked for ours. We are doing the very best we can for you. I don't want to hear another disrespectful word about her, or about me, for that matter!"

Liandra shrunk down and pulled the sheet up protectively around her chin. She looked frightened, and Maida had a sudden surge of fear as well. What have I done? she thought. This is King Anglewart's daughter. "I'm sorry," Maida said, her voice much smaller now. "I shouldn't have spoken to you like that." She turned and ran down the stairs from the loft.

When Liandra called Maida to help her dress that evening, she was quiet. They both were. Mother Peg and Rafe had gone off on one of their expeditions. Liandra descended the stairs, sat at the table opposite Maida and ate one of the open-faced sandwiches Maida had made from cured meat that had come in the box of supplies from the Castle. Then she reached across the table, offering the other half quietly to Maida. Maida, shocked, looked into the Princess's face for confirmation. What she saw was the first little inkling of humility she had seen there. She accepted the sandwich with thanks.

GLEVE

"Gleve," Father Mallory called from inside the cabin.

"Coming," Gleve called back from the garden.

"Hurry," the old man said. Gleve picked up his basket of herbs and vegetables and ran.

The patient's eyes were open, peering through the still-swollen yellow bruises. He gripped the edge of the blanket with his broken hands and stared in puzzlement around the room, stopping to study Father Mallory as he stood beside the hearth. His brow was creased, clearly trying to figure out who the old man was.

Gleve carefully sat down on the edge of the pallet. "Hello," he said. "We've been waiting for you to wake up." The troubled eyes left Father Mallory and peered at Gleve. The young Healer suddenly felt a little shiver travel through him. The patient's eyes were a clear, jewel-like colour of blue, startling in contrast to his dark hair and the even-darker stubble of beard that now covered his chin.

The patient tried to speak. "Where …?" was all he managed to say before his voice disappeared into a croak.

"You are in the cabin of Father Mallory, a Senior Healer, and I am Gleve, his Apprent … Co-Healer. We are caring for you." Gleve paused while the beautiful blue eyes studied every inch of his face. "Who are you?"

The young man's brow creased again, now with a look of panic. "Don't know …can't remem …"

"It's all right," Gleve told him. "Are you hungry?" The patient nodded, stiffly. "All right. I'll get you some soup and then we'll see if you can sit up to eat it."

The meal took the rest of the night, as Gleve slowly, gently, helped the patient to sit up and carefully spooned soup into his mouth. He was clearly ravenous. After Gleve had wiped his chin, straightened the sheet and helped him settle again, the patient rewarded him with a tiny smile, soon ended by a wince of pain from his damaged face. The young King's Man then fell into a deep sleep.

Gleve studied him. As his face healed it became obvious that it was long and fine-boned, probably handsome. His hands, too, as the broken bones healed, emerged as unusually long and delicate, not the usual build of a King's Man travelling the roads of the Realm. More like an artist or musician, the kind of King's servant that rarely left the Castle.

Gleve felt awe at his Teacher's skill and patience. According to the Order, he and Father Mallory were both fully qualified Healers, but could he have set all those fine, bird-like bones back into their original places? The patient was lucky; he would probably have full use of his hands again, important if he were an artist of some sort.

JESSA

On Sunday afternoons, the residents of the Women's Retreat House wereallowed to see visitors, even the servants if they had relatives outside. Each season, Ev's mother's sister gathered as many family members as she could and brought them to fill the visiting room. And fill it they did, from wall to wall, most of them standing because they outnumbered the chairs. They shuffled uncomfortably in their coarse clothes, a tightly clustered group of dark-skinned Earth People, out of place in the realm of the fair-skinned Sisters. They stared with big eyes at the fixtures in the room, the few furnishings, the shiny paint on the walls.

Jessa, hidden in the dark hallway, studied them through the open door. Ev made her round of the room, hugging and greeting each aunt, uncle and cousin. She had a few words with each, news of their lives, words to, from or about others who could not come. Her mother's sister, as always, waited until last. She always stroked Ev's face and hair as they talked, as though her love was too great to be carried by words alone, or as if she could cast spells as she spoke. Jessa knew that this woman would have been a witch if starvation had not forced the family to come to the town and sell themselves as servants. Ev's mother, too, had witchcraft in her and the longing to cultivate it, as did Ev herself.

This time there was a very old woman with Ev's aunt, a dried-apple face shrouded by a heavy cloak and hood, a knarled walking stick held in an equally knarled brown hand. Ev did not seem to know her. There was clearly an introduction going on, and Ev bowed her head in respect. Next Ev's aunt patted Ev's arm and moved away, leaving her in conversation with the old woman.

MOTHER TESS

She was small and plain, this great-granddaughter of the famous Calla. She kept her face down as manners required in the presence of an Elder, but glanced up to Tess's face from time to time, obviously curious. These moments gave Tess a glimpse of large, serious and surely intelligent eyes. "I understand you are the daughter of Stella." The girl nodded slightly. "Who was the daughter of Remaude." Again a tiny acknowledgement. "Daughter of the great Healer Calla."

The child surprised her by looking up, directly into Tess's eyes. "Have you come for me? Is it time?" she asked, her voice tight with held breath.

"What are you talking about, child?"

"My mother, she told me the Old Ones would send for me when it was time."

Tess's mind raced. What on earth was this about? It must be important. Her Healing sense was tingling. "Time for what?" she asked.

"The Key," Ev said, dropping her eyes again.

JESSA

Jessa heard the swish of a gown brushing the hall floor. She ducked behind the door just before Sister Alfreda arrived to announce that time for the visit was up. Ev and Jessa suspected they gave this notice before the time allotted was really gone, knowing that it took the family almost as long to say goodbye as it did to say hello.

Sister Alfreda went into the visiting room and began shooing Ev's relatives out like so many chickens in a dooryard. Behind her back, Jessa stepped into the doorway again. The old woman was clutching Ev's arm, staring hard at her. Ev pulled back a little and Sister Alfreda came right between them, taking the old woman by the shoulders and turning her toward the door. The crone almost lost her balance. Several nearby family members converged to hold her up, but she twisted back around, seeking Ev. Instead she saw Jessa standing in the doorway.

Her eyes widened and her mouth dropped open, displaying gums without teeth. She made a move as if to come forward, but the people around her did not let go. They cast frightened glances at Sister Alfreda and began to half carry the crone backwards toward the door. Alfreda, however, had caught the old woman's reaction and whirled toward the hallway in a swirl of grey skirts. Before she finished the motion, Jessa had flown into the stairwell and away.

20 MOTHER TESS

Tess crumpled toward the pavement. The strong lads on either side of her guided her to a nearby mounting block and carefully set her down. One of them supported her while the other called to one of the young women to fetch water from the courtyard pump. Remaude's other daughter, Marle, was at her elbow. "Mother Tess, what's wrong?"

Tess could not take in enough breath to speak. She reached for the leather bag that hung from her belt, held it out toward Marle.

"Something in here?" Marle opened the pouch, held it out. Tess pointed at a small bottle of Shock-Remedy. Marle lifted it from among the other items in the pouch. "Drops," Tess managed to say, and opened her mouth. Marle carefully opened the bottle and used the little stick inside to place several drops on the old woman's tongue. Even struggling with her breath and heartbeat, Tess noticed the woman's confident hands. Yes, she would have made a Healer.

The remedy moved through her pathways, calming and healing. Marle knelt before her holding her hands. When Tess recovered enough to walk, still with the support of Marle's strong sons, they made their slow way back to Marle's rooms in the carriage house of the wealthy home where she worked as a servant. When Tess finally sat before Marle's fire, a cup of hot tea in her hands and only the two of them present, Marle asked, "What was it you saw?"

"A dream," Tess said. "Come to life. An omen."

"What does it mean?"

"I don't know."

By the next evening Tess could still not answer Marle's question, but she had certain pieces: the young King's woman from her dream, Ev's Mother's message that someone would send for her when it was time, the Key, she had said. Whatever the Key would unlock, Ev seemed to know what and where it was.

"How often do you see young Ev?" she asked Marle.

"At least every season."

"Could you go back to her soon? Would those awful Sisters let you?"

"Of course. They know I'm Ev's next of kin. They let me visit when I please."

"Go to her," Tess said, fiercely, "Tell her that yes, the time has come. I am sending for her. Can she leave there?"

"No."

"She must find a way. We must find a way."

21

JESSA

"Who is that old woman? Jessa asked Ev as she plopped her mop back into the bucket. They were washing the floor of the hall outside the kitchens.

"She's a Healer, an Old One. Her name is Mother Tess."

"Is she a relative of yours?"

"No. My Aunt Marle brought her. She wanted to meet me."

"Why?"

Ev leaned on her mop, frown lines between her brows. "I thought I knew, but she didn't seem to know what I was talking about."

"What do you mean, you thought you knew?" Ev turned away, bent her back over her work. "All right, all right," Jessa said. "Earth People secrets." Ev gave her a sharp look, but just kept on sliding her mop in big crescents across the flagstones. "And why did she look so shocked when she saw me?"

Ev stopped mopping. "Is that what she reacted to? You? In the doorway?"

Jessa nodded. "So what was that all about?"

Ev shook her head and leaned on her mop, studying her friend. "I have no idea. I really have no idea."

After a few minutes, Ev reached down to wring out her mop and returned to systematically sloshing it across the floor. "So why do you spy on me every time my family comes to visit?"

"You've got some handsome cousins," Jessa gave her hips a little swish. "Who's the one with the big, broad shoulders?"

Ev concentrated on her work. "That's my cousin Giffe, Marle's son. He's a cattle-herd for the Sotta family."

"He looks so strong."

"He is."

"And the one with the long, slim hands, with the red trim on his jerkin?"

"That's Rolof, son of Uncle Strond. He probably would have been a musician in the Old Times. He knows hundreds of songs."

"What does he do?"

"He's a house servant in the Liet family mansion, in Von." Ev gave Jessa another sharp look. "So, you were looking over my male cousins?" Jessa blushed. "Why, Jessa? Even if you lived outside and had family you would never be married to one of us."

"Well, I can wonder, can't I? What it would be like to be touched by their strong, dark hands? What's the harm in that?"

"Oh Jessa! What harm?" Ev stopped mopping and turned to face her friend, her back rigid. "If any of them was caught looking back at you, he'd be out in a field tied to a Dragon stake by sunrise."

Abruptly serious, Jessa pushed her mop out of the pool of water that had formed around it and began to sweep it back and forth along the floor next to the swath Ev had already cleaned.

MAiDA

Rafe and Mother Peg arrived home a couple of hours before dawn. Peg asked Rafe to put her down next to Maida, who was weeding the garden by the lantern light. "I'm glad you're out here," she said. "I don't want to face the ice queen any sooner than absolutely necessary." Peg glanced toward the window and stopped in amazement. "That's not … no … surely I don't see mending in the grand lady's hands?"

Maida smiled. "Actually," she said, "There was just a tiny little bit of melting of the ice queen tonight, and yes, that's sewing. This evening she suddenly volunteered to work on my growing pile of mending. Apparently she is well trained in fancy stitchwork, and you can imagine what she had to say about our torn clothing! But, she's been working away at it, doing a far better job than I have ever done!"

"That wouldn't be hard," Peg sniffed. "So what happened?"

Maida brushed the soil from her tools with her hands, and placed them in the basket beside her. Then she stood up and wiped her hands on her apron. "Rafe," Maida turned to him. "Take the goats to the stable. We'll be there in a few minutes."

When he had gathered the goats and gone, Maida smiled triumphantly at Peg. "I told her off."

Peg's face went slack with horror. "You what?"

"I know I took a big risk, but I just couldn't take her disrespect any more, and it actually worked. Apparently there's a little streak of humility in there somewhere."

"Surely she didn't apologize."

"Oh no, not that, but she shared some of her food with me."

The Healers eyebrows went up. "Well," she said. "Well then."

GLEVE

Gleve had just helped the patient to the table for breakfast when the young man suddenly remembered his name. "Keiran!" he exclaimed. His face, almost returned to its normal shape under the colours of healing bruises, lit up with delight. He looked from Gleve to Father Mallory and back again. "I'm called Keiran!"

Father Mallory reached across the table to gently pat the bandaged hand. "Good. Your memory is starting to come back. By the time you have healed enough to travel to your home, you will know where it is."

In the weeks that followed, Keiran's body healed steadily. His broken bones knitted well. He could soon stand and walk, bend and lift with less pain every day. He became Gleve's helper, fetching water, firewood and food, trimming meat and vegetables for cooking, washing clothes and sheets, hanging them to dry on the line in the yard.

As Father Mallory predicted, his memory began to return, surfacing in sudden bursts. One day in the garden, he remembered the names of all the vegetables he could see and then more that were not there, including some that could not be grown this far north. He rhymed off a list of names one evening, apparently people he knew, although he could not say who they were or where he had known them. At bedtime, Gleve would sit on the side of the pallet, carefully smoothing salve on Keiran's healing wounds, and encourage him to talk. Bits and pieces would come out, moonlight on a multi-paned window under a thatched roof, a new pair of boots made of leather, the smell of flowers he later remembered were roses.

The rest of Father Mallory's prediction, that by the time he could travel he would remember where he lived, seemed just as far off as it had the day it was spoken. When Father Mallory fetched the clothes Keiran had been wearing when he came, carefully unrolling the small bundle of tattered fabric, Keiran brightened and said, "I serve King Anglewart."

"Do you live in the castle, then?" the Old Healer asked him.

Keiran's face clouded over again. "I must."

"Not necessarily. The King has servants in many places."

"I suppose. I'm sorry, I can't remember."

Later, in his own bed, Gleve shut his eyes and imagined that he was still smoothing salve on that fair, fine skin, his hands tingling with a warmth that slowly spread through his whole body.

"I'll be glad when we don't have to be so careful about what we say to one another at home," Father Mallory told Gleve as they walked along a narrow road deep in the Northern forest. They had received an urgent message the night before. Both Healers were needed in this out-of-the-way place.

"I know. There's so much we must not let him know. When he remembers who he is, and goes back …"

"You don't want him to go, do you?"

Gleve looked into his Teacher's eyes, twinkling in the faint light of the travelling lantern. He sighed, then blushed, then smiled. "You Old Ones," he said. "How do you read minds like that?"

The Old Man laughed. "Sometimes it's not that difficult."

Gleve blushed harder. "I'm trying not to be attracted to him. He is King Anglewart's man. I know it's just not …right … possible even."

"Dear boy," Father Mallory said, his eyes radiating love and respect for his co-Healer. "I shouldn't tease. I know it's not easy."

24 MELISANDE

Imelda sat on the edge of the bed as Melisande sipped a cup of strong herb tea. She had not sent for the King's Healers, but for a lowly chambermaid, a Woman of the People. The small, dark servant came running with the knowledge she had picked up as a child from her mother, a Healer, and a packet of herbs secreted in her apron pocket.

"Perhaps you will soon feel like eating again," Imelda remarked.

"Mmm. I think so, soon."

"But now you are tired," Imelda crooned to her charge, setting the cup on the table beside the bed. "You must sleep again."

Melisande's eyes began to close and then shot open. "No, not this time. Imelda, there is something I must do." She pushed the covers away, shifted herself until she was sitting tentatively on the side of the bed.

"No, dear Mel, whatever it is, surely it can wait until you are better."

"No, it must be now, while everyone thinks I hover near death."

"You do hover near death."

"Not quite so close now. Please, Imelda, help me dress. I must look very much like a Queen."

Imelda opened her mouth to object again, but then took in the determination on Melisande's face, a look she had seen there since the Queen was a toddler. There were moments when no one stood in this woman's way. Imelda sighed, lingered another moment in protest, and then went to select a dress.

Robed in yards of carefully crafted blue silk, her husband's favourite colour, and hung with jewels, Melisande checked herself in the mirror. She did look every inch a Queen, despite her deathly pale face. She had to move very slowly, but she could still manage the regal posture that made her look taller than she actually was. She accepted Imelda's arm for a visit to the chapel and knelt in front of the Warrior God while Imelda sat, head bowed, on the bench behind her.

The Little Dragons

The Warrior God towered above the altar, fully armoured and standing on a Dragon with his spear through its neck. His handsome marble face was bearded and fierce. He looked a little like Anglewart although, given its age, the figure must have been meant to suggest Anglewart's great-great-grandfather.

In silence Melisande walked slowly, leaning still on Imelda's arm, to the door of the passageway that joined the King's and Queen's rooms. Only four people were allowed to use this secretive hallway, the King, the Queen, Imelda and the King's Head Bailiff, Ermin.

The Queen turned to Imelda, gathering all the strength she had. "I'll go alone."

Imelda opened her mouth to object but Melisande shook her head. The Waiting Woman bowed her head and stood back.

The Queen moved slowly through the narrow hallway, her silk skirts rustling quietly around her feet. It was dank, made of grey stone like the rest of the castle. Once, when they were young, it was the passageway to love and sensual pleasure. It used to beckon to Melisande with its promise of warm reward in the light of morning. For the past nine years, ever since Farrell's birth, it had been deserted except for the occasional message carried by Imelda or Ermin.

The door at the King's side was now locked, probably to prevent Melisande or Imelda interrupting the King's new pleasures. Melisande listened. She could hear Anglewart's voice and that of Torrie, their eldest son and heir to the throne. She waited. She did not want Torrie to see her, much as she would like to see him. She could not hear the words, but their voices were angry. Fortunately Torrie was soon dismissed and Melisande heard the door close as he left the King's chamber. Now she heard only Anglewart's voice and Ermin's. She shivered. Ermin was a cool, menacing man with quick, calculating eyes. Melisande knocked.

"Who is there?" It was Anglewart who responded.

"Melisande."

There was abrupt and total silence on the other side of the door, then footsteps and the sound of the key in the lock. Ermin opened the door, his face shocked and almost as pale as her own. The King had risen to his feet, his face an echo of Ermin's.

Melisande gave them a moment to hide their surprise, then addressed the King. "I wish to speak with you my Lord." She cast her eyes in Ermin's direction. "In private."

Anglewart nodded to Ermin and he quietly left by the main door. He probably turned around immediately on the other side and put his ear to the wooden panel, but that was a chance Melisande would have to take.

"My Lady, please be seated. You are not well." Anglewart moved a chair forward and held it for her. She seated herself with great dignity. He took a chair facing her. "I hope your recovery progresses …"

"Anglie, let's not pretend with one another in private. We have done enough pretending in public to fill three lifetimes." The King fell silent. "I don't want to make any comments about my 'illness,' as you call it …"

Anglewart began to sputter. "I don't know what you mean. I …"

Melisande held up her hand. "Stop. That's not what I came to talk about." She waited until he calmed and gave her his full attention. "I know you want to marry a woman with more noble standing than I have. It probably would have been the right thing to do in the first place, if we hadn't been so much in love." She studied his face for a moment, still handsome but creased now with worried lines, the burden of his power. "But that's not what I came to talk about either. I know I am worn out, and have no further use here. Farrell will go to the barracks in a year or so. The other boys are doing well there. Liandra is gone, and when she returns she will be married to Prince Lochiel and go to live with him in the Southlands."

To her surprise, Melisande noticed a small frown of pain cross her husband's weathered face at the mention of Liandra. So, he still felt something for her, their first-born, their love-child, the one he held and played with before the weight of leadership fell unexpectedly on his shoulders.

"And Ortrude …" She was glad to see the pain in his eyes deepen. He did, then, feel something about losing his lively second daughter to that failed experiment with the Dragon egg. She allowed him a second to feel it before she went on.

"I would like to leave the role of Queen behind me as much as you would like to see me gone from it. No, don't interrupt!" She cut short his sound of protest, a daring move given the kind of cold and ruthless ruler he had become.

"I know you would have sent me to the Women's Retreat House long ago if you were a lesser man, and not so much in the public light." She paused for effect. "And you know I would be happy there, don't you?" She raised her eyebrows and waited until he gave her a small nod. "So now there is an opportunity. Everyone knows I am very ill and will surmise that I could die, which may well happen yet. Who would question you sending me to the Women's Retreat House for nursing care?"

The King threw his head back and laughed. The little signs of feeling she had seen earlier fled from his eyes. "Foolish woman. The priests have ultimate control of the Retreat Houses. If you live, how long do you think it would be before they realize that you are there under false pretenses? Even if you lingered on as an invalid, they would never condone my marrying another woman until they knew you were dead." He rose and looked down at her with complete disdain. "Now go."

Melisande kept her straight back and her dignity until the passageway door closed behind her, then managed a few more steps before she crumpled. Imelda, anxiously listening from the other door, rushed in to help her back into her room and her bed, where she could hold her and receive her tears.

ANGLEWART

As soon as the heavy wood and iron of the door thudded into its frame, cutting off the glimmer of blue silk skirts, the official door opened and Ermin, silent as ever in his deerskin-clad feet, stood before the King. Anglewart studied the narrow pale face before him, the eyes flicking here and there even in this tense moment. He let his Head Bailiff stew for a few moments, watching fear, anger, worry, determination pass through the servant's eyes. He knew Ermin well. They had been together since they were noble-born boys struggling over their lessons and clashing wooden swords in the practice yard. He had shared more of his life's hours with Ermin than with his wife, probably even more than he had spent alone in his own company.

Ermin, of course, knew his master too. What did he see in the King's dark eyes at this moment? The tangle of anger, fear and old love that had been triggered by Melisande's surprise visit? He had heard everything, of course, through the door. Ermin's ears heard almost everything in the Kingdom. He was the capable and clever head of the King's spy network. Did he see weakness in his Master, his Monarch, his old friend?

Before Melisande, they had had an encounter with Torrie, strong and headstrong eldest son. Anglewart sometimes had to shake his head in Torrie's presence, blink his eyes hard to erase the image of a bright-eyed young lad dogging his father's steps, so keen to learn everything he could about being King. Now it was an impatient young man who stood before him, one who would judge the King's thoughts at this moment to be weakness.

Torrie wanted his father to give him permission to rally the young warriors and challenge the Dragons in their mountain lair, as Anglewart's generation had done, as his father's and grandfather's generations had done before that. What had it gained them except a shallow glory in the eyes of their sons? Along with terrible pictures burned into their memories for life, their friends, brave, skillful young warriors, lying mangled on the battlefield, dead or screaming in pain, blood red or burned black, or worse, their screams fading as the scmitar claws of a Dragon carried them away. Torrie knew nothing of his father's scarred memories, or his growing regret for the destruction of the Dragon Priestesses, his persistent suspicion that it had been a mistake. The Heir would surely see such doubts as weakness. And what would he do, if he did know?

If Anglewart continued to live and rule, he imagined that his heir would someday issue a Challenge. Rarely used in the Kingdoms, a Challenge allowed an older son to take on his father in single combat. If he won, he would take over rulership of his father's lands. The father, if he survived, would live on as a dependent in his son's household, or live out his days in the Men's Retreat House.

Torrie, however, did not yet meet the conditions for a Challenge. He would have to marry and have a son of his own. He was moving in this direction and, the Warrior God knew, it was time to be thinking about a wife for him. Unfortunately his eye had come to rest on a young woman whose hand in marriage would be another kind of challenge for his father. He wanted to marry into the Rodolphs, the house his father should have married into, if he had been more attentive to power and less to love in his youth. He wanted to marry his father's mistress. Did he know the King was bedding the beautiful, young Thalassa Rodolph? It had not been more than a few months. Was it that obvious? Did Torrie already have his own spy network? Surely nothing like that could get by the ever-watchful Ermin, unless, of course, Ermin shifted his loyalty from father to son. That would make a quick end to the rule of King Anglewart of the Westlands.

Speaking of the ever-watchful Ermin, his eyes were on the King, a slight sheen of sweat broken out on his brow. Time to let him off the hook, renew his loyalty. "So," said the King, "She lives."

"Shall I have the agent executed?" Ermin's eyebrows rose in question. The King nodded assent. Ermin went on. "That serving woman, Imelda, had one of her witch friends treat the Queen, sire. I didn't think the woman could possibly have enough skill. Shall I send another agent?"

"They will be doubly on guard."

"I will wait, but not too long. Your heir is restless. Time to catch the little silver fish while you have the chance." So Ermin was still loyal to the father, for the time being.

The King gave his servant the faintest of smiles. Ermin had been a spymaster so long he could not speak in anything but code. "No, not yet," the King said. A frown passed over Ermin's brow and then disappeared just as quickly into his faithful servant mask. "I need to think," Anglewart said, nodding dismissal. Ermin, ever alert to his signals, took a backward step to the door, bowed and left.

Anglewart dropped his head into his hands and rubbed his aching eyes. It didn't help; too many rings. He held his hands up and studied them, thick and calloused, still the hands of an active soldier preserved by daily battles with his Sword-masters in the exercise yard, but hidden behind all this thick gold. That was his life, he thought, a soldier masquerading as a King.

Dawn began to colour the view from the open window. It looked across the hills and valleys of the Westlands toward the rougher Northlands. In the far, far distance were the tips of the mountains' black teeth against the lightening sky.

As he watched, the first tiny silhouettes appeared, stretching their almost invisible wings in the grey sky before snaking away, fanning out over the Kingdoms. Foul worms, emerging from their mountain lair to terrorize his people for another day. If the stinking creatures had any consciousness at all they would be laughing at him. The obsession of three generations of rule, the goal of his life, his father's, his grandfather's, was their eradication, and all they had succeeded in doing, it seemed, was to help the Dragons thrive. Every effort to kill them just robbed the Realms of good, courageous soldiers while filling the Dragon's bellies. Even now that he had turned his attention to learning about them, thinking about those damned witches and their ability to control the devils, all he had succeeded in doing was to kill one daughter and wound the other.

The King clutched the expensive fabric covering his muscled belly as a vivid picture came to him, his sweet and cheerful second daughter, the one who loved him without question, as if he were just a man and not a King, and his beautiful older daugher, who remembered him when he was just a man and not a King. Their faces, of course, echoed the youthful face of their mother when they were young and in love, and he had to admit, even older, even deathly ill, she was still beautiful. No wonder he had not looked at her in months, even as she sat by his side fulfilling her official duties as Queen. How could he bear to kill her if he looked at her?

Time to close the shutters, call a valet to remove the rings and heavy robes and guards to watch his door through the day. Would he go to Thalassa? His angry words with his son had pricked the urge to lie with her, enter and conquer once again the object of his son's immediate ambition. On the other hand, Melisande's beautiful face in his mind's eye threw cool water on his desire, peeled it back to reveal the layers beneath. Briefly he glimpsed his own loneliness, the loss of a love that had gone far deeper than his love of power. How could she still weave this spell over him? He abruptly dropped the handful of fabric he had been crushing, formed his hand back into its fist and pounded the glossy wood on his desk. Damn her. He would go to Thalassa. Now. Fully robed and raging. And take her.

MELiSANDE

Later that night King's Men arrived at the Queen's door with an arrest warrant. Imelda tried to block them. "No, you can't take her. Can't you see how ill she is?" It made no difference. One of the soldiers scooped the Queen out of bed. Imelda demanded that he pause long enough for her to tuck a blanket around Melisande and gather up a few things. He gave her a few moments, then she followed them into the stone hallway.

In the dungeon there was a private room for highborn prisoners. Although it was grim, dark and closed in by iron bars like any other cell, it had a large and comfortable bed, with curtains for some measure of privacy. It had been freshly made up, the women were glad to see. The King's Man deposited the Queen into it. Imelda placed the few things she had managed to bring carefully on an empty shelf on the wall and hung a dress for the Queen on a hook she found beside it. As soon as the men were gone, she crawled in beside Melisande. The two women clutched one another in fear and despair. Neither could imagine sleeping.

"Imelda."

"Yes dear."

"When I was so ill with the poison, going in and out of consciousness, I kept reliving the worst moments of my life, vividly, as if they were happening to me at that moment."

"Sh, sh, sh."

"No. It helps to tell it. I remembered giving birth to all of the children after Liandra and … the horrible humiliation … all those officials in the room – as if anyone could or would switch babies behind their backs!"

Imelda began to rock Melisande, as if she were still a small child. " And the awful pain when Farrell was born. I thought I was going to die!"

"And, above all." Melisande voice tightened with tears. "Ortrude and Liandra … lying in the snow … the blood … and the Dragon going over the wall, chain and all."

Imelda continued to rock and rock her beloved, hurting child well into the day.

GLEVE

Gleve started out of a deep sleep. Daylight peeking through the cracks in the shutters lit Keiran's anxious face above him. He could feel Keiran's hand on his arm. For a second, his heart and body leaped together toward the handsome young King's Man, but Keiran was not there for him. "Gleve, Gleve," he whispered urgently. "I have a brother. He's ... he's hidden. I left him. I told him not to leave the basement. I stocked it with food, but how long have I been here? He must have run out by now. When he gets hungry, he'll leave the house. I must go home. I must ..."

Gleve slid out from under his blankets and took Keiran by the shoulders. "Keiran, Keiran, calm down." He heard Father Mallory's feet hit the floor. There was a pause. Gleve could picture his Teacher fumbling for his slippers and cane. Then there was the tap shuffle tap shuffle of the Old Man coming to help.

In moments he was there, his cloud of white hair wild about his head. He reached out to lay his hand on Keiran's arm. "My son, what's wrong?" he asked.

Keiran turned and sat down beside Gleve on the edge of the bed. Gleve put an arm around his shoulder. Keiran was trembling. "Father Mallory, I remembered, my brother, he's in danger." He repeated what he had just told Gleve.

The Old Man now sat on the edge of the bed as well, on the other side of the agitated Keiran. "Your brother was hidden? Why?" His voice trailed off as he considered various possibilities. Keiran fell uncomfortably silent. "Remember, my son," Father Mallory told him. "We People of the Land don't hide away family members who are 'abnormals' as you call them."

Keiran let out a breath, calming in the Old Man's presence. "He's ... yes, an abnormal. He's not safe. He's ..."

"You must find him," Father Mallory said. "But we don't know where, do we?"

The Little Dragons

Keiran leaped to his feet, pacing back and forth in the tiny room while both Healers watched him. "I can almost remember."

Gleve led Keiran to the kitchen table and set about making tea. Father Mallory sat down opposite him. Keiran dropped his head into his hands and was silent.

The teapot was empty, the biscuits were eaten, and Gleve was thinking about urging Father Mallory to go back to bed. In fact, he was thinking longingly about going back to bed himself, when Keiran suddenly leaped to his feet, roaring, "Hanford! I live in Hanford!"

MAiDA

Rafe and Maida fed the animals and cleaned the pens while Peg sat on her stool reading through her notes. Rafe ate his supper in no more than three bites, it seemed to Maida, and then was ready for bed. As he disappeared into the loft, Maida sat down to milk and Peg carefully closed the Journal in her lap, her face creased into a frown.

"Anything new tonight?" Under Maida's strong hands the milk hit the bucket with a rhythmic whit, whit, whit.

"Everyone has a story or two about this or that Dragon Priestess that they knew or knew about when they were children." She sighed, deeply. "But no key that would unlock the door. No sign pointing to how they found the Little Dragons and learned to communicate with them."

"Well, I have a little piece of information to cheer you up." Maida paused in her milking. Peg's eyebrows went up, her attention caught. "The scars on the Princess's back? I was right. They were made by the captive Dragon."

"Did she tell you the story then? What happened?"

"She and her sister and two friends, other children of noble houses, were playing with it in the castle courtyard when it got very excited and upset. It's eyes changed colour. Did you know their eyes were like rainbows, with colours moving in spirals?"

"Yes, I knew that."

"Oh." Maida paused, disappointed that she her prized piece of information was old news to Mother Peg.

"Go on girl."

"And it raised the crest on its head, the first time they had seen it do that. It was a blue Dragon, by the way." Peg nodded. "Anyway, at that point it suddenly turned on them, growling and slashing with its claws. They ran, but it followed, tearing its chain out of the stone wall. It killed Liandra's sister and one of the other children, knocked Liandra on her face, jumped on her and clawed her back, then flew away over the wall."

"Was it perfectly tame up until then?"

"I don't know. It must have been, or would Anglewart have allowed the children to play with it like some sort of pet?'

"How old was it then? How big? How big was it when it first hatched? What was it like? Did they learn anything about it during the time they were playing with it?"

Maida rose to put one goat back in the pen and fetch another. "Mother Peg! I don't know! I tried to ask more questions, but she clammed up tighter than a locked box!"

Mother Peg sighed again. "Oh, I want so much to know!"

"Well, I think she's slowly coming to trust me a little. Maybe she'll tell me more as time goes on."

EV

Ev tried to calm her breathing. There wasn't much air in the stuffy depths of a laundry cart full of dirty sheets. Marle had known that the bedding from the Women's Retreat House was washed in an open-air laundry down by the river. They had come up with a plan: Ev would find out where the laundry carts waited to be wheeled away. Once down at the river, they often sat untouched for several nights, since it took most of the week to wash and dry their contents.

When the laundry servants left for the day, Ev would slip out and hide somewhere under the wharves along the river. This would be the most dangerous part. Even though the wharves were only a few hundred meters from the laundry, a hunting Dragon would easily spot a young woman running down the cobbled street between the two if it happened to soar overhead. It would be important to listen, watch, spot doorways, overturned carts or anything else she could hide under if she were caught along the way. When darkness fell again, she would make her way to Marle's rooms.

Marle explained that whatever the Key was, knowledge of it must have been lost in the times of the Terror, but the Old Ones were working to put the puzzle back together again, and Mother Tess was sure that the Key was an important piece. It was indeed time. Mother Tess had sent for her.

Ev's chest hurt from trying to suck in enough air, She felt as if she were suffocating. Could that happen under a pile of sheets? Would it be possible to black out and then die from lack of air? She ached to stand up, shake the sheets from her shoulders and fill her lungs.

A metal latch rattled, followed by the groan of hinges and heavy wood. There were voices in the hallway where the full laundry carts stood, lined up along the wall. Ev didn't recognize them. They must be laundry servants who worked down by the river. She also couldn't hear what they were saying, the words muffled by the folds of linen all around her. She clutched her own knees, curling tighter to fight her panic.

In a few minutes she regretted that she had burrowed right down to the floor of the cart. As it began to roll it bumped and lurched, grinding her bones against the wooden boards. Ev bit her lip to keep from crying out, but the next bump nearly drove her teeth through the flesh. She settled on gritting her teeth together hard.

After an endless, bruising journey, the cart rattled to a halt. "Over here," someone shouted, and the cart moved again until it banged into something, probably another cart. This brought an "oof" out of Ev, but apparently no one heard her under the crash of the two carts, because no one investigated.

MELISANDE

The bag of herbs from the chambermaid was dwindling, but it had done its work. Melisande was clearly recovering. By the third night in the dungeon, she felt well enough to put on the dress Imelda had brought for her and move to one of the simple wooden chairs that furnished their cell. Imelda shook out the covers and re-made the bed.

"I wish I could have my embroidery," Melisande told her. "Something to do with my hands."

"I'm sorry. I had only a few minutes to grab what I could."

"I know. I'm not criticizing. You were a Godsend that night, as always. It would just be nice to have something to keep busy, make the time pass, worry less."

No sooner had those words left Melisande's mouth, when they heard the scrape of the iron door at the end of the corridor, heavy boots on the stone floor. Two of the King's Men appeared at the barred door to their cell, unlocked it and entered. Behind them came Ermin, cloaked and evil-looking. Melisande stood, her regal stance, while she cringed inside.

"You will come with us, your Highness," Ermin had a smooth voice, understated. "Are we coming back here, or should Imelda take our things?" Melisande asked.

Ermin sneered and shrugged his shoulders. "Take your things if you like. You're not coming back." Melisande's skin tightened into goosebumps. Imelda gathered up their few possessions once again.

At the door leading out into the courtyard, Ermin picked up something dark from a hook on the wall. As he turned, he unfolded a pair of travelling cloaks and held them out. Imelda helped the Queen put one on, then pulled the other around her own shoulders. The armed men escorted them out into the darkness. Imelda glanced at the stars. It was close to morning. Were they to be tied out for the Dragons?

MAiDA

Aden, the King's Bailiff, came with four men carrying two wooden boxes filled with fresh supplies for the Princess's meals. Rafe, as always, disappeared from sight as soon as the flicker of their lanterns appeared far down the trail. As they entered the clearing, Liandra ran out into the barnyard, ignoring her already-ruined shoes. "Aden, take me home!" she commanded.

"It's nice to see you too, my Lady," Aden responded.

"Just take me home," she insisted.

"You know I cannot do that, my Lady, but I have food and wine for you, the best the Castle has to offer. Also, some fresh clothes." Aden was too well trained a servant to look at the wreck of a dress Liandra was wearing, or her hair tangled and flying free, but the contrast to the clean and neatly dressed party from the Castle made everyone think the same thought.

As Aden and Peg conducted their business, exchanging full boxes for the empty ones, discussing arrangements, Liandra continued to storm about, now demanding, now begging to be taken home. Aden ignored her until it was time to leave, when he politely wished her well.

The Princess screamed and ranted until the Castle party was well out of sight, then collapsed on the front step, sobbing. Maida considered comforting her, but a little shake of Mother Peg's head warned her away. Maida and Peg went about their business.

Suddenly the Princess shrieked. "Who's that?"

Maida ran out of the kitchen. "Who?" she asked

"There! There's a man looking at me from the loft of the barn. He's gone now, but I swear he was there."

Maida paused, then decided there was no alternative. "That's Rafe," she said."He lives here."

"Oh, I thought there was someone else here, an abnormal."

Maida took in a startled breath.

"He's frightened of me, isn't he?" Liandra looked thoughtfully at the dark barn. Suddenly she called out in the direction of the open loft door. "Rafe! It's all right! I won't hurt you!" Maida started again, then she smiled at the Princess, who, amazingly, smiled back before returning to the kitchen.

That morning, when Maida went to the stable to milk, Rafe was restless. "'Cess!" he said to Maida.

"Yes, that was the Princess."

"'Cess," Rafe repeated.

The next evening, Peg was in her room preparing for that night's journey. Rafe crept cautiously to the kitchen door. Liandra was sitting in her usual place by the hearth, her breakfast coffee in her hand. Rafe stared at her through the door, his eyes as round as dinner plates.

"It's all right, Rafe," Liandra told him. "I won't hurt you." Rafe continued to stare. Liandra turned to Maida. "He lived in the Westlands before, didn't he?"

"I don't know," Maida responded

"He's telling me now."

"He's …?" Maida searched for words.

"I can hear him, in my head, not in words, exactly, but I can hear what he means," Liandra told her. "That's why he's frightened of me, because he knows I'm from the Castle." Liandra paused, then understanding dawned on her face. "He was left out for the Dragons, wasn't he?" Maida was too shocked to respond. Liandra turned back to Rafe. "My father's men did bad things to you, but I won't hurt you."

"Now that's a promise you'll have to keep," Maida told her.

"What do you mean?"

"Think! Rafe was left out for the Dragons. Hiding him here means breaking your Father's laws. If you ever mention that Rafe is here, you will put him and us in grave danger, even yourself, if you don't report him right away."

Princess Liandra blanched slightly at the thought of what could happen to anyone caught breaking her Father's laws. "Oh," she said. "I hadn't thought of that."

"Well now you must not only think of it, but remember," Maida warned her.

The Little Dragons

It was the next morning, after Peg and Rafe returned and joined her in the stable, that Maida had her first opportunity to report on this conversation to Peg. Peg turned to Rafe. "Was she right?" she asked him. "Is that what you told her?"

Rafe grinned at her and grunted.

"Do you suppose it's because they are both King's People?" Maida asked. "Do they read each other's minds?"

Both women looked at Rafe. He stopped forking hay, grinned at them and said, "'Cess!"

EV

The night was endless. There was, thank the God, no more banging around, but the sheets began to press down on Ev in the suffocating dark. She tried not to imagine throwing them off, gasping in a big breath of cool night air. Instead she tried to doze, but the wood underneath her bit into her flesh making even light sleep impossible. She occupied her mind by remembering good times, visits from her family, long sessions of working and chattering with Jessa. This thought made her eyes prickle. There would be no going back. Would she ever see Jessa again?

"Is there time for one more?" Ev jumped as a loud voice called out just beside the cart in which she hid. She couldn't hear the response. "The Bird Star is still over the horizon," the nearby voice said. Again she could hear no response, but suddenly the cart lurched into movement again.

No, no, Ev thought, panic rising into her throat. You don't have time for one more. Wash it tomorrow … but before the thought was even complete the cart went over with a crash and abruptly she was plunged into painfully hot water.

The wet sheets wrapped themselves around her, clinging, pulling her down. She flailed against them, entangling herself even more. Her skin felt as though it was burning off of her bones. There was no controlling the panic now. She tore at the fabric clinging to her face, began to cry out, but boiling water rushed into her mouth, choking her.

The sheets settled, then began to rise again. Ripping and tugging against the sheet that covered her head, Ev rose with them. Just when she thought her lungs must explode, her hair was grabbed from above. She was lifted. If she could have screamed from the pain of it, she would have. The wet linen was pulled from her face and she gasped hoarsely for air. All around her was a fantastical world of rising steam lit by a row of dancing torches. Her lungs hurt; her skin hurt; her scalp hurt and a large face loomed in front of her own, dark wisps of hair escaping from a grey servant's headscarf. "What's this then?" it said.

KEIRAN

Keiran walked quickly along the narrow road. At first he had followed a map Gleve had drawn for him because, although he had remembered the name of his village, he had no idea how to get there. As he came closer to home, however, the lantern Gleve and Father Mallory had given him picked out familiar landmarks that in turn triggered memories. Now he knew that the road he was following would become a side street of Hanford and, well before that, he would come to the cottage that was his home. It had been built near the town but out of sight of the other houses because of Aymeric. He had also remembered his brother's name along the way. Aymeric.

His injuries, barely healed, were aching from the hard walking but he kept going, even picked up his pace, his heart rising into the back of his throat as he got closer and closer. Aymeric. How long had he been away? What had become of Aymeric?

Another lantern approached, coming slowly in the opposite direction. Keiran called out, "Hello. Who goes there?"

"I am the Widow Elnord. Who are you?" The voice was that of an old woman, the name familiar.

"I am Keiran of Hanford." The Widow's lantern stopped moving forward and there was a moment's silence.

Then suddenly it was coming more quickly. The Widow stopped a few feet away and held it higher, peering into the darkness. As soon as he saw her face Keiran remembered, a neighbour, a friend. "Why so you are. We were told you deserted from the King's service." There was movement as she made the sign for the Warrior God's protection. She quickly snuffed out her light and looked behind her toward the village. "Quick!" she hissed. "Put out your light." When Keiran hesitated in confusion, she said, "Now!" her voice so full of urgency that he immediately dropped the hood of his own light.

They stood silently in the dark roadway. As his eyes adjusted to the faint light of the stars, he could see her looking back toward the village, listening. She put a hand on his arm and whispered, "This way. Quiet as you can."

He followed her a short way into the woods, tripping over roots and hummocks. "Shh," she hissed. A few yards in they came to a small clearing created by a large fallen log. She paused to listen again. "I don't think anyone saw us," she whispered, then sat down on the log to catch her breath.

"What's wrong?" Keiran asked her.

"You've a price on your head."

A bolt of shock travelled through Keiran's whole body. "Because they think I'm a deserter?"

She paused to listen again for anyone who might be coming along the road, then continued in a low voice. "That, and because a month or so after you left on the King's expedition to the mountains, a young man came out of your house. I think he was looking for you, but he couldn't speak right. You're charged with hiding an abnormal."

The Widow paused again, partly to listen to the road, partly to take in his response in the dim light. Keiran had frozen with fear. "What happened?"

"As soon as people realized what he was, they called the King's constables. He put up a fight, probably frightened out of whatever wits he had. A good fight too; he was a big lad."

"Was?"

"They put him out for the Dragons. What else would you expect?

Keiran closed his eyes tight and held his breath, holding in the cry that wanted to come from his belly through his throat.

After a minute or so, she asked, "Was he your brother, Aymeric?"

"Yes," Keiran breathed the word, his throat clenched.

"I thought he might be. When he was four years old or so your mother told everyone he had died of a fever, held a funeral and everything. So she kept him hidden all those years."

Keiran felt a shock run through him. He suddenly had a vivid picture of his beloved mother. She, too, had been wiped from his memory. "My mother," he whispered to the Widow Elnord. "Where is she?"

There was a sudden stillness beside him, then a rustle as she got to her feet. She made the Warrior God's protection sign again and began to back away. "Your mother has been dead for almost ten years," she hissed and turned to make her way quickly back to the road.

MELiSANDE

It seemed the carriage had barely begun to roll when it stopped again. Melisande and Imelda gave each other a frightened look. One of the King's Men opened the carriage door and Ermin appeared there, offering his hand. They stepped out onto cobblestones in a dark alley. There was a high stone wall beside them and an open door. As they stepped through Melisande caught her breath. It was the back door of the Women's Retreat House.

With rising hope, Melisande followed Ermin's narrow back down a short passage and into a simple but comfortable reception room. Waiting for them there was Head Mother Mabonne, dressed in the simple grey gown of the Women's Retreat House and the white veil of her rank. "Your Majesty," she said, lowering her head and taking Melisande's hand.

"I wouldn't bother with 'Your Majesty,'" Ermin cut in abruptly.

As soon as the women sat down, he began. "This is the King's command. You …" he turned to Melisande, "… will live out your days here. Your life as Queen is behind you, including your name. The Head Mother will assign you a new name and that is all you will be called by, ever, by anyone."

"Only seven people know who you are," he glared at Imelda, "The four of us, the King, and the two men-at-arms who escorted you here. By tomorrow, only five people will know." Melisande narrowed her eyes over the cruelty of it. Ermin watched her with satisfaction. He had only told her to get her response, Melisande realized, just as he had kept their destination secret until they arrived at the door.

"You are all sworn to absolute secrecy. If this information ever emerges beyond the five people named, you will all die for it." He paused for a moment for this to sink in. "The Queen's funeral will be held in a few days …"

Melisande suddenly gasped. "But my children! Are you saying that my children won't know? They will think I am dead?"

"That is what I am saying Madam. The Queen is dead."

Melisande began to rise to her feet, but instead slid to the floor in a faint.

When Melisande woke up she found herself in a small, clean bed. She looked around her. It was a plain but comfortable chamber. An open window let in a fresh night breeze. A plain grey dress hung on a hanger on the wall, a black veil on a peg beside it. Of course! She was in the Women's Retreat House.

A slender young girl dressed in grey with a matching kerchief tied over her hair let herself in, balancing a tray, and quietly closed the door behind herself. When she turned, Melisande felt a jolt of shock. "Liandra!" she said, struggling up into a sitting position.

The young woman almost dropped her tray in surprise. "No, Lady. My name is Jessa."

"Oh!" Melisande's eyes filled with tears, which she quickly controlled. "Of course. Come here."

"I've brought you some broth from the kitchen. I was told if you were sleeping to leave it …"

"Come here, Jessa." The young girl came and stood by the bed. Short and naturally rounded, her spare diet had nonetheless made her much thinner than Liandra. But the face, the hair, the quick, capable hands.

Melisande leaned back against the pillows. She patted the bed. "Sit here for a minute." Jessa obeyed, clearly embarassed under the scrutiny of this latest Widow to arrive at the Retreat House.

Melisande slowly raised her hand and laid it on Jessa's cheek. The young woman remained still, although there was alarm in her eyes. "Jessa," Melisande said, while stroking the young woman's face, once, twice. Then she lowered her hand. "Thank you for the broth, Jessa, beautiful child."

"You're welcome, Lady." Jessa leaped up from the bed and was out of the door like a sprite.

JESSA

Jessa stood against the wall in the corridor outside the new Widow's room. She held her own hand where the Lady's hand had been. Her cheek burned. Later she slipped down to the pantry where Ev had been assigned to a month of peeling potatoes. "Why would she do that?" Ev asked.

"Who knows? She's very strange."

Eve's hands never ceased in their work, even as she spoke. "It's going to be interesting waiting on her."

"An adventure!" Jessa's eyes lit up. "A high-born lady called me beautiful!"

MAIDA

Liandra handed Maida the finished mending, neatly folded and piled. "Now what shall I do to keep from dying of boredom?" she asked.

"You're so good with a needle," Maida ran her hand over an almost-invisible patch on the uppermost item in the pile. "There's lots of fabric upstairs, you know. People who spin and weave often give Mother Peg lengths of linen or wool in return for Healing and, as you know, I avoid sewing it up as long as I possibly can."

"It's rough," Liandra commented when she felt the fabric lengths Maida pulled from a trunk in the loft. She studied Maida's dress. "So, would you like a new bodice and skirt?"

"Everything I have is still good, especially now that you've done such a nice job of mending them." Maida paused, looking at the tattered silk dress Liandra wore, still the same one she had arrived in. "What about you? Wouldn't you be more comfortable here in something not quite so fine?"

"Oooo—next to my skin? It would be all scratchy!"

"You have other court dresses in your trunk. Why haven't you worn those?"

"They're too good. They'll just get ruined."

"There are silk chemises in your trunk. You could make yourself clothing like ours and wear one of those underneath."

"Hmmm," Liandra pulled out the finest piece of linen she could find and rubbed it between her fingers. "I suppose I could."

"And our clothing is better for pregnancy. You just let out the lacing as your belly grows …"

"My belly is not going to grow!" Liandra snapped. "I am not pregnant!" She dropped the linen back into the trunk and stomped down the stairs.

GLEVE

Lynna followed Gleve everywhere. He went to the garden to gather a few things for their midnight meal. She dug up too many beets. He said nothing. As he bent to pick up the harvest, she bent faster, gathering everything into her folded apron to carry back to the house. She watched him begin to wash the vegetables at the pump in the yard, then offered to do it. She watched him begin to trim and cut them at the board in the kitchen, then offered to finish. Gleve dropped into a chair at the table and caught Father Mallory's eye. The Old Man's face was scrunched up, obviously trying not to laugh. This deepened Gleve's annoyance.

"There's almost no water left in the buckets and dawn will soon be here. I'll go and fetch some," Lynna offered.

"Sure. Thanks," Gleve told her. She clattered out to the yard with the buckets and in a minute the squeaking of the pump covered any conversation that might take place in the kitchen. Gleve sighed. "I guess I'll have to have a talk with her."

"I guess you will."

"Stop laughing."

"Me? Laughing?" Father Mallory let a small giggle slip out.

Gleve smiled, just a little.

"At least she keeps you busy and annoyed enough to stop you from dwelling on how much you miss Keiran."

Gleve's smile disappeared into sadness.

"I'm sorry," Father Mallory said, reaching across to hold Gleve's hand for a moment. "I know you could love him, but it would be so dangerous."

"I know. You're right." He sighed. "I just wish she wouldn't make those cow's eyes at me all the time."

"There's quite a lot to talk with her about."

Just then the pump stopped and Lynna called out to them, "There's someone coming. Someone sick or hurt."

Gleve and Father Mallory rose and looked out through the kitchen window. There was indeed a lantern weaving and stumbling along the path as if held by a drunkard. Gleve quickly lit the lantern they kept beside the door and ran out into the night, Lynna at his heels. Father Mallory waited in the open door of the cottage. As they approached the entrance to the path, the lantern Lynna had spotted clattered to the ground. A tall young man sank to his knees beside it, his face filthy and scratched, twisted in pain.

"Keiran!" Gleve said. He dropped to his own knees, set down his lantern and threw his arms around his exhausted friend. Lynna stared at them open-mouthed.

38 MELISANDE

Melisande sat as straight as she could while propped against her pillows. Head Mother Mabonne sat on a chair facing the bed. "Two servants have been assigned to keep your room and bring your meals to you until you are well enough to eat in the dining hall. You must keep an eye on Jessa, the fair one. She is a restless child, constantly in trouble. This isn't the right place for her, but what choice is there? She was abandoned as a baby on our doorstep.

"Her friend, Ev, does not belong here either. In fact, she tried to escape recently. She is a child of the Earth People and should be among them, but she is the orphan of a bond-servant and inherited her mother's bond. The Warrior God sent them both here and here they shall remain."

Melisande nodded.

"And now I have been given the task of choosing a name for you. I was wondering if you would like to be called Peace. That is what I hope you will find here, my Lady. It is well known that your life up until now has been … stormy."

"Peace," Melisande said the name thoughtfully. "Will that not be too obviously an assumed name? People may wonder what name I came with. Would it be acceptable to take my mother's name, Merrit? It's common enough that no one will wonder why my name was changed, it will honour her memory, and I also hope to achieve merit while I am here."

"All right then, Lady Merrit. And what would you like to do, after you are well again, of course, as I have no doubt you will be. Most of the Widows work in the embroidery room, since most have been trained, as you have, in fancy needlework. The Women's Retreat House earns much of its keep by selling tapestries and embroideries to noble houses and churches."

"I could do that, and would like to do it. My first choice, however, would be to learn to work in the copying room. I have all my life longed to be able to read."

"Usually those selected to work in the copying room are Sisters, and younger than you are, with a long life of manuscript work ahead of them. I don't want to draw attention to you, or cause trouble for you or myself. How old are you, if you don't mind me asking?"

"I have thirty-six years."

"Ah well, you are young yet. I will think about it, Your Maj ...I mean, Lady Merrit."

Melisande nodded. A sudden thought struck her and she held up her left hand, her gold wedding band still in place. "Why do I still wear my wedding ring? I thought all jewelry belonging to Widows was sold to support the Retreat House."

"All except wedding rings. Widows continue to wear them in honour of the permanence of the married state."

"Well, I don't want mine." Melisande began to pull it off of her plump finger, then stopped. A sudden memory touched her, Liandra, saying that when Melisande's ring came to her after her mother's death, she would wear it and remember her mother every day. Along with the memory came an idea.

"Or maybe I do," Melisande said and pushed the ring back into place.

JESSA

"I thought I was to have two servants," the Lady Merrit said to Jessa, "But so far I have only met you."

"The other one is my friend Ev," Jessa said. "She's finishing up a punishment, a month of peeling potatoes in the scullery."

"A month of punishment? That's a long time. What did she do to receive that?"

"She tried to leave here," Jessa said. "Her punishment for that would have been even longer, but she was burned, too. They figured the pain was the rest of her punishment."

"Burned?"

"She hid in a laundry cart, but they dumped her into the tub with the sheets."

"Why did she want to leave?" Lady Merrit asked.

"There's a old witch, in her family I think. She sent for Ev."

Lady Merrit had been casual until now. Her eyes suddenly fixed intently on Jessa's face. "Do you know the name of the witch, as you call her?"

Jessa suddenly realized she was chattering again, and to a Widow, one that she was supposed to be serving. She could hear Sister Mattia's voice: "A servant is silent, no more obvious than the curtains on the window."

"I'm sorry, Lady," she said, dropping her eyes to the tray she was about to pick up. "I talk too much."

"But the witch, do you know her name?"

The Lady's voice was so urgent, Jessa looked up at her again. "No, Lady, I'm sorry. You will have to ask Ev."

"This is my friend, Ev." Jessa pushed Ev a step closer to the bed, but the strange Lady Merrit just nodded in a friendly way.

"I'm pleased to meet you, Ev," said Lady Merrit. Both young

women waited for the question about the Healer's name, but Lady Merrit turned back to the embroidery hoop in her hand.

Jessa paused for a moment, but couldn't stop herself. "Did you ever meet the Queen? Her funeral is today. Head Mother is going. I wish I could, and see all the fine people, in their clothes and jewels …"

"Jessa!" Ev hissed.

Jessa's fair skin blushed scarlet. "I'm sorry," she said and dropped her eyes to the floor, turning to do her work.

MELISANDE

Melisande had to wait for a few days before the young Woman of the Land came into the room without the talkative Jessa. "Come here for a moment," the Lady said. As she had with Jessa, she patted the edge of her bed. Ev sat where she indicated, looking uncomfortable. "I gather from Jessa that you have contact with your relatives outside?"

"My family comes to visit me sometimes."

"Including at least one Healer." Ev nodded. "Jessa says she's an older woman." Ev nodded again.

"She isn't, by any chance, one of the Old Ones?" Melisande asked. As she expected, the young woman's eyes widened. There was a great deal of secrecy around the Healers, and no wonder after the murdering rampage the Kings had carried out against the Orders of the People of the Land. This young servant would not expect Melisande to know anything about them, or call them anything but witchs. "You don't need to tell me," Melisande reassured her, "But I want to know something. Could you arrange to have a small package taken to one of the Old Ones, a Healer called Mother Peg?"

MAiDA

A few nights after Aden's visit Maida was packing cheese into molds in the kitchen, her hair tied up in a clean kerchief, a fresh apron protecting her dress. Liandra was sitting by the hearth sewing.

"Where did you learn to make such good cheese?" Liandra asked.

"My family are cheesemakers. I was apprenticed to my father before I …" She stopped abruptly, lifted a dripping basket of curds to her stone worksurface. The warm whey ran down its pitted grey surface and dripped into the stone sink.

Liandra's needle paused. She watched Maida. "Before you what?"

Maida looked at her for a moment, then dropped her eyes in shame. "You might as well know," she said. "I wanted to be a Healer. I ran away, went to the Healer's School."

"And what did they say?" Liandra asked, but Maida had turned to look out through the kitchen window. Her eye had been caught by a single lantern approaching along the path from the West. She rinsed off her hands in the basin on the counter and wiped them on her apron.

The traveller was Aden. "Sir!" Maida exclaimed. "We weren't expecting to see you again until it is time for the next box of food."

"No, I was not expecting to come so soon again either." Aden looked past Maida to Liandra, who was now on her feet, her sewing dumped in a heap beside her chair. "I have news for the Princess, news that I am loathe to deliver, your Highness."

Liandra sobbed on and off through the night, Maida comforting her as best she could. Aden had left a small decorated box, saying it was something of Liandra's mother's that her father thought she might like to have. When Liandra opened it, her tear-stained face took on an expression of puzzlement. "It's just a necklace," she told Maida "I thought it would be her wedding ring. It's traditional that the ring is passed to the eldest daughter."

GLEVE

Gleve tenderly washed days of dirt and sweat from Keirans body. He had stoked the fire into a roaring blaze and pulled the tin bathing tub as close to the hearth as he could but Keiran still trembled. "More hot water," Gleve barked at Lynna, who stood by tending a huge pot of it set right beside the fire.

"No, stop," Father Mallory said from his chair on the other side of the hearth. "You don't want to cook the poor boy." Gleve shot the old man a worried glance. "It's not the cold that's making him shiver," Father Mallory told him.

Gleve paused in his task and studied his patient for a moment. There were tears running down Keiran's cheeks. No, not cold, upset. "Oh Keiran, what's happened to you?" he asked. When Keiran did not respond, Gleve went back to his careful washing.

It was only later, when Keiran was clean and dry, dressed in Gleve's extra nightshirt and wrapped in a blanket, with a large cup of steaming broth in his hands that he spoke through the tears he couldn't hold back. "I shouldn't have come here. I'm putting you in danger. But I couldn't think of anywhere else to go."

"No. You must always come here when you need shelter," Gleve told him, and Father Mallory nodded.

"Danger?" asked Lynna.

In bits and pieces Kerian's story came out. "You could be executed for giving me shelter," he concluded.

Father Mallory laughed. "My son, you know how far we are from anyone who would tell the constables that you are here and how much warning we get of travellers coming. All you need do is hide in the cellar under the kitchen until we know who it is that approaches our cottage. You'll be safe enough here, as will we. You are not the first person, illegal in the eyes of the King, to stay here." Gleve gave him a sharp look, but the old man gave no sign of regret at slipping out secrets.

Keiran's bed in the loft was now Lynna's, so Gleve gave his own bed
to his exhausted friend. He removed the warm stones he had placed in
the bed earlier to take the chill off and helped Keiran climb in under the
covers. "Roll over," he instructed, "And I'll massage your back. Keiran
turned to face the wall and curled up, his breathing rough from the tears
that continued to bubble up from time to time. Gleve began gently to
work the stiff muscles in his friend's back and shoulders.

Daylight began to peek through the cracks in the shutters. Gleve
heard Father Mallory say goodnight to Lynna and close the door to
the room next door. There was some rustling and bumping as the Old
Man changed and climbed into bed. He heard clattering pots as Lynna
cleaned up the kitchen and put the bathing tub away. Then there was
some shuffling and swishing. Gleve realized she was pulling the pallet
out of the storage closet, unfolding it on the floor in front of the hearth
and making it up with sheets and blankets. For him, of course. That was
thoughtful of her.

After Lynna's steps disappeared into the loft the cottage fell silent.
Keiran's muscles were relaxing, his breathing calming into the regular
rhythms of sleep. With practiced skill, Gleve slowed the movements of
his hands, finally stopping so quietly that Keiran would not notice even
if he was still conscious, which it seemed he wasn't. The next steps were
very familiar – withdraw his hands, pull the covers up and tuck them
carefully around the back of Keiran's neck, tiptoe out of the room. But
he did not do this. Instead, he carefully lifted the covers and crawled in,
curling himself against Keiran's back. After a moment's pause, he slipped
his arm around Keiran's waist.

He instantly regretted this action as Keiran jolted into wakefulness.
The tension so carefully soothed from his back muscles returned in an
instant. Gleve waited, hoping Keiran would relax again, but he didn't.
Instead, he turned to face his friend. The faint light from the cracks in the
shutters showed the puzzlement and caution on his handsome face. The
two young men studied each other, barely breathing, for what seemed like
a long time. Gleve was flooded with love for his friend and gratitude for
his return. It filled him to the point of pain. He could not stop himself.
He leaned forward and gently kissed Keiran on the lips. Keiran froze in
surprise, his eyes flooded with confusion.

As quickly as he had filled with love, Gleve suddenly filled with
panic. This was dangerous. This could not happen. It was what he
had held back for all the months Keiran had lived with them while he

gradually healed from his injuries.

Gleve scrambled to escape from blankets that suddenly conspired to hold him captive. Thrashing himself free he hit the floor with a thump and ran from the room, controlling himself just enough to shut the door quietly. He dived under the covers Lynna had carefully arranged on the pallet, pulling them over his head. He curled there, frozen with panic and regret.

ANGLEWART

"And how did she take it?" King Anglewart asked Aden, his most trusted Bailiff after Ermin, who stood, as always, a wary presence by his side.

"Just as you would expect, Your Highness," Aden said, "Consumed by grief."

The King nodded. "As we all are," he said. Aden never removed his eyes from the floor in front of his feet. Was he genuinely sad for the loss of his Queen and the grief of her daughter? Melisande was popular among the servants, he knew, for the same reason she was popular among her vast network of friends – her kindness, her thoughtfulness, her sense of humour. Even knowing she was not dead, he was surprised to feel her absence, and he did regret that Liandra was left to grieve in exile for the mother he knew she truly loved.

The right amount of time had passed to change the subject. "And the reward—have any come forward?" Aden had been assigned the responsibility of questioning anyone who responded to the King's offer of payment for information about the Little Dragons and the Dragon Priestesses.

"Yes, Your Highness, some have come forward."

"With any information worth getting?"

"Not yet, Sire. All have stories, but nothing we have not heard a hundred times before."

The King allowed another silence to fall between himself and his retainer. Aden did not become uncomfortable as some did, which the King took as a sign of steadiness and honesty. "Keep on with it, then," he said. "You are dismissed."

Aden bowed his grizzled head and backed away the requisite number of steps before turning and striding from the room.

MAiDA

Comfort came quickly to Liandra. After sleeping through the next day, she came down the stairs from the loft looking peaceful and composed. "Are you all right?" Maida asked her.

"My mother is still alive," Liandra told them. "I don't know what's happened, but I know she's all right."

"How do you know that?" Peg asked her.

"Rafe told me, and I believe him."

A few days later, confirmation arrived in a small, paper-wrapped package carried by a drover from the west. "This is for you, Mother," he said to Peg. "It comes from the Women's Retreat House, with a message. I memorized it. Hope I've got it right still: 'The Lady is well. Tell no one.'"

Peg thanked the man and asked if he would stay for a meal, but he was in a hurry to move on. When he had gone, Peg opened the packet. She frowned in puzzlement as a gold ring slid into her hand.

"My mother's ring!" Liandra leaped to her feet and came across the room. She showed Maida and Peg the inscription in the ring, "Anglewart" and "Melisande," joined by ornate scrollwork. "She found a way to send it to me." She clutched it to her heart for a moment before slipping it onto her finger.

"What is going on here?" Maida asked Mother Peg as soon as they retreated to the stable at chore time. "She thinks she's reading Rafe's mind somehow. And how would he know?" The Healer shook her head, looking as puzzled as Maida felt.

Rafe, hearing his name, stopped in his task of carrying a pan of water into the chicken pen. Maida turned to him. "Rafe, Rafe, I wish you could talk to us." Rafe grinned broadly and looked back and forth from Peg to Maida.

Peg sighed, "Go on with your work, lad."

To Maida she said, "I'm preparing a package to send to the Healer's School. Word has spread that I am looking for information about the Dragon Priestesses and now I'm getting messages that various people farther east would like to talk to me, although most of what they want to talk about is probably their ailments! At any rate, I want to take Rafe and make a journey of a few nights into that part of the Forest. That will take me very close to Sister Loka's practice, and I know she plans to travel to the School soon. I want to send the interviews I've done so far with her, and I also plan to ask if others have noticed activity among the Dragons. I think more are going over here than have for some time."

"I think so too."

"I'll also write a letter to Sister Holly, the Librarian, and ask if she knows of anything, in any of the Journals there, about mind-to-mind communication, or strange knowledge in someone who doesn't even seem to register normal everyday things."

MELISANDE

The smell of candlewax and the music of women's voices drifted in from the Chapel where all the Sisters and Widows had gathered. In the anteroom behind the Chapel, Melisande and Imelda sat side by side on wooden chairs, dressed for the first time in the grey gowns of the Women's Retreat House. The snip snip of a pair of scissors echoed against the walls as lock after lock of long hair landed on the floor, Melisande's golden blond mingling with Imelda's white. The ceremony was solemn, for Melisande, a mixure of sadness and relief.

When the quiet Sister with the scissors was finished, Melisande and Imelda studied one another, taking in their newly shorn heads. Two Sisters approached with their veils, black for Melisande, to signify her Widowhood, grey for Imelda, who had decided to begin the long process of becoming a Sister. They offered their hands to lead the new entrants to the back of the Chapel aisle.

Beneath a statue of the Warrior God and his dead Dragon, the Head Mother stood at the foot of the altar steps, waiting for them. There was a pause in the choir, a shuffling of feet, a clearing of throats. The Sister who directed the singers raised her hands. When she brought them down the Chapel filled with a joyful hymn of welcome.

Melisande, now Merrit, and Imelda walked back to their adjoining rooms hand in hand, equals. As they turned into their hallway, they heard young voices and paused. It was Jessa, telling Ev what rumours she had heard about the Queen's funeral, who was there, what changes have come about in the royal and noble families, what they wore. Her cheerful chatter disappeared down the hallway in the other direction.

Imelda gently squeezed Melisande's hand, but the former Queen burst into laughter, quickly controlled. "I shouldn't laugh at her, poor child. How ironic that I have just shed all of that, with relief and gratitude, and she craves it!"

GLEVE

The next evening Father Mallory gave Gleve a critical look. Gleve realized he must be haggard and hastened to excuse it. "I didn't sleep all day," which was true. Father Mallory nodded, but assessed him for another moment or two. "You should look in on your patient."

"He's exhausted. I think I'll just let him sleep."

A brief frown crossed Father Mallory's brow, but Gleve ignored it. Lynna also gave him a look, a concerned one, but said nothing as she placed a basin of warm water on the counter for him to wash his face and began to prepare breakfast.

A couple of hours later, Father Mallory raised the issue again of checking on Keiran. Gleve knew he could avoid it no longer. He picked up a small lantern and carefully entered the bedroom. "Keiran, are you awake?" he asked as he closed the door behind him. There was a rustle as Keiran turned toward the wall. "How are you feeling?" Gleve asked. No response.

Gleve sighed and stood uncomfortably beside the bed. He didn't even set the lantern down on the side table. After a few moments, he spoke again. "Look, Keiran. What I did, I shouldn't have. It was unprofessional, for a Healer, that is. I …" His words died away. What else could he say?

Keiran's rusty voice emerged from the piled blankets. "I know what you think I am."

This took Gleve completely by surprise. "What do you mean?"

There was a long pause, then Keiran pulled back the blankets from his head and turned to look at Gleve. Now his features were distorted by anger, hurt and shame. "You think I'm a faggot."

"A faggot? Keiran, no. People of the Land don't use that word. We don't think there is anything wrong with men loving men. We don't have insults for them, I mean, us."

"Us?"

"I mean, me. I am a man who loves men, always have been. So is Father Mallory. It's not a problem for our people. I'd forgotten what it would mean, for you, that is. I'm so sorry."

There was a movement behind Gleve. He had not heard the door open or close, but suddenly Father Mallory was there beside him. He studied Keiran's troubled face for a moment, then asked, "What have you remembered now, my son?"

Keiran's face crumpled. He curled up again, although facing them this time, and released a deep, desperate sob. Father Mallory lowered himself to the side of the bed and laid a calming hand on Keiran's shoulder through the covers. "It's all right. Tell us."

"I remembered…the beating. They were King's Men, other King's Men, like me. We were camping. They were teasing me, calling me a faggot. And they were drinking. It just got more and more violent. They …" His voice was choked off by another sob.

"I know what they did to you," Father Mallory told him. Keiran's eyes widened. "You forget, I'm the one who cleaned you up and salved your wounds." Keiran flushed scarlet, turning away. Father Mallory sighed deeply. "I have watched you both work so hard to resist becoming fond of one another. For you, Keiran, the problem is that you believe men loving men is a sin. For you, Gleve, it's a matter of being unprofessional as a Healer and knowing it might be dangerous to share too much with someone who might someday return to King Anglewart's service. But think, both of you. All is now changed. Keiran cannot return to his world. He is a wanted man; to return would mean death. And what is there for him to return to anyway? His beloved brother is gone. He will stay here, find some destiny among us." He turned back to Keiran, "Among a people who value the love between men, if that is part of your destiny."

A long silence followed this speech, Father Mallory looking back and forth from one troubled young face to the other. Finally he rose to his feet. "I think you should talk." He started toward the door, but turned back, to Gleve. "And you must have a talk with Lynna as well. You can't put that off any longer."

Gleve nodded and the old man left, softly closing the door behind him. Talk, but Gleve could think of no words. He found it difficult even to look at Keiran. After a short time there was a rustle as Keiran turned away and pulled the covers over his head. Gleve stood there awhile longer, but eventually there was no choice but to turn and leave.

Apparently Father Mallory had said something to Lynna, or she had overhead some of their conversation. Gleve winced when he saw the pain on her face. She said nothing. Nor did he, since he couldn't think what to say. She did not look either of the two young men in the eye for weeks and her disappointment radiated from her in waves, affecting the whole household.

As Keiran recovered his strength, though, he began first to help her with the heavier tasks, such as hauling firewood and water, then took them over altogether. Then he began to help more and more with the cooking, gardening and cleaning. This left Lynna free to study Father Mallory's collection of Journals. Both Healers devised questions and tests to reinforce her growing store of knowledge. When there was Healing to be done, either patients treated by Father Mallory at the cottage or those Gleve visited all over the district, Lynna became a constant presence, watching, questioning, assisting, trying her hand at the skills she must learn to become a fully qualified Healer herself. She was gifted. Their appreciation for her grew and they never forgot to let her know. In turn her confidence grew. She found her place as an Apprentice in this ancient craft and gradually let go of her dream of a different kind of partnership with the handsome young Gleve.

The handsome young Gleve, however, was miserable, since he also could not have the partnership he wanted. He bitterly regretted ever showing his feelings to Keiran, and the tension between the two young men seeped into every crevace of the small cottage.

MAIDA

Mother Peg and Rafe departed for their journey with a rare feast in their pack. Liandra had decided that all of her food should be shared, so the travellers carried cured meats, fruits and cheeses rarely seen among the People of the Land, even a flagon of beer. Liandra and Maida stood side by side in the yard as the journey-lantern disappeared up the path to the east.

"Would you normally go with them on a Healing trip like this?" Liandra asked.

"I would go if we planned to be back the same night, but not a longer trip like this. If I went, who would care for the animals?"

"I suppose so. I was just afraid maybe you were staying because of me. I'm not as afraid of being here as I was at first."

Maida smiled at her, "I know."

Maida had set up two planks across a pair of sawhorses against the side wall of the cabin. A pair of lanterns hung from hooks on the wall, lighting the rough work surface. Two stools stood beside it, and baskets of freshly harvested herbs sat in a row on the ground. "Show me what to do," Liandra said to Maida as they approached this improvised worktable.

Maida showed the Princess how to sort the herbs and tie them in bundles for drying, collect seeds and spread them to dry for planting the next year. Liandra soon gathered up the tattered lace on her cuff and tucked it into her sleeve because of its tendency to brush plants and seeds off the table.

Maida pulled some parchment scraps from her pocket. A quill pen and inkwell already stood on the outside window ledge. She began to make labels.

"Was it hard to learn to read and write?" Liandra asked.

"At first."

" But the King's laws make it illegal for women to learn."

"Long ago when King Gallward decreed that Healers were to be protected in the Realm he also made an exemption for female Healers to learn to read and write, and to be useful to a Healer, a servant has to know a bit too, for example, to be able to make labels for herbs."

Maida returned to writing her label. Liandra sighed. "I would like to learn to read."

"Well, why not? I could teach you a little while you're here. We already have one secret about a breach of the King's laws."

"That would be wonderful!" Liandra went back to her work smiling. "I wish my mother could meet you. She always wanted to read and write. She wanted it so badly she tried to learn secretly when she was a child. Fortunately, she was found out by her nanny, who loved and protected her. It would have been a lot more serious if someone else had caught her."

There were a few moments of silent work. Liandra broke it: "I wonder what happened, why it was announced that she died, why she's in the Women's Retreat House. I wonder if Imelda is with her—Imelda is the nanny who raised my mother and us as well."

"Maybe you'll find out when you go back."

"I hope so. It will be difficult, though. Clearly it's a secret, and as soon as I go back, I'll be involved in preparation for my wedding, and then the wedding itself, and then I'll go off to live in the Southlands." She had lost her smile.

"Do you want to marry and go to the Southlands?"

"I did want to. Prince Locheil is very handsome, and wealthy, and he kisses well!" She giggled.

"And how do you know that?"

"We were allowed to take a walk together, to get to know each other. There were chaperones following, but they fell behind, and there were trees …"

Maida laughed. Liandra continued. "He is also second in line for the throne of the Southlands. I could possibly be Queen some day. But I'm not so sure now, about wanting that."

"Now?"

"Well, after the Dragon attack, and losing Ortrude, and now whatever has happened to Mother and Imelda, and … being here. Life is different here. I'm …"

"Changing?"

"Yes, I guess I am."

"Speaking of changing, when will you be finished sewing your

Woman of the Land outfit?"

"I'm nearly done. Just the holes for the lacing to finish edging. I can probably do that this morning."

"Can't wait to see you!" Maida teased.

As morning light began to brighten the kitchen window, Maida finished cleaning up supper and putting away the milk while Liandra finished her new outfit. She stood and held up the blouse. "How do you like it?"

"Beautiful!" Maida walked over and felt one of the seams. "I could never sew like that."

"Well I'll probably never read as well as you."

"Let's have a reading lesson this morning, before we go to bed." Maida went into Mother Peg's room and emerged with Folk Tales of the Westlands in her hands.

Liandra looked hungrily at the book. "Yes, let's! But first I want to try on my new clothes." She ran up the steps to the loft. Maida set the book down on the table and followed.

Maida undid all the hooks on the back of the ruined silk dress, with difficulty, since the stitches that held them were stretched almost out of the fabric.

Liandra took a fine silk chemise from her trunk and pulled it on over her head. As it fell over her belly, Maida was sure it was rounder than before.

Maida helped the Princess pull the blouse over her head, step into the skirt and shrug her shoulders into the bodice. She threaded new laces through the carefully edged holes Liandra had just finished making. She began to tighten them.

"Liandra …you measured for this … how many weeks ago?"

Liandra looked down at her body, placed her hands over her belly and paled a little. "You're not saying … No … no … I've just gained a little weight while I've been here."

"Liandra, it could be …"

"No!"

"When you kissed Prince Locheil, was there more?"

"Well, we felt a little under each other's clothes, but that's all, there were chaperones!"

"Have you ever felt under any other man's or boy's clothes?"

"Well, a little, in play, with noblemens' sons, even servants' sons. Doesn't everyone do that? But I've never 'lain with a man.' God, you sound like my mother."

"Well, you don't have to actually lie with a man to …"

The Princess raised her voice. "I don't want to talk about this any more." She began pulling off her new clothes and throwing them into a corner of the loft. "I'm going to bed. Leave me!"

Maida woke suddenly on her pallet in the kitchen. Someone had screamed. "Liandra?" she called out. There was no response, but she could hear whimpering coming from the loft. She threw back her cover and hiked up her shift to climb the stairs. The Princess was curled tightly into a ball, the covers pulled up over her head. The whimpering came from her. Maida sat on the side of the bed and laid a hand on her shoulder through the blanket. "Liandra, what's wrong?" The princess went on whimpering and now Maida could feel that she was shivering as well. She began to rub the trembling shoulder.

Gradually, Liandra calmed. Eventually, she uncurled and emerged from under the blanket, her eyes red. "I … I am pregnant, aren't I?" Maida nodded, not sure what to say. "But I don't want to give birth!" Liandra shuddered. "My mother nearly died having my youngest brother. She screamed and screamed! I know. I was there!"

"What do you mean, you were there?" Maida asked her.

Liandra sat up, and Maida helped pull a pillow up behind her back. The princess drew her long hair back from her tear-stained face. "A royal birth isn't private like the childbed of other women," she told Maida. "The King assigns some of his Bailiffs as witnesses, so they can testify that the child is truly an heir of the royal house. Otherwise, someone could switch babies, or take the real heir, or who knows what. And as they come and go, other people can come in if they want, like curious older sisters."

"So you were there when your youngest brother was born? And it was a difficult labour?"

"I had gone back to my own room by the time he was born, but I could hear her all the way down the hall." Liandra shuddered. "It was terrible."

Maida had assisted Mother Peg at difficult births. It could be terrifying. Death always hovered in the room during a birth, animal or human, but you could almost feel her breathing on the back of your neck during a difficult one. She gathered Liandra into her arms. "Oh my dear, it's all right. It's all right. First of all, very few births are like that.

Most go smoothly, just as they are supposed to. Second, Mother Peg has brought many, many children safely into the world. She must have midwived hundreds in her life. She's considered one of the best midwives in all the Realms."

"But even the good births hurt a lot. I was there when my second youngest brother was born too."

"There are ways to help with that. Mother Peg uses teas that ease the pain. Some are strong enough that women say they feel like they're floating, that the pain is far, far away. Also, Women of the Land give birth squatting on the floor, not lying in a bed like the King's women do. It helps the baby come faster."

"Really? Don't the woman's legs get tired?"

"The assistant sits behind the birthing woman and helps hold her up. That's my job when I help Mother Peg. And another thing, there are exercises, breathing exercises, that help you move the pain through you and out, into the Earth beneath you."

"Can you teach me?"

"I've watched Mother Peg teach them often enough. But now, sleep." Maida helped Liandra ease down into her bed again.

The Princess turned to the wall and curled into a tight ball. Maida began to tuck the blankets in, but stopped. After a moment, she lifted them instead and slid into the bed behind Liandra. She began to massage the Princess's neck and shoulders. Her hands worked down Liandra's back, easing the tension from the muscles. Liandra gradually relaxed, began to doze. Maida, her hands tiring, curled against Liandra's back and slid an arm around her waist.

Liandra tensed again and, after a moment, pulled away and turned to face Maida. "What are you doing?" she hissed. "You aren't filled with Dragon Spirit, are you? The Warror God condemns women like that."

Maida was now wide awake as well. "What are you talking about?"

"You know, women who touch other women like men."

"What? Your Warrior God condemns women who love one another with their bodies?"

"Of course. It's wrong. Unnatural."

Maida laughed, softly. "What is unnatural about love? Lots of women touch and caress one another, in all kinds of ways. For some it's sweet friendship, for others release or pleasure. For some it's a life-long bond of love together."

"But the Warrior God ..."

"We follow the Earth Mother. We are all part of Her, including our bodies, especially our bodies, and she loves being touched."

"Really?" Liandra studied Maida's face in the day-lit loft. She tentatively stroked Maida's brown cheek, once, again. When Maida began to unlace the front of Liandra's night shift, the Princess stretched forward to receive the young servant's gentle hand on her breast.

48 MELISANDE

Melisande sat at a writing table set against the wall of her room. She had a small book open before her, a list of words beside it. She struggled, joyfully, to read. Gradually becoming aware that her back was aching, she stopped to stretch and turned around to smile at Imelda, sitting in a chair just behind her. Imelda put down the piece of embroidery she was working on. "You are happy, my child?"

"Very. You, more than anyone, know how long I have dreamed of learning to read."

"But is it difficult? At your age?"

"I suppose it's difficult at first at any age. It starts to come easier when you understand what sound comes from each letter."

"What are you reading?"

"It's the story of the Warrior God killing the Dragons. It helps that I've heard it a thousand times in Chapel." Melisande stood up and walked thoughtfully to the window, looking down over the courtyard where servants and Sisters moved back and forth at various tasks, their lanterns bobbing. On the other side lanterns shone in tiers of windows just like her own. "Imelda, do you think the Warrior God really killed Dragons when he was on earth?"

"How would I know that, my Lady?" Imelda looked up from her work, startled by the question.

"The Kings and Nobles always portray themselves killing Dragons in tapestries and paintings, but I've never heard of one really doing it. In fact, it's the other way around. The Dragon kills the knight! Or the knight barely escapes with his life."

"My Lady, I suppose it was one of the Warrior God's miracles."

"I tried to say this to Torrie, did I tell you?"

Imelda's hands were still. "I don't think so."

"It was just before the night of the poison. I came upon him in the chapel, on his knees before the Warrior God. All I could think of was how much like a baby bird he looked, with his hair cut so short and that scraggly little mustache he was trying to grow, but he was deadly serious. He was praying that his father would let him raise an army of young men to go after the Dragons. 'It's our generation's turn,' he told me. 'The Dragons multiply and grow stronger if we do not challenge them. Each generation must do what it can to drive them back. Someday there will be a generation that finally ends their rule of the Realms,' he said, obviously hoping that it would be his. I tried to tell him that it is the Dragons that drive us back in each generation. He could not hear me."

"Why won't Anglewart let him raise an army?" Imelda asked. "He's right. Every generation of young nobles takes their turn at it."

"I wish I knew, although I'm glad he's holding them back. I don't want another generation's blood feeding the roots of the mountains, especially the blood of my own beautiful sons." Melisande shuddered, then took a breath and sighed deeply. "I wish I knew Anglewart's mind on anything. There was a time when we would talk late into the night …" The Queen's voice petered out, lost among her thoughts. Imelda had gone back to her embroidery before her mistress spoke again. "They are beautiful, in a way, aren't they?"

"What?"

"Dragons … When I think about that creature Anglewart had chained to the wall of the small courtyard, usually all I can think of is Liandra and Ortrude lying face down in the snow, and the blood …"

"My Lady …" Imelda began to set aside her work and get to her feet.

"It's all right. I can finally say such things without weeping – sometimes." Imelda, seeing that Melisande was truly all right, settled back into her chair, but did not pick up the embroidery hoop again. Instead she gave her former mistress her full attention.

Melisande continued. "I sometimes think about him before that terrible day, when he was small and tame. He was so beautiful! Remember how the sun sparkled on his scales, bringing all those colours out in a background of sky blue? Elegant creature – he moved with such grace. And remember his eyes? They glowed, and so expressive …"

"Remember how Liandra could sooth the little thing? How she would call up to the window for us to watch as she rubbed his belly? He would lie on his back with his eyes closed and purr like a kitten. He would watch for her, run to her when she came into the courtyard … Why do we want to kill them Imelda? Don't you think about what it must have been like before our people came here, when the Dragon Priestesses of the Earth People knew how to tame them?"

Imelda shrugged her shoulders and watched her former mistress, whose eyes were far away.

MAIDA

Mother Peg and Rafe came home just after midnight. "That looks better," Mother Peg said when she saw Liandra wearing her new outfit. Then when Liandra helped Maida prepare food for them, Peg's eyebrows rose up to her hairline.

When they had eaten, Liandra picked up a folded length of linen she had left on the stairs. "Rafe," she said, "I think you need a new shirt." Maida and Mother Peg looked at the one he was wearing. She was right; it was pretty ragged. Rafe grunted his delight at being the centre of attention. Liandra told him to stand up and hold out his arms. He hesitated. "Don't worry," she reassured him. "I won't hurt you. It's just so I can make you a new shirt." She unfolded the length of homespun linen. "See?" Rafe grinned, delighted, straightened his back and held his arms out as far as he could. Liandra began to work with a length of cord, tying knots to mark the measurements she was making.

"You do know what you're doing," Peg remarked.

"All the girls at the castle have to learn how to sew," Liandra said. "Silly, since the servants make all our clothes." She continued to work. "Yes, that's right," she said, "At the Castle."

"Pardon?" Maida asked.

"I'm talking to Rafe," Liandra told her.

Maida studied the pair of them. Rafe did not seem to be communicating. In fact, he was staring out the window as he stood with his arms held straight out. Suddenly she realized that Liandra was talking to her. "Does Rafe have a longer name?"

"I don't know," Maida said. "We named him Rafe. Is he telling you what his name was before?"

Liandra stopped working and frowned in concentration. "There's something," she said. "Something long … but I can't make it all out."

"Surely she can no longer deny she is pregnant," Mother Peg said when she and Maida had retreated to the stable.

"No, she's accepted it now," Maida told her, "And I don't think she was quite as innocent about men as she made herself out to be."

Mother Peg studied her servant sharply. "Do I see a sparkle in your eyes?" Maida flushed darker and looked down. Damn her mistress for being able to read her mind!

Peg chucked, then became serious again. "Maida, is this wise? She is Anglewart's daughter, destined to marry a Prince. There are things she should not know, including the woman-love of the Earth Mother. Many King's people think that's a myth, and we encourage them to think it. Their Warrior God is not kind to women who touch other women."

"I know," Maida responded, troubled, but that night Peg noticed that the pallet by the hearth remained folded neatly away.

MELISANDE

Melisande approached the Head Mother and knelt to kiss her hand. "Rise, daughter," Mother Mabonne told her. "Come, be seated."

Melisande took one of the comfortable chairs set in a small circle in front of the Head Mother's desk. The room was better appointed than most in the Women's Retreat House, but by Castle standards, it was still a very simple room.

The Head Mother did not go back to her seat behind the desk, as Melisande expected she would, but sat in another chair in the circle. "I hear good things about you," Mother Mabonne told her. "The embroidery mistress is delighted with your work and Imelda's too. She says she can assign the two of you to anything, no matter how difficult, and you do a perfect job of it."

"Thank you, Mother, although I wouldn't say perfect."

"Also the Sister teaching you to read and write says you are an eager pupil and learning fast."

"Thank you, Mother."

"Are you happy here?"

Melisande looked up at her for the first time and smiled. "I am."

"I am glad of it. Now, what can I do for you?"

"Mother, I have a favour to ask, a very large favour." The older woman nodded, waited. "My only grief in leaving my old life and coming here is my eldest daughter, Liandra. A Queen loses her sons at the age of ten, when they go to the barracks to become soldiers, but her daughters are close to her until they are seventeen, eighteen, perhaps nineteen or twenty. Even after they are married, they come to visit, and a mother is usually allowed to visit as well, especially when a daughter goes to child-bed."

"You grieve that your daughter believes you are dead."

"I do. She is the only one I have left."

"So what do you propose?"

"Liandra is currently visiting relatives. As soon as she comes home, she will be married to Lochiel, Second Prince of the Southlands. On the way home, her party will be very small and they plan to stay at inns along the way."

"And you propose to cross her path at one of those inns?"

"Yes. No one in her party will know me. I will simply be a travelling Widow from the Women's Retreat House."

"A rare enough occurrence to draw attention."

"But it happens."

"Yes, sometimes it happens. And what of Liandra? The agreement with your husband … that is, your former husband, is that if knowledge of your true identity goes beyond the five people who know already, we stand to lose our lives. Knowing the King, I have no doubt that he would keep his word."

"I trust Liandra. She learned court politics young. All children of a King do. And why would she want to put my life at risk, or Imelda, who raised her, or her own, for that matter?"

"True. What of the cost? Such a journey would bring the expense of a carriage, a travelling party, inns."

"How much money did my husband … former husband, that is, give to the Women's Retreat House for my upkeep here? For all his ambition and cruelty, he is very generous."

Head Mother Mabonne opened her mouth to respond, then closed it again. She rose to her feet. "This is a risky thing you ask."

Melisande slid from the chair to her knees. She clenched her hands and put all of her longing into the look she gave her superior. "Please."

The two women remained in that position, eyes locked, for a long moment before Mother Mabonne began slowly moving her head from side to side. "You are convincing, my Daughter, but the risks are too great. I cannot possibly allow such a thing."

51 GLEVE

One early morning Lynna and Gleve were returning from setting a farmer's broken arm. They had stayed over several days with the farmer's family, because it was a long journey and because they wanted to be sure the infection that had set in before they arrived was under control. Lynna asked questions all the way home, stopping only when the lights of the cottage appeared through the woods.

Father Mallory met them at the door, kissing both of them on the cheek. Keiran sat by the hearth. He and Gleve greeted one another with a wary nod before Gleve noticed the stones of the hearth itself. They were covered with drawings. He walked over to look and shuddered. Lynna came down from the loft where she had deposited her pack and, responding to the silence, came over to look as well. "Oh!" she exclaimed.

The stones on the floor in front of the hearth were covered with Dragons. These were not the vague shapes one usually saw in artwork, or in the badly worn stone sculptures that survived from the Old Times. These Dragons were fully formed. They curled gracefully and ominously around one another, every scale, every point on their spines, every claw, every whisker drawn in awesome detail. Their eyes glittered not only with sharp awareness, but with a range of expressions – curiosity, malvolence, humour, wariness.

"Where did these come from?" Gleve finally asked.

"Keiran drew them," Father Mallory told him.

Gleve looked at Keiran, who shrugged his shoulders. "I don't know how I know what they look like, but suddenly I started to see them."

"He took a piece of charcoal out of the fire," Father Mallory said, "Fell to his knees and started to draw. He kept it up for hours."

"These aren't beginner's drawings either," said Gleve. "Do you remember being an artist?"

"I must have been," said Keiran.

JESSA

Jessa heard the soft brushing of linen hem on stone. The sound stopped
as the day-watch Sister paused at the door of her tiny stone cell. She
heard the wooden cover of the peephole slide up, then back down, and the
swishing gown continued on its way.

A moment later the door softly opened and closed again. Jessa sat
up. It was Ev, shivering in her light nightdress and bare feet.

"What's wrong?" Jessa whispered.

"I can't sleep."

"But the day-watch sister …"

"She's just gone by."

"I know, but she'll be back soon."

"I left my blankets piled up so it looks like I'm in the bed."

Jessa giggled. It was usually her role to come up with rule-breaking
schemes. "Come here," she said, holding up the edge of her blanket. Ev
ran the few steps to the cot and climbed in. "Yikes, your feet are cold!"
Jessa complained. "We'll have to look like one person," she whispered,
snuggling close and pulling the blanket over their heads. They stifled
giggles.

Becoming serious again, Jessa asked, "Why can't you sleep?" Ev
was silent. "It's something to do with that old Healer woman, isn't it?
And the reason you tried to escape? What's going on, Ev?"

"I can't tell. It's a secret."

"But I'm your friend!"

"I know, but it's between me and my mother, a promise I made
when she was dying. I haven't kept it … yet."

"But she's dead."

"It's still a promise." A few moments of silence went by then,
"Jessa."

"Um hm."

"How does the Lady Merrit know so much, like about Healers,

things King's People usually don't know?"

"She's strange."

"She watches you all the time."

"I know. It feels weird." They fell silent and Ev began to doze off. Jessa shook her shoulder. "Tell me your secret."

"No."

"If you don't tell me, you're not my friend."

"Jessa, that's not fair."

"Tell me."

Both girls froze as the day-watch Sister passed in the hallway. As soon as her steps faded away, Ev said, "No."

Jessa gave her a firm push out of the bed. "You'd better go."

MAIDA

One early morning, Liandra, Maida, Peg and Rafe sat at the table sharing the morning meal before Rafe and Maida went out to settle the animals and Rafe in the barn for the day. Their plates were filled with vegetables from the garden spiced with slices of sausage from Liandra's box, their cups filled with goat's milk. In the midst of satisfied chewing and scraping of spoons on pottery, Liandra suddenly asked, "Can you tell me about the Dragon Priestesses?"

Mother Peg looked startled, narrowed her eyes at Maida, who shrugged and shook her head.

"What do you already know about Dragon Priestesses?" Peg asked, a sharp edge to her voice.

Liandra looked up at her, surprised and confused. "Is that something I shouldn't have said?"

"No, it's all right," Maida told her. "We just don't talk about them much because during the time when the Kings were killing them it was dangerous.

"Rafe said something," Liandra told her. "Something about the bond between the Little Dragons and the Dragon Priestesses. Sort of like a deep love."

All three women turned to stare at Rafe. He had been bent over his plate, intent on shovelling the last of the good stew into his mouth with his spoon. Suddenly the centre of attention, he straightened, looked from one of them to another, first wary, then delighted that all eyes were on him. He broke into his characteristic grin.

"From everything I have heard, I believe that is right," said Mother Peg in a low voice. "I think it was the closeness of their bond and, in turn, the closeness of the bond between the Little Dragons and their cousins, the Great Dragons, that allowed them all to make the Agreement, so we could share the Land in peace together for so many generations."

"They must have been powerful women," Liandra said. "More

powerful even than my father. I bet they could do anything they wanted."

"Not quite," Peg told the Princess. "The Dragon Priestesses committed their whole lives to their work of communicating with the Dragons, resolving conflicts and breaches of the Agreement, tending the cattle to feed the Dragons. They had little life of their own in which to do 'whatever they wanted.'"

"But the power to direct Dragons …"

"It's a different kind of power. It's not the power to make people do as you say, like your father's power. It's more like a power that's given to you to serve the people, and the Dragons, and in turn it owns you. It tells you what to do."

"Really? What a life! Just like a servant!"

Mother Peg sighed. "Not quite, because it was a choice to serve. And think of what they had in return. Every account I have ever heard says that the Dragon Priestesses were loving, wise, deeply satisfied women, and they had a strong community among themselves. Just think, in all those generations, none of their secrets got out, one little bit. Think of what kind of trust was involved in that."

"Why were they all women?" Liandra asked. "Men can be Healers, even though most are women, and the Leaders were both women and men, weren't they?"

"Yes they were," Mother Peg told her. "No one I've ever spoken to, or read, has been able to say why only women became Dragon Priestesses. It was part of the secret."

MELISANDE

Melisande bent over an embroidery frame in her room, carefully stitching a Dragon's eye, thinking about how many more colours there were in the real thing than one could possibly create with needle and thread. She straightened and turned when the door opened behind her. It was Ev, a bucket of cleaning equipment in her hand. "Oh," she said when she saw Melisande, stopping in the act of stepping into the room. "I didn't know you were here. I'll come back later."

"No, my dear. Clean it now. You won't bother me. Where is Jessa?"

"In the kitchen."

Melisande studied the young servant's unhappy face. "I haven't seen the two of you together for some time. Is something wrong?"

"No, Lady Merrit." Ev's whole demeanour denied the words, but Melisande knew better than to pry further.

"So you must clean all the rooms alone?"

"It's no problem, Lady." With that Ev turned her attention to her work. A minute later, so did Melisande.

Suddenly Melisande felt watched. She realized that she had not heard movement behind her for some time, although Ev was still in the room. She turned. The young woman was watching her, twisting a cleaning cloth in her hands.

"Is there something you want to say, Ev?" Melisande asked, shifting to face her.

"I want to ask you … how do you know about Healers? I mean People of the … Earth Healers?"

"I don't know any personally."

"How did you know how to send that package to Mother Peg? Do you know where she lives?"

"I'm afraid not. It was your aunt who knew how to send the package."

"Oh."

Ev worked the cleaning cloth between her hands. Melisande broke the tense silence. "Ev, my dear, why did you try to run away?"

Ev twisted the cloth harder. "My mother," she said. "I was eight years old when she died. She taught me something, a sort of poem, made me repeat it over and over again. When the time is right, when the Old Ones send for me, I'm supposed to tell them the poem. An Old One has sent for me, but I can't leave."

"Why didn't your mother give the poem to one of the Old Ones herself?"

"She was a bond-servant, Lady. She couldn't leave her household any more than I can leave here, and besides, no one sent for her. It wasn't time."

"Can you get someone to write it down?"

"I'm not supposed to tell it to anyone else, just one of the Old Ones."

"Oh." Melisande knew she shouldn't push farther, but could not help herself. "Is it something about Healing? Herbs or spells or something?"

"No, Lady. It's ... like directions to go somewhere. There's a traveller, sort of, in it."

"Sometimes poems with travellers in them are about a spiritual journey."

"Are they?" Puzzlement crossed Ev's face. "I always thought they were real directions ... Is there a place called Theta's Well?"

"Yes there is. I went through there many times when I was young. It's a good, fresh well at a clearing where several roads and paths meet. It's been an important stopping-place for travellers for many generations. There's a small market there, a blacksmith shop and an inn. Is it in the poem?"

Ev nodded. As if she felt she had said too much she quickly gathered up her bucket and left.

GLEVE

As they shared the morning meal in the presence of the Dragons sketched on the hearthstones, somethin teased the edge Gleve's memory. Finally it popped to the surface. "Keiran, when you came back from your journey to Hanford … tell us again what your neighbour told you. Wasn't there something about King Anglewart's expedition to search for the Little Dragons?"

Keiran looked blank for a moment, then understanding dawned. "Yes! It's true. She said I was wanted because I had deserted from the King's service during the expedition to search for Dragons!" He looked at Gleve, awe written on his face. "That's why I was so far north with other King's Men. That's why I know what Dragons look like. What an amazing memory you have."

Gleve blushed hard as he continued. "I had thought of that expedition before, when I was wondering how you came to be in the Foothills Spring campsite, but then I would always think it just couldn't be. The men chosen for an expedition into the mountains would have been the roughest, strongest fighting men the King had. I don't mean you're not strong …" Gleve glanced at Keiran to see if he had offended. Keiran simply looked deeply lost in his own thoughts. "… but you are fine boned, your hands always make me think 'musician' or …"

"Artist," Keiran finished the sentence.

"Would the King have sent an artist to record what they found?" Lynna asked.

"I wish I could remember!" Keiran scrunched his face in the effort to come up with something more.

"Don't try too hard," Father Mallory told him. "Memories come in their own time."

"Don't I know that!" Keiran smiled at him.

MAIDA

Maida and Liandra sat under a lantern in the yard shelling peas. Mother Peg and Rafe were gone on yet another journey to Heal and ask questions. Liandra glanced around, then bent forward and kissed Maida on the lips. She giggled. Maida smiled, then returned to the work. Liandra sighed. "What's wrong, Maida?"

Maida opened a few pods in silence, letting the peas rattle into the bowl in her lap. When she looked up, the lantern light shone on the wetness in her eyes. "Liandra, I can't let myself love you like this. Every time I look at your belly getting larger, it reminds me that our time will soon be over. When you go your way and I go mine, we will probably never see each other again." Suddenly Liandra's eyes, too, filled, and she returned without comment to her task.

Sometime later she asked, "Maida, why aren't you a Healer? I thought that's what you were when I first came here. Your voice is more soothing than hers."

"She can be soothing when she wants to be. In fact, she can put people into a trance so deep they can't feel her stitching a wound or setting a bone, just using her voice."

"I think you could do that." Maida paused with an open pod of peas, but did not look up. "So why aren't you a Healer?"

Maida blinked hard, surprised by the anger that rose in her to meet Liandra's question. She did not try to keep it out of her voice. "Because Mother Peg refuses to believe that anyone who does not come from a long line of Healers can become one. At the School I was examined by the oldest of the Old Ones and she said I could be a Healer, but Mother Peg just laughed at that."

"So why don't you go back there, to the School?"

Maida sighed. "It's not that easy."

"You ran away once."

"From my family, which ended my Apprenticeship as a

cheesemaker, but if I ran away from Mother Peg the School would have to discipline me for disobedience. They would never accept me as an Apprentice then."

"I don't understand why they don't discipline her, the old witch!" Maida was very still, said nothing. "But you are angry about it, aren't you?" Maida nodded, her eyes blurring. She blinked again to clear them. "So isn't there anything you can do?"

"Wait. She's very old. If I serve her well, the School will assign me to someone else when she dies, hopefully as an Apprentice."

"But she might live to be really, really old."

"I know. I do try to learn everything I can. I hope if—when—I become an Apprentice I'll already know a lot."

Liandra snorted and popped a pod so vigorously that the peas jumped out of the bowl and scattered on the ground. "You're a lot more patient than I am. Some day you'll just explode, rebel in some way no one could imagine." She bent to pick up the peas but couldn't reach them over her large belly. "When I am Queen of the Southlands," she said, "I will send for you to come and be my personal Healer." Maida laughed and began gathering the peas scattered on the ground.

Suddenly, a man's voice shouted from well down the eastern path. "Mother Peg! Where is Mother Peg?" Maida set her peas aside and stood up. Now she could see a lantern coming down the path, bouncing and twisting.

Two men came into the clearing, disheveled and wild-eyed. Between them they carried a third man, cut and bleeding. Liandra, too, had risen to her feet. "Mother Peg," one of the men said through his gasps for breath. "He was attacked by a Dragon. We've carried him all the way from Tummel."

"Mother Peg isn't here," Maida said.

"But you're her Apprentice, aren't you? You can take care of him."

"I'm just ..." Maida began but Liandra cut her off.

"We'll take care of him."

Maida stared at her, shocked, but the confidence in Liandra's voice carried her forward. She ran into the house, pulled out the pallet and laid it on the floor in front of the hearth. The injured man groaned as his friends set him down upon it and continued to whimper as he lay there. He had been slashed and bitten all over his chest and legs. Like all Dragon wounds, the gashes were puffed up and bright red. Liandra stood over him studying the cuts, her face pale.

Maida found some bread and cheese and poured a flagon of milk. She sent the two men out to the yard with them to eat and rest. "What are we going to do?" Maida whispered to her.

"I know exactly what he is feeling," Liandra said. "His cuts are burning like fire." She looked up at Maida. "What would Mother Peg do?"

"Cut off his clothes," Maida whispered. "Cover him with a sheet and wash him very carefully with warm water."

Maida and Liandra finished washing his wounds, working slowly because he winced and whimpered each time they touched one of the bloody gashes. "Now, a salve," Maida said. "But I have no idea which one."

Liandra closed her eyes for a minute, then rose and went to the storeroom. She came back with a pottery jar. Maida read the label. "Licorice?"

"It will work. Watch." Liandra scooped out some of the salve, warmed it for a moment in her hand, then began to smooth it on the terrible wounds. As she worked, the man began to calm.

Maida joined Liandra in smoothing on the silky cream. When she looked at the first gashes Liandra had salved, she thought the redness was already fading.

"How did you know?" Maida asked.

"Rafe told me."

MELiSANDE

A Librarian quietly tapped Melisande's shoulder. "You have a visitor, Lady." She looked down at her fingers holding the quill, stained with ink. "You are to come quickly," the Librarian said. No time, then to clean her hands. A Sister waited to guide her to the visiting room.

When they entered, a man in a full, roughly made cloak sat in one of the wooden chairs, his back to them, his large hood pulled forward over his head. He was slumped in the chair but this could not disguise his height. He did not turn to greet them.

The Sister bowed and left. Melisande had a sudden urge to go with her, or at least ask her to stay, but it was too late. Her footsteps disappeared down the hallway outside. She knew the woman could have stayed to spy through the large keyhole, she had heard of others doing this, but apparently this Sister had other duties to attend to.

Perhaps the man knew about the keyhole too, because he still did not turn. "Sir?" Melisande addressed him. A hand emerged from the cloak and beckoned her to come around to the other side of the chair. The moment her eyes fell on those long calloused fingers, Melisande's heart leapt into double its previous rhythm. How is it he could still affect her like this? "My Lord," she whispered.

The hand beckoned again and she came around the chair, beginning to kneel in front of him. "No, no," he whispered and reached forward to grab her forearm. Her skin warmed under his touch. "You are no longer required to do obeisance to me. In fact," and his eyes crinkled just as they always had in laughter, only with more creases, and deeper ones, than there used to be. "You are no longer even alive. And I am some rough journeyman come to speak to the Lady Widow in the Women's Retreat House."

He rose and brought a chair forward, setting it close in front of his own. Melisande sat. When he was seated again, they studied each other's faces for a long time in silence.

"This is a terrible risk," she said, finally. "Why?"

"I need to know," he said, and paused. "Do you hate me?"

What a storm of emotions rose up to meet his question—anger, sadness, longing, nostalgia, even love, but not hate. "No," she told him.

He nodded. "And are you happy here?"

"I am happy here."

He studied her again, seeming to search for truth or lie in the depths of her eyes. He nodded slightly, affirming that he had found truth. "I wanted to tell you before you hear—I am going to marry Thalassa Rodolph."

This was not a surprise politically, but at the level of the heart? "And are you content to do so, when you know I am still alive?" she asked him.

"No, but I must."

"And the Warrior God? "

"It is not the first time I have disappointed Him. I hope, when the time comes, He will understand. He, too, was a King."

She nodded. "And our son? How does he respond?"

"He does not yet know. I'm sure he will be angry. I am looking for another young woman for him, equally highborn, equally beautiful, equally ..." She knew the missing word – sexy—was glad that he didn't say it.

This was the cynical, power-craving King. She did not want to talk to him.

"And I want to ask," he said, returning suddenly to her Anglewart again, "Is there anything I can do toward your happiness here?"

Her eyes jumped to his. "Yes," she said.

GLEVE

As Father Mallory predicted, Keiran's memories did come, some of them painful. The men on the expedition were the roughest fighting men the King had. The beating in the Foothills Spring campsite had not come out of the blue. Father Mallory had time to listen, and his healing presence drew the poisonous memories from his young patient. Keiran shared the taunts the King's men had heaped on him, the tricks they had played on him, the dangers they had exposed him to just to hear him scream, only to pull him back to safety at the last moment, laughing at him.

One evening he ran to the hearth and pulled a piece of partially burned wood out of the fire so quickly he singed his fingers. He ignored the heat in his haste to sketch the image in his mind's eye on a large flagstone. The rest of the household watched, fascinated, as the picture took shape – a female dragon curled protectively around her clutch of eggs.

Later Father Mallory approached Gleve. "Those new Journals you brought from the School, did you not tell me that one of them is for information we discover on the Little Dragons? Should we give it to Keiran as a sketch book, to record his memories of the Dragons as they emerge?"

"Give a Healing Journal to one of the King's People?" Gleve reacted with instinctive hesitation. Even the existence of the Healing Journals was considered a secret kept from the King's People. They had burned so many important books during the conquest.

"He will never go back to his people," said Father Mallory. "You know that."

"But he will never be one of us either."

"No, he must find his destiny somewhere in between. However, I have a feeling that his memories of King Anglewart's expedition, as they continue to emerge, will bring important new information." Gleve considered for another moment. "I'll take full responsibility for the decision," Father Mallory added.

"All right. We have one of the large Journals, intended for illustrations. Let's give him that."

When Gleve put the Journal in Keiran's hands, the artist fell silent and his eyes filled briefly with tears. Then he began to explore its textures, reverently running his fingers over its soft leather cover, it's neat stitching. He opened it and touched the smooth surface of the paper. His brow creased in concentration, an expression the household had learned meant more memories about to emerge. Suddenly he looked up, his eyes wide, staring into the distance. "A sketchbook," he said. "I had one." He thought again. "It was with me on the expedition. It was wrapped in leather and carried in a special pocket inside my oiled leather jacket to keep it dry."

Gleve looked at Father Mallory. "You don't suppose …"

"The Foothills Spring campground," Keiran completed the thought.

"Yes, you must go and look," Father Mallory agreed. "Lynna is a capable young woman and an able Apprentice. She and I will be all right on our own."

"Do you mean…both of us?" Gleve looked uncomfortably at Keiran, who looked away.

"It would hardly be safe for Keiran to make a journey like that alone," Father Mallory frowned at Gleve. "And maybe, as you travel," he turned his gaze to Keiran, then back to Gleve, "You can come to some better way of dealing with the feelings between you." Both young men blushed fiercely.

"But what if you must travel to Heal someone? Gleve fretted.

"They'll just have to come to me, or send someone to carry me to them. Don't worry."

And so it was that Keiran and Gleve departed soon after sunset the next night, dressed and provisioned for a long journey.

MELISANDE

Four women jostled and bumped over the rough road. Head Mother Mabonne had given Melisande permission to make the journey, but not before pacing furiously back and forth across the carpet in her study. "I don't know how you managed this," she said, "An order straight from the King. You're a fool. He's a fool. The risk of your secret, and his, getting out is great. Or you'll be eaten by Dragons out there or the Earth People will eat you themselves." Melisande restrained herself from laughing.

The Head Mother objected to Melisande's choice of servants. "The one has tried to escape before. What if she leaves you high and dry in some backwoods inn? And the other wouldn't know a rule if it bit her hand."

"I will take responsibility for them," Melisande told her.

"Well I suppose it would be little loss to this House if they do become a Dragon's breakfast …" Head Mother Mabonne abruptly clamped her mouth shut, as clear a statement as any that she knew she had gone too far.

The Men's Retreat House usually organized any travelling done by residents of the Women's Retreat House, but Mother Mabonne wanted to attract as little notice to this journey as possible. She had one of her own trusted servants quietly rent a small, battered carriage and hire a driver and guard from a livery stable on the edge of the town. The rest of the arrangements were left to Melisande.

Melisande noticed that Ev and Jessa sat as far apart as they could. They stared out of opposite windows, excited by every tree, every stone, every cottage caught briefly in the light of the lanterns swinging on the corners of the carriage. Neither had been outside of the Retreat House since they had been taken into it, Ev nine years ago, when she was an eight-year-old, and Jessa when she was newborn.

When the sky began to pale, the carriage stopped. It's four occupants stepped down, exhausted and bruised, in front of a small inn. The carriage turned down an alley close by. The men would sleep in the stable with the horses.

The women sat at a table in a quiet corner of the inn's main room long enough to eat a simple meal, but it was uncomfortable. The locals, almost all men, stared openly at them. Women dressed in the plain grey robes and dresses of the Women's Retreat House were a rare sight in such a rough place. Ev and Jessa were not sitting apart now, Melisande noticed. In fact they leaned together, their shoulders touching. They seemed torn between fear and curiosity, their eyes now fixed to the top of the table, now flicking up and around at the crowded room. Of course, she thought, they were so very sheltered at the Retreat House. Jessa would only have ever seen men from a great distance, if at all, in her life, and Ev had seen only her male relatives since the age of eight. As soon as possible, she asked the innkeeper's wife to show them upstairs to their rooms, two small wooden chambers, not terribly clean, each with a barely adequate bed.

Before Melisande and Imelda disappeared into their room for the day, Melisande asked Jessa and Ev to attend them for a few minutes. The two young women stood, because there was nothing but the edge of the bed to sit on, and Melisande and Imelda occupied that. They fidgeted nervously. The Widow Merrit had proved strange indeed.

"Ev," Melisande addressed the young Earth Woman. "This is Theta's Well."

"Oh!" Ev gasped, as her friend looked at her in surprise and puzzlement.

"And when night falls again, there will be a couple of people arriving to see you, your Aunt Marle, and with her, Mother Tess." Ev's breath caught in her throat with a little squeak.

I plan to tell the men from the livery that I am unwell and we must stay over here a night and another day before we go on. I will ask the innkeeper's wife to make up a packet of food, and then the two of you will be free for the night. It is indeed the time, Ev, to see if your poem does describe a real place. It may mean something completely different, of course, but if it does lead to something, something the Healers should have or know about, you can give that information to Mother Peg."

"Mother Peg?" Ev was almost in shock.

"That is where we are going, to see Mother Peg," Melisande told her. "You must not tell anyone—not now and not when we get home. Can I trust you?"

Ev nodded vigorously, her eyes wide. Melisande turned her attention to Jessa. She was clearly puzzled. Ev must not have told her about the poem inherited from her mother. But Jessa, too, was nodding.

"Good. I wouldn't have brought you if I didn't think I could trust you completely. And," the Lady looked meaningfully from one to the other, "Whatever has come between you, I would like to see your friendship healed."

"Yes, my Lady," both girls said in unison, and then looked cautiously at one another.

MAIDA

Maida could not sleep. She lay on one side for awhile, then the other side, then tried lying flat on her back. Everything was equally uncomfortable. Liandra, curled around her large belly, seemed oblivious to Maida's restlessness.

Roald the Shepherd, for that was his name, had left a few days after he had come, limping, but on the mend, his two friends supporting him for the journey back to Tummel.

Before long Maida could no longer avoid the need to walk through the passage to the toilet. This she did as quietly as she could, slipping from the bed and down the stairs, moving softly in her bare feet and carefully closing the door behind her. Once up, she did not feel like lying down again. She looked longingly at Mother Peg's shelf of Journals. Mother Peg had been absent from the cottage a great deal lately, but with Liandra here, there had been no time for study of the Journals. Maida quietly dipped herself a cup of milk and sat down at the table.

After a minute, she gently pushed one of the shutters open, just a few inches. The window looked out over their little dirt courtyard toward the barn, quiet and shuttered in the dangerous daylight. The pastures were a little brown this time of year. No wonder the goats came in looking for hay even after a night of grazing. The garden, too, was dry looking. She must remember to take out a bucket or two of water tonight and give the plants a drink.

Suddenly a long shadow came slipping over the pasture, the barn, the garden. Maida jumped up and stepped back from the opening between the shutters, holding her breath. She had not heard the flap of wings. The Dragon must be gliding. Maida heard a moan from upstairs, and the rustle of the Princess turning in her bed as the shadow passed by.

Maida knew she should just close the shutter again, but it was so tempting to look at her garden in daylight. There were blossoms, bright spots of colour in the neat rows of vegetables and herbs. At night when she worked among the plants, she barely noticed the flowers. Some were closed at night and the rest were colourless grey or black in the darkness.

Then the shadow was back, darker and much larger. She could even make out the shape of the Dragon's long snout as it came between the sun and the packed dirt of the courtyard. Oh no, thought Maida. It must have seen me. She stood well back from the window while the sinuous length of the creature passed overhead. As soon as it was gone, she reached out and closed the shutter, but not before she caught a glimpse of its glossy blue tail undulating through the sky beyond the barn. She shuddered. It was far too low.

There was another moan from upstairs, followed by a whimper. Maida quietly crossed the floor and climbed the steps to the loft. "Liandra?" she whispered "Are you awake?" The Princess whimpered again. "What's wrong?" Maida asked her.

Liandra was curled up, holding herself tightly. "It hurts."

"What hurts?"

"My scars. They burn when a Dragon flies over."

"May I look?" Liandra nodded and Maida gently raised the Princess's shift to look at her back. "Oh!" Maida exclaimed when she saw the scars. "They're very red and sore looking."

"They hurt!" The Princess repeated.

"What about the salve that worked so well on Roald? Would it help your scars?" Maida got to her feet and moved toward the steps.

"It goes away as soon as the Dragon leaves," Liandra told her and, sure enough, by the time Maida returned with the jar of salve, the scars had returned to the puffy pink-white of months-old wounds. Since she had fetched the salve, Maida offered to rub it on the scars anyway. "It may help if another Dragon flies by," she told Liandra.

As Maida worked, carefully spreading the cool salve on the scars. Liandra began to speak. "At first my father's Dragon was so cute," she said. "He glittered in the light of the torches. We say he was blue, but his scales were really all the colours of the rainbow. And his eyes. They were brilliant. You knew what he was feeling just by looking at them."

"How did you know?"

"They changed colour, light and dark, and shape, a little. But mostly, when you looked straight into his eyes, you just knew. Oof!" The Princess squirmed, curling tighter.

"Did I hurt you?" Maida removed her hand from the Princess's back.

"No. It's the baby. It's moving, kicking or something."

"Really? That's good," Maida said and returned to smoothing salve on the scars.

"It's scary, when a Dragon flies over and the scars hurt. Sometimes I think he left his mark on me to claim me. He always knows where I am. I can't get away. Someday he'll find me." Liandra buried her head in her pillow.

"Oh sweetheart," Maida comforted her. "Surely not. You're safe here and then your father will protect you once you go home, and then your husband in the Southlands."

"Rafe says he'll always protect me."

"Really? He does?" Maida paused. There was no end to the discoveries of what went on in the mind of the silent, apparently simple, Rafe.

Liandra nodded.

"Well, he will, then. There, I'm finished." Liandra sat up, pulling her shift back into place and pushing a pillow in behind her back. Maida put the lid back on the jar of salve. "You know, you've never told me about the day the Dragon attacked you."

"I've never told anyone." Liandra's voice sounded choked and Maida looked up to see a tear escaping down the Princess's cheek.

"I didn't mean to upset you." Maida crawled in under the covers and sat beside Liandra, an arm around her shoulders.

"You're the first person I've talked to about anything important since my sister Ortrude. She was just a year younger than I am. We told each other everything."

"Was?"

"She is the one the Dragon killed when it escaped." Tears were now flowing freely down Liandra's cheeks. "And you know the worst thing?"

"What?"

"I think she was killed just by accident. It was me he was coming for. He just kind of slashed her on the way by, but by the time everyone got there to help us, she was dead."

Maida held her closer.

JESSA

Jessa and Ev sat on their bed, their nightgowns tucked around their feet. Daylight outlined the shutter on the window and poured through the cracks in the wood, lighting up the dust motes floating around the tiny room. They were too excited to sleep.

"But why wouldn't you tell me about this before?" Jessa demanded.

"You know. I told you. My mother said not to tell anyone until I could find one of the Old Ones."

"But now you'll have to tell me the poem."

"No, it's a secret!"

"How can I help you find out if it contains real directions unless you tell it to me?"

Ev fidgeted with her toes, curled up in the fabric of her nightgown. After a few minutes she said, "Swear to me that you will never tell anyone. Swear to me."

Jessa took on a solemn tone. "I swear, on our friendship, which is the most important thing in my life, never to tell anyone even one single word of your poem."

"Is it?"

"What?"

"Our friendship, the most important thing in your life?" Jessa held Ev with her serious grey eyes. No need to speak. Ev sighed. "All right, I'll tell you, but don't forget and let it slip out. You do that sometimes!"

"I know, but this is too important. I won't tell a soul."

"All right." Ev took a deep breath. "It goes like this:

Oh ye who would the secret seize
At Theta's Well, face mountain breeze.
Forsake the road you walk with ease
For stone-lined path, well marked with threes.

Twelve thousand steps before ye'll see
A cottage hid by apple trees.
Upon the hearth, fall on your knees.
Beneath its stone lie Dragon keys.

With the last word, Ev let out the remainder of her breath. The two young women stared at one another, thinking hard.

"Mountain breeze—that must mean north," Jessa said.

"How will we know which way is north?" Ev asked.

"The main road, the one we're on, goes east and west."

"What do you suppose 'well marked by threes' means? And what are 'Dragon keys'? I hope they aren't something dangerous."

"I have no idea. Maybe your aunt will know, or the old Healer that's coming with her."

"I can't believe we're going to see them—tonight!"

Jessa looked thoughtful. "Ev, this poem is at least as old as your grandmother's time, right?" Ev nodded. "What if the 'cottage hid in apple trees,' if it really existed, isn't there any more? Or someone else lives in it?"

"We can't know until we go, can we?" Ev clutched her knees to her chest. "I'm so excited I can hardly breathe. I'm not going to be able to sleep."

"I guess we should try. It could be a long night." With that Jessa pulled up the covers and the two friends snuggled under them together.

Early that evening Lady Merrit asked the innkeeper's wife to send a message to the stables that they would not travel that night. She also asked for a packet of food and a small travel lantern for the young women and for meals to be served to herself and Imelda in their room. Jessa saw a glitter when the Lady's hand left the pouch at her waist. She must have paid well for the innkeeper's wife's service. Everything was done as Lady Merrit asked.

As soon as darkness made the roads safe, two heavily cloaked figures came up the stairs, slowly, for one was bent and supporting herself on a stout walking stick. Once in the room shared by Lady Merrit and Imelda, they pushed back their hoods. Ev ran into Marle's arms. Her aunt briefly stroked her hair, then pushed her far enough away to smile into her eyes. Ev then turned to the Old One and curtsied to her as she would to a grand lady. The old woman chuckled. "Come here, lass," she said, taking

Ev's hand in her knotted one. "You are a Woman of the Land. Don't bow to me. Give me a kiss." Even short Ev had to bend a little to place a kiss on the Healer's creased cheek.

"And you are young Ev's sister-adventurer," the old woman said, turning to look carefully at Jessa.

Lady Merrit told her Jessa's name and the Healer nodded. Jessa found herself wary, the elderly Woman of the Land had reacted very strangely to her that day in the Visiting Room, but she followed Ev's lead, giving the Healer her hand and bending much farther than Ev had to place a light kiss on the Old One's soft cheek. As she straightened, Tess continued to hold her hand and study her face. Jessa began to blush. "I have dreamed of you," Tess told her. That, then, would explain her reaction in the Visiting Room, the careful study of Jessa's face now, but what on earth did it mean?

There was no time to wonder. Lady Merrit handed them the packet of food and lantern, then took Jessa's and Ev's hands in turn and looked straight into their eyes. "Be careful," she said, "And come back well before daylight." Both girls nodded vigorously.

Lanterns shone from the windows of the inn and three or four cottages scattered along the road. Lights also flickered in the inn yard where jingling and the voices of men commanding horses told them travel preparations were under way. A brightly-lit room at the back of the building gave off the clattering and banging of meal preparation. In front of them was a small gathering place of pounded earth, probably the site of the weekly market. Right now it was deserted. Marle and Tess led Jessa and Ev toward a low circular stone wall in the centre of this space. As they got closer, they saw that it enclosed a covered well. "This is Theta's Well," Tess told the young women as they approached it. There were four openings in the wall around the well and it was low, worn smooth on the top, obviously designed as a place to sit and talk. Marle and Ev helped Tess lower herself into a spot facing away from the inn. The others arranged themselves around her.

"And so, young descendant of the great Mother Calla," Tess addressed Ev. "What is this Key you spoke of?"

"It is a poem, Mother. My mother made me repeat it over and over again until I knew it by heart. She said to tell no one until the time was right and the Old Ones sent for me."

"Many chains were broken during the Times of Terror. The Old

Ones have forgotten this Key of yours, if they ever knew. Perhaps it was something Calla meant to tell the School, but died before she could. However, no matter. I sent for you. I believe the time is right. Tell us, child."

Ev closed her eyes and allowed the dark small noises of the dark woods around them to close in, as if still sheltering the words she had hidden all her life, and her mother and grandmother before her. Finally she took a breath and repeated the poem softly to Mother Tess.

When her voice died away, Mother Tess looked at Marle. " I think Mother Calla was giving directions to her own cottage. It was north of here, and twelve thousand steps would be four or five miles, which would be about right."

"Do you think she hid something, then?" Marle said. "In her own cabin?"

"It sounds like that, doesn't it? As if something is buried under the hearth stones." The old woman's brow creased even more deeply, faintly visible in the shadow of her hood. "But that cabin was burned by the King's Men in Calla's own time. I can't imagine what would be left."

Marle sent an anxious glance in the direction of the eager young women. "The hearth stones would likely survive, unless someone dug them up for building materials in the years since. The apple trees, they might have survived."

"Yes, yes. Calla was famous for her apple orchard. There may be trees still there." Tess sighed, turned to Ev and Jessa. "Well, my young ones. All you can do is try. Count your twelve thousand steps and search for ancient apple trees and hearth stones set into the ground, perhaps under the remains of a burned cottage. You must start now, for the night will not protect you for long. Come, we will bless you."

Ev and Jessa knelt before Marle and Mother Tess. Both put their hands lightly on the tops of the young women's heads. "Earth Mother," said the Old One, "Protect and guide these young servants of your ancient Dragon Priestesses, and bring them safely back with whatever Calla left for our generation. It is time."

The two older women accompanied the travelers to the north side of the open space where several paths disappeared into the forest. Most were dirt pounded by many feet, but two were carefully paved with stones. "'Stone-lined path," Ev whispered. "But which one?"

Jessa held out the lantern. Ev found the flint and stone all servants carried in their pockets and lit it. The four women examined the openings of the paths. In a moment Mother Tess pointed to the large stone set crossways in the opening of one of them. Ev held the lantern beside it. There were worn marks on the rock, three spirals. Ev looked into the Old One's face, her own brimming with excitement. "Marked with three?"

Mother Tess nodded. "Off you go then," she said. "Save your energy for counting."

They ran for the first two hundred steps, when another cottage came into view, sitting in a small clearing just off the path. Smoke rose from the chimney and lantern light shone through the windows. The girls hid their lantern and tip-toed past, counting under their breath.

From here on the going became a lot more difficult. The path was overgrown with dense thickets. They pushed their way through, sacrificing their arms to the brambles to protect their faces. In some places they had to crawl on their hands and knees to follow the ancient paving-stones among tangles of roots. "I don't want to think about what I just put my hand in," exclaimed Jessa, scrubbing her hand against her thigh.

Ev giggled. "So that's why you're taking it home on your skirt?"

Jessa made a face at her, barely distinguishable in the faint light of the lantern.

When they encountered streams, they took off their stockings and shoes and waded across. The stones under the water were slippery; the hems of their skirts were dipped many times. Soon their legs and feet were soaked, stockings, shoes and all, despite their efforts to care for the soft leather.

Sometimes the path disappeared entirely. When that happened, one girl would stand on the last stones they could find and the other would go ahead, casting about in the brush with the lantern, until she located paving-stones again. Sometimes many yards of the path were buried or gone, and both girls despaired of losing it altogether.

Their spirits really fell when they began to lose count.

"Sixteen-hundred!" Jessa announced.

"No, that's fifteen-hundred."

"Sixteen-hundred. Fifteen-hundred was back at that brook, remember?"

"No that was fourteen-hundred."

Jessa sat down and put her face in her hands. "Oh dear. Now what do we do? We can't go back and start over."

"I know," Ev said. "When this happens we'll take the lower number. Better that we start looking for the 'cottage hid by apple trees' too soon rather than too late."

They stopped to rest more and more often as they went along. When they were hungry, they opened the package from the innkeeper's wife. Lady Merrit must have paid well. There was a generous quantity of cheese and bread, even a few pieces of fruit.

When they reached what they thought was twelve thousand steps, they looked around themselves in dismay. There was nothing to distinguish this spot from any other they had passed, trees, brush, the remnants of the stone path. They pushed on, casting the light of the lantern as far as they could from side to side, but found nothing.

Jessa threw herself down on a log beside the path. "I don't believe it. We've come all this way for nothing."

Ev dropped beside her. "What time do you think it is?"

"I don't know. People say they can tell what time it is by the stars, but I've never learned how." Jessa looked up at the small piece of sky they could see from their log. "Oh oh."

Ev looked too. The sky was definitely growing lighter. "We can't look any further. We have to go back."

They picked up their lantern and pack and began retracing their steps, trying to hurry, but they could not make any more speed than they did coming the other way. The light relentlessly grew, moving across the sky from east to west. Soon it was not necessary to use the lantern.

As they hurried across a small clearing, Jessa suddenly grabbed Ev's sleeve. "Get down!" She pulled her off the path. Spotting a low, spreading tree, she dived under it, pulling Ev behind her. "Dragon," she whispered, as the two of them crawled deeper under the umbrella of branches. As they crouched there, the unmistakable, sinuous form of a Dragon passed overhead, its long snout stretched in front, its wings beating at a leisurely pace. In silhouette they could not see anything more than its shape. It was, fortunately, very high in the sky.

Ev put her arms around Jessa and the two of them crouched there as the Dragon disappeared into the east. A few minutes later, another followed it.

"Now what do we do? We can't continue on," Ev said. "In fact, I'd say we have to find some better hiding place than this." She released her hold on Jessa, levered herself onto her knees, and looked around. "I think there's a thicker tree over there." As she put down her hand to crawl in that direction, she suddenly stopped. "Jessa."

"What?"

"Look."

Jessa did. All around them was a carpet of windfall apples.

Jessa watched the sky while Ev explored farther into the bush around the apple tree. "Another apple tree!" the Woman of the Land announced and, a few minutes later, "Another one!"

A hundred yards or so off the path, Ev found the collapsed remains of a tiny cottage. Jessa joined her. A pile of stones marked the location of the chimney. Jessa continued to watch the sky while Ev carefully pulled aside stones and pieces of wood.

Fortunately, the cottage seemed to have fallen away from its chimney, so the heaviest beams lay on what once would have been the front wall. The area around the hearth was not too deeply buried, but still it took Ev most of the day to pull everything aside. Several more Dragons passed, but Jessa spotted them far off and both girls crawled in among the fallen beams. The Dragons did not seem to be hunting in any event. They were winging their way slowly from west to east, some alone, some in groups.

By mid afternoon, Ev was tired and filthy, her dress torn almost to rags and her hands bleeding. She did not seem to notice. She examined the hearthstones, felt carefully around them with her fingers. "Jessa," she finally shouted. "This one's loose!"

The sun was declining well into the western sky. Jessa gave up her watch and helped Ev work away at the stone. It was true. The other stones were mortared, but this one was held in only by a rim of well-packed earth. They used a stick to dig the earth away, and then a larger one to pry. Just as Jessa was beginning to think about lighting the lantern again, the stone finally swiveled and crashed aside.

Beneath it lay a small, flat metal box. Jessa helped Ev to pry it out of its place, then lit the lantern. Ev used the stick to pry open the lid of the box. Books! It contained three, small, leather-bound books.

ANGLEWART

King Anglewart straightened himself to his full height, making it clear he stood above his son's crimson face and clenched hands. Torrie was young, lithe and very strong, a package of pure muscle, but his height was a legacy from his mother. "I will gladly take your suit to one of a dozen suitable young noblewomen," the King said.

"But you knew I meant to ask for Thalassa."

"You had not said as much," the King kept his voice low and calm, a deliberate contrast.

The young man opened his mouth to respond, but then closed it again, his face scowling even more deeply. The King knew it was dangerous to tempt his heir to such anger, but not as dangerous as letting him make the crucial liaison with the Rodolphs and, for the moment, the young man was helpless. He stood before his father visibly struggling to control himself. The King, guessing that Torrie wanted to leave but did not trust himself to speak, nodded. The heir spun viciously on his heel, almost taking a piece of the carpet with him as he strode from the room. Shortly there would be the clash of swords in the yard, Anglewart knew, release of rage and practice in hope of a Challenge to come.

He himself would release elsewhere. He would search out his young bride-to-be. But one did not hold on to one's rule just by marrying the most powerful bride available. He took in a deep breath, let it out slowly, and turned to sit at his huge wooden desk. He glanced up at Ermin, ever at his elbow, ever expressionless, or was that the tiniest hint of a twitch at the corner of his Spymaster's thin lips?

"There are new reports from Aden's questioning of the peasants, my Lord," Ermin turned and lifted a stack of parchments from a bench by the door, placing them on the desk.

"I don't want to read them, Ermin, unless there is something new." The King looked up at his servant, raised an eyebrow.

"No, my Lord, nothing new. The same old farmers with Dragon

Priestess aunts. A hundred goggle-eyed descriptions of the way their eyes rotated and their scales shone, forgetting that you have seen one of the beasts closer than most." There was a slight catch, Ermin perhaps remembering a moment too late his Monarch's pain that would follow on such a statement. Neither would dream of acknowledging it.

"Then take it away," the King said. "Have Aden file it all in the library and keep looking." He watched as Ermin lifted the pile back to the same spot on the bench it had occupied a moment earlier. "Has Aden questioned that old hag Liandra is staying with?"

Ermin looked up. "Not yet, Sire."

"Tell him to get on with it. She's as old as the mountains. If anyone knows something, she does, although those old witches are tighter than clams with information, probably to hide how little they really do know." He chuckled, watched Ermin pick up the next document on the bench. "So, what next?"

 63

GLEVE

For the first few days there were cottages to stay in. The People of the Land were wary of the tall young King's Man, but everyone knew Gleve, and so welcomed Keiran for his sake. As they travelled further north, the last of the human dwellings petered out and they were left to find safe hiding places as each dawn approached. They spent the days in logs, caves or under the roots of trees, trying not to touch one another in the crowded quarters, disguised by the earthen colour of the travelling cloaks wrapped around them. Keiran was plagued with a stream of memories prompted by the landmarks they passed. At times he couldn't sleep and sat up during daylight hours sketching madly, filling pages of his precious journal with hauntingly life-like Dragons. He also sketched the men of the expedition, in one case carrying an improvised stretcher bearing a huge egg. "Was that the egg that King Anglewart hatched at the castle?" Gleve asked him.

"Must have been," Keiran replied.

They approached the Foothills Spring campground cautiously, ready to hide and wait if anyone was camped there. As they studied the log shelters arranged in a semi-circle around the springhouse, Keiran suddenly doubled up and vomited. Gleve knelt beside him, wanting to touch him but not daring. "I'm sorry," Keiran whispered when he could speak. "This is a place I'd rather not remember.

"I know," Gleve said. "We won't stay. We'll just try to find the sketchbook, all right?"

Keiran nodded. By now it was obvious that the camp was empty, although they would have to pay attention to the paths coming from both directions. There might be a party of soldiers or drovers headed for these shelters before daylight, hoping for a safe and comfortable place for the day.

"The drovers told Father Mallory they found you in the woods behind the camp, although that gives us quite an area to search," Gleve said. "Let's walk into the bush in different places, about ten feet apart, searching as we go. If we find nothing in the first spot, we'll move ten feet along and try again." Keiran nodded, rising and shouldering his pack.

They searched carefully and systematically, keeping an eye on the paths and the sky as well. They had reached a point about two-thirds of the way around the clearing, behind one of the shelters, when Keiran called out. Gleve pushed through the bushes between them, joining his friend beside a small clearing. It stank, clearly a place used by travellers to relieve themselves. Keiran held up his lantern so Gleve could see what he had found – a stocking entangled in the bushes, torn and shredded, but blue, the colour worn by King Anglewart's men.

The two young men circled slowly outward from the shreds of stocking, carefully searching the ground under their feet and the branches around them. Gleve found a battered glove, black, as anyone's glove might be. They began to watch the sky, nervous as it began to lighten. "We have to find a hiding place for the day," Gleve said. He looked at the rough bunks in the shelters. "You're sure you couldn't consider sleeping …?"

"'No," Keiran cut him off. They left with no further word, finding a space under a large fallen log nearby. There they shared a little dried bread and cheese and curled up at opposite ends of the log to catch what sleep they could in the daylight hours.

MAIDA

Mother Peg read her thick letter from Sister Holly in the stable while Maida and Rafe finished the morning chores. After Rafe went upstairs to prepare for bed and Maida began to gather what she needed to carry to the house, she set it down carefully on her lap.

"What news?" Maida asked her.

"Interview notes are pouring in from all parts of the land, with plenty of information about the Dragon Priestesses, some of it new, but no one has yet found the secret of where they found the Little Dragons and how they learned to communicate with them. There is plenty of information about mind-to-mind communication in humans, though, too much to summarize. Holly says I should come and read it for myself. And finally, yes, others are reporting more activity among the Dragons, but no one knows why."

Maida paused to check the sky before crossing the courtyard. "Look at that!" she said, standing back so that Mother Peg could see. In the eastern sky, just beginning to glow with the first hints of dawn, at least twenty Dragons were already in the air.

"Quickly! Let's get to the house," Mother Peg said, stepping stiffly into the courtyard.

Maida took one last look before she closed the cottage door. Several of the Dragons were coming in their direction. "There are so many Dragons out there!" she said to Liandra.

"They're not hunting, though," the Princess responded. "They're looking for something."

Maida and Mother Peg turned to stare at her. The Old One's expression was as surprised as Maida knew her own was.

GLEVE

They were both awake well before sunset. "It could have been any King's servant's stocking," Gleve said, chewing on another small piece of hard dried bread. "I'm sure King's men go through here all the time, and that is the latrine area. If someone were going to lose a stocking, it would be there."

"Maybe," Keiran answered, thinking. "But I've remembered something. While I was being beaten and ..."

"Raped," Gleve filled in, since Keiran still had trouble saying the word.

"I can remember the smell of shit. I think they might have caught me literally with my pants down." He shuddered. "I just can't help thinking that was my stocking." He paused, thinking. "Gleve, I want to go back and search again."

"All right."

"I mean now, before sunset."

"In the light? Here? So close to the mountains? The Dragons will be coming back to their lairs for the night."

"I know, but the bush is thick and the camp shelters are right there, four steps to safety at a run."

"I don't like it."

"Then you stay here, or in one of the camp shelters. I'll go on my own."

"Keiran ..."

Determined, Keiran put a few scattered things in his pack, shouldered it and scanned the sky. Gleve rushed to close and shoulder his pack as well. "I can see you won't be stopped. And I won't let you go alone."

Keiran smiled at him. Gleve frowned back.

Looking up, they darted from one clump of trees to another, pausing in each move until they were sure the sky was clear. Dragons passed over, high above them, winging their slinky way back to their mountain caves. None seemed to be looking down. Perhaps they all had full bellies.

When they reached the camp, they started across the open space and then heard the flapping of large wings. They ran the last few steps to the nearest shelter and flattened themselves against the inside wall, holding their breath, as the dark snaking shadow of a huge beast passed over the grass. They waited, but it did not come back to investigate. They were soon able to run into the woods behind the camp.

Gleve stood guard, scanning the sky as Keiran searched the ground. Starting at the ruined stocking, he circled slowly outward again. When Gleve spotted a Dragon, even far off, he would hiss a warning and both young men would lie still on the ground under the thickest tree they could find.

Keiran suddenly straightened, thinking. He moved around to the other side of the latrine clearing and started to search there. Darkness was falling. Just as Gleve began to think about getting the lanterns out, Keiran called. Gleve ran to him. Keiran was pulling the remains of a well-made oiled-leather jacket out from under a pile of brush. He felt it and let out a triumphant, shout. "It's still here! In its pocket." He rolled the remnants of the jacket tightly around the hard square of the sketchbook and tucked it under his arm. "Now let's get out of here. The quicker the better!"

They paused only long enough to light their lanterns and they were off, Keiran striding ahead with his long legs. "Wait," Gleve called out after awhile, puffing. "I can't keep up." Keiran paused and turned. "The sketchbook," Gleve gasped. "Can we take a minute to look? I'm dying to know if it survived the weather."

"Not yet. I feel so sick and frightened there. I want to get as far away as I can." Keiran turned and started off again.

INTERLUDE: THE DRAGONS

The roots of the mountains tremble
Sun shimmering around us
As we beat Air with our wings
The new approaches
Little Brother
The old approaches
Ttime from before
Come, Dragonkind, and dance
Change takes wing among us.

JESSA

When Jessa and Ev arrived at Lady Merrit's room, she cried out and ran to them, throwing her arms around Jessa. "Oh, we were so worried! I was sure I had lost you. I rehearsed a hundred ways to tell Head Mother Mabonne." She released Jessa and hugged Ev. "Oh my dear!" She stepped back to look at Ev. "What has happened to you?"

Ev grinned with delight. In fact, both girls had been grinning all the way back. Ev pulled what looked like a white rag from under her arm. It was a large swath from the hem of her chemise, torn off to protect and hide their treasure. She set it down on the bed.

Lady Merrit and Sister Imelda stepped closer to stare down at it. Before they could ask, Ev carefully unwrapped the ruined chemise and opened the metal box. Lady Merrit took in her breath when she saw the ancient books inside. She reached out to touch the fragile leather cover of the one on top, but withdrew it before making contact. Then she turned and looked out the window at the faint hint of grey in the sky. "We must get Marle and Mother Tess over here before it gets light," she said, hurrying to the door. She closed it carefully behind her before they heard her footsteps descending the stairs.

"I sent the coachman for them," she said when she returned. "And I asked the innkeeper for a basin of warm water for you, Ev."

This arrived quickly. Lady Merrit wrung the cloth that came with it and began gently cleaning Ev's face. Ev pulled away. "Please, Lady."

Lady Merrit laughed. "Oh Ev, you have always done the serving, haven't you? Well you have had a great adventure and done an important service for us all. It's your turn to be waited on. Sit still." Ev did not look happy about it, but she let Lady Merrit bathe her face, hands and feet. Jessa went to get clean clothes for both young women.

After that, they waited. Lady Merrit sitting on the bed, beside the open metal box, staring at the books as if entranced.

"You can read them, can't you?" said Ev. Lady Merrit nodded.

The Little Dragons

"Open one," Ev urged her. "Read what it says."

Lady Merrit looked up at her, amused. "Patience, my dear. We must wait for Mother Tess."

The two young women sat on the floor, Marle, Imelda and Lady Merrit on the edge of the bed. Mother Tess was the centre of attention, enthroned on a simple wooden chair brought by the innkeeper. Reverently she lifted up the top book. It seemed to Jessa that her hand was as old as the leather. She opened it and frowned. "Oh dear," she said, and held it out for the others to see. "The water must have leaked into the box. This one is damaged." And they could see she was right. The soft parchment of the pages was stained a dark brown and as she gently ran her thumb over their edges, it was obvious that they were stuck together in a single block. Jessa gave Ev an anxious look and saw that Ev's expression was equally alarmed. Were they too late? Had the secrets been erased by water and time?

Tess set the damaged book aside and reached in for the next one, her face a mask of concentration. All six women in the room let out a breath together when she ran her thumb along the edges of the pages and they ruffled. Then she opened the first page and tilted it so they could see. It was undamaged. "This is Mother Calla's Healing Journal," Tess said. "It must have been her last one, the one she was using when she died."

She set it gently aside and picked up the bottom book. When she opened it, her eyes became larger. She looked up and, to Jessa's amazement, tears trickled along the deep creases in her cheek. "This is it," she whispered, and began to read:

"I, Sister Rena, a Dragon Priestess of the People of the Land, have chosen to break the Rule of Secrecy of our Order. I do this after much thought and prayer, because the Kings have killed almost all of us. Only a few remain, and we are in hiding, doomed to die, if not today, then tomorrow, the next day, or the day after that. Our Secrets are the key to life in a Land ruled by Dragons. They must not be lost …"

After only two hours of sleep Jessa and Ev were exhausted and sore but Lady Merrit was at their door when the sun was still a half-hour above the horizon urging them to get up, pack and eat. Then the Lady yelled at the driver and guard to harness the horses. Ev caught Jessa's eye, her own brows raised high. Neither of them had ever heard the Lady shout like that before.

The minute it was dark enough, they descended to the inn yard where the carriage waited. Then they were on the road again, the young women's sore bones painfully jouncing while Lady Merrit fidgeted. Every few minutes, it seemed, she asked the driver how soon they would arrive at the village of Tummel.

GLEVE

It wasn't until the sky began to lighten again that Keiran finally stopped. Gleve bent over to still his pounding heart and nearly toppled the rest of the way. They waited until Gleve had recovered a bit, then began looking around for a safe place to spend the daylight hours. The best they could do was a tree with low branches spread out like a skirt, touching the ground. They crawled into the space underneath and leaned on the rough bark of the broad trunk. Gleve was still breathing hard. Keiran apologized to him. "I'm sorry, my friend."

"I understand," Gleve responded, his mind latching firmly to the words "my friend."

By the time they had rested briefly and shared a few road provisions, the light of the sun was seeping through their feathery canopy, bathing them in soft green light. Tired as they were, their first concern was the rescued sketchbook. Keiran had set the leather jacket down on the rocky ground in front of them. Now he carefully unfolded it. Its tough oiled outer layer was still intact. He found the inner pocket and gently pulled out the flat square package. One at a time he unfolded the corners of the soft leather wrappings until the sketchbook sat exposed in his hands. The lower edge was stained with water, but the rest of it seemed little worse for its months in the outdoors. He carefully opened the front cover. There, in a neat artist's hand, was printed: "Sketches: King Anglewart's Expedition to Search for the Little Dragons, Summer, Year of the Kings 128, Keiran of Hanford, King's Artist."

Keiran began to turn the pages, slowly, carefully freeing each one from the water stain at the bottom. The early pages were filled with sketches of the King's Men on the expedition, their rough faces and hard hands, a line of them making their way through the forest, each with a large pack and tall walking stick, or circled around a fire cooking a meal, the fire lighting their faces as the first hints of dawn grew in the sky behind them. Keiran shuddered when they reached some drawings of the

Foothills Spring campsite. "Those were done on the outward bound trip," he remarked. The beating was on the way back."

"It's coming back to you now?"

"As I see each drawing I can remember where I was and what I was thinking as I did it."

More pages. In spite of their exhaustion, neither young man could imagine getting any sleep on the sharp rocks beneath the tree even if they weren't totally engaged in the drawings before them. They barely breathed as each page revealed more of the story. Now the drawings showed the men working their way up the slopes of the mountains, climbing from rock to rock. The style of the sketches here was rougher than before. "My hands got banged up from the climbing," Keiran explained.

Pictures of the men at rest were obviously done in caves. They huddled together in small rooms in the rock of the mountain face. "We had to choose small caves," Keiran said. "If it was big enough for a Dragon you risked walking right into a den and becoming the Dragon's supper before you even had a chance to turn around."

"Oh!" Gleve gasped, as a turning page revealed a scene of terror. A Dragon's claws grasped an unfortunate member of the expedition, his face twisted with fear and pain in the moments before he was taken away. The next page showed members of the expedition tending to the terrible wounds of men the Dragon had injured but not taken.

"We had to stay in that little cave for days," Keiran shuddered. "The Dragons knew we were there. We had to wait until they lost interest."

'The men," Gleve asked. "Did they survive?"

"No. Dragons don't leave ordinary wounds. They burn and fester. Both men died after a couple of days."

"I know. I've only helped Father Mallory treat Dragon wounds a few times. Most of the patients recovered, but the wounds still burn when a Dragon is nearby. For the rest of the person's life."

On the next page, there was a sketch of a narrow doorway into the mountainside, intricately carved on both sides. "Oh," Keiran exclaimed. Then, "Oh," louder, startled.

"What is it?" Gleve asked.

"How could I have forgotten this? It was the most amazing place, a sort of ... palace, carved into the rock. See?" He began to turn the next few pages. It showed the members of the expedition walking, awestruck, through decorated passageways. There were rooms, too, with furniture and hangings. "Some of the rooms were too small for Dragons to get into, so we were safe there." He paused, studying his own drawings. "The carvings and embroidery, look at it," Keiran turned another page. "All Dragons. Wonderful, dazzling pictures of Dragons. The artists who did these were … beyond words."

Gleve stared, breathless, at the unfolding glory of this hidden place in the mountains. He knew what it must be. "Keiran, have you heard of the Dragon Priestesses?"

"The Dragon Priestesses, of course I've heard of them. They were evil women who turned the Dragons against humankind, used them to gain the power of Kings."

"Well, not quite."

"Another difference between King's People and the People of the Land?"

"Big difference, this one. I'll explain later. Anyway, I think you must have found their School. They had one in the mountains."

"Like the Healer's School by the Eastern Sea?"

"Yeah, like that."

"Hmm. Look at this room here." The next page showed a room with what appeared to be a low wall on the far side. "There were several of these, rooms looking out into a huge natural cavern. It was full of Dragons." He turned another page. "During the day, when the Dragons were gone, the men closed in one of those look-out places with stone, leaving a space too narrow for the Dragons. We started to use it as a watching-post. We hung a large lantern on a stick just outside. The Dragons didn't like it, but it was protected by an outcrop of rock. They couldn't get at it. That's when I started doing studies of the Dragons."

Keiran turned page after page, each one filled with detailed sketches of Dragons. This was where his memories had come from, the ones he had drawn on the hearthstones of Father Mallory's cottage. There were Dragons eating, sleeping, snapping at one another, curled up together, looking annoyed, or quizzical, or content. Their sinuous forms wound around one another and the rocks with evil grace. "How I wished I had paint with me!" Keiran exclaimed. "Although I could not really have reproduced their colours – red, green, blue, gold, all sort of luminous, like really fine silk, but more translucent, and more solid at the same time. Full of rainbows." His voice had become dreamy. Gleve studied his face. It had filled with wonder.

"What happened next? How did they get the egg?"

"The egg, yes. While we were watching from our lookout, several female Dragons began to make nests on ledges around the outside walls of the cavern and lay eggs in them. One chose a balcony room of our palace. They didn't leave very often, not like the all day hunting of the others, but they did go out sometimes to stretch and groom and eat the food the males brought to them. It was very risky, but the men fashioned a sort of bag, or net, and while our mother Dragon was out taking care of herself, they managed to get it around one of her eggs and drag it back into the passageway behind. That part of the story comes later. I drew lots of pictures of them lowering the egg in its net from the entrance of the palace-cave and carrying it back down the mountain and through the woods. I knew these would be the pictures the King would be the most interested in, the ones that showed his men being heroes, bringing back the egg. Before we get to that, though, I did more exploring and sketching in the palace-cave … I mean the school … and look at what I found."

MAIDA

Liandra went into labour no more than an hour after Mother Peg and Rafe departed on a journey to Rose Creek. A farmer had come with a message that a Healer was needed and they had gone with him. They were not expected to return until the next evening. Maida sent out a little prayer that they would return by then. A first labour was rarely quick, so Maida had confidence that Mother Peg would be there by the time she was needed.

She turned her attention to taking care of Liandra as she had many labouring women under Mother Peg's supervision. She heated water and helped her friend have a warm bath. When she emerged from the tub, Maida produced a light shift woven from thistledown, soft and comfortable. They walked slowly, arm in arm, around the room, around the yard outside. They did breathing exercises together. They talked. Liandra lay down from time to time, seeking a comfortable position. Maida massaged her lower back and sang to her. There was always a full, warm cup of tea, make from the herbs Mother Peg used to ease the pain of labour. Liandra became very dreamy.

The day had come and gone when Liandra suddenly curled up and groaned. "What's going on?" Maida asked her.

Liandra remained curled tight for a moment, then pushed herself into a sitting position. "Maida, I feel sick."

Maida helped her to her feet and down the withy passage where Liandra lost whatever remained of her last meal. When they returned, Maida gave her water, then more tea.

Liandra doubled up again. "Ooooooooh!" she moaned. "Maida, I feel like pushing. What should I do?"

Maida worked to remain calm, sent out a thought: Oh Mother Peg, please come home.

Liandra closed her eyes and moaned again. When the contraction passed, she looked into Maida's eyes. "Mother Peg isn't back yet."

"Don't worry, she will be."

"If she doesn't, do you know what to do?"

Maida paused, and the very pause told Liandra the answer.

"It's alright, Maida. I know you've helped Mother Peg deliver babies many, many times. You know everything you need to know."

"That's right," said Maida, and tried to sound as if she believed herself.

Maida worked with Liandra, breathing through the contractions and finding comfortable positions. The Princess's favourite was on her knees on a cushion on the floor, her elbows on the seat of a chair. Maida urged her to sip more tea between contractions, until the Princess's eyes were glazed.

When her waters broke, Liandra's contractions became much more urgent. In spite of the pain-dulling tea, with each push she let out a long groan, moan, sometimes even a wail. Now Maida helped her into a squatting position and sat behind her, holding part of her weight. Maida was so busy coaching Liandra's breathing she didn't have much time to think, but did wonder how she would get into position to catch the baby if Mother Peg didn't come. Dawn must be approaching. Maybe Mother Peg had decided to stay over the day. Perhaps she could urge Liandra to lean forward with her elbows on the seat of the chair again, receive the baby from behind and hope it just popped out all by itself, as many babies seemed to do.

Just then there was a welcome sound in the courtyard, footsteps, voices, the rattle of the lantern. Liandra groaned and the sounds outside stopped. "Mother Peg," Maida called out. "Send Rafe to the stable to do the chores and come quickly!"

There was shuffling outside and Mother Peg's voice instructing Rafe. Then the door opened and the Realms' most famous midwife was there to take over. Maida felt light with relief, although she didn't pause for a moment her gentle guidance of Liandra's pushing and breathing.

Mother Peg surveyed the scene, Maida with her strong arms around the Princess, holding her up, Liandra squatting, knees wide apart, her whole body heaving with effort. The Healer dropped her cloak, leaving the lantern, still lit, beside it and went to the counter where everything was arranged—warm water, clean basins and towels, scissors and string. She washed her hands and put a clean receiving-cloth over her arm.

"I think it's coming!" Liandra took two quick breaths and then shifted immediately into another push and groan.

"All right, just in time then," Mother Peg said. "Let's see what's happening."

The Old One pulled up a low stool and set her still-burning lantern beside it. She awkwardly lowered herself into position. As the Princess went into another massive push and groan, Peg gathered up the front of the light birthing-shift. "Can you hold this too?" she said to Maida, lifting the gathered fabric over Liandra's heaving belly into Maida's hand.

Then Mother Peg stopped, completely frozen. She looked at Maida, who raised her eyebrows in question and alarm at the old woman's expression.

Now the young birthing mother caught on that something was amiss. "What?" she said. "Is something wrong?" The last word was almost lost as she went into another long push and groan.

GLEVE

Keiran turned a page to reveal sketches of a large room, open to the Dragon cavern at one end. "I had to be careful. The Dragons could have come in, but they seem to be sound asleep at night and, come to think of it, I never did see one in this room, or any sign of one. Anyway, I made these sketches with my lantern as low as I could keep it and still see."

In front of the wall opposite the opening was a large raised dais. The wall itself was completely covered with huge carvings. Keiran had reproduced them in detail. Over everything floated a magnificent Dragon, its neck, tongue, claws, tail, curled protectively around the other figures in the scene. There, Dragons mixed with women dressed in long cloaks with miniature Dragons on their shoulders, in their arms, or at their feet. "There they are!" Gleve exclaimed. "The Little Dragons! If only we knew, where they found them, how they tamed them ..."

Keiran had turned a page. "Your answer to that question might be here. This was the centre of the carving." A stone woman stood there, her face knowing and peaceful, her hair floating free around her naked body, her hand resting on her very pregnant belly.

"And on one side of her, this." He turned another page. To the left of the pregnant woman, another naked woman lay on some kind of sloping couch, her hair also floating gently around her, and above her, curled around her, his lower belly between her legs, a Dragon.

"And on the other side, this." Keiran turned the page to reveal, on the right side of the central pregnant figure, another pregnant woman lying on the same sloping couch, surrounded and supported by other women, her legs spread. From between her thighs emerged the head and shoulders of a miniature Dragon.

Gleve could not leap to his feet in their tiny shelter, so he leaped to his knees. "Keiran! That's it! The secret of the Dragon Priestesses! They didn't find the Little Dragons, they ..."

Keiran finished the sentence, "... gave birth to them."

MOTHER PEG

Mother Peg was almost afraid to touch it, for what emerged was not the round head of a baby, but a slender rainbow-sheened reptilian muzzle. As she hesitated, the eyelids opened, revealing glowing, multi-coloured eyes.

"What's wrong?" the Princess asked again, then groaned into another heave, this time ending with a wail as a pair of gossamer wings, tightly folded, came into the world.

"It's all right," Mother Peg said, recovering the proper tone for a Healer. "One more good push now." She overcame her awe enough to put her hands around the creature's body, supporting its weight lest it slide to the floor. The Princess gave one more great effort, finishing with a relieved squeak as the hind legs and tail slid out.

The Old One partially wrapped the beautiful little creature in the receiving cloth and held it up for Liandra and Maida to see. Both of their faces registered complete shock, and then the Princess broke into a joyful smile.

Mother Peg slid a clean cushion of folded cloth under the Princess and Maida carefully lowered her into a sitting position. Liandra reached out for her treasure. It stopped squirming and, in turn, studied her as she held it in her arms. "His name is Roxtrianatrix, and that's why the Dragons are here, to greet him."

Peg and Maida suddenly became aware that daylight had arrived and no one had closed the shutters. Shadow after long shadow passed over the courtyard.

"Oh!" the Princess exclaimed, looking up at Maida. "It's his voice! That's what I've been hearing all along in my head!"

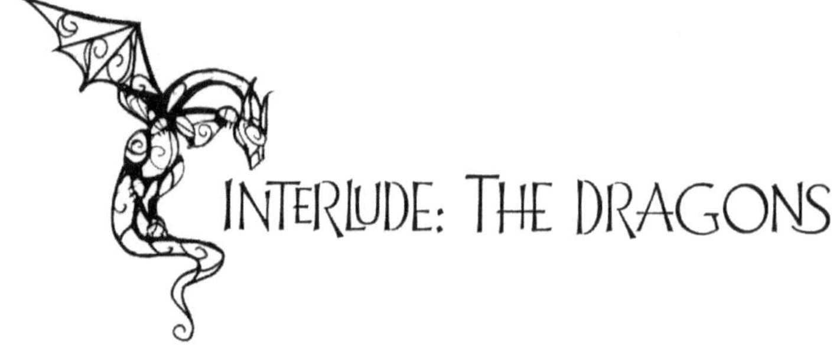

INTERLUDE: THE DRAGONS

Lithe bodies
Twist, turn
Dance shimmering celtic knots
In the sky
Blue, gold, green
Bronze, black, red
Weaving wreaths of joy
The Little ones
Live again
Our Keepers
Return
Hallelujah.

71 MOTHER PEG

Liandra sat in a chair by the hearth cradling her sleeping Little Dragon in her arms. It was two nights since the birth, and the smile had never left her face. It might soon, though, Mother Peg thought. There were some difficult decisions to make. Liandra and Roxtrianatrix must surely go to the Healer's School and work with the Order of Healers to re-create the Order of Dragon Priestesses. But what of her father and husband-to-be? The King would soon be sending Aden to fetch her. If he were to find out about the Little Dragon, he would be quick to take both of them back to the Castle and into his control. Could they hide her from them? If they tried it might trigger another purge of the Order to find her and punish the Healers. Very soon they must rouse the Princess from her idyll and discuss the future with her.

Rafe had been looking out through the kitchen window. Now he turned to Mother Peg and pointed. She looked. There were lanterns coming through the forest, along the path from the west.

"Liandra," she said. "There's someone coming. Go to the loft—quickly!"

Without question, Liandra gathered up her precious bundle and disappeared up the steps to the loft.

Peg and Maida went out into the yard to greet their visitors. Strangely, there were four women, all dressed in the garb of the Women's Retreat House. Two wore gowns, one with the grey veil of a Sister, the other with the black veil of a Widow. The other two wore the grey dress of servants, with matching grey kerchiefs covering their hair. They walked behind the two older women, hidden in their shadows, but it was obvious that one of them was a Woman of the Land.

The shorter of the two gowned women, the one wearing the black veil, approached the old Healer. She dropped her eyes to the ground. How did she know what was considered polite among the Earth People? "Mother Peg?" she asked.

"I am Mother Peg." As soon as Mother Peg saw her clearly in the light of the lantern, she guessed who the stranger was.

"I am ... " The woman paused, seemed to think for a moment. "My name is Melisande." One of the servants in the shadows gave a little gasp and raised her hand to her mouth. "But now I am called Lady Merrit."

"And you are here to see your daughter," Mother Peg said. She noticed that Maida was staring strangely at the woman who had gasped.

"Has she ...?"

Mother Peg paused. Lady Merrit's eyebrows suddenly came together in a frown. "Is she all right?"

"I don't think we can let you see her," Mother Peg said.

"But why not?" Lady Merrit looked close to panic.

Just then there was a shout from the door of the cottage. "Mother!" Liandra came running into the courtyard and threw her arms around the former queen. They held one another tightly, but in the next moment Lady Merrit looked over her daughter's shoulder and her eyes widened. The Sister brought her hand to her mouth and the young servant woman let out a small shriek, for from the open door of the cottage burst Roxtrianatrix, all glittering blue scales and rainbow translucent wings. "Oh," said Liandra, turning. "You can fly already." The Little Dragon circled the amazed group in the courtyard once and then settled on Liandra's shoulder and began to preen himself. Mother Peg scowled.

"But that's a ..." One of the serving women, the one who had shrieked, had stepped out from behind the two older women. Now it was the turn of the residents of the cottage to stand wide-eyed and open-mouthed.

"Yes," said Lady Merrit. "Liandra has a twin."

Mother Peg suddenly laughed. "Well," she said. "Well then, a second-twin. The one your people believe is such bad luck. But I don't think she is bad luck now."

As the visitors settled themselves around the hearth, Maida picked up the bucket to draw fresh water for their tea, but before she could take even a step toward the door, Lady Merrit said, "Mother Peg, I know it is rude among you to speak of important matters before food and drink are served, but this cannot wait. There is a third surprise this night." Maida stopped, the bucket swinging slightly from her hand. Lady Merrit nodded at the dark servant, who stepped hesitantly forward, her eyes fixed in some mix of hope and fear on Mother Peg. She reached into the purse hanging from her waist and took out a cloth-wrapped bundle. She pulled the cloth away from a metal box, opened the lid and held it out to Mother Peg. It contained three, small leather-bound journals.

"Oh!" Peg exclaimed.

Melisande spoke. "These were written by Mother Calla and Sister Rena, a …"

Before she could finish, Mother Peg interrupted her. "I know what they are," she said and reached out for them. "And who are you?" she addressed the young Woman of the Land, "And how did you come by these?"

"We have much to discuss," said Melisande.

JESSA

The cottage was crowded. Every chair, every stool, even Maida's pallet was in use as the six women sat in a circle around the hearth. They ate and drank and listened intently as each story was told.

Jessa's eyes were as round as pottery plates as she learned of her origins as second-twin to Princess Liandra, allowed to live because of the love her father bore for her mother, placed on the steps of the Women's Retreat House instead of being left out for the Dragons. "If I had known, I would have come to see you much sooner, please believe me," Melisande said.

Mother Peg gently caressed the covers of Mother Calla's journals, frowning slightly every time she touched the damaged one, as Melisande helped the shy Ev tell the story of the Key. Well into the day they sat in complete silence as Mother Peg read aloud part of the Journal of Sister Rena, Dragon Priestess. She had to stop reading from time to time, when her voice choked and tears began to trickle down her face. The journal was a manual of sorts. It seemed to provide all the information that the Healers and Liandra would need to know to raise and care for Roxtrianatrix, and, through him, communicate with the Great Dragons.

Later, as exhaustion began to dim the excitement, Mother Peg spoke to the whole company. "We all have secrets now, things that we must not say to anyone outside of this room, or we will put our own and one another's lives in danger." She looked slowly around at each face in the circle. The women all nodded in agreement. "And we have some decisions to make about the future."

Melisande turned to Liandra. "My dearest, your father must not know. He will send armed men to capture you. He will never let you go free knowing you are the key to communicating with the Great Dragons."

Liandra's face abruptly lost the delirious joy of the past few hours and days. "I know," she said. "I don't know what to do. If I try to hide, I will put all of you, and perhaps all Healers, in terrible danger."

The Little Dragons

So, she had been thinking about it too, Mother Peg thought. "We are all very tired," she said. "Perhaps we should sleep, and think, and try to weigh our possible paths in the evening."

"Yes," Melisande agreed, then looked directly at Jessa. "Dear child," she said, "Can we talk a little before we sleep?"

Jessa and Ev lay curled up together on Maida's former pallet on the floor in front of the Hearth, wide awake despite their exhaustion. Imelda shared Mother Peg's large bed, while Maida slept on a thick folded blanket beside them on the floor. Melisande had asked to share Liandra's bed in the loft. Their voices drifted down, softly whispering together, but not the words.

"What did she say to you?" Ev asked.

Jessa pulled the covers up over both of their heads. "She said the first key was your poem, but the second key is me."

"What does that mean?"

"She says that Liandra must go to the Healers School with the Dragon, so they can raise it and learn how to communicate with the Great Dragons in secrecy, and the only way that can happen …"

"Oh," said Ev. "If you take Liandra's place." Jessa nodded in the dark, close space under the blanket. "Oh Jessa," Ev said, suddenly breathless. "This is your dream. You're the daughter of a King. You'll marry a prince, probably be a queen one day." There was a tight stillness beside her. "Jessa?" Ev reached up to touch Jessa's face. It was wet. "Jessa, what's wrong?"

"It was all right as a dream," Jessa whispered between sniffs. "But now that it's real, I don't want to go."

"But Jessa …"

"Ev, we've known each other since we were nine. You're my best friend. There will never be anyone else like you. There can't be. And how will I ever see you again?

Ev gently stroked Jessa's cheek. "I know. But there might be a way … and Jessa, just think, no more scrubbing, no more Dungeon, no more potatoes …" She stopped as a small sob broke from her friend.

GLEVE

Their bellies were blessedly full and their cold, tired bodies soaked up the comfort of Father Mallory's cottage fire as they showed the Old Man what they had found. His breath became so ragged that Gleve worried about him. Tears ran down the Old Healer's face. He wrapped his arms around Keiran. "The Goddess surely sent you to us, and then sent you back to us. You must carry this treasure to the Healers' School, and stop to show Mother Peg along the way."

Gleve's face turned troubled. "A King's Man? The Healing School?"

"My son," Father Mallory answered. "How can you ask it? He is chosen, a very special calling."

"How will he get there?"

"You will take him."

"But what about you?"

Father Mallory turned to Lynna and put a hand on her shoulder. "Apprentice Lynna has already become a very able assistant. She will care for me and work with me." Lynna's face shone with pleasure.

MELISANDE

Rafe sat by the Hearth in his glory, with the full attention of two women. Roxtrianatrix liked Rafe, and by the time he was a day old Liandra had discovered that if she needed her hands free, the beautiful Little Dragon would play with the big farmhand to the point of exhaustion, then fall asleep in his lap. Tonight Rafe had made a toy out of a length of string and a large cork. He moved it around the floor, in and out of his feet and the legs of the chair, making squeaking noises. The lithe little creature would stalk it and pounce on it like a kitten. Unlike a kitten, he would then fly up with it and try to tug it out of Rafe's hand before dropping it and swooping to the floor to start all over again. Imelda and Melisande watched the game, laughing with delight.

Maida had gone to Tummel to send a message to the Castle that Liandra was ready to come home. Mother Peg sat at the table, one of Mother Calla's Journals open in front of her, alternately reading and watching the game at the hearth.

Imelda turned to her. "You told us that Dragon Priestesses had to learn to live with a Little Dragon on their shoulder every minute of their lives, but Liandra has a nanny!"

All three women laughed.

JESSA

The laughter came up from below. Liandra and Jessa were in the loft. Liandra's trunk lay open and a rainbow of court dresses were spread across the bed and part of the floor. Liandra held a green silk gown up to Jessa. "We'll have to take these in a little. You're not as plump as I was when I came. Of course, I'm not either. You mustn't get lazy at court and fall into eating more than you really want. It's easy to do." She picked up a rust-coloured dress. "Try this on," she said.

As she evaluated the fit of each dress, Liandra kept up a running commentary, all the things she felt Jessa would need to know to take over her role in life. "You will hardly ever speak with my … our father. He doesn't ever come near the women's quarters. But should he ever be near you and say 'Rumple-Elves,' those are little creatures he used to pretend he could see and I couldn't when I was very small. I don't remember much of it, but I guess he played a lot with me before he became King."

"Rumple-Elves," Jessa repeated.

Liandra described her one meeting with Prince Lochiel in great detail, trying to recall everything they said in the exact words they had used. When she came to the part about outpacing the chaperones and sneaking a kiss behind a tree, Jessa squealed. "Really?"

"It was kind of exciting." Liandra blushed at the memory, "Although that was partly the risk of getting caught! He was gentle, and a passionate kisser! He touched my breasts for a second, just a brush."

Jessa blushed along with her. "It makes me squirm to think of it."

"I hope he's a good lover," Liandra said, "And that you learn to love one another. And that he doesn't become cold and distant like my father did after he became King." She paused and looked Jessa straight in the eyes. "Oh I wish we had been able to be sisters all along. I wish I had even known about you!"

"Me too," Jessa said. "And now maybe we'll never see each other again."

"Who knows. We're only seventeen, and as you said, life will change if we can make a new Agreement with the Dragons. Maybe as old ladies we'll sit in your quarters at your Southlands castle and sip tea and talk about when we were young."

Jessa laughed with her briefly, then turned away to hide the tears that suddenly stung her eyes.

Lady Merrit and Imedla took much longer than they normally would standing in the courtyard, travel lanterns lit, bidding farewell to Liandra, Peg and Maida. They wanted to allow Ev and Jessa as long as possible to say goodbye. The two friends held one another tightly and shed tears into the shoulders of each other's plain grey dresses.

Finally, Lady Merrit approached them and placed a hand on Ev's shoulder. "Come," she said. "We must go while there is still enough of the night left for a safe walk to the village of Tummel." She folded Jessa into her arms, holding her for a long time. Then she held her at arm's length and looked into her wet eyes. "Go well, my darling. I am proud of you. And I think we will meet again."

Jessa and Ev wiped their eyes with the fabric of their sleeves. Several times they turned to look at one another once more as the Women's Retreat House group crossed the clearing and started along the trail to Tummel. Even when she could no longer see them, Jessa watched until their lanterns flickered out of sight.

MAIDA

When Maida roused herself to do the evening chores, she found the pallet in front of the Hearth empty. "Mother Peg," she called. "Liandra. Come quickly." Bed frames creaked, bedding rustled as it was thrown aside. A few minutes later, all three women stood staring with horror at the empty pallet, it's blanket neatly folded. "Completely cold?" Mother Peg asked. Maida nodded.

MELISANDE

Mother Tess blinked hard a few times, then gave up and allowed the tears to trickle down along the deep creases in her cheek. Marle took her hand, stroking it gently, a delighted smile on her own face. "Who ever would have believed …" she whispered, but apparently could not find the words to complete the sentence.

Melisande, Imelda and Ev were also smiling, at Tess and Marle, at each other, quiet now that they had told the story of their visit to Mother Peg's cottage. Mother Tess pulled a bit of her sleeve over her hand to wipe her face. "Oh that old Peg," she said. "Won't she be proud now? Is she on her way to the School with her prize?"

"That is the plan," Melisande said, "As soon as they see our Jessa off to the palace posing as Liandra."

"And she will take Maida with her? It's about time that young woman was given a proper apprenticeship as a Healer." Melisande, Imelda and Ev looked at each other. None of them knew. "Ah well," Tess said, "I will find out. I am now very anxious to travel to the School myself, see a Little Dragon with my own eyes before I die." Marle glanced at the door and her hand on Mother Tess's tightened for a moment before she let go and reached out for a steaming cup of tea Ev handed to her. Tess glanced at the door as well. "You're right," she said, as if Marle had spoken. "I guess we shouldn't be saying it aloud. Anyone could be listening at the door."

Ev served the other women as well, then poured a cup for herself before setting the thick peasant teapot back on the small table in the centre of a tiny upstairs room in the inn at Theta's Well. The innkeeper's wife had produced the tea and a plate of biscuits, along with chairs for the three older women. Marle and Ev shared the side of the bed.

Marle turned to Melisande. "Lady Merrit, how will you explain to Head Mother Mabonne that Jessa will not be with you?"

Melisande's smile faded. "I haven't thought of anything yet."

"Everyone is talking about how many Dragons have been flying overhead in this region for the past few weeks. Oh! I just realized. It probably has something to do with the arrival of the … " Marle gave the door a guilty glance. "Sorry. Anyway, there have been a few more Dragon attacks than usual lately too. Could you say Jessa was carried away?"

Ev spoke. "We did have a close call, at Mother Calla's cottage …"

Melisande studied her eager young face. "But what reason can I give for her being outside at daybreak?"

There was a pause, the sloping timbered ceiling reflecting back the hard thinking of every woman in the circle. Mother Tess's eyebrows went up. "You could say the two of them, Ev and Jessa, slipped out to try and find us.

Melisande frowned again. "But Ev will be with us … oh." She stopped as Tess's thought became her own. "I could leave Ev here with you."

Ev sat up straight, took in a sharp little breath. "To apprentice as a Healer?" she said and looked at Melisande with eyes full of hope.

Marle, too, fixed her eyes on Melisande. "I think it is what she was born to do, " she said, "If her mother had not fallen on such hard times …"

Melisande nodded. "Of course. It makes perfect sense."

Ev leaped from her seat and threw her arms around Melisande's neck, then stepped back with a look of horror at what she had just done. Melisande laughed, took her hand. "Go with my blessing," she said.

"And mine," added Imelda, grinning broadly.

JESSA

As soon as the rhythmic breathing of sleep surrounded her in the little cottage, Jessa had quietly slipped away. She followed the trail as far as she could, but there were Dragons passing overhead. They were very high, but she dared not risk it. She made her way into the woods and hunted for a sheltered spot. A large fallen tree, hollowed by time, gave her what she sought. Wincing away from the crumbling rot beneath her hands and knees, she crawled inside. At least it was soft. More quickly than she imagined possible in such a place, she was asleep.

She awoke as twilight fell and crept out, brushing bits of the forest floor from her skirt. She studied the clearing around her with growing concern. From which direction had she come? Where was the trail? She must find it quickly, for she had no lantern to light her way.

She decided to search in systematic circles out from her daytime refuge in the log. After four circles, she found the trail, but following it by feel in the darkness proved harder than she imagined. She lost it, found it, lost it, found it, lost complete track of the time. Then her spirits leaped up as, along with the first streak of grey in the dawn sky, she spotted the lights of Tummel.

The noise from the inn met her before she even crossed the square to reach it. Its main room was filled with travelers, all men, celebrating the end of another night's journey with ale and the generous food of the place. Jessa did not want to enter. She peeked as carefully as she could around the edge of the door, searching for any woman to be found there. In a few moments a stout older woman swept through the door from the kitchen, steaming bowls of stew on a tray in her hands, and began pushing and swearing her way to a table where a group of soldiers waited with loud impatience for their food. As she placed the bowls before them, she was facing the door and Jessa stepped forward a bit to get her attention. The woman saw her, and in a moment came over, the empty tray now swinging by her side. "The women from the Retreat House?" she said. "No, dear. They went on last night."

Jessa watched her disappear again into the kitchen, completely at a loss. As she tried to imagine what to do next, her eyes fell on the table of soldiers just served with their stew. One of them was staring back, disbelief and confusion written on his rough face.

MOTHER PEG

"The little minx. The deceptive, lying, sneaky little minx!" Mother Peg banged her stick on the ground in helpless anger. Maida and Liandra stared at her, their faces shocked, by Mother Peg's language or the betrayal of Liandra's twin, Maida couldn't say and didn't care. "Well, she couldn't have gone far, unless a Dragon got her." The two younger women continued to stare, the Little Dragon shifting nervously on Liandra's shoulder. "Well, go and look for her," the old Healer shouted. As the two younger women lit their lanterns, she added, speaking to Liandra, "And you, if you encounter anyone, stay out of sight."

Maida and Liandra found no sign of Jessa, alive or eaten by a Dragon. It was a grimly silent supper in the little cabin in the woods. When the dishes were washed and put away, Mother Peg cleared her throat. Maida looked up from tidying the kitchen, Liandra from the sewing in her lap. "The King's Bailiff will come in two, perhaps three, nights. You, Liandra, be ready to hide in the barn, up in Rafe's room, in the loft behind the hay."

"What will you tell him, Mother?" Maida asked.

"I will have to think of something. Your job, my girl, will be to keep silent." Maida nodded.

JESSA

Terror opened up like a trap door under Jessa's feet and she fell into it, kicking, biting, scratching, writhing, anything to tear free from the hands of the soldiers. She got some satisfying yells, winded "oof" sounds and vicious swear words in return. "Careful now," said one of them, and she suddenly realized they were not actually hurting her. The one that had urged caution maneuvered himself behind her and wrapped his muscular arms around her, pinning her upper body solidly against his chest. Not her feet, though. She slammed her heel into his shin, knocking a cry from him, followed by "Hey now, Your Highness."

Your Highness? In a flash she understood.

"Her feet, Treen, get her feet," the man said, his voice loud in her ear. Someone grabbed her feet, held them still. The smell of sweaty men rose around her in a foul cloud, choking her. "Get the Captain," he said, his voice even louder.

"Maybe she's gone crazy, like they said," another voice said from below, the man holding her feet.

A short, solid bull of a man now appeared in front of her. His massive head seemed to grow right out of his even more massive shoulders. Another soldier held a torch up for him and he looked closely at her face, squinting the weathered skin around his small eyes. "You're right," he said to the man who held her. "It's her." Then he addressed Jessa directly. "Your Highness, what are you doing here?" His eyes traveled down her body. "And dressed like a servant in the Women's Retreat House?"

Since she had no idea what to say, Jessa decided that silence might serve her well. She glared at him. "She's gone mad, just like they said," the voice of the man holding her feet rose again.

"Shut up, Treen," the Captain snapped. He studied Jessa for a few more moments. "I don't think so," he said, "But it's not our business. It's the King's." By now a crowd had gathered in the tight hallway and the main room beyond. "Innkeeper," the Captain bellowed over his shoulder. An older man pushed forward toward them. "Do you have a room with no windows, where we can keep this young woman under guard?" The innkeeper nodded that he did. "Good," said the Captain, "And some food and drink for her." The innkeeper nodded again.

MAiDA

On the third night after Jessa's disappearance, the King's Bailiff came.
They were the noisiest party to approach the cabin since Liandra arrived
all those months ago, heavy male feet, mutters as they stumbled over
roots and stones. Maida gave Mother Peg a worried look. The old
woman seemed completely composed. She must be confident of her plan,
whatever it was. "Quickly," she snapped, and the two younger women
disappeared into the barn, Roxtrianatrix clutching Liandra's shoulder.

They made their way quickly and quietly up to Rafe's room,
where he grinned at them, pleased to have visitors. "Shhh," Maida
cautioned him, forgetting how many times he had hidden there before.
He sat crosslegged on the floor. Roxtrianatrix left Liandra's shoulder
and crawled into his lap, curling up and closing his eyes. Good, thought
Maida. Not that he would make much noise anyway, but if he were lively
there could be bumps or scratches, something knocked over. The two
young women sat side by side on the edge of Rafe's wooden bed, holding
hands and listening.

The party of King's men made their noisy way into the courtyard.
Maida listened for the rattling and clunk as they set down the sedan chair,
but only heard the softer clatter of lanterns. "Greetings," said Aden's
voice.

"Greetings in return," said Mother Peg. Followed by "Sir, I have
very bad news."

"I know," he said.

After a moment's silence, Mother Peg said, "You know?"

"We met a group of soldiers traveling west. They have captured her.
They are on their way to take her back to the King."

"Oh," said Mother Peg.

"What happened? They seem to think she's gone mad," Aden said.
"And all she did was scowl at me, and I've known her since she was a
child."

"Well, it's been very hard, what she's been through. She ran off into the woods. We couldn't find her. I'm just glad she's safe."

"And can you explain why she was dressed like that?"

"Like what?"

"Like a servant from the Women's Retreat House."

There was a suitable pause. "A servant? From the Women's Retreat House? Are you sure?" He must have nodded, because she continued. "I have no idea. Could she have met someone? Traded clothes?"

"A servant from the Women's Retreat House? Travelling alone? Out here? I don't think so," Aden responded.

"Could she have had it with her all along, planning an escape?" Another silence. Maida could picture them, the tall, white haired King's man, the tiny, dark Healer, shaking her head in puzzlement. "Well, however she laid her hands on such clothing, I am relieved that she is safe. They will take care of her, the soldiers?"

"Yes of course. She is the King's daughter. They will take her to him. And the child? All was done as we asked?" Again Mother Peg must have nodded, because there was no reply.

When they were gone, Liandra and Maida returned to the cottage. Mother Peg was in a good mood. "That was easier than I thought," she said. "Now we must depend on the young twin's acting skills."

"I hope she'll be all right," Liandra said.

"That, child, is out of our hands," Mother Peg told her. "Our task, yours and mine, is to get you and that precious Little Dragon of yours as quickly as possible to the Healer's School." Maida's hopes flared, only to be doused again. "And you, my dear," Mother Peg addressed her, will keep the place here, with Rafe.

ANGLEWART

The young woman in front of him jerked the King's heart in a way he would not have expected. Dressed humbly, in a ragged grey servant's dress from the Women's Retreat House, her eyes fixed to the floor, she was so like Liandra, yet so unlike. His princess daughter was plump and soft, spoiled by her life in the Palace. This child was strong, reared on hard work. He took a step towards her and held out his hand. She started slightly, controlled it, frightened and brave. Then she stole a questioning glance at his face. He smiled, and she hesitantly put her hand in his, calloused and hard, as he knew it would be. "Will you walk with me?" he asked her. Her eyes sought his face again, questioning, just for a moment before bowing again. He dropped her hand and turned, walking toward the door, knowing she would follow.

He was grateful that Ermin was busy elsewhere. The Head Bailiff did not know about the second-twin, born as she was in his days of privacy and love, before the battle for the Crown but, Spymaster that he was, he would notice every detail that separated this strong young servant woman from his soft Princess daughter.

In the hallway he turned toward the tower steps. He would walk with her on the battlements. One would think more readily of the garden for walking with a young daughter, but this time he wanted to be sure no one was listening. The battlements were one of the few places that offered a clear view of anyone nearby.

It was windy when they emerged from the tower. The guard, startled, saluted both King and then, with a slight hesitation, the small figure following him. The King nodded and went well past him, out of hearing, before turning. She had clearly been looking down into the torchlit courtyard, but stopped when he did and dropped her eyes again. "No need to be so humble here, child," he said to her. "We are alone, not King and subject, but father and daughter." She raised her face to him, pale and tense, but curious. "What is your name?" He watched shock pass through her expression. Her lips began to form the name Liandra. "I know who you are," he told her, "But I do not know your name."

She hesitated. He could almost see her mind racing behind her eyes. "Jessa," she finally said, in a tiny voice.

"Jessa," he repeated. "And do you know who you are, Jessa?"

"I know I am second-twin to your daughter Liandra." She dropped her eyes again to the dark stones of the walkway.

"And how long have you known this?"

"A few days, Your Highness."

"And who told you?"

"The Lady Merrit."

"And what do you know about her?"

"She is a Widow who came to the Women's Retreat House this spring."

"How did it come that she told you who you are?"

The young woman looked up at him again – gauging or puzzling? "She took me travelling with her – I have been her servant since she came to the Retreat House. She left me in an inn in Tummel and went somewhere. When she returned, she told me who I am and said that I must come and present myself to you as my sister."

"And you agreed to come?"

"No. I ran away."

"And my soldiers caught you before you even left the inn in Tummel."

"Yes, Your Highness."

Anglewart studied her. She may know more than she was saying she did, but it might be better to wait until she was less on her guard. And clearly it was time for another interview with Melisande. What was she up to? And where was Liandra? Whatever her use to Melisande, however, this young one would be of use to him as well. This may even be what Melisande was thinking. "Jessa," he said, "Look at me." She did, her eyes shining a bit in the starlight with tears held back. "Tell me truthfully, are you a virgin?" She gave that tiny start again, but recovered and nodded, solemn and without hesitation. "And can you keep secrets?" She nodded again. "All right," he went on. "No one besides you and me can know that you are not Liandra. To my closest advisors, I will say that you tried to run away and switched clothes with a servant from the Women's Retreat House who was also running away. For everyone else, it will be a mystery, where you have been and how you came to be dressed this way. There will be rumours, of course, but silence is always best. Do you understand?" She nodded again. "And meanwhile," he said, and reached out to cup his hand under the chin of her serious young face, "Welcome home." The tears that leaped into his own eyes caught him by surprise. In part to cover them, in part because he wanted to do it anyway, he stepped forward and folded her into his chest.

LiANDRA

The trail was endless. Liandra followed the bent figure of Mother Peg through trees so huge they disappeared into the night sky, far beyond the piddling circles of light cast by their travel lanterns. They whispered out there in the dark, though, and sometimes reached down to brush Liandra's face with twig fingers. There was a chorus of singing voices in the dark, too, the insects that serenaded them in the clearing where Mother Peg's cottage stood, only louder and more sinister. Their lights flickered and bounced, picking up a root here, a stone there, casting weird, dancing shadows.

Mother Peg hobbled along, the tread of her soft leather-clad feet followed by the click of the wooden stick she used to balance herself—pad, pad, click, pad, pad, click. Every now and then she would catch her foot on something, grumble her annoyance. If it hadn't been for Roxtrianatrix, clinging tightly to her shoulder, exchanging thoughts, she would have either lost patience or given in to terror.

What's that? she would ask him.

Little, harmless, good to eat, he would answer her.

Will this old woman even make it where we are going?

She's tough, the Little Dragon would say.

Liandra stopped herself just in time to avoid crashing into Mother Peg, who stood looking at an oddly-shaped stone standing at the side of the trail. "This is the marker," the old woman said. When Liandra did not respond, Mother Peg frowned at her. "This marks the trail to the last Dragonstone remaining in the Eastlands. We must make a thank offering there."

Liandra raised her lantern higher and studied the woods. When she looked closely, she could barely make out what might have been a path. "How far is it out of our way?" she asked.

"Not far," Mother Peg answered.

"That's what you always say."

Mother Peg pushed the brush aside, set her foot on the faint side-trail. "Come," she said.

"No," said Liandra.

Mother Peg raised her own lantern, studying Liandra's face. Her own in its light was glowering. "You will," she said.

"I won't."

"This is a holy place and, because of you, a holy time. What will the Great Mother think if we don't make a Journey-Prayer?"

"You can barely walk. We are traveling only a few miles a day. We can't afford any side-trips."

Mother Peg banged the ground with her walking stick, glared at Liandra as if the fierceness of her expression could force the Princess to bend to her will. Liandra crossed her arms, her lantern dangling low by her side. Roxtrianatrix stirred on her shoulder.

"Ask your Little Dragon then," Mother Peg said. "What does he say?"

Roxtrianatrix immediately spoke in her mind. You should go, speak to the Dragons. Whatever you say to a Dragonstone, they will hear you.

But, the journey, it's so long, she's so slow.

You would make better time in the daylight.

Liandra turned her head to look at him in surprise. "What?" said Mother Peg.

You have me with you. The Dragons will not harm you.

She said aloud. "Roxtrianatrix says we should go to the Dragonstone."

"Well," Mother Peg looked smug. "Well then."

"And he says we should travel in daylight, that because of him we're safe from the Dragons."

Mother Peg's expression changed to surprise, became thoughtful, then folded into a frown. She turned and began to feel out the almost-invisible trail with her stick. "Let us go and make our prayer. We can talk about this further when we stop to rest."

84 MAIDA

The goat Maida was milking bleated and kicked the bucket. It clattered aside, a pool of milk spreading across the milking stand, pouring over the edge into Maida's lap. Maida leaped to her feet, holding her skirt out in front of her, and abruptly burst into tears. Rafe dropped his hayfork and shambled to her side, his big, round face a comic mask of concern. Maida did not see the humour, though. She dropped onto a hay bale and buried her face in her hands. Rafe shuffled from foot to foot in front of her. She could hear his big, clumsy feet, feel his panic. Wiping her eyes with a last, dry corner of her apron, she tried to reassure him. "It's alright. I'm alright, Rafe. I just … miss them is all."

Rafe seemed to calm down a bit. He sat on another bale beside hers, clutched his big, red hands between his knees and stared at her. When she looked up, big tears gathering at the corners of his blue eyes.

ANGLEWART

Daylight would be well advanced over the distant mountains by now. All of the servants, even Ermin, had been sent to bed, and still the King sat in the Chapel of the Warrior God.

His last business of the day with Ermin was to review the wedding arrangements. He was pleased to see that Jessa's was well advanced. Must get her married quickly, he thought, before she makes a slip and someone guesses that she is not Liandra, before Ermin sees her and figures out that something is amiss, before some wretched servant seduces her. He had never found out who fathered Liandra's child, despite questioning, spying, even a little torture in the ranks of the servants. He knew Ermin was as frustrated as he was with their failure to uncover that information, a slap in the face of Ermin's professional pride as well as a maddening puzzle.

Then there was his own wedding, which seemed to be running into one mysterious delay after another. He had begun to wonder if the Warrior God himself was displeased.

He studied the face of the Diety, portrayed as his ancestor, so much like his own face. Some claimed they could hear the Warrior God speak to them when they prayed. Probably just a story, or imagination, something desired so strongly it became real. He fervently wished it were true, that a two-way conversation were possible with the God.

Bending, he set the kneeler on the floor and, sliding forward, lowered his knees to its padded surface. For the first time in many months, in fact, since the terrible grief of losing Ortrude, he propped his elbows on the wooden wall in front of him, folded his hands, rested his forehead on them and prayed from his heart.

All-powerful Warrior God, Melisande lives, and yet, for the well being of the Realm, I am to be married again. Two living women. Two wives. A gross violation of your all-wise law for the conduct of human lives. Please forgive me. It is for the well being of the Realm. It is for …

He could not think what else it was for and, as he considered this, his mind wandered into questions that had been circling in his head ever since Jessa had come back into his life: Where was Liandra?

Aden reported that his Princess had run away from that old witch in the after the birth of the child, and that the child had been given to a peasant family to adopt, as had been agreed from the beginning. Aden said the crone seemed surprised about the Women's Retreat House outfit. Were both his daughters running around in the woodlands at the same time? No, that couldn't be. This was part of someone's intricate plan for something, but what? And who?

He would love to send someone to question that old witch in the woods. Aden was the one who knew the way, but if he were told about the two daughters, if anyone were told, the secret would not be long reaching Ermin's ears. At one time, he would not have dreamed of keeping anything from Ermin, his Spymaster, ally, servant and friend, but things were changing. Or rather, he, Anglewart, was changing and Ermin had not. Or perhaps he had, but in a different direction. For a time, Ermin had seemed in complete agreement that outright warfare against the Dragons was just a recipe for dead warriors. Now, he had begun to suggest that with the advances in smithing armor, with the longer-flying arrows, with stronger alloys in their swords, with the larger horses they had been breeding over the past decade … Would he have tried to poison Melisande without Ermin's urging? Would he be planning his marriage to Thalassa? Yes, the Rodolph alliance was important, but, at the price of his Melisande?

Melisande. She was the other person who could be up to something here, but what? And why? He couldn't think of a way to question the crone for now, but he had accomplished a meeting with Melisande once before. But would she tell him? There was only one way to find out.

LiANDRA

It was midnight, and Liandra lifted her lantern to peer into the woods along the road. "I think we should find a place to sleep for the rest of the night," she said. "In the morning, we can try traveling in the daylight."

Mother Peg planted her walking stick. "You say your Little Dragon says it's safe."

"He does."

"How do I know you're telling me the truth?"

Liandra placed a hand on her hip and let out her breath. "Why would I lie and put both of us in danger?"

"Humph."

"Oh for the God's sake."

"The Goddess's sake."

Their argument had become so loud that neither heard the drover until he came around the corner, his lantern swinging from the shaft of his handcart. Startled, Roxtrianatrix, on Liandra's shoulder, arched his back, raised the crest on his head and made a hissing sound. The drover's eyes popped wide open, his mouth formed an O, and he dropped his hand shafts. His cart clattered to the stones. His lantern bounced into the road and went out.

Liandra instinctively doused her lantern too and stepped off the path into the darkness among the trees. By touch she found a particularly large trunk and, slipping behind it, stood still, her hand around Roxtrianatrix's muzzle to silence him.

The drover fumbled for his light and re-lit it, holding it up and peering around him. "Mother Peg?" he said.

"My son, you frightened me." Mother Peg had not moved from the spot where she had been standing, could not.

"Mother Peg, I thought I saw ..."

There was the slightest pause. "My son, do you suffer from waking dreams?"

"Ah, no, never have before, anyway."

"Well it's something you should perhaps talk to a Healer about. Now, if you'll excuse me." She hobbled past him and his cart and continued on down the road.

Light from the drover's lantern shone into the woods, briefly lighting up the forest floor on either side of Liandra's hiding place. She shrank down and held her breath. The light moved away. After a few minutes, she heard the drover pick up his shafts and move on. His light disappeared down the path towards the west. By now Mother Peg's had long since disappeared in the opposite direction.

Liandra waited a little longer before feeling her way back to the road. She lit her lantern and hurried after Mother Peg. The old woman had not gone far. "That was close," Liandra heard the trembling in her own voice.

"Much too close. We must be more careful."

Liandra found a small cave not far from the trail. "You can do what you like," she had told Mother Peg. "I'm going to get some rest and then try traveling in daylight in the morning." She grumbled quietly as she hunted for soft pads of moss and fern by lantern light. You'd think the old woman could do just a little bit of the work. Liandra, after all, was a princess and had the burden of Roxtrianatrix perched on her shoulder. When the bed was ready, Mother Peg simply curled up inside her cloak with her back to her traveling companion.

Liandra made a face at the old woman's back and sat down, leaning against the rock wall at the cave's door. She unlaced her bodice and shifted Roxtrianatrix around into position to nurse. He suckled for a few moments and then squirmed away, climbing back up to her shoulder and looking around at the dark woods. What's wrong? she asked him with her mind.

Hungry, he said.

So come back down here and nurse, she thought back at him. My breasts are full enough to hurt.

The Little Dragon crawled back into her arms and suckled, but switched his tail back and forth, restless. Not enough anymore, he said into her mind. Need more now.

Like what?

Meat.

Oh. Liandra sighed. She had wondered if her Little Dragon would need to eat like a Great Dragon someday, and what to do about it.

Hungry, said Roxtrianatrix.

You'll have to wait until we get to the School. The Healers will help us figure something out.

MAiDA

The young boy actually knelt before Maida. She winced as his bony knees struck the stone floor of the cottage with a bruising sound. "Please, Apprentice, everyone says you can heal my mother."

"Get up," she said, more sharply than she intended. "You're mistaken. I'm not an Apprentice. I'm just Mother Peg's servant."

"But you help her, at births, stitching up wounds, setting bones. You know what to do. Everyone says."

His eyes looked so big and frightened in his thin dark-skinned face. Maida softened, just a little. "What did you say happened to your mother?"

"She fell into the well. Her leg is bent funny and it's swelling. And she's in so much pain she cries all the time. It must be broken."

"Is the skin broken? Is she bleeding?"

"No." He shook his head. "Please come, Sister."

"I am not a Sister! But all right. If the bone is broken it must be set to heal properly. I have watched Mother Peg do it many times. You live on the Tummel road, you say?" The boy nodded. She took a small pack to the pantry and tried to think what would ease the pain, speed the healing. As she gathered up her cloak and traveling lantern, she worried about Rafe. She had never before left him here alone.

"Go on ahead," she told the boy. "Care for your mother. You've given me good instructions. I will be there as soon as I can."

When his lantern had disappeared down the path, she allowed him some time to get well ahead of her, then went to find Rafe in his hiding place in the barn. She gave him careful instructions: finish moving the last of the manure pile to the garden. I've left some bread and cheese on the counter in the kitchen for you to eat. Take the chickens and goats into the stable as soon as the sky begins to turn even a little bit grey. Feed them and wait for me there. I'll be home in time to milk and make your supper. Do you understand?

Rafe nodded. "Wait," he said.
"Yes, exactly, and don't worry. I'll be home very soon."
"Soon," he repeated.

LiANDRA

They walked slowly that first morning they traveled in daylight, their lanterns hanging from their belts, bouncing blindly against the fabric of their skirts. It seemed more important to study the shades of green in forest canopy, smile at a little grey bird that sat on a branch and sang to them, study a tiny, glowing flower growing beside the trail than to walk. Liandra watched Mother Peg feel the bark of a tree, running her knarled fingers over the dips and creases in its rough skin, admiring the hundred shades of brown and grey. Her face was open, taken over by amazement like a small child's. Liandra imagined her own face looked that way too. It was a wondrous world open before them, and they could see so much of it. Glade led to glade as Liandra peered through the forest, light sloping into small clearings and picking out jewels: a berry, a mushroom. The smell was different too. At night the woods gave off an earthy scent, soil and moss, fungus and dampness. In the daytime the sun warmed the swaying fans of the evergreens and gave off a waft of resin, piney and sharp. Who could have imagined a world so beautiful?

As the morning went on, they began to walk with a little more purpose, learning to peer in amazement at their surroundings and take steps at the same time. Roxtrianatrix was right. They could make much better time in daylight, without roots reaching out of the night to grasp their feet and shadows to trick them into stumbling when there was not anything there. Roxtrianatrix danced above them, landing on branches, taking off again, playing like any young thing in the bright day that was his natural habitat.

A small group of dragons circled high above them. Liandra shivered when she looked up, but each time Roxtrianatrix reassured her. They love you, he said. You are a Dragon Priestess. And it was true. At the Dragonstone two nights before, Liandra had felt love pulsing from the stone, surrounding her, caressing her. She felt like lying down and curling up, sleeping in its warmth and safety. Does that come from the stone? she asked Roxtrianatrix.

From the Dragons, he said, through the stone.

They stopped to eat a bite of lunch on a large flat rock in a clearing. Maida had packed their food carefully, each day's allotment wrapped separately in waxed cloth. As they ate, a Dragon circled down toward them, a little lower with each pass. They stared at him, fascinated. He was a bronze-brown colour, but as he turned his sinuous body, catching the sunlight from different angles, his scales came alive with layers of rainbows. His wings, too, displayed every colour of the spectrum, shimmering as if alive as they gracefully moved the long body through the air. Roxtrianatrix rose to fly in matching circles above their heads, but still below the tips of the trees. The light flashed off of his glittering blue scales so brightly that the two women had to raise their hands to protect their eyes, not accustomed to the full light of the sun.

On the next pass, the Dragon looked down at them and Liandra gave a little squeak of recognition. "Look," she said. "His eyes. Like jewels. Like opals. I remember that from the Dragon at my father's castle."

Just then the dragon swooped so low that his belly brushed the tops of the trees encircling the clearing, bending them slightly. Both women instintively ducked. Roxtrianatrix chattered aloud in excitement. In the Dragon's wake the pointed tips of the trees sprang back, swaying. Liandra and Mother Peg looked at each other. Liandra could see fear in Mother Peg's eyes to match her own. "Roxtrianatrix keeps telling me it's all right," Liandra assured the Old One.

"I should certainly hope so," she responded, still nervously scanning the sky.

Later that day they took a detour through the trees to avoid a small cottage sitting in its little clearing in the forest. It was obviously occupied—a pail by the pump, an ax wedged into a chopping block. The inhabitants were probably asleep at this hour, but it was well not to assume so. Bad enough that the drover had seen them on the road the night before. You never knew when someone might decide to curry favour by taking word to the King.

The Little Dragon was not, however, cooperating. He flitted into the clearing, sniffed about, hovered over a small shed that stood near the edge. "Get him back here!" Mother Peg hissed to Liandra.

"I'm trying!" she snapped back, and it was true. She was saying everything she could think of to get him to come back to her, coaxing, commands, threats.

Feathered things in there, Roxtrianatrix signaled back. Like Maida's. Do you mean chickens?

Hmmmm—to eat, he said.

Well you can't get at them in that shed. We'll have to find some later, when we get to the School.

Just then the shutter on one of the cottage windows swung open. The face of a woman appeared there, sleepy and annoyed. As soon as her eyes fell on Roxtrianatrix perched on her chicken coop, she shrieked and slammed the shutter closed.

Come, Liandra threw the thought at Roxtrianatrix. Quickly! She took Mother Peg's elbow and pulled her toward the path. As soon as Roxtrianatrix realized they were leaving, he abandoned the chicken coop and followed just above them.

As they were about to leave the clearing, Liandra looked back. Two shutters stood wide open, the woman's face in one, a man's face in the other, watching them leave.

A few hundred meters along the path, Lianda's eye was drawn to something light coloured in the brush by the trail. A chicken crouched there, probably left behind when the people in the cottage put the rest of the flock in for the day. No sooner had Liandra spotted the bird than her thoughts drew the Little Dragon's attention to it. A flash, a crashing of branches, a dismayed squawk, and Roxtrianatrix shot upward with the chicken in his claws. He settled on a high branch in a cloud of feathers. His mistress could feel his triumph and need to eat.

A moment later, Liandra fell to her knees on the trail, grinding her fists into her eyes and shouting, "Stop! Stop! Stop!"

"What's wrong?" Mother Peg was instantly at her side.

"Blood and insides. He's tearing it apart." She bent over, now pressing the heels of her hands into her eyes. "I can see it even with my eyes closed."

Mother Peg put her hands on the younger woman's shoulders. Liandra could feel the Healer's calming energy flowing through her body and into the ground beneath her knees. The terrible images were still there, but her panic eased, and shortly the chicken was gone, leaving a bloodstain on the bark. At this point, she realized she could look down, past the branch, and see herself kneeling on the path, Mother Peg bent over her. She looked up into the tree, and the minute her eyes settled on Roxtrianatrix, her vision clicked back into the proper perspective, through her own eyes. "I was looking through his eyes," she said to Mother Peg.

"Yes, there's something about that in Mother Calla's journal."

"There is?"

"It's clearly another gift of the tie between Dragon Priestess and Little Dragon, but one that you're going to have to learn how to control."

"Does she say how, in the journal?"

"I didn't read that section in detail. I hope so." Mother Peg helped Liandra to her feet. The Princess brushed the dirt off of her skirt and turned again to the tree branch high above them. Now she could feel waves of satisfaction coming from her charge. Happier now? she asked him.

Yes, oh yes, he said. Sleepy now.

Well, come back down to my shoulder, but clean that blood off your claws first!

They reached the edge of the Barrens the next day, pausing where the path left the shelter of the trees to cross the open ground. Are you sure? Liandra asked Roxtrianatrix. The Little Dragon was snaking along ahead of them, circling back, chittering to them impatiently. "Is he sure?" Mother Peg asked. "We could stay until evening in the Healer's cabin we just passed, wait for darkness to be absolutely certain."

Come, come, of course it's safe. They love you, Roxtrianatrix said in a singsong voice in Liandra's mind.

"He says he's sure it's all right," she told Mother Peg.

Mother Peg gave one more nervous look at the Dragons circling overhead. They did seem to be very high in the sky. "All right, then. He is a Little Dragon. He should know." She firmly set her stick on the path ahead of her and took the first steps out on to the Barrens. Ignoring the shiver she felt along her spine, Liandra followed.

They were no more than a few hundred meters out onto the Barrens when there was a deafening flapping sound immediately behind them. Liandra turned just in time to see a set of long, reptilian fingers, tipped by curving claws, opening under a vast shadowed ceiling of glittering blue scales. They closed around her. She screamed as her feet left the ground, shut her eyes as tightly as she could. It's all right, it's all right, he won't hurt you, said Roxtrianatrix in her mind, almost drowned out by the sound of her heart beating in her throat.

He's gentle. You're not hurt, said Roxrianatrix. Open your eyes.

The wind whistling past her ears was deafening, punctuated by the flap, flap of massive wings. The scales on the Dragon's belly were not cold, as she would have imagined, but warm against her back

As she opened her eyes the wind instantly drove tears from them. She was held in the scaly claws as if in a basket. The Barrens were disappearing below her, wheeling as the Dragon climbed in slow circles. Roxtrianatrix flew at her side. She could feel his excitement, his joy. The Little Dragon continued to offer a litany of comfort: You're fine. He won't hurt you.

She caught sight of Mother Peg, as tiny as a child's doll, her walking stick more like a match stick dropped on the path beside her, looking up, waving her arms. Her mouth was moving. And then she was gone. All Liandra could see now was a carpet of green treetops rolling gently up and down over hills and valleys, passing beneath her, her glittering Little Dragon keeping pace by her side. Whump, whump, whump went the powerful wings. It's all right, Roxtrianatrix repeated, They love you. And now she could feel it, surrounding her, holding her up like the scaly blue claws that held her gently to the Dragon's breast, the same warm, powerful love she felt at the Dragonstone.

MOTHER PEG

As her heartbeat slowed, Mother Peg felt faint. She had been waving her arms at the disappearing Dragons, yelling at them to bring the child back. Her stick lay beside the path. She managed to retrieve it and prop herself up on it while her aching lungs struggled to catch her breath. The Little Dragon had betrayed them. Was he working with the Great Dragons? Did they tell them to lure the two women onto the Barrens in full daylight?

Her anger and alarm turned to fear. Out in the open on the Barrens, in full daylight. She must make her way back to the Healer's cabin as fast as she could. And yet … She scanned the sky above her, the huge, blue vault of it, empty. They could easily have taken her too. There had been at least ten Dragons. It was just Liandra they wanted.

In the Healer's cabin, Mother Peg sat heavily on the side of the bed, relieved to be off of the Barrens. She had puzzled about it through the whole struggling hobble back to safety: What did the Dragons want with Liandra? Was it Roxtrianatrix they wanted, and thought he would never go with them without his mother, if you could call the Princess that?

At least – and here she felt the inside pocket of her skirt to be sure – she still had Mother Calla's precious journals, safe in their metal box.

MAIDA

"Rafe!" "Rafe!" Maida called over and over again.

The Healing had gone well, despite her nervousness. It was a straightforward bonesetting. The pain-killing herbs had worked quickly and well. She had closed her eyes and found that she could feel through the skin without touching, judge the direction and pressure needed to put the bone back in place. She had watched Mother Peg do this so many times. She slipped into the reassuring Healers' tone with ease, giving confidence to herself as well as her patient. She had left the woman resting well, her leg held in place by a splint and bandages, packets of herbs for pain and healing on the table beside the bed, and had made her way home with much of the night still remaining.

She had quickly found that her charge was absent from the barn and house. Another half-hour confirmed that he was not working in any of the fields around the cottage. Now she checked each of the trails leading to the clearing, as far as she dared, given the approach of dawn. Her lantern cast wild shadows among the trees, but no sign of Rafe. Her throat was sore from calling.

She should not have left him alone.

91

LiANDRA

Liandra was half frozen, her eyes watering as the Dragon carved through
the colder air of the Northern mountains. She did not want to close
them, because each lift of the massive wings revealed another awesome
panorama of rocky peaks crowned with snow, their lower flanks carved
by steep wooded valleys. Other Dragons flew around them now. She
lost count of the fierce armoured snouts, the opal eyes, that came close
to look at her. They seemed to greet Roxtrianatrix with a flick of their
mighty tails and then, with a flash of belly scales in every shade of
blue, green, bronze, black and gold, they would join the honour guard
conducting her to the heights. Her hands were tiring from gripping
the scaly blue toe that supported her chest when she noticed they were
dropping, skimming along a ragged cliff. They rounded a corner and the
dark mouth of a cave gaped before them, with more Dragons flying in and
out, a great, glittering cloud of them.

It took a minute for her eyes to adjust to the darkness, although
the musty smell of the place almost overwhelmed her. It was a relief,
however, to be out of the wind. The Dragon hovered for a few minutes,
and she caught glimpses of a huge cavern dotted with rocky perches, each
one hosting a Dragon, landing, taking off, or just sitting and watching
them. On one side a scattering of smaller caves caught her eye and held
it because they were arranged in straight rows, three levels of very small
openings, twenty or so in each row, and below them two larger ones.
Beside these, and slightly lower, was a much larger opening with some
kind of platform projecting forward into the cave.

The Dragon approached the top row of small holes, and Liandra saw
that each had some kind of fence set into it. He approached the one on
the end, lifted her and carefully placed her just behind the fence, which
turned out to be a balcony railing. As his fingers unfolded from her, her
legs began to buckle. She turned and grasped the railing hard. It was
sturdy, made of polished hardwood. Roxtrianatrix landed beside her on its

smooth surface. Are you all right? he asked.

As the feeling came back into her legs, she stood straighter and looked out over the gigantic room before her. Dragons sat on every ledge she could see and many more hovered in mid air. Every pair of kaleidoscope eyes was focused on the two of them. The feeling of love—no, stronger than that, adoration—was intense.

Alethilion says welcome home, Roxtrianatrix said.

Who? she asked, but did not need to wait for the answer. She looked into the eyes of the Dragon immediately in front of her, the lithe blue Dragon that had carried her here, and recognized him. Her eyes dropped to his back leg, neatly tucked under his belly. Yes, a ring of scar tissue, the mark of an iron manacle. What is his name? she asked.

Alethilion, Roxtrianatrix repeated.

Behind the balcony was a sleeping chamber. Liandra explored it in the dim light that entered from the larger cave outside. The room was dominated by a bed, made up with sheets and a comforter, musty with time and full of the smell of the outer cave. Beside that was a small table and on it, thank the God, a lantern and flint. Fortunately there was fuel in it, although the wick was dry. After two or three tries, it lit. Now she could see the rest of the room. There was a sturdy wooden chair, a cupboard holding two dresses and a cloak, and several shelves lined with books. The only decoration was a small tapestry of a hovering blue Dragon on the wall. When she touched it, a puff of dust billowed from its old fibres. There was also a thick layer of dust on the floor. When she looked back, she could see her own footprints.

Roxtrianatrix stayed perched on the railing, delighted to visit with his Great Dragon relatives. Holding her lantern aloft, Liandra entered the corridor behind the simple room. It led past rows of doors. Each one she opened revealed another sleeping chamber, identical in furnishings, but revealing the individuality of their long-disappeared inhabitants. Some were immaculate; some piled with a jumble of belongings. Some bookshelves were empty, or held bouquets of dead flowers or small sculptures. Others were piled so high with books they were bending slightly under the weight. Dresses and cloaks were hung neatly in the cupboards or tossed across beds or chairs, or lying in heaps on floors, all identical in cut but differing in colour and size, from tiny enough for a child to voluminous enough for the heaviest of breasts and the best-fed of bellies.

In the middle of the corridor a spiral staircase descended, passing two more corridors identical to the first and ending in a landing between two large rooms. One side was a library, judging by the floor to ceiling shelves of books, the small desks, the circle of comfortable chairs around a huge stone fireplace. On the other side was a dining hall filled with tables and chairs. They were clearly intended to be set in rows, but half of the room was in disarray, its dust scattered by recent use. She thought of her father's expedition to steal the Dragon egg, Alethilion's egg. The soldiers must have found this place.

Each of these rooms, the library and dining hall, had a long balcony overlooking the Dragon cave. Alethilion hovered just outside the dining hall balcony, watching her. He had been following her explorations. She shivered. All her life the sight of a Dragon so close, paying you that kind of attention, would mean your life was not going to last beyond a few more minutes.

A large door in the back of the dining hall led into a vaulted ballroom, or something of the sort. As she stepped through the door, there was an excited chittering sound behind her. It came from Alethilion, who was flapping his wings noisily just off the edge of the balcony. "Don't worry," she said aloud. "I'm coming back."

An echo in her mind repeated her words, Roxtrianatrix passing them on to the big blue Dragon. He calmed and disappeared from the opening. Liandra felt relief. Maybe he would go and rest, stop watching her every move.

The reception room was as disordered as the dining hall had been, the old furniture pushed aside to make room for the soldier's sleeping pallets in the centre of the floor. On her way through, she spotted a worn pair of black doeskin pants discarded in a corner, definitely from the uniform of one of her father's soldiers.

The reception room had a door on the far side as well, with light in it. There, Liandra found an outdoor platform, probably large enough for a Dragon to land on. Immediately she was proven right, as Alethilion landed in front of her, flicking his tail in what she took to be greeting. She smiled at him and he flicked harder. Behind him the clear light of the mountains was fading, the sun heading for rest behind the vast peaks.

This sparked hunger in Liandra. She hadn't eaten since breakfast. Where there is a dining room, there must be a kitchen, she thought, and her father's soldiers had been here not that many months ago. They may have left behind something to eat. She headed back to look. On the way through the reception room, she noted a particularly large and well-finished passageway leading away into darkness on one side.

The kitchen was off the dining hall, apparently the only room with no balcony overlooking the Dragon cave. It looked as though it had survived a storm, everything knocked about and dirty with crusted food. Men! Liandra thought, as she waded into the mess looking for something edible. There were several packets of the hard biscuits that served as soldiers' rations. She collected them together into a tin box she found sitting on a shelf. There were five altogether, not enough to last her for long. She would have to figure out what to do about food, not only for herself, but for Roxtrianatrix.

She opened one of the packets. The biscuit inside was too hard to chew. The point, she guessed, was to work at it slowly. When she did, her hunger faded. It made her thirsty, though. The pump was not hard to find, set beside a stone sink with a drain. A row of tin cups hung on hooks on the wall. She helped herself to one. The water was cold and good.

Still chewing on her soldiers' biscuit, she picked up her lantern and continued to explore. Small rooms off the kitchen seemed to be offices or Healing rooms, one containing four beds. One long passage led out of the mountain to a stable with a large storage room half-full of hay. The stable opened into a sheltered meadow with a fence around it. As soon as she stepped out, Alethilion was there beside her, flicking his tail like a dog. Clearly there was no protection from Dragons here in the meadow. Either the animals in the stable grazed at night or there was an agreement that they were not to be eaten. Out here Liandra could see that darkness was falling. It had been a long day, filled with wonder and emotion. She was exhausted.

On her way back to the sleeping chamber where Alethilion had placed her, she made another discovery. At the end of each corridor there was an indoor toilet, better even than those at the castle. A small pump filled a basin for washing hands and face. When the plug at the bottom of the basin was pulled, the water ran through the toilet, carrying whatever was there away to some clever cesspool elsewhere in the mountainside.

At the sleeping chamber, Roxtriantrix waited on the railing, happy to see her. She found a nightdress in the closet and adopted it, glad to strip out of her filthy traveling clothes. She was too tired to mind the mustiness of the bedding and fell instantly asleep, Roxtrianatrix curled on a small rug beside the bed.

MELiSANDE

"Marle, welcome!" Melisande held her hands out to her visitor, surprised to see her so soon after their parting in the inn at Theta's Well. She stepped back and indicated the chairs in the Visiting Room, sent for Imelda and a pot of tea before asking, "Is something wrong?"

"No," Marle told her. "I mean, yes and no." Imelda arrived and greeted Marle warmly. A few minutes later, a young Servant arrived with the tea. As the grey-clad girl shut the Visiting room door, Marle nodded her head slightly at it. "Is it safe to speak here?" Her voice was very low, just loud enough for Imelda and Melisande to hear.

Melisande had not heard the Servant's steps disappear from the hallway. "It is a delight to see you," she said loudly, covering the slight rustle of the parchment scraps she pulled from her pocket, along with a charcoal stick wrapped in a bit of light fabric to keep the user's hands clean. "Be careful," Melisande wrote.

Marle reached out for the writing tools. While Imelda and Melisande kept up an innocuous conversation, she wrote: "Word spreading quietly among Healers. Great excitement. But on road to School with M. Peg, L. & Rox. taken by Dragons."

Melisande's face lost its colour as she read the note. Imelda reached out to cover Melisande's hand with her own, frowning at the message she could not read.

"And how are our friends in the Eastlands?" Melisande asked aloud, as Marle bent to write again. "Not attack – took carefully. Rox. went willingly. Tess thinks Dragons up to something – will not hurt L. Thought you should know. Will come if hear more. Keep ears open here too."

Melisande read the note several times, nodded.

"All is well in the Eastlands," Marle said aloud.

"Thank you. It's important to get news from friends," Melisande said, also aloud, covering the rustle of her skirts as she rose and carried the notes to the fireplace. "We look forward to seeing you again."

The Little Dragons

Two days later, Melisande was not surprised to find the tall man in the rough cloak slouched in one of the Visiting Room chairs, his back to the door, his hood pulled up over his head. He was in front of the fire, as if craving its heat, and had pulled another chair alongside his own, very close, she noticed. He indicated with his hand that she should sit there.

Slouched as he was, he did not tower over her. He turned sideways to face her, holding the hood out to cover any glimpse of his face someone at the keyhole might be seeking. He had aged, she saw. His eyes looked tired.

She bent to whisper behind the shelter of his hood. "My Lord."

That brought a momentary smile. "Not your Lord any more." It disappeared again. "Where is Liandra?" he asked, and watched her sharply for her response.

She knew she could fool the Court by substituting Jessa for Liandra but, if he was paying attention at all, not the King. She had thought about what to say, planned to give the same story about Liandra she had given Head Mother Mabonne about Jessa. Now it was true. She had only to let her real worry for Liandra show through her words to convince him. "She was taken by a Dragon." In fact, having to carry the knowledge as a secret from all but Imelda had caused the worry to build. She found tears leaping to her eyes, looked down to allow them to escape, running down her face. She had lost so much. The fire crackled in the silent room.

After some time had passed, Melisande pulled a linen handkerchief from her pocket and blew her nose. She did not miss his glance at the handkerchief. As Queen it would have been silk. "I was very happy to find Jessa here," she whispered. "You told me she was all right, and I believed you, of course, but it was good to see her with my own eyes."

"She has grown into a lovely young woman," Anglewart said. "And soon she will marry Prince Locheil of the Southlands."

"And no issue about her virginity," Melisande whispered.

"Thank you," he said. So he believed what she had hoped he would, that she had sent Jessa for the sake of the marriage to Locheil. Men, and their all-important power games! She kept her eyes firmly on the crumpled handkerchief in her lap, so he would not read the anger there. "The Dragon," he said, "The one that took Liandra, do you know if it was blue?"

"You mean …" – this had not occurred to her before—"The one in the courtyard?" He nodded. "I don't know. I wasn't there when it happened."

"Where did it happen?"

"Somewhere near the witch's cottage."

"How did she get outside in daylight?"

"I don't imagine the old woman could have stopped her if she decided to run away."

"And what became of the child?"

What did he know? What had Peg told Aden? "I don't know," she said. It was safest.

"So did you see her when you went?"

"No, I was too late." The tears had dried up with the anger, then the worry about what he might already know, but her nose was still quite full. She lowered her head and used her handkerchief to blow it again.

MOTHER PEG

Word of the Little Dragon and Mother Calla's journals spread quietly but quickly among the Healers. Every day brought another Senior Healer to the School to see for him or herself, join the discussion of what would happen next.

Mother Peg was in her glory, the centre of many conversations in the Dining Hall. She told the story over and over again of Roxtrianatrix's birth, the discovery of the Journals. Every session was the same, first excitement at these two leaps forward in their efforts to discover the secrets of the Dragon Priestesses, fading to dismay that the possible new Dragon Priestess was gone, along with her Little Dragon, to who knew what fate and, although the second of Sister Rena's journals had survived, full of information on how to raise, train, control and communicate with Little Dragons, it was the first journal that must have contained the information about how the Priestesses became pregnant with their Little Dragons in the first place. And the first journal was damaged beyond reading.

GLEVE

Keiran and Gleve walked as quietly as they could, listening for the tread of foot or wheel ahead of them or coming up behind. They had had some close calls with merchants and soldiers. Soldiers, in particular, were a worry because so many of them had been shown the poster advertising the price on Keiran's head. Anyone else could have seen these as well, and even if they hadn't, the sight of a Man of the Land traveling with a King's Man would be enough to cause suspicion.

They were dirty and rank from sleeping wherever they could find a log or cave to give them shelter. They used a lantern only when necessary and tonight found they had enough light from the moon to guide their feet along the road. The moon was setting, though, and a pale greyness had entered the bowl of the sky. Gleve paused and looked around. "Time to find a hiding place for the day," he said.

Keiran nodded, a gesture lost in the darkness, and scanned the roadsides. "Oh dear," he said. On either side of them were steep, rocky walls.

"I think the land opens up again a bit further on. I see sky," said Gleve.

"A long way ahead," Keiran said.

The two young men picked up their pace, heading for the open area while still scanning the verges, one on each side, as had become their routine, looking for a side path or some other spot where they could safely leave the road.

Before they had gone far, however, they heard the distinct sound of marching feet coming along behind them. They glanced at one another, and now there was enough light to see expressions. They picked up their speed, but the troop behind them must have been quick-marching to reach wherever they were going to spend the day. They were gaining ground.

The rock walls on either side of the road were closer, higher, steeper, and the two travelers gave up looking for an escape off the road. They fixed their sights on the ever-brightening open sky in front of them and broke into a jog.

The open area turned out to be a broad river, moving swiftly under a long bridge. The sky was beginning to turn blue; the sun must be up. It was no time to be out in the open on a bridge. They looked at each other. The footsteps were coming up on them from behind. No choice. They ran.

As they reached the middle of the span, Gleve glanced over his shoulder. The soldiers had arrived at the end of the bridge and were halted. They were not looking at the fleeing travelers, however, but had fixed their eyes on something upstream, with unmistakable horror. Gleve followed their eyes and stumbled to a stop. A green Dragon was bearing down on them, jaws open, claws spread.

A blast of sulfurous breath, a deafening flap of gigantic wings, a blinding flash of brilliant green belly scales, and the creature had plucked Keiran from the road in front of him. He shouted, but later could not remember what words came out of him. All he could remember was Keiran's wildly kicking legs as the Dragon lifted him over the bridge railing, momentum carrying both captor and captive a few hundred meters downstream.

The Dragon curved its tail under its belly, beat the air a few times, turning to go back over the bridge and away, upstream. It didn't go, however, but hovered, its attention caught by something at the spot where the road disappeared into the woods at the far side of the bridge.

Gleve heard a roaring voice and a very large man appeared, running onto the bridge. He was clumsy, stumbling over his own oversized feet as he came, but not caring as he shouted at the Dragon.

Then there was a sharp chittering sound and all of them, Dragon, soldiers, the big man and Gleve, looked up with mouths hanging open. Descending upon the Dragon was a miniature of himself. A small, lithe creature, covered in blue scales. A miniature Dragon. And then comprehension – a Little Dragon. It could be nothing else.

It descended on the Great Dragon and circled around its head, apparently scolding. The Great Dragon, obviously cowed, lifted itself to the bridge again with one mighty flap of its wings. Then with a series of small hovering motions, it deposited Keiran in a heap directly at the big man's feet. The big man was grinning and shouting. "Kee! Kee! Kee!"

The Dragon lifted away and Gleve began to run toward Keiran's motionless form, but a moment later the Dragon turned toward him and breathed out a curl of fire. The heat and whoosh of it drove Gleve back a few steps. The Dragon came toward him again. There was no choice but retreat. He ran back, straight into the midst of the soldiers, who were also retreating, all order lost.

The Dragon caught up to them and snatched the last of the running men into his claws, then flew up and away. The soldiers stopped, watching their comrade disappear in a glitter of green light. Gleve looked back across the bridge. It was empty.

MAiDA

Maida heard Rafe before she saw him. Besides the irregular thump, thump, thump of his feet on the path, even more clumsy than usual, he was shouting, "Kee, Kee, Kee!" It sounded like an imitation of a bird for a moment until she remembered. This was one of his words, repeated often in his first months with them, always with "Ma" and "Ric." She and Mother Peg had concluded these were names, probably his family.

She went to meet him, lantern held high. When he burst from the path into the clearing she saw the reason for the stumbling gait. He was not only trying to run, but also carrying someone in his arms. His face was not alarmed, though, but delighted. "Kee, Kee!" he said to her, presenting the limp body of a young man like a prized trophy.

Inside the cabin she pulled the pallet from its storage place and dropped it on the floor in front of the fire, then lit an extra lantern while Rafe gently placed "Kee" on the pallet. He was alive, she saw, but very pale, breathing shallowly. His back was bleeding, and when she turned him on his side, she saw a criss-cross of Dragon claw marks. He had been attacked. How on earth had Rafe found him?

There was a pot of warm water already on the hearth. She sent Rafe for clean rags and bandages, fetched Liandra's salve for Dragon wounds. The cottage was quiet as she washed the wounds, applied the salve and bandaged them. The danger in Dragon wounds was always infection. At least these were still fresh. She carefully removed what was left of the young man's traveling clothes. Here was another puzzle: he was blond and fair skinned, but his clothes were those of the Earth People. She checked for broken bones and found none. He did not seem to have hit his head. He had probably fainted from shock and blood loss. Judging by the stirring and slight groans while she worked on him, he was not far from consciousness.

"We'll have to keep him warm," she told Rafe. "Fetch the blankets from Mother Peg's bed." He leaped to obey her and went on to tuck the blankets over the injured young man with exaggerated care. "He'll need liquids," she said, more to herself than to Rafe, but instantly he went to fetch a cup. She bent over the patient. "Hello," she said, patting his cheek, "Can you hear me? I need you to wake up." He took a breath, moved slightly away from her hand. She patted harder. "Kee?" she said. This brought Rafe back to her side, cup in hand, staring earnestly down at the young man on the pallet.

"Kee!" Rafe said, and the young man's eyes opened, already searching. "Kee!" Rafe repeated, and lunged as if to gather the patient up in his arms.

"No Rafe!" Maida put a hand out to stop him. "He's hurt. Leave him be."

Now the young man on the pallet spoke, wonder in his voice. "Aymeric?" and Rafe, although obeying Maida enough not to pick him up, threw himself upon the young travelers chest. "Aymeric! Aymeric!" the voice was muffled in Rafe's bulk on top of him.

"Rafe, sit up. You'll suffocate him," Maida barked, as sharply as Mother Peg would have in the circumstances. Rafe obeyed and sat back on his heels, but his eyes remained fixed on the slight figure in the bed, his face bursting with delight.

His pleasure was matched by that on the patient's face, shining through the tears trickling down it. "Aymeric, I thought I would never see you again."

"Ric," said Rafe, looking at Maida. This drew the patient's attention to Maida as well.

"Oh, you are a Healer. You're caring for me."

"My name is Maida, but I am not a Healer."

"Oh," he said. "Maida. You are a friend of my friend … oh." His face transformed into an expression of alarm. "Gleve. Where is Gleve? There were soldiers, and a Dragon …"

"Were you traveling with Gleve?"

"Yes, we were coming here, to see Mother Peg. Where is Gleve?"

"I don't know," Maida said. "Rafe, was there another man with … is your name Kee?"

"Keiran. That is Aymeric's way of saying it. Did you call him Rafe?"

"We didn't know his name so we gave him one. Is he …?"

"He's," the young man paused, probably, Maida thought, from long habit of secrecy about Rafe. "He's my brother."

"And 'Ma'?"

"Our mother. She's dead now. But how did Aymeric get here?"

"Some drovers found him … it's a long story, one of many, obviously, and you are weak. You need rest."

"But Gleve, I must find Gleve." Keiran tried to rise, but instantly fell back, the bit of colour that had returned to his face during his reunion with his brother fleeing once more. "Yes, clearly I must rest, but someone must search for Gleve."

"Rafe, I mean, Aymeric …

"Ric!" said Rafe/Aymeric, obviously pleased that Maida now knew his name.

"…was there another young man with Keiran?"

Rafe/Aymeric's brow crumpled in exaggerated concentration. "Drag'n," he said.

"Yes, there was a Dragon."

Rafe/Aymeric brightened. "Ro'tric!" he said.

"Roxtrianatrix?" Maida said. Rafe/Aymeric nodded vigorously. Maida turned to Keiran. "Do you remember what happened?"

"No, I was snatched by a Dragon. All I saw was green fingers, with claws. I think I fainted immediately."

"Did you see Roxtrianatrix?" Maida asked Rafe/Aymeric. He nodded again.

"Who is Roxtrianatrix?" Keiran asked.

"Another long story. First you must rest. Rafe, help lift him up."

Rafe moved behind Keiran and lifted his shoulders, as tenderly as possible propping his brother against his chest. Maida helped him take as many sips as he could manage of a tea made from pain-easing, sleep-inducing and infection-fighting herbs. His eyes drooped, then opened again. "My jacket," he said. "Where is it?" Maida handed it to him. He felt for the square package Maida had already noticed deep in one of the pockets. "All right," he said, and tucked it close beside the pallet. His eyes began to close again.

"Let him rest now," she said, and Rafe lowered him to the pallet to sleep and pulled up his stool. He was not going to move any farther from his rescued brother than he had to.

GLEVE

"And who are you?" asked the King. After days of being marched westward, Gleve stood, filthy and sore, at the foot of the throne in the King's reception room, his head bowed even before the officer guiding him pushed it roughly downward. For days he had been looking at the ground because they had his hands tied so tightly behind his back it forced him into the bent posture of an old man.

"Speak up," the officer prodded him. His name was Pitley. He had been in charge of the band of soldiers on the bridge. Just before coming into the room, he had instructed Gleve to address the King as "your Highness" every time he spoke, if he was required to speak.

"My name is Gleve, your Highness. I am a Healer." Hopefully the provisions of the treaty protecting the Healers would save him from torture, or at least make it a bit lighter.

"Look at me," said the King. Gleve tried, but his bent back would not allow it. "Untie him," said the King.

Pitley made a point of cutting Gleve's wrist lightly as he slashed away the ropes binding him, not deeply though. Probably blood on the expensive carpets would get him in trouble, Gleve thought. His spine and neck objected sharply, but Gleve forced himself to straighten, his shoulders also complaining as his hands dropped to his sides for the first time in many days. He looked at the King, saw a careworn and aging face, still handsome and imperious, framed with neatly trimmed grey hair and beard. "So what to you know about this incident on the Deep River bridge?"

"Very little, your Highness. I was traveling with a companion, hurrying to make it over the bridge before daylight, when he was snatched by a Dragon." Gleve's throat tightened. He fought to speak as if nothing important had happened. "The events that followed were as surprising to me as they were to your soldiers."

"And what were those events, as you saw them."

"A large man came onto the bridge from the far side, waving his arms and shouting, and then a… miniature Dragon appeared and flew in circles around the Great Dragon's head. It dropped my friend and came after us – me and your soldiers – and I saw no more, your Highness."

"Was it a Little Dragon you saw?"

"I don't know, your Highness. I have never seen one. Nor my parents or grandparents."

The King leaned sideways on his elbow, stroked his beard and studied Gleve. "Why did my soldiers arrest you?"

"It seems they think I have something to do with the amazing events on the bridge, your Highness."

"They also report that the reason you were on the bridge in daylight was because you were running from them."

"We were running to reach cover beyond the bridge, your Highness, as I assume your soldiers were as well."

The King nodded. He turned to the shifty-eyed official who stood beside him. "Put him in a cell," he said, then more quietly, so only the people immediately around him could hear, "With good care." The official scowled, but his face was turned away from the King.

Gleve felt tentative relief. Did that mean no torture? "I will want to talk with you again," the King said. Oh, so maybe the torture would come later, after the King found out all he could by kinder methods.

"Bow," said Pitley, poking him roughly from behind. Gleve bowed, then the officer turned him around and marched him out of the hall.

A pallet and two buckets seemed to be the extent of the furnishings in Gleve's cell, one of them, fortunately, reasonably clean and half-filled with fairly clear water, the other empty and coated with dried filth. His toilet, clearly. The smell of it joined with the dampness and mould to make the air in the tiny room sickening. But at least, Gleve reminded himself, he had not been tortured – yet.

He could see little through the barred door, just a narrow stone hallway, but there was obviously a lot of life in the place. It reached him in the form of racket, hard boots on the stone floor, clanging and jingling of metal objects, large and small, and a great deal of shouting.

"Hey, you," a voice bellowed from nearby, echoing along the corridor. "What are we doing in here? We're faithful soldiers of the King. What have we ever done but serve him?" Gleve recognized the voice. It was Pitley.

"I'm just your guard," came the response. "Don't know nothing. King wants you here; you're here." The voice faded during this speech, accompanied by the thump of heavy boots as the guard walked away.

"What the hell?" Pitley said, more quietly.

ANGLEWART

"He knows more than he's saying," Ermin said.

"Exactly. And this time we are going to try a different approach. Since when did torture ever get us good information?" Anglewart glared at Ermin from his full, impressive height. The Spymaster looked angry, but knew enough to keep his mouth shut when the King was in this mood. "Better to let him worry awhile, then approach him with kindness. He'll spill everything he knows. Make sure the scribe made note of his name. Gleve, was it?"

"Yes, your Highness. And what about the soldiers?"

"Do you think they know any more than what they're told us?"

"No," Ermin said.

"Me neither. So let's just keep them away from the whisper network. I'm sure they've blabbed their story in every inn's common room along their way, but without them to provide eye witness accounts, hopefully it will blend in with the hundreds of other rumours of Little Dragon sightings that seem to be circulating."

"Yes, your Highness," Ermin dropped his eyes, his face returning slowly to its normal colour.

"Meanwhile, I think we finally have a legitimate sighting of a Little Dragon."

"Yes, Your Highness."

The King thought about this for a minute, then took on a more cheerful tone as he changed the subject. "So, wedding plans. Now that we have a date for Liandra and Locheil's wedding, I trust the preparations are on track?"

"Yes, your Highness."

"And my own blessed day? Are we close to having a date settled?"

"Well," Ermin hesitated. "There is a problem."

The King's eyebrows lowered over his sharp hawk's eyes. "What problem?" he asked.

"The meat sellers, your Highness. They say that they cannot provide that much good roasting meat so soon after supplying the first grand feast."

"What? I've never heard of such a thing before."

"There is a shortage, Sire. They say there was disease among the cattle this spring and ..."

The King cut him off. "So how long before they have enough for a second feast?"

"Three months, your Highness."

"Three months? That's ..." Anglewart suddenly heard himself, how loudly he was roaring the words. Whatever the problem, shouting would not help. He took control of himself. "All right then. I guess they must do the best they can. See if you can speed them up. Lord Rodolph is waiting to negotiate a date."

As Ermin bowed himself out the door, Anglewart watched him leave with narrowed eyes.

MAIDA

Keiran healed quickly, with no infection in his wounds. Rafe, whom Maida was trying to remember to call Aymeric, did most of the care. The love between the brothers was moving to see.

Despite being from different peoples, trust between Keiran and Maida grew quickly because of their mutual caring for Aymeric and worry over Gleve. Keiran shared his errand with Maida, although he did not show her the sketchbook. If he had, Maida might have shared the story of what had come to pass in this very cottage so recently, but she did not. Despite Aymeric's insistence on trying to tell her something about the Dragon attack that included "Ro'tric," she had resisted telling Keiran what "Ro'tric" was, letting him think it was a person with an unusual name.

Keiran wanted to return to the bridge and search for Gleve. "But would he still be there?" Maida asked. "Between the Dragon, or Dragons—there might have been more than one – and the soldiers, what do you think might have happened to him?

This was a depressing refection, for what were the possibilities? A second Dragon took him? The Dragon that snatched Keiran dropped him in favour of Gleve? The soldiers would have no reason to kill a Healer, would they? But they might have taken him with them.

"If Gleve were free and uninjured, where would he go?

"He'd come here," Keiran reluctantly admitted.

"And he may yet," Maida said, "But meanwhile, I think the important thing is to get that sketchbook of yours to the School. It might be very, very important. We're lucky it wasn't damaged or lost already."

"But what if Gleve …"

"If I hear of him, I will go and get him if I can," Maida promised, "And if he turns up here, I will send him after you. Wouldn't he want you to complete your joint mission?"

"But at the School, I'm a King's man. Why would they believe me?"

"Ask for Mother Peg. Show her the sketchbook."

The evening he left, Keiran was slow and reluctant. Maida reassured him, there was nothing to be gained for Gleve by staying. She had prepared a pack for him with food for the journey, freshly filled a travel lantern with fuel. Keiran finally hefted his pack to his shoulder and wrapped his arms around Aymeric, held him for a long time. As the hug continued, Aymeric's face transformed from delight to concern. Keiran stepped back. "You be good," he said. "I'll be back soon."

"No," said Aymeric, shaking his head. "Go."

"No, dear brother. You must stay here and take care of Maida."

Aymeric folded his arms across his huge chest and shook his head. As Keiran turned to go, Aymeric followed. "No, no, Aymeric. You must stay here," Keiran insisted. Aymeric just planted himself and waited, too large for either Keiran or Maida to restrain by force.

"Time is passing," Maida said after awhile.

"I don't think I can go without him," Keiran said.

"Obviously," Maida said. "Wait here." She ran to the pantry and quickly prepared another, larger, pack of food. Returning to the courtyard, she silently handed it to Aymeric, who instantly displayed the delighted expression he had worn since Keiran was restored to him. "Take care," Maida said, kissing them both. "The Mother be with you." And she watched them disappear, the rambling giant and the slender youth, into the forest.

ANGLEWART

Ermin stood before his King's desk with several pieces of parchment in his hand. "We have two people in the Eastlands trying to claim your reward, Your Highness," he said. "And their descriptions match—a young woman, an old woman and a blue Little Dragon, traveling eastward on the trail to the Healer's School. One report comes from a couple in an isolated cottage along the road, the other from a drover, who identifies the old woman as that witch from near Tummel." A shiver traveled up Anglewart's spine. "All of this matches reports from a spy I have placed as housekeeper for a witch here in the Westlands. She says there are stories among them about a Little Dragon and some connection with that old Crone." He lowered the papers, looked expectantly at the King.

Anglewart ran his hand over his tired eyes. "These aren't the usual vague rumours, are they? How are we going to find out more?"

"It's that old witch we need to question."

"You know the law won't allow us to interfere with one of the witches." Ermin's eyebrows rose. "Come now, we would never get away with arresting a senior one like her."

"What about the young one that lives with her? She's got to know what's going on. We could snatch her for some questions." He said questions with a twist of his mouth, a little torture, he meant.

"We'd be little more likely to get away with kidnapping a witch in training."

"She's not a witch in training. Just the old woman's servant."

Anglewart's eyebrows went up now. "Is that all she is?" Ermin nodded.

100 ODD AND GIMLIN KING'S MEN-AT-ARMS

"So what do you think of this?" Odd said, swinging his lantern as he walked.

"Not much," said Gimlin, his companion. "Would you hold that bloody thing still?"

Odd let his light stop swaying. "So we're supposed to snatch a servant away from one of them witches? You know what they can do to you?"

Gimlin shivered." Everyone knows that, turn you into anything they want."

"Hate men too, don't they? Fancy going home with no balls, Gimlin?"

Gimlin shivered again. "So we got to be very, very careful, like they told us. Get her when she leaves the place, so the old witch thinks she just got lost in the woods, hurt herself, got et by a Dragon."

"Yeah, simple." It was Odd's turn to shiver.

MELiSANDE

On the night of Jessa's wedding, Head Mother Mabonne invited
Melisande and Imelda to her reception room. When they got there, they
could hear the organ playing joyful music in the Cathedral. The large
set of double doors that Melisande had always wondered about stood
open. Propped inward, they revealed a shallow balcony with an ornate
railing and a view of the High Altar of the Cathedral. Melisande looked
down and realized they were completely hidden from the congregation
gathering in the large church, not only because of their height above
the floor, but because the opening was covered by a filmy curtain. Head
Mother Mabonne pointed out an identical balcony, except without the
curtain, facing this one from across the nave. It belonged to the reception
room of the Head Father of the Men's Retreat House, she explained. This
pair of balconies allowed the Head Father and Mother, along with anyone
else they saw fit to include, to observe services they were not allowed
to attend. In the case of the Head Father, these were only the services of
the Women's Retreat House, because they were allowed to attend public
celebrations and royal events. The women, on the other hand, could
attend only their own services.

Melisande and Imelda watched intently as glittering nobles filled
the pews, their voices rising along with the music. "Will you be seated?"
Mother Mabonne asked. There were three padded chairs arrayed behind
them. They did as they were asked, but leaned forward, their elbows
on the railing, so they could see everything unfolding in the nave. Most
people they knew, of course, and they exclaimed back and forth, pointing
out one or another of their friends or acquaintances below.

Just before the wedding was to begin, the two royal families about
to enter into this important alliance were guided up the aisle by the ushers
and seated in the front rows – Prince Locheil's brothers and sisters were
there, along with four pews full of extended family. "They always were a
handsome lot," Imelda remarked.

The royal family of the Westlands included Anglewart's brothers and sisters and their families and, of course, Melisande's relatives. "Oh Imelda," she whispered at the sight of her own sisters and brothers still dressed in mourning black. "It hasn't been quite a year since my 'death,' has it?"

"Look," Imelda whispered. "Your Aunt Amaris. That woman never ages."

"Oh what I wouldn't give for a visit with her," Melisande said, and Head Mother Mabonne gave her a disapproving glance.

Last of all, Lochiel's mother, Queen Calantha, entered on the arm of her oldest son and was guided to her seat in the front row. Behind her came her husband, King Leo of the Southlands.

The door on the far side of the altar opened and the groom's party entered the church. Lochiel came first, tall, slender, displaying his nerves by rubbing one hand in the other. Melisande studied him. She could not see his face very well from so far away, but she remembered meeting him when he and his parents came to negotiate the union. He seemed a gentle, if perhaps shy, young man. She fervently hoped that he would provide a loving union for her beautiful Jessa.

Behind him came his best man, Melisande's second oldest son, Eldrin. They were the same age and had been friends since they were very young. Melisande took in her breath at the sight of Eldrin. A passionate rider, he had grown into the straight, confident posture of the skilled horseman. "Look how tall and strong he's become," she whispered to Imelda.

"We tend to remember them as they were when they were much younger, don't we?" Imelda whispered back.

Behind Eldrin came his brothers Torrie and Farrell. "Oh look at them," Melisande raised her handkerchief to her mouth and could not say more. They were indeed handsome young men. Torrie and Eldrin were, in different ways, images of their father, although Torrie, to his own dismay, had interited Melisande's short stature. Farrell was in all ways a young male version of herself.

There was a pause, filled with shuffling and expectation, then the organist leaped into the traditional wedding processional. Below them, all heads turned to watch King Anglewart, tall and powerful despite his aging face and greying hair, dressed every inch the monarch he was, advance up the aisle with Jessa on his arm. Despite herself, Melisande's heart gave a little lurch at the sight of him.

The Little Dragons

Jessa carried as much ivory silk as a skilled seamstress could possibly fit on her small but sturdy body. Her face, of course, was veiled and four serving women, all close young relatives, carried her train. She held a huge bouquet of blue and white lilies, the colours of Anglewart's house, and Melisande thought she could see the flowers trembling in the young woman's hands. What a weight we put on our children, she thought, the full load of our royal blood, our family pride, our ruling power, our aspirations to dynasty.

The music faded as they reached the head of the aisle. The Priest stepped forward and asked the ritual question: who would give this woman to this man? Anglewart responded in his deep voice and stepped back to take his place in the front row. The priest reached for Jessa's hand. She turned to give her bouquet to one of the women who had just arranged her train in a becoming curve down the altar steps. The Priest placed her strong young hand in Lochiel's. Melisande imagined that she could sense the young woman's joy or. at least. she hoped that was what Jessa was feeling. Under the stern eyes of the Warrior God the ancient words meant to tie a young woman's fate to that of her husband began.

102 ODD AND GiMLiN KiNG'S MEN-AT-ARMS

"So's that her, then? The one we're s'posed to take?" Odd muttered to his companion. He and Gimlin crouched in the bushes beside the path. Ahead of them the trail opened out into a tiny clearing. Light shone from the windows of a cottage. A woman of the Earth People walked across the yard, her lantern casting a bright circle on the packed earth. She entered another building, likely a barn, because they could see her light shining through the cracks between the rough boards of the walls.

"I reckon," whispered Gimlin. "But what I want to know is, where's the witch?"

"Bet she's in the cottage. She's old, remember? They can live to be a hundred, maybe two hundred years old."

Gimlin shuddered. "I don't care how old she is. I don't want to meet her."

"We won't, idiot." Odd spat into the dirt beside them. "We'll get the young one when she comes out of the barn."

"What if she yells?"

"That's your job. I'll grab her. You put a hand over her mouth."

"Right."

"Right."

"So now we wait?"

"Now we wait."

They waited. And waited. Gimlin stretched his legs. "Shh," hissed Odd.

There was no sound from either cottage or barn. Odd said: "Don't s'pose they know we're here? You know those witches can see through walls, don't you?"

Gimlin shifted his weight.

"Shh," Odd hissed again.

A shadow passed by, visible in the cracks between the boards of the barn. "There, she's coming," said Odd. Both men raised themselves from where they were sitting on the ground to a squatting position, and waited. And waited.

"How do we know the witch isn't in the barn?" whispered Gimlin.

"Shit," muttered Odd.

"Shhh," Gimlin admonished this time. He craned his neck to try and glimpse the stars between the trees above them. "What time do you s'pose it is?"

"Night was already part gone when we got here, damn those cowards in Tummel." It had taken some time to find anyone ready to tell them which path led to the witch's clearing. A little boy finally pointed it out, just before his mother jerked him away and made the sign of the Warrior God, the same as everyone else they had asked. "I think I see light," Odd looked hopefully into the trees to the east of them.

Gimlin stared uncomfortably in the same direction. "Yeah, I think so too." He looked back at the cottage, where nothing had changed. "All right, we'll go back to Tummel and put up at the tavern for the day, then come back tomorrow night. Hey!" he exclaimed as Gimlin started off down the path to Timmel before he had even finished. "Wait for me."

ANGLEWART

At the reception following his daughter's wedding, King Anglewart looked down from the high table at his hall filled with revelers. It was not his usual angle, because the high seats normally occupied by the King and Queen had been given, as tradition dictated, to the young couple. On the far side sat King Leo and Queen Calantha beside their handsome young son. Beside him, in her mother's former chair, sat Jessa, flushed and excited and as beautiful as any young woman he had ever seen, except, of course, her mother. His heart was stabbed by an unexpected dagger of love and sadness mingled. As if aware of it, Jessa turned to look at him. Her hand was resting on the arm of her chair, under the table. He reached for it, held it in his own. The callouses were fading, but her hand would probably always show the legacy of hard work she had endured growing up. Oh my daughter, he thought, you will have to keep them covered to pass as the pampered Princess you are supposed to be. He squeezed it. She smiled at him, joy and trepidation mingled in her eyes.

The King turned his attention again to the room before him and something caught his eye. By the wall two men stood, heads together, consulting intensely. One head was young and wore the heir's crown. The other was sprinkled with grey – Ermin. The King's eyes narrowed. Since when did they know one another so well?

The next evening, shortly after bidding farewell to the Southlands party as they departed for home, Jessa one of them now, Anglewart called Ermin to him. "Is the date set for my marriage to Thalassa?" he asked.

"There are some problems, your Highness."

"The meat vendors?"

"Yes, also some scrambling to find enough fabric for the ladies' dresses. You know women; they can't wear the same thing to two weddings."

A beat of silence went by before the King roared, "I don't care about the women's dresses, nor the meat for that matter. Let's get this wedding date settled and the ceremony arranged. Now!"

Ermin blanched, then bowed deeply and started toward the door.

Next Anglewart summoned the Heir. "It's time you did some work with a group of soldiers in the field," he said. "Pack your things. As of tomorrow, you are taking over command of the border patrol between the Westlands and the Eastlands."

Torrie opened his mouth, but no words came. He tried again, "But, your Highness, Father …"

"No buts," the King said through clenched teeth. "Go."

104 MAIDA

The sky was lightening. Maida rushed to finish her milking. There was so much work without Rafe to help. She was constantly running behind. On top of that, there was a weight of loneliness upon her. With Mother Peg, Keiran, Rafe and her beloved Liandra all gone, the cottage echoed with emptiness. The clearing seemed abandoned. And where was Gleve? With no conversation to fill her nights, and sleeping poorly during the day, she worried about what had become of him. Her concern washed away the last of her anger over his broken promise to talk to Mother Sarah at the Spring Equinox Gathering.

The sun was uncomfortably close to rising when she picked up her buckets at the stable door and prepared to run across the courtyard. She checked the sky and could see a faint outline of a Dragon on the eastern horizon. Slopping milk in her haste, she scurried across the yard.

She had set the milk pails on the counter and pulled the shutters of the kitchen window closed when there was a huge racket in the yard, a beating of air, a scraping and scrabbling. Maida froze, afraid to even peek.

A second later, there was a knock on the door. "Maida? Are you there?"

Maida gasped and lunged for the door. "Liandra!" She grabbed Liandra's sleeve and pulled her over the threshold, then stopped as if turned into a statue, horrified. The yard was completely filled with the feet and tail of a glittering blue Dragon.

Liandra put her arms around her shocked friend and began to laugh. "Maida, dear, it's all right, really." At that moment, Roxtrianatrix slithered through the open door and darted in circles around the two of them, chirping in what could only be delight.

As Liandra released her, Maida wiped her eyes with the back of her hand.

The Dragon in the yard bent over to peer in through the door, its reptilian snout filled with teeth and its eyes filled with slowly turning colours, like a spinning pinwheel. Maida gasped and leaped back, farther from the door, trying to pull Liandra with her. "This is Alethilion," Liandra said, indicating the Dragon at the door with her hand. "Roxtrianatrix's father."

Maida made breakfast while Liandra told her the story. "Where is Mother Peg?" she asked.

"I last saw her on the Barrens. I assume she made her way to the Healers' School."

"You assume?"

"She wasn't very far away from it, was she? I have no way of checking, and I don't want to talk about her. I want to talk about us. Please, Maida, come to the mountains with me."

"But Mother Peg told me to take care of the cottage."

"Maida, look at how she treats you! Besides, she may not come back for months, even years, maybe never."

"But I've started doing some Healing of the local people. They need me."

"Mother Peg refused to see you as a Healer. Even now, at the School, they will be figuring out who will cover this territory."

"My garden …"

"I got here in less than half the morning. We can come and care for your garden and harvest when it's ready – in the daylight!"

"What about my friend Gleve? We don't know what happened to him. He may show up here needing care."

"We can search for him better by Dragon."

"My goats …"

"There's a stable and pasture there, at the Dragon Priestess's caves. We'll make slings to carry them in."

Maida gave a suspicious look through the door, which Liandra had left open. The blue Dragon was curled up, apparently sound asleep, filling every inch of the courtyard.

"For the God's sake, Maida, it's time to rebel against that old crone and the Healing Order. What value do they give you, that they didn't take you back and apprentice you to someone who would give you the respect you deserve? Besides, I need you. You know I can't feed myself …" This brought a laugh from Maida. "… and we can be together." She reached for Maida's hand and squeezed it. A moment later they were on their feet, wrapped tightly in one another's arms.

Maida swept the cottage and drained the pump. She used every basket she could find to pack food and medicines from the pantry. She took some of her cheeses from the aging room and left the rest in their neat rows. They could come back and get more. Meanwhile, Liandra sewed slings from a length of homespun she found upstairs in the loft.

When they were ready, Liandra asked Roxtrianatrix to call a few more Dragons. Maida held her breath while a shiny black one carefully closed its claws around her parcels and baskets and lifted them away into the sky. The goats were panicky, but hung well in their slings, only turning slightly in the air as a group of five Dragons picked them up and slowly made off with them. Finally, only Alethilion and a small green Dragon waited in the courtyard. Maida could hear her own heart pounding as she closed the cottage door and walked out. "It'll be all right. You'll see," Liandra reassured her as the green claw-tipped fingers closed around her, gently supporting her as she was lifted from the ground. She had thought she would want to screw her eyes closed as hard as she could, but her attention was immediately held by the cottage, the stable and the garden, tucked neatly into their clearing, disappearing beneath her. And then the Tummel road, and the village itself, the river, the bridge – days of travel by foot passing by in a single beat of the Dragon's mighty wings.

105 ODD AND GiMLiN KiNG'S MEN-AT-ARMS

They had made good time coming back from Tummel because they were now familiar with the path. The night was not very old when they settled themselves in the woods to watch the clearing. "Why's it all dark?" Odd whispered close to Gimlin's ear.

"No one home?"

"Shit."

"Maybe they're in there waiting for us."

Odd shivered. They lay quietly in the undergrowth. After some time, Odd shifted his position. "What are you doing?" Gimlin whispered.

"Trying to get a hard biscuit out of my pocket. I'm hungry."

Gimlin grunted.

Odd took it as agreement and continued to squirm. When he got the biscuit in his hand, he broke it in half and handed part to his companion. Time went faster sucking on the bit of travel ration.

More time went by. Gimlin looked at the stars. "Night's going," he said. "I don't think there's anyone here."

"You ready to look?" Odd's face was pale in the starlight.

Gimlin didn't respond, but quietly rose to his feet and, with exaggerated caution, approached one of the shuttered windows. He peered through a crack, then turned to where Odd remained hidden and shrugged his shoulders. Next he tried the door. Locked.

Now they sat openly in the clearing, although they didn't light their lanterns. "So we go back to Tummel and come again tomorrow night?" Odd asked.

106 ANGLEWART

As Anglewart sat at his high table presiding over supper, there was a commotion at the back of the hall. The company parted to reveal Torrie, dressed in full armour, marching on a straight course for the front of the room. He stopped before his Father, his face deathly pale, jewels of sweat standing on his brow, but his back rigid and his voice strong.

"My King," he said, "I hereby Challenge you…" He raised his left hand and began to pull the thick leather fighting glove from it "…for your Kingdom." The glove came free and he slapped it down on the table in front of the King.

Anglewart suddenly discovered that he couldn't breathe. His face was probably as pale as his son's. This he had not foreseen. He could rule this Challenge illegal. Torrie was not yet married, after all, and did not have a son, but surely that would look cowardly. At this moment, with more than a hundred people in the Hall watching in complete silence, his mind scrambled to find an alternative. He looked into his son's eyes, so young, so determined and, beneath that, so terrified. Oh my dear boy, he thought, you're making a terrible, terrible mistake.

There was no choice. He stood, drew himself up to his full height, picked up the glove and put it on. "Your time and place?" he asked.

"The next full moon," Torrie said, "At nightfall."

107 ODD AND GIMLIN KING'S MEN-AT-ARMS

Word of the Challenge reached Odd and Gimlin at the inn in Tummel. Odd turned to look at his companion. "So," said Gimlin, "What would happen if, say, the old witch had been at home and, say, she caught us watching her cottage and, say, she turned us into mice?"

Odd thought about it for a minute or two. "We'd disappear, never be heard from again, by any human, anyway."

"Right. So what do you say, that's what happened?"

Odd took some time to register what Gimlin was suggesting. When he did, he laughed. A few minutes later, though, he because serious again. "That's called desertion," he said. "You know what happens to deserters."

"We're way the hell out in the woodlands and the King's been Challenged," Gimlin said. "No one's going to be looking for us for a long time. I'm sick of watching a witch's empty cottage. So, let's say we spend our lodging money on a pair of axes and some woodsman's clothes and head for the northern borderlands. Lots of jobs for log cutters there."

Odd slapped his knee, laughed again.

# MAIDA

Maida felt as though she had not blinked in hours, there were so many wondrous things to see, the land passing far beneath her, the colours of daylight, the mountains, awesome beyond what she could have imagined, and then the mountain opened up into a cave so huge it disappeared into its own darkness, rustling with hundreds of Dragons. Finally, she saw orderly rows of openings in the far wall, the School of the Dragon Priestesses.

They immediately settled the frightened goats into their new quarters, closing the door to give them comforting darkness and no further sight of Dragons. "Old hay," Maida exclaimed, her nose buried in a handful of the stuff stacked in the feedroom beside the stable. It wasn't mouldy, though, and by searching she found some that was slightly appealing to her goats.

She was appalled at the state of the reception room, dining hall and kitchen, almost rolled up her sleeves immediately to start cleaning. "No, not now," Liandra pulled her away, leaving the baskets of food in the middle of a long table to be unpacked later. "There's a hallway I meant to look at yesterday," she said, pulling Maida by the sleeve behind her.

The passage from the reception room was obviously not just for everyday movement between rooms. It was high and decorated with painted walls and ornate torch brackets. It descended on a gentle slope, turned, and opened into a circular space with an empty stone bath or pool, a decorated pump standing beside it and a small firebox set into its side.

On the far side of the room with the pool, they felt the cool breeze and clinging smell of the Dragon cave. They entered a large room. "This is the one on the lowest level you can see from out there in the Dragon cave," Liandra whispered, "With the platform jutting out." As if in response, a Dragon landed on the platform, filling the far end of the room. Their lanterns bounced light off of golden scales. It lowered its head and made a snuffling sound at them. Immediately another Dragon landed beside it, equally curious, a black one this time. All they could see was the sparkle of their lights on its scales and eyes.

On either side were large, circular stone pits. Maida looked into one. It was blackened, clearly used for fires. There were torch brackets as well, high up, matching the ones in the hallway and bathing room. Between the two fire pits, against the back wall, was a raised dias and an altar of some sort, although it was set with one of its short ends toward the platform where the Dragons sat, the other toward the back wall, not sideways like the altars in churches. It was also much higher where it came closest to the wall and had a rounded ledge on the lower end.

The two women did not spend much time studying the strange altar, though, because their attention had been drawn by the carvings covering every inch of the wall. Beside them their lanterns picked out stone Dragon Priestesses with Little Dragons on their shoulders beating drums and singing. Above them a Great Dragon flew, wings spread wide, head and tail lowered. "Look at that." Liandra said, holding her lantern higher. A long, slender, curved thing hung from the stone Dragon's belly. Roxtrianatrix chose that moment to slide into the room, circling them and landing on Liandra's shoulder. His penis, he said into Liandra's mind. He's about to make a Little Dragon.

Liandra told Maida what Roxtrianatrix had said. They moved to the end of the room, behind the strange altar. Above it was a carving of a naked, pregnant woman, her hand resting on her belly, her face peaceful. Over her arched a huge Dragon, curled protectively around her and all the other scenes on the wall.

On one side of the altar was a carving that made its use obvious. While more Dragon Priestesses and their Little Dragons stood in attendance, a naked woman lay on the sloping altar, midwives on either side holding her hands, another holding a cup of some medicine. She was frozen in the act of giving birth to a Little Dragon, its elegant head and neck supported by a fourth midwife squatted at the end of the altar, its furled wings emerging.

On the other side, more stone Priestesses sang and drummed behind a side view of the same altar. This time a naked Priestess lay on it, knees bent and spread, while a Great Dragon arched over her, its long, curved penis disappearing between her legs.

"So, that's how they did it," Maida breathed the words rather than said them.

"The Dragons are happy," Liandra said.

That evening they sat on the balcony in the Dining hall, two chairs pulled up to the railing, the remains of their first meal in the School of the Dragon Priestesses forgotten on the table behind them. Roxtrianatrix perched on the balcony and translated to Liandra and Liandra repeated the words to Maida as the Dragons told them stories of the Dragon Priestesses of old, who had borne which Little Dragon, fathered by which Great Dragon and what they had done in the world. The names were so long they quickly became just a jumble of syllables to the young women's ears.

They spoke of their hunger and how the Dragon Priestesses had raised cattle to feed them. "They say we would be safe in the daytime if we had farms like those again."

"I don't know how to set about that," Maida said. "No one even knows yet that we're here."

They expressed their joy again and again that the Dragon Priestesses had returned. "I guess that's us," Liandra said.

"Us?" Maida asked.

Liandra listened to an involved conversation among the Dragons, channeled through Roxtrianatrix. "They want you," she said, finally. " I guess there is a senior Dragon, a leader or King to them, who is upset that Alethilion was the first to father a Little Dragon. He wants to 'marry' you."

"Marry me?" Maida's skin tightened into goosebumps.

"That's the word they're using."

"Which one is he?" Liandra passed the question on to Roxtrianatrix.

There was a commotion in the cave. A number of Dragons that had been perched on rock ledges took off and circled around in a cloud of moving wings. In a few minutes, they parted and a huge Dragon came snaking slowing through the centre of them. He shone, a dark golden colour, like old gold jewelry. He hovered before them as the other Dragons moved back, forming a multicoloured aura around him. He brought with him such force of presence that Liandra and Maida spontaneously stood up.

"This is Glenardinaliat, Lead Dragon," Liandra said.

109

JESSA

Jessa could hardly believe the softness of the bed. It puffed up around her like clouds in the sky, the mattress and comforter both stuffed with soft down feathers. Queen Calantha had chosen this large chamber in the Southlands castle for her second son and his new bride. Her gift to them was a set of tapestries to cover the stone walls and capture any drafts that might sneak in to chill them. Jessa was not fond of the scenes on the tapestries, images of battle, men killing one another and Dragons, but she found that if she squinted her eyes she could turn them into brilliant, cheerful swirls of colour.

Her arm was losing feeling, but she didn't care, because it was Lochiel's head resting on her shoulder, his nose nuzzled into her neck. He slept like a child, an expression of joy on his face. She breathed in his scent of sweat, leather and their mingled bodies. Just a few days ago she had been afraid of what would happen after the wedding. There were dire tales among the serving staff, just as there had been among the servants in the Women's Retreat House but, as soon as they were alone together for the first time, Lochiel had made a little speech to her, one he had obviously rehearsed in advance: "Beautiful Leandra, I am honoured that you have accepted me as your husband. I never want to hurt you. I want you to come to love me with the love I see between my parents."

Both of them knew that consummating their marriage on the first night was unavoidable. The serving women would be checking the sheets in the morning looking for signs of their union and her virginity. Young royal men were usually assigned to older women well before their marriage so they would know what to do in bed. He had been taught by a woman named Magnilda, he told her, a former prostitute who was taken in by his mother as she grew older and given a position as a serving maid. She had taught him well, because he had been exquisitely patient and gentle, talkative and funny, and he listened to her when she spoke to him. There had been a little pain, but it was lost in the excitement of discovery.

And now, just a few days later, her heart swelled up whenever she looked at him.

She lifted her hand, briefly admiring the fine lace that decorated the edge of her nightgown sleeve, and ran her fingers through the tousled dark meadow of his hair. She had dreamed of this, short months ago, thinking it absolutely impossible. The memory gave her a pang of missing Ev. Would she ever see her friend again? It was possible, for surely Liandra's Little Dragon would change everything.

MAiDA

Through Roxtrianatrix, the Dragons told them how the Dragon Priestesses conducted what they called a "Dragon marriage." They lit the torches and the fires, the Dragons remembered, filled the round pool with water and heated it for a purifying bath. They padded the sloped stone altar with blankets and pillows, and the Dragon Priestess bride was wrapped in a robe the colour of the Dragon she was to marry. On one trip to the room with the bathing pool, Liandra and Maida found a cupboard filled with soft blankets and pillows, and robes in each of the Dragon colours.

The Cave of the Sacred Marriage, for this is what the Dragons called it, would be filled with drumming and chanting for the whole of the ceremony, they said, just as it would be nine months later, for the birth of the Little Dragon conceived in the Sacred Marriage.

Glenardinaliat did not shadow Maida the way Alethilion did Liandra, in part because of his size, in part, they gathered, because he had responsibilities as Lead Dragon. From time to time, however, Maida would catch him hovering, in the darkness of the cave, in front of the balcony of the Dining Hall or the bedroom she and Liandra had chosen for its double bed and its proximity to one of the wonderful bathrooms. He always shocked her all over again. He was immense, and gave off an intense energy. He terrified her.

"Become a Dragon Priestess with me," Liandra would ask, whispering into Maida's ear in their cozy bed. Maida's instinctive response was to curl into a ball, in fear and disgust, defending her body from the very thought. "Please," Liandra would beg until she tired of Maida's stubborn silence.

111 ANGLEWART

Torrie's challenge had come just barely past a full moon, giving King Anglewart almost a moon cycle to prepare. He had always kept his body and his fighting skills exercised, but the responsibilities of state were greedy for his time. He could barely stand the sight of Ermin now but, as the only servant capable of taking over many of the routine tasks of government, he needed his help. Ermin agreed, as Anglewart knew he would. After all, if Torrie won the battle, who would inherit the task of teaching the new young King how to govern besides the faithful Ermin? He also needed Ermin to speed the planning of his wedding to Thalassa Rodolph. It could not be done in one moon, but he would publically declare his confidence in victory by planning the wedding for two weeks after the Challenge fight. In this, too, Ermin cooperated, as Anglewart knew he would. The Spymaster and Heir were probably thinking that if Anglewart died in the battle for the Kingdom, Torrie could simply step into his father's shoes and walk down the aisle.

Anglewart was determined that would not happen. He worked hard every day, gymnastic exercises, riding, running, followed by practice fights with every master swordsman in his army. He would have his razor edge honed by the time the moon was full, along with his sword.

KEIRAN

Keiran and Aymeric made good time across the Barrens. They reached the Healer's School before midnight. Maida had instructed them not to approach, but to wave their lantern back and forth until someone came to find out their business.

Keiran had dared to imagine that somehow Gleve had made it to the School before them and would be the one sent out to see who they were. He knew it was an image with no reality, invented to give himself comfort, but still he was disappointed when the young man who came was a stranger. His curious face closed in suspicion when he saw that they were Kings' men. He seemed nervous of Aymeric, probably because of his size and clumsy way of moving.

Yes, the young Healer said, Mother Peg was here. Yes he would fetch her.

A long time later a lantern appeared again, coming toward them on the path, very slowly. They could hear the Old One grumbling before they could see her. "…pull me away from my studies …" "…all this way out…" "…slowly, Dawkin, I'm not young like you."

"Hold the lantern up," she said to Dawkin as they approached. Surprise was obvious on her face when she saw Aymeric, immediately replaced by displeasure. "Rafe," she said, "What on earth are you doing here?"

Aymeric, who would once have physically cowered away from her sharp tone, said, "Kee!" and pointed at Keiran.

Mother Peg was already studying him. "I don't know you," she said.

"Mother Peg…"

"How do you know me?"

"Maida sent me."

"What does the girl want?"

"She said I should show you something, some sketches…"

"Whose sketches?"

"Mine, they …"

Mother Peg lost patience. "I have no time for this," she barked. "I was doing important work in the Library and this young fool dragged me all the way out here on my old legs for a King's man and an idiot." She turned and began hobbling back toward the School. "Bring that lantern," she barked over her shoulder at Dawkin.

Dawkin shrugged apologetically. "There's a cabin just across the Barrens," he said.

"We stayed there on the way here," Keiran said before Mother Peg interrupted with another demand that Dawkin bring the lantern.

113 ANGLEWART

Before the Challenge battle, King Anglewart warmed up carefully, bringing himself gradually to his mental and physical peak. Before going to the field, however, he took a few minutes in the chapel. He knelt before the Warrior God, so like himself, and prayed to continue ruling the Westlands. "He is young yet," the King told the God, "And rash. He will make a ruler one day, but not yet." In return he promised to try his best to win the fight by injury rather than death.

The field had been roped off and surrounded by torches burning in high stands. There were rows of benches and chairs for the nobles, open spaces for the peasants to watch. The crowd was huge and noisy, excited by the possibility of blood, spilled from the King, the Heir, or both, excited by witnessing history.

Early in the fight, experience ruled. Anglewart worked carefully, defensively, watching sharply for openings. He put his sword through one gap in Torrie's guard and drew blood from the boy's shoulder, although not, unfortunately, on his sword side. The Heir, too, was playing it defensively, attacking only enough to keep the fight moving, more often staying out of sword range. The strategy was clearly intended to wear out the older man, but Anglewart knew he was in peak condition.

The fight went on and on. Every hour the referee, Anglewart's Head Swordmaster, called a break and the combatants retreated to opposite sides of the field where they could sit while servants washed their faces and offered them sips of warm, sweet juice. After each break they took the field again, renewed.

As they entered the third hour, Anglewart's muscles were sore. He had not fought this hard, this long, with his life at stake, for many years. He made an error, left an opening, and Torrie caught it, driving the point of his sword into his father's thigh. The wound bled freely, spilling blood on the grass and forcing Anglewart to mistrust his footing on that side.

His leg began to fail him, his speed and agility compromised by a limp. The crowd roared. Anglewart began to feel lightheaded. It must be the loss of blood. He asked for a break, a sign of weakness, but he had no choice.

After the break, he rallied, caught his opponent with a nasty cut in the ribs. It was not deep, but the blood flowed crimson over the young man's armour, drawing a huge shout from the crowd. Torrie came back wildly, and Anglewart hoped the boy had lost his cool thinking. It was the Heir's greatest weakness as a fighter and, if he gave in to his rage, the King would win. But this did not happen. Torrie kept on fighting, quickly but with thought, and Anglewart could feel himself tiring.

His sword arm slowing, the King left an opening, and his son's weapon cut through the muscle on the back of the other thigh. To his horror, the King discovered he could not lift that leg off the ground. He must fight in one spot. He could no longer attack, so he turned his attention to defence. He parried a swing aimed at his upper body, then shifted to catch a vicious upward stroke. Torrie danced to a position behind his father. Anglewart spun to face him, dragging his useless leg. The noise of the crowd battered his ears. His vision wavered and then he caught the flash of Torrie's sword at the edge of it. The last thing he knew was the crunch of his wounded body meeting the ground.

MOTHER PEG

Mother Peg leaned heavily on her stick and frowned at the length of the hallway in the guest wing of the School residences. The Librarian had told her another of the Old Ones had arrived, her old friend Tess. Last room on the right, a Sister just outside had told her. "Why is it always the last room?" she grumbled. "I swear the point is to make an old Healer walk as far as possible."

"Is that you growling out there, you old coot?" Mother Tess was suddenly in front of her in the hallway, as bent as Peg and leaning on her own stick.

"My dear," Mother Peg greeted her old friend, taking Tess's statement as affectionate teasing. However, Tess's face did not display affection. It was, in fact, clouded with anger.

A young Apprentice emerged from the room just behind Tess. It was the one who had found Rena's journal, that great-granddaughter – or was it great-great-granddaughter? – of Mother Calla. "Peg, you'll remember Ev," she said.

"Of course," Mother Peg said. "Are you an Apprentice now?"

Ev flashed a smile at Tess. "Yes, Mother Tess has taken me on."

"Ev, my dear, will you go back to the kitchen and get pitchers of hot water? We would both benefit from less road dirt."

"Certainly, Mother," Ev gave a little curtsy, then blushed. "Sorry."

After she left, Tess explained that Ev had yet to unlearn the habit of curtsying to her "betters," learned as a Servant in the Women's Retreat House. "And now come in here and sit down," she said, indicating her room. "We have some things to talk about."

Peg was annoyed by Tess's tone, but entered the room and took a chair beside the fire. Tess sat in another chair, facing her. "I'm sorry you lost your Little Dragon along the way, with his Priestess."

"If that's what you're angry about, I couldn't help that. I'm hardly able to fight off a Great Dragon."

"I know, I know. I'm not blaming you, just sorry. But as for some other things that have happened lately, what are you thinking, you arrogant old woman?"

"I'll not take that kind of talk," Peg said, thinking about making a grand exit but, before she could get her old knees to lift her out of the chair, there was a knock at the door.

"Come in," Tess said. The door opened to admit an unsmiling Mother Sarah. Peg's brow creased. Something was afoot. However, there was nothing to do but greet the oldest of the Old Ones. Tess rose and pulled up a third chair for Sarah.

Once they were settled into their uncomfortable circle, Tess addressed Peg again. "I've asked Sarah to come because there are some things you need to answer for. First, what did you think you were doing sending young Ev back to the Women's Retreat House without even a thought for her future? She is a great-granddaughter of Mother Calla, one of the best, and her Aunt Marle has strong Healing gifts, although her circumstances denied her the training that was her due. Instead, she has taught herself by watching and listening."

"There is no such thing as a self-taught Healer," Peg spat out.

Tess ignored her. "Did it not even occur to you to bring Ev here?"

"But the Queen ..."

"Shhhh! She's the Lady Merrit, and she was quite happy to arrange things so that Ev could accept an Apprenticeship as soon as I offered. I gather you didn't even think to ask." Tess paused and glared at Peg, but Peg was too busy huffing to come up with a response, so Tess went on. "Second, where is Maida?"

"Why, back at the cottage."

Now Sarah spoke. "Did it not even occur to you to bring her here?"

"Someone has to take care of the place."

"And could that not have been arranged? With neighbours perhaps?"

"We've been through this before, Sarah. She is not a Healer!"

"Yes she is. I won't repeat it all here, but I'm appalled you didn't even think about bringing her."

"You can't tell me what to do with my own servant."

Tess spoke again. "Third, you don't even know where Maida is and what has happened to her."

Mother Peg stopped growling, looked at Tess in surprise. "What do you mean?"

"There is no one at your cottage. It is closed up. Even the goats are gone."

"What? Well that faithless girl."

"Maida is not faithless. If she is gone, something has happened to her, and if you were determined to leave her there, you should at least have seen to her safety, asked someone to keep an eye on her, and asked a Healer from here at the School to go back and stay with her, seeing to the needs of the People in your area."

"I can't imagine what has become of her. I left the hired hand …" Mother Peg stopped, shock on her face. "The hired hand!" she said.

"What now?"

"He turned up here, and I didn't even think …"

"That is point number four. I met him and his brother …"

"His brother?"

"…at the Barrens cabin on my way here. They did not know what has become of Maida – she was there when they left your cottage – but they have an important document with them, one that I suspect will help fill in more pieces of the Dragon Priestess mystery, one Maida told them to bring here. And you sent them away! Did you not respect Maida's judgement enough to at least find out what they had come to say? And I see you didn't even think to ask why Maida's hired man was here without her."

"I couldn't bring a King's man here to the School, and certainly not that idiot."

Sarah entered the conversation again. "The task of piecing together the Dragon Priestess mystery is important for all the peoples of the Land. If a King's man has something to contribute, or even an 'idiot,' as you insist on calling him, we need everything. It was you who pushed us all to collect information and now it is you who is closed to some important tidbits that have drifted our way."

Peg began beating her walking stick rhythmically on the floor in front of her chair. "I'll not listen to this, I'll not listen, I'll not listen."

"Now you're being childish," Sarah told her.

"I'm leaving." And with that, Peg stumbled to her feet, not caring how ungraceful the movement was, and made her way into the hall and away, back to her own room. There she slammed the door and dropped to the side of her bed, furious and ashamed in equal measure.

115 MELISANDE

In a small bedchamber in the Men's Retreat House, Melisande sat beside the dying King. Her eyes were fixed on his profile, outlined in the light of the lantern on the other side of the bed, so painfully familiar. She had been given special permission by Head Mother Mabonne and the Head Father of the Men's Retreat House to be here. Shortly after beginning her vigil, she had sent a note to the Head Mother, asking a favour. She wondered if Mabonne would think her request mad.

She studied the lifeless hand resting on the blanket, calloused and bloody, but still the long, artist's hand of the young man she had fallen madly in love with so long ago. She picked it up and held it. It was cold.

There was a soft knock on the door. "Come in," she said, and it opened to reveal a young Brother. He did not step in, but stood back to allow a hooded figure to enter the room. As soon as he left, closing the door behind him, a capable hand reached up to drop the hood. Melisande set Anglewart's hand on the side of the bed and rose to her feet. Her request had been honoured. "Marle!" she said, as she crossed the floor to hug Ev's aunt.

The attending Brother brought the hot water and clean cloths that Marle requested. "Do you think we can ask him to wash the King's wounds?" she asked, nodding at the door as it closed behind him.

"No," Melisande said, dropping a cloth into the steaming water and rolling her sleeves out of the way. "I would rather assist you myself."

Together they stripped the King of the last remnants of his fighting clothes and the dirty bandages wrapped around his wounds by the palace doctors. "What are they thinking?" Marle hissed. "All this dirt!" They washed the wounds in a tea Marle made from herbs she had with her, and Melisande held the edges of the worst gashes together while Marle stitched them with a slender needle and silk so fine it could have been spun by a spider. They smoothed a thick layer of healing cream over the injuries and wrapped them in fresh bandages, then washed the rest of the Kings body. They even did the best they could with the blood and dirt caked in his hair. Between them they managed to put a clean flannel nightshirt on him and settled him under blankets warmed by the fire.

Marle studied Melisande's face for a moment. "Do you still love him?" she asked. Melisande creased her brow, questioning. "I mean, are you still angry with him, after what he did to you?"

Melisande felt her heart for a moment. "No," she said. "I was angry, but now, seeing him broken like this, it has flown." And then she had a sudden thought. "In fact, the anger has moved on, to another."

"Oh? And who would that be?"

"My son, Torrie. What arrogance, challenging his father like this. What is he thinking? He broke the Rule of Challenge by doing it before being married and fathering an heir, although I think I know why he was in such a hurry. He's much too young to rule, and too rash."

"I understand. Don't think about that now. It will interfere with our Healing. Think about the man lying here, needing our help. I return to my question: Do you love him still?" Melisande's eyes filled, and a moment later there were tears working their way down her cheeks. "I see you do," said Marle. "All right, I need you to love him now." Melisande nodded, unable to speak.

Marle pulled a chair to the foot of Anglewart's bed and showed Melisande how to cup her hands around his feet but not touch them. The Healer instructed the former Queen to think about the earth under the floor of the building. "Think of rock," she said, "Think of roots and little streams carving their way through total darkness. Think of creatures that burrow, long twisting tunnels under trees."

Marle sat at the head of the bed and cupped her hands around the King's head, not touching, just as she had instructed Melisande to do at his feet. She took a deep breath, closed her eyes and became very still. Her breathing slowed and became shallow, in counterpoint to the struggling gasps of the wounded man. Melisande felt her own breathing matching Marle's. The tears dried on her cheeks, ignored.

In a few minutes she felt warmth between her hands, flowing into her. When she remembered to think about things under the earth, it flowed through her, warming, soothing, healing. How did the Earth People learn to do these mysterious things? But it felt good, and right. She remembered Marle healing her after the King's attempt to poison her. She had no doubt the servant had saved her life, and now she hoped fervently that she could also save Anglewart's. What the future would hold after that, who knew? She wasn't about to worry about it just now. Her task at this moment was to think of the earth and love her husband, and this she found easy to do.

116 KEIRAN

Aymeric sat perfectly still at a table in the dining hall of the Healer's School. He looked around with big eyes, a puzzled frown on his face, as Healers bustled around him. Every few moments, he would check Keiran, who sat in one of the big chairs by the fireplace, as if afraid his brother might disappear again if he took his eyes off of him for too long. Mother Tess and the ancient Mother Sarah sat in the chairs beside Keiran, silently studying the sketchbook.

A young Apprentice came from the kitchen with a bowl of stew and a biscuit on a plate. She set it in front of Aymeric. Suddenly his broad, delighted smile broke out, like the moon after the passing of storm clouds. Food was something he knew what to do with. He picked up the bowl and tilted it, slurping some of the stew. Keiran grimaced at him. He stopped, looking apologetic, set the bowl down and picked up a spoon, making no less mess, but imitating the manners both Keiran and Maida had tried to teach him. The young girl laughed. Keiran, too, could not resist smiling. "Perhaps a napkin," he said to the young girl, who went to get one.

Mothers Tess and Sarah did not notice this exchange. They turned the pages of the sketchbook, studied them, reverently. Finally Sarah looked up at Keiran, her eyes shining. "This is it," she said. "This is the secret of the Dragon Priestesses. Bless you for bringing it to us. Perhaps we can even draw Peg out of her room with this."

"Is Mother Peg still here then?" Keiran asked

"Oh yes," said Tess, "But hiding in her room." She chuckled.

117 ANGLEWART

The King floated through something heavy, dark and cold. Air or water, he could not tell. It was deathly still around him and, as his eyes cleared, he began to make out men, standing in ragged rows, fully armoured and staring blankly into space. At least those with eyes stared, for every man among them was horribly wounded. There were gashes and ragged holes, limbs missing, faces missing, flesh torn. Blood flowed everywhere, soaking the men, their armour, the ground around them. Why did they not scream and cry? They must be dead, but why did they not fall?

Near him stood a tall, grey haired man, his left arm a bleeding stump, cut off by a blow that continued into his chest, slicing between two ribs to cleave his heart. With a jolt Anglewart remembered that blow. He had been so proud of the instant, powerful death he had meted out to the Earl of Enclist. That was a battle over the boundary line between Eastlands and Westlands. He had been very young.

A thought crossed his mind and he looked more closely at the other men. His vision wobbled in and out of focus but, as he looked, he remembered other blows, other enemies dropped on the field. These were men he had killed. Above them and behind them rose a shadow. He flinched, remembering. It was that Bronze Dragon that hesitated, about to eat him on the field of combat. As he wildly swung his sword, no hope of touching the beast, it had stopped, studied him. That was the first time he had seen the whirling rainbows in a Dragon's eyes. The second time was the Blue one, the one that killed Ortrude. The Bronze Dragon had, for some reason, spared him. He claimed for years that he fought it off, but he knew it wasn't true. It had simply turned and flown away.

So this must be the realm of the dead and he himself was dead, floating in a white nightshirt among all these men he had killed. Had he taken so many lives? He should have died on the field at Torrie's hand, more honourable to be bleeding in this lost realm, still dressed in his armour.

Torrie. Was Torrie here? No. He remembered. There had been a chance, a moment when Torrie's ribs were exposed to his sword to be sliced like the Earl of Enclist. He had struck, wounded, but not with full speed or force. He had held back from killing his own son and Heir. Was that weakness? Perhaps he deserved to lose the Challenge.

Something caught the King's eye, pulling his mind back to the field of carnage all around him, a slight figure, standing just at the edge of the blood-soaked grass, dressed in white. He picked his way over the mutilated bodies in his path to get closer.

An invisible spear of pain plunged into his heart and her name broke from his lips. "Ortrude." He moved more quickly to reach her, tripped over a severed leg, went down on one knee in the reddened mud. She looked at him, her face passive, eyes empty. "Ortrude!" he called to her again. Her brow creased, a scrap of attention entering her blank eyes. Faintly, she smiled, then pointed upward, into the roiling slate sky. Struggling, stumbling, Anglewart reached her. My daughter, he said, and stretched his arms out to pick her up. She melted into a smoky vapour between his hands and was gone. He dropped to his knees, threw back his head and wailed a cry of pure grief. Then he remembered her pointing finger and looked up.

Above the broken men and the shadow Dragon, he could see a light in the sky. Not the moon, but more like a flickering torch. Curious, he floated upward, the bloody field disappearing into mist beneath him. The thick substance must be water, because he broke the surface into light. He caught his breath, for what he entered was a bubble of pure pain. Throbbing heat ran through his limbs, stabbed into his head. He would have cried out, but he couldn't move. He opened his eyelids just a crack. There were torches dancing, coming down from the walls to attack the small fire burning in a grate against the wall. The fire drew itself together to strike back and the King was sucked down again, into the dark water, no pain, no vision, but just before he went under, he heard a woman's voice.

It was Mel. His Mel. Where was she? Was she here in the Realm of the Dead with him? Mel! Mel! He tried to call out, but she was gone. Mel, in the Realm of the Dead. But of course. He had killed her with his own hand. Poison. He had allowed Ermin to poison her. Oh Mel, my beautiful Mel, how could I have done that?

He could see her, young and shining. Once they had lain together in a field full of flowers. She knew what they were called, some sort of flower that bloomed at night, releasing its sweet scent. Ever after he could smell that fresh sweetness on her skin when he buried his face in her flesh. That was so long ago, before he was King, before Servants watched their every move, before Farrell's birth tore her and gave her months of pain that made her shrink from his touch, before he began to look at her as a liability in his quest for power. Fool. Power-hungry fool.

I killed her. I killed my beautiful Mel, he thought, as he floated through endless silent darkness. This isn't just the Realm of the Dead. This is Hell. The Warrior God has sent me, deservedly, to Hell. My Lord, I regret. I would give anything – my Kingdom, all that foolish power – to have my Mel again.

MELISANDE

"Excuse me, Lady Merrit," the Brother assigned to Anglewart's care this day spoke to Melisande. "His eyes are open."

Melisande, who had been dozing in a chair beside the fire leaped to her feet and bent over the King. His eyes were indeed open, although unfocused like those of a newborn child. She picked up his hand where it lay on the blanket, squeezed it between her own. "Anglie," she said.

He heard her. His eyes cleared a little and searched for the source of the voice. They settled on her face. "Mel?" he whispered and his lips quirked up slightly at the corner, just the smallest hint of a smile. He squeezed her hand.

119 KEIRAN

"You have done us a great service," Mother Tess said. She and Holly, the Sister who served as Librarian, sat at one of the long tables across from Keiran. Aymeric sat very still in one of the chairs by the fire, watching their exchange with curious, slightly worried eyes. Keiran sent him a reassuring smile. He had been through so much, this different brother of his. Keiran knew how much he hated anything outside of his set routine. He had done amazingly well in this new place, ready to obey whatever Keiran told him to do. The only time he fussed was when Keiran moved out of his line of sight. It was clear that, having lost his beloved brother once, he was not going to risk it happening again.

Keiran turned his attention back to Mother Tess. "We have something for you," she said. "Holly?"

Keiran had not noticed until now that Holly had one hand behind her back. Now she drew something out from behind the folds of her dress and set it in front of him. Keiran drew in his breath. It was the most beautiful book he had ever seen, very thick and solidly bound in red leather. The Healers were famous for the quality of their books.

"This is for me?" he asked.

They both nodded. He reached out and touched it, opened the front cover, thinking of the sketchbook he had left behind at Father Mallory's cabin. This one was larger, thicker. The parchment was clear of imperfections. On the first page was written: "Presented to Keiran, in deepest appreciation from the Healers School." Kerian's eyes were wide with wonder. "Thank you!"

"And now," said Mother Tess, "What do you want to do? We would be honoured to have the two of you stay with us for a time. Perhaps Aymeric would like to work in the stables, as he did for Mother Peg and Maida? Perhaps you would like to continue exploring our library? There is much interesting artwork in it. Or we could put you to work sketching the life of this place."

Keiran's face darkened. "I want to find Gleve."

"Ah yes," Mother Tess said. "I thought you might. But where would you start?"

"Back at the bridge, where we were separated."

"What would you do there?"

"Find the nearest houses and inns, see if anyone saw or heard anything of him."

"And what if the soldiers took him with them, or, Goddess forbid, the Dragon?"

"Then … " Keiran dropped his eyes to study the table. The grain of the wood swam in his vision.

"Keiran, I can see how much you love him." Keiran could feel himself blushing, one of the disadvantages of the light skin of the Kings people, he thought. The Earth people blushed, certainly, but it wasn't so obvious, at least not to him. He opened his mouth to say "it's not what you think," but he couldn't.

"Keiran, I think if Gleve is not in the hands of the King, or the claws of the Dragons, we will hear as soon as anyone. You have a sense for our communication networks around the Realms. They are extensive and swift." Keiran nodded. Tess reached with her knotted hand to pat his. "Stay here, dear boy. If he is to be found, we will find him." Keiran nodded, causing a drop to splash on the polished surface of the table beside the beautiful new sketchbook.

120 MELISANDE

"So, he is married then?" The King sat in a large chair in front of the fire in his chamber, supported by several pillows and warmed by a blanket.

Melisande pulled up a smaller chair and sat beside him. He freed his hand from the folds of wool on his lap, reached out to her. She automatically clasped and caressed it. "Yes, he is married, to a Rodolph, no less. Mabonne let me watch from her balcony over the altar."

"To a Rodolph. My father's dream fulfilled."

"Not your dream?" There was a sharp edge to her voice.

He looked at her, sadly. "No," he said.

"Mabonne represented the Women's Retreat House at the reception. This morning she called me in to tell me that he used that gathering to announce his intention to make war on the Dragons. He is calling all the warriors of the Realms to him."

"Oh dear. He thinks that the advances we have made in bows, arrows and swords since we last tried to fight them will make a difference."

"And will they?"

"No."

"He has appointed Eldrin as his second-in-command. Torrie is young; Eldrin is barely more than a child."

"More than a child, my dear, but you are right, too young to go into battle as second-in-command. Oh, Mel, it will be slaughter, Torrie's reign launched in blood as mine was, and my father's before me." Anglewart's face looked extremely old at this moment, ravaged by dread of the future as well as the journey he was currently making along his road of pain. Melisande squeezed his hand and reminded herself that it was a miracle that he was alive, and a credit to Marle's amazing gift as a Healer.

He was looking at her, the light of a smile in his eyes. "And you, my pretty nurse. Perhaps you might consider marrying me?"

"I might, except I'm dead."

"Well that's fine," he said. "I'm dead too." But his smile faded. They both knew that there was no precedent for those committed to the Retreat Houses to be released again.

"At least I think Mabonne is ready to allow me to continue visiting you."

"It will have to be enough, then." He turned to the fire, giving her the view of his profile, so patrician, yet so vulnerable, so proud and so broken. It tore at her heart.

121

JESSA

As soon as they were alone in their bedchamber, Jessa fixed her questioning eyes on Locheil's face. "Must you go?"

"I have no choice. I was allied to your brother anyway, but now I am his kin through our marriage. When he calls me to arms, I must go."

"But it's such a stupid plan. The Dragons have killed so many fighting men, in every generation since our people came here. I know there is a better way."

"You know there is a better way?"

Jessa stopped short. She wanted so much to tell him, but knew she must not. He was also bound to tell his ally anything he knew that could be considered military intelligence. Damn Locheil's excessive honour! Her knowledge would just send that bloodthirsty Torrie on a campaign to seek out Liandra before she was ready.

But ready to do what? March in from the Healer's School and announce herself as the founder of the new Order of Dragon Priestesses? Would the new King then turn around and kill her? And when would she be ready? In time to stop this useless bloodshed? And would some of the blood shed be Locheil's? Her eyes filled. She looked down at her hands in her lap, which spilled the tears into her nose. She sniffed, hunting for a handkerchief in her sleeve.

"Oh Liandra, dearest," Locheil said. Hearing tears in his voice, she looked up. His eyes, too, were full. They put their arms around each other then, and held on, sniffing into each other's shoulders.

"And so I must stay here and pray for your safety, like any good royal wife," Jessa said.

"I don't think you have any choice either."

A few minutes later, Jessa stiffened. "What?" said Locheil, feeling the change. He let go and held her at arm's length, studying her face.

"Take me with you," she said. Then she giggled, thinking that his eyebrows just might hit the ceiling.

# MAiDA

Liandra sat hunched over on the edge of the bed, clutching herself and screaming. Maida sprang up and went to her, sat beside her, held her. "They're tearing something apart!" Liandra sobbed. "A deer, I think." Maida squeezed her, hard. "At least it's dead now, but they're tearing it to shreds."

They had discovered that Dragons, even Little Dragons, did not have to eat very often, but when they did, it was a bloody frenzy. They had tried everything they could think of to shut off Liandra's ability to see through Roxtrianatrix's eyes. Even when she was sound asleep or in a stupor from Maida's sedative tea, when the Little Dragon became upset or excited, his vision broke through into hers.

Liandra leapt to her feet and blundered around the room, her eyes open but blind to what was around her. "No," she shrieked. "Stop." Maida tried to hold her back from running into things, but Liandra was strong in this state. By the time her panic faded and she threw herself down once more on the bed, her shins were bruised and bleeding a little from violent encounters with the furniture.

Maida sat beside her exhausted lover, rubbing Liandra's shoulder. "How long has it been since Roxtrianatrix has spent more than a few minutes with us?" Maida asked.

They both thought back. "Weeks," said Liandra. "I don't know what to do. It's like having a young son who has gone running with a gang of thieves."

"Are you ready to think about going to the Healer's School yet?" Maida asked.

"And be under the thumb of that crabby old woman again? There's got to be some other way."

Maida sighed. They had gone over this ground many times. She thought they needed to consult Rena's journal; Liandra did not want to go.

JESSA

Jessa clomped around the clearing imitating of a male walk. Stopping in front of Locheil, she made a great show of scratching her crotch, then cleared her throat and spit into the woods. Locheil lay back on the moss, laughing so hard he could not take in breath. Their horses watched from the trees where they were tied, ears twitching at this strange human behavior. Jessa's too-large helmet fell down over her eyes. She pulled it off and dropped to the forest floor beside her husband. Men's clothes felt very strange, she thought, but very freeing.

Locheil sat up, wiped his eyes on his sleeve, then became serious. "Liandra, dearest, you're funny, but I can't let you do this."

Jessa, too, became serious. She planted her fists on her hips. "I don't think you can stop me. Would you put me in your father's prison?"

"No, of course not, but, but … it's impossible."

"I don't think so."

They studied each other through a long silence. Locheil's eyes faltered first. "I see you're determined," he said, followed by a sigh and another long pause, his eyes this time on the moss at his feet. When he lifted them again, it was clear to her that he had stopped resisting, at least for now. "Gerth," he said. "I must remember to call you Gerth. And this is my faithful servant, Gerth." He waved his arm, introducing her to the horses and suddenly began to laugh again.

"I was afraid your father was going to ask to see Torrie's letter," Jessa said.

"Me too. It would have been a challenge to reproduce his seal."

"A challenge? Try impossible."

"'I need my dear sister by my side in these difficult times …'"Locheil tried to immitate Torrie's voice.

Jessa joined his laughter. "Oh stop."

They ate their lunch sitting on the moss. The horses lost interest and turned their attention to their hay. Too soon, it was time to travel again. As she packed what remained of their bread and cheese into her saddlebag, Jessa pulled something out. "One more thing," she said, and held up a pair of shears in the lantern light.

"Oh no, must we?" Locheil objected.

"We are making a choice that was not offered to us. I think in this, there truly is no choice." She sat on a rock with her back to him and held out her long, shining braid of hair. He paused, then took a deep breath and closed the shears on it. It fell away in his hand. A short boy's bob fanned out around Jessa's ears. "How do I look?" she asked.

"Like my faithful servant, Gerth," Locheil replied, smiling. Then he looked down at the limp braid in his hand. "Maybe I'll take it with me, in my saddlebag."

"I don't think that would be a good idea. What if someone found it there? You could not claim to be carrying your wife's hair. They would assume you have a mistress. Besides, you don't have any extra space."

He sighed. "You're right, of course."

"It will grow again," she said.

They left her braid hanging over the branch of a tree a few steps away from the clearing, joking that they would look for it when they came back. "If the birds don't take it for their nests," Jessa said, and Locheil kissed her. "Won't be able to do that with your faithful servant," she said, "Or the rumours will be worse than a mistress."

Jessa had insisted Locheil put a convertible saddle on her horse. He took off the lady's horn, stowed it in the saddlebag, pulled out a stirrup and clipped it in place. "Have you ever ridden astride?"

"I'd hardly ridden at all before you began to teach me."

"I don't know how you, a King's daughter, escaped riding lessons."

"By being very, very bad at it."

"You're not bad at riding, quite the opposite."

"Well thank you."

"Anyway," he said, giving her a leg up. "I think you'll find riding astride easier than sitting a lady's saddle."

She settled herself into the curved leather seat. He was right. It was a much more secure position on horseback, although spreading her thighs so far apart felt strange, and would probably cause some sore muscles by the end of the day.

Locheil clipped his travel lantern to his stirrup and mounted. "And so, onward, faithful servant Gerth," he called out as he nudged his horse to a walk.

MAIDA

"All right, all right, we'll go," Liandra said, exhausted and tearful.

"I think we must," said Maida, standing behind Liandra, massaging her lover's rock hard shoulder muscles. That afternoon the Dragons had caught a man trying to sneak through the forest. Liandra's throat must be sore, Maida thought, she screamed so much.

"Perhaps we can take the goats to Father Mallory and Lynna. They are the nearest Healers to here. I hope they can care for them," Maida said. She paused, rubbing a gentle circle on Liandra's skin. "And then we'll go."

Liandra sighed, her reddened eyes closed. She nodded.

GLEVE

Gleve walked in a tiny circle around his cell. At first he had paced this route in anxiety, cot to buckets, buckets to cot, but then his training as a Healer took over. It would just sap his health to be in a daily panic, he knew. Whatever happened, the wise course would be to maintain his body and mind. He called on all the mental discipline he had learned during his training as a Healer. He meditated and exercised, controlling his mind as he walked by remembering every trail he had ever travelled in minute detail.

The food was ghastly. The smell was worse. He lost track of time, although the guards' routine at least told him when it was evening and morning. He had stopped waiting for something to happen a long time ago because, day after day, nothing did.

Some of the guards who had brought him here had given in to panic or deprivation or the torture they had suffered in a ridiculous effort to retrieve more information about the events on the Deep River Bridge. Their bodies had been carried without ceremony from their cells.

Pitley, the Captain, was still alive in the cell next door and still occasionally demanded that the guards tell him why his troop was here when they had done nothing but faithfully serve their King. He seemed to know some of the guards and would ask them for news of the outside world. This is how they learned of the Challenge, the death of King Anglewart, and now a new war on the Dragons.

Surely they had been forgotten down here in the bowels of the castle. Surely they would die here and never see those they loved again. Father Mallory, Keiran … Gleve could feel his heart speeding, panic again. He paused to run his filthy rag of a sleeve over his eyes, took a deep breath and increased his pace. Walk, walk hard. Drive despair away. Hang on to hope. Walk, walk hard.

JESSA

One of the other pages was looking at Jessa. She shrank inside herself, bending even further over Locheil's shield sitting on the wooden bench in front of her, polishing even more industriously with the rag in her hand. For at least the twentieth time she doubted her judgement, coming here to this castle where she was identical to the other King's daughter, who had spent almost all of her life here. She had thought of packing rags inside her page's helmet to make it fit better, but at the moment was thankful that she had not done it. As she leaned forward it slid down on her forehead, covering most of her face. After a few minutes she sneaked a quick peek. He had gone about his business.

"How often would the pages have seen you?" Locheil whispered during one of their stolen conversations in his tent. "And how close?"

She didn't know, of course, but told him, "Not very often or very near."

"It would be so far from possibility anyway, a Princess turned into a page boy. People don't make leaps like that in their minds," Locheil told her.

"I certainly hope not," she said. "It makes me nervous."

He looked around, assuring himself that no one was approaching the tent or hanging around outside it, then reached over and kissed her. His hand lingered on her face. "I look over at you sleeping there on your pallet and long to have you in my bed with me."

"Me too."

"Especially with our marching orders for the day after tomorrow. After the battle, who knows if one or the other of us, or both …"

"Shhh," she said, laying a finger on his lips. "Don't say it. I couldn't bear to lose you."

"Nor me you."

MAiDA

Just as the sun was setting, a red Dragon set Maida down in a clearing a little distance from Father Mallory's cabin. Roxtrianatrix had instructed her to curl up there and sleep, waiting for Maida to return at dawn so she could carry her back to the mountain. Maida walked through the Northern forest, so tall and dark compared with her home country in the Westlands, as darkness fell.

"Lynna?" Maida said as the young woman opened the door, light pouring out around her.

"Maida! Come in." She turned back toward the cozy front room, allowing Maida to walk past her. "Father Mallory, it's Maida," and in the next breath, to Maida, "Where did you come from? They all say you disappeared from Mother Peg's cottage. How did you get here?"

"My child!" Father Mallory had struggled to his feet and came slowly toward her, supporting himself on his walking stick. "It is so good to see you. Everyone has been so worried." He held out the arm that was not supporting his weight on the walking stick and Maida walked into it to receive his hug. "How did you get here?" he asked.

"I came …" she hesitated, it seemed so strange to say it, "…by Dragon."

Father Mallory broke Lynna from her pose as a surprised statue by telling her to get tea for their guest. Maida he invited to sit in the chair facing his own by the fire. "My child, what a long story you have to tell us," he said.

The early part of the night was gone when Maida finished telling it. Lynna had served first biscuits, then a milk soup, then more tea.

"So you and your friend, the first Dragon Priestess, are living in the old Dragon Priestess's School in the mountains?"

She had told him this, but now confirmed it.

"Oh my," he said. "What will happen now?" Father Mallory was frowning deeply.

"What do you mean?"

"The new King, King Torrie, has declared war on the Dragons. He will be marching soon, any day now, to attack their lair in the mountains."

"What?" Maida's cup slipped from her hand and clattered onto the wooden table.

"Did you not know?"

"How would we know? We have been alone up there in the mountains for months. We have heard nothing. What happened to King Anglewart?" Father Mallory told her about the Challenge battle. "Is he dead then?" she asked.

"We heard they took him to the Men's Retreat House to die, but we haven't had news of his death. Nor has there been a royal funeral that we know of." Father Mallory looked at Lynna, as if checking to see if she had heard more than he had, but she shook her head. Maida's thoughts flew to the Queen in the Women's Retreat House, but this she could not talk about. Only the group that came together that amazing day at Mother Peg's cottage knew that the Queen was not dead. They and, obviously, the former King, if he still lived.

"But war on the Dragons? That will just provide a feast for the Dragons," Maida said, her mind jumping to thoughts of Liandra. Maida would have to bear the news that her father was certainly injured and may be dead, and if it came to a battle between her brother's army and the Dragons, how terrible it would be for her to witness it through Roxtrianatrix's eyes. So many of her relatives would be there, and other nobles she would know. "What kind of a fool is this King Torrie?"

"One determined to follow in his father's and grandfather's footsteps, I guess." Father Mallory shrugged his bony shoulders. "Is there something you can do to stop the slaughter, from up there in your mountain School?"

"I don't know," Maida's voice lifted into a kind of wail. "We don't know what the old Dragon Priestesses knew. It's more than just having a Little Dragon perched on your shoulder."

"Can we help in any way?"

"I had come to ask you to take my herd of goats and care for them so Liandra and I could travel to the Healer's School and learn what we can from Mother Rena's journal, but now … I don't know. Would we be better at the Healers School? Or is there something we can do here, to stop the killing?"

There was silence for a few minutes, only the fire crackling in its grate. "I can't tell you, my child. Only you and your friend Liandra can answer that, if anyone can. If you do decide to go, I think we can manage your goats."

Before she left, Maida asked about Gleve. Father Mallory's face fell now into lines of deep sadness. "We have heard nothing," he said. "Only a letter from Keiran telling us what happened at the bridge, nothing more."

"Oh dear." Maida leaned forward in her chair and took his skeletal hand in hers. "I suppose in the absence of information, we can only hope."

"At least Keiran and his brother are safely at the School for the time being."

"Are they? Did they accept Rafe there … I mean Aymeric?"

"I still shake my head over it, that it was Keiran's brother who was helping you in your stable all that time."

"Me too."

"And yes, they have given him work in the stables and gardens at the School, the same kind of work he did for you."

"I'm glad. I don't think that would be Mother Peg's idea."

"I know it was not. Sarah made the decision. She's a little older than Peg, you know."

"Only by six years, as Mother Peg loves to say."

"I guess I will have to go down on my knees in humility before Peg next time I see her. She was right, more than right, about this Dragon Priestess business."

"She'll like that," Maida said, and they smiled at the thought, despite their worries.

LiANDRA

When the Dragons began to stir in the morning, Liandra could feel their excitement through Roxtrianatrix. Instead of the usual gentle rustle of stretching wings, the twitters and chirps of Dragons chatting back and forth, the close air of the cavern swirled with wing beats, punctuated with high-pitched cries. The soft light in the entrance was broken by lithe shadows as one Dragon after another launched into flight.

She rolled over and roused Maida. "They're coming," she said. "Where's Roxtrianatrix?"

"Still in the cavern, but getting ready to fly with them. I've asked him not to go, but he's ignoring me." Maida gave her a horrified look and both women jumped from the bed and began to pull on their clothes.

On one of their explorations in the library they had discovered a small doorway leading to a long spiral staircase. Following it upward until their legs ached, they had discovered a small opening high up on the mountainside. It looked down the long valley to the south, the way anyone on foot would have to come to reach the Dragon cave and the School.

This day they ran until they could stand the tight muscles in their calves no longer, and then barely slowed, their gasping breaths echoing off of the stone walls. They came to the opening just as the sun emerged over the horizon. A steady stream of Dragons emerged from the cavern beneath them and, in a thunder of moving wings, disappeared down the valley. In the distance, they could see a growing crowd of Dragons circling in the air, the new day glinting from the moving kaleidoscope of their scales.

"Can you tell where they are?" Liandra asked. She had not been out of the School since Alethilion first brought her here. Maida, on the other hand, had so recently made the journey to speak with Father Mallory.

"There's a big, circular meadow, just where the valley widens out to leave our mountain, before it narrows to pass that smaller peak on the horizon there. A logical place for your brother to challenge the Dragons."

"Oh no," Liandra said, and reached out to steady herself against the solid rock of the mountain wall beside them. "Rox is getting excited." She closed her eyes. "My brother's army," she said. "You're right. They are spread out in the meadow, lined up in straight lines as well as the curve of the valley walls will allow. They're all looking up, pointing spears and bows toward the Dragons. There are lots of flags. It's all gay at the moment, like tournament day."

"Can you see your brother?"

"I'm dizzy; Rox is circling." Liandra began to lean more heavily on the rock wall beside her.

She could feel Maida clutching her arm. "Liandra, this is a precarious place. I think we should go back down."

Liandra ignored her. "There they are, my brothers, on horseback, Torrie in the lead, of course, Eldrin beside him. Oh no, they brought Farrell. But he's so young." Through Roxtrianatrix's circling eyes she tried to focus on Farrell. He was armoured like the others, but she could see the terror on his pale face. A strange stew of feeling bubbled up in her, anger at Torrie, fear for all these young men waiting like sacrifices in the meadow and a sudden burst of overwhelming love for Farrell, her youngest brother, a child playing soldier.

As this feeling coursed through Liandra, Roxtrianatrix paused, stopped his excited circling, focused his attention on Farrell. Alethilion, flying beside Roxtrianatrix, paused as well. Liandra could see him observing the Little Dragon as he hovered. The blue Dragon gave out a cry and in a few moments was darkened by a large shadow. He and Roxtrianatrix looked up. Huge Glenardinaliat hovered above them, looking down.

"Maida," Liandra whispered. "My love for Farrell made them hesitate for a moment."

"Look for other men you care about, then."

"Who? I've hardly met any men besides my father and brothers."

Maida thought for a moment. "The one you were going to marry?"

Liandra scanned the army below her, looking for Locheil. Her brothers stood out because they were mounted. The men on foot were one, large mass from the air, matching pale faces, matching metal helmets in a multicoloured swirl of cloth tabards and hoods.

129 MOTHER PEG

Holly appeared at Mother Peg's door. Peg saw immediately that what she held so protectively to her breast was Dragon Priestess Rena's Journal. "Well," she said, "Well then," a hint of satisfied smile on her lips.

"Just for an hour," Holly said, setting the Journal on Peg's table.

"Humph," Peg scowled at her. She considered the Journal hers, since she had brought it to the School, but when the others gathered in the Library to read aloud from it every night, she refused to leave her room. Tired of the argument, Mother Sarah finally ruled that Peg could study the precious book for one hour each evening.

Holly arrived promply to take the Journal back. "Listen to this," Peg said, obviously reluctant to close it and hand it over.

"We talk to the Little Dragons, and through them the Great Dragons, through our minds, but even more important is what we say with our hearts. The whole of Dragonkind can pick up what we feel. If we love a person, he or she is completely safe from harm in the presence of any Dragon. On the other hand, if we feel anger or hatred for anyone, an individual or group, they are in danger.

"This makes it crucial that a Dragon Priestess discipline herself to discharge her anger only in the appropriate way, in a ritual designed for this purpose, where these dangerous feelings can be expressed, written on paper and safely burned. Peace in the Realms depends on the Dragon Priestess's learning to love everyone, in all corners of the Land, like us or different from us, friend or someone with whom we find it easy to be in conflict."

Mother Peg looked up, her eyes glassy. "That couldn't have been easy."

Holly bit her lip and reached for the book.

JESSA

Jessa stood behind Locheil holding his spears. From one of them the pennant of the Southlands fluttered in the cool breeze. Locheil was armed with his bow. He held it loosely before him, an arrow nocked, ready to raise the moment the Dragons came within range. Around them were Locheil's brothers and cousins, all armed with bows, all backed by pages holding their spears. Pennants matching theirs snapped and blew all around them. It was amazing to see all the colours of the men's fighting regalia in the daylight, so vivid and bright.

Like the men around her, however, Jessa could not spend much time admiring the colours of the army, for overhead circled more Dragons than she could count. Their colours outshone the humans on the ground by far. The sun rippled off of their scales as they slithered through the air. They were all looking down, studying the army that was watching them.

The swirl of Dragons expanded, spreading outward, increasing their speed. Their moving shadows darkened the meadow. Then, as if in response to a command, they descended, claws outstretched like bouquets of daggers.

The moment the Dragons came within range, a storm of arrows shot into the air. One Dragon yelped and soared away from the field of battle. Jessa thought it had taken an arrow in the eye, but most of the arrows clattered harmlessly off of hard scales. Jessa choked back terror and turned her attention to Locheil. He had dropped his bow and reached back. She placed a spear in his open hand.

A melée of Dragons fell on them. Men sheiked as they were pierced and torn. The ground became slippery with blood and entrails. Jessa lost her vision as her helmet dropped forward over her eyes. She pushed it back with her forearm and took a spray of blood across her face. This she wiped away with her sleeve just in time to see Locheil's open hand waiting for a second spear.

131 MAIDA

Liandra's eyes stared blindly into the open sky and her words tumbled over one another as she gave Maida a running account of the circling Dragons and the gathered army. Maida's fear grew. She held Liandra's arm and tried to coax her to go back down the stairway. Liandra couldn't hear her.

When Liandra bent double and began to shriek. Maida wrapped herself around her lover, helpless. She tried to push Liandra back, into the opening in the mountain, although she was also terrified of falling down the steep stairs.

Liandra tried to run forward. Maida threw her weight against her lover's chest, barely forcing her to stagger to a halt. The distraught Princess clutched herself tightly and screamed again and again. Maida could not move her. It was if she were rooted into the stone beneath her feet.

Then Liandra arched her back and shrieked, "Torrie! Oh Torrie!" With inhuman strength she tore herself from Maida's arms, ran a few steps and flung herself forward from the ledge into the bue sky.

It was Maida shrieking now. She threw herself to her belly and pulled herself to the lip of the platform just in time to see Liandra's tiny, far-off form turning and twisting in slow motion through the air before disappearing among the thick trees lower down on the mountainside.

Her lover would be lying down there, surely hurt badly. She had to get to her. She ran into the mountain and down the stairs, slipping on the old stone, catching herself, calling Liandra's name over and over again and hearing it echo up and down the narrow tunnel.

132

JESSA

Without warning, the Dragons began to make piercing calls. They abandoned the battle and rose into the sky on their huge wings. They turned, hundreds together, and began to beat their way back toward the mountain.

As their strange shrieking noise disappeared up the valley, a complete hush fell on the bloody field below. Men froze into statues, weapons still raised but mouths agape and eyes bulging.

The only sound now was the groaning of the wounded, and it was this that snapped Jessa back to consciousness. She searched out Locheil's eyes. He was searching out hers at the same time. Neither of them was hurt.

There should be commands, but nothing came. The horses still on their feet milled in a group to one side, their reins held by pages but no one on their backs. At the same moment Jessa and Locheil laid down their arms and began to tend to the wounded men around them. Others saw and joined them. Jessa straightened and looked around. Behind the main scene of battle, along the edge of the clearing, there was a clean grassy area sheltered by a few tall trees. "Tell them to sort living from dead and take the wounded over there, where we can tend them," Jessa whispered to Locheil. He rose, looked where she was pointing, and lifted his voice to repeat what she had said. His commanding tone was instantly obeyed.

133

MAIDA

By the time Maida ran out through the big reception room doors, the air was filled with high-pitched screams. The Dragons streamed up the valley toward her and circled in a milling mass above her head. She was about to leap from the flagstone ledge in front of the door and tumble down the mountainside as best she could, when a glittering blue back and beating wings emerged from the trees below her, Alethilion. Around him flittered his smaller Blue likeness. Roxtrianatrix shrieked unceasingly, a higher-pitched sound than the Great Dragons all around him.

As Alethiliion rose to Maida's level, she could see that he cradled Liandra in his front claws. "Here. Bring her here," Maida shouted, but her voice disappeared into their keeing. Alethilion flew past her and entered the Dragon cave.

Maida ran through the Reception Room to its balcony. Alethilion had landed just below and beside her, on the ledge in front of the Sacred Marriage Cave. "No," thought Maida. "The supplies to care for her are up here."

She ran back into the Reception Room and down the passage to the Cave, thinking to grab a torch as she went. The Cave was filled with the voices and scraping belly-scales of many Dragons. She immediately noticed that their screaming had found some sort of weird harmony. They were singing.

She ran to light two or three torches and stuck the one she had into a bracket. She turned in time to see Alethilion lay Liandra gently on the altar. As she ran toward her lover, there was no missing the odd angle of Liandra's head as it lolled to the side.

Still disbelieving, Maida stroked the battered side of Liandra's face with one hand while placing the other on the pulse in her neck. There was nothing. Roxtrianatrix had landed on the other side of the altar and watched her intently. She moved her fingers to Liandra's wrist, which was clearly broken. Nothing again.

The Little Dragons

With the strange dirge of the Dragons all around her, Maida threw back her head and wailed. Roxtrianatrix joined her. Out of breath, she fell forward on to Liandra's still chest and sobbed, clutching her lover's broken hand. She felt scales against her shoulder. Roxtrianatrix had fallen across Liandra too, his head nestled against Maida's arm.

Maida, Alethilion and Roxtrianatrix grieved through the night, surrounded by an ever-changing chorus of huge attendants moving into the cave, joining the song and, after awhile, leaving to be replaced by others. Glenardinaliat was with them much of the time.

At one point Maida became aware that Roxtrianatrix was pushing something into the hand that hung by her side, the one not clutching Liandra's. She looked down to find the Blue cape from the closet in the room with the bathing tub. There was no doubt what he wanted her to do with it. She arranged it over Liandra's body, tucked neatly at her chin. Bruised as it was, she couldn't bear to cover the Princess's face. Roxtrianatrix again rested his scaly head on Liandra's chest, his eyes closed, and Maida went back to kneeling beside the altar, alternately moaning and sobbing.

When the first glow of sunrise lightened the darkness of the Dragon cave, Glenardinaliat touched Maida lightly with his vast muzzle. She could feel his warm breath on the back of her neck and it made her shiver. He left the Sacred Marriage Cave. In a few minutes, Maida could hear the rustle of many wings, swirling in the Dragon Cave, then disappearing out into the open air.

JESSA

In the morning, the Dragons returned, circling above them. Torrie's body lay under his shield and cloak in the forest just behind the clearing, the other dead soldiers, row upon row, around him, covered with whatever cloaks could be spared. At the edge of the clearing on the other side lay the wounded, protected by a row of trees. Jessa was exhausted from tending them through the night, as had many others.

The next of Liandra's brothers, Eldrin, was now in command, with her youngest brother, Farrell, by his side. They and their officers were mounted on the few remaining horses, their much smaller army in rows behind them. Jessa stood behind Locheil once again, holding his spears while he nocked an arrow and lifted it toward the glittering hoard above them. She had remembered to fold a rag into her helmet, but it still did not feel very firm on her head.

The Dragons descended. Arrows were shot upward at them and then bows were replaced by spears and they were engaged in close, bloody battle once again. Surrounded by shrieks and clashes, her feet mired in mud and blood, Jessa flocussed on one thing, Locheil's hand, reaching behind him for another spear, and another, and another.

Before she could hand the fifth spear to him, the front edge of a vast bronze wing knocked them both off their feet. Jessa landed on her side. A steely bronze claw dug into the bloody ground inches from her face. She saw another pierce Locheil's shoulder. He screamed in pain. She twisted to look upward just as the Dragon twisted to look down at Locheil.

Jessa scrambled to her feet. Her fear fled, leaving her mind cold and clear. Her helmet tumbled from her head as she rose. She drew Locheil's spear back over her shoulder as she had seen the men do and looked up, searching for the Dragon's eye.

The Dragon spread its wings to lift off, Locheil now firmly grasped in its claws, but it stopped and stared at Jessa, it's eyes whirling. It brought its wings downward just as Jessa threw the spear, lifting its head out of range, but it released Locheil and dropped him at her feet. The spear clattered off of the scales on its leg. She picked up another from the ground and held it poised, but the bronze Dragon was now too far away. It did not leave, however, but circled, its eyes fixed on Jessa. Then, one by one, the other Dragons disengaged from the field and circled with it, just out of range, all looking down at Jessa.

Shortly, Jessa saw a blue flash and a moment later Liandra's Little Dragon hovered among them, also looking down.

"Roxtrianatrix!" Jessa shouted and lowered her spear. He made a chittering sound. Jessa became aware that silence had fallen once more upon the battlefield. She shouted his name again. "Roxtrianatrix!"

The Little Dragon floated downward, in range now, but not a weapon was raised. Every eye was fixed on this impossible creature of story and legend. He peered into Jessa's face and made that chittering noise again. A shadow slipped over both of them and a huge golden Dragon, surely the largest of any here, circled above the bronze Dragon.

Roxtrianatrix landed lightly in front of Jessa. She held out her hand to him. He laid his head in her palm and looked up at her. Inexplicably, his touch filled her with deep sadness.

It seemed a long, long time that they stood like that, dirty, bloodied page and brilliant blue Little Dragon, surrounded by silent men, a host of Dragons circling above them. Eventually, Roxtrianatrix rose into the air again and departed toward the mountain, the huge golden Dragon just behind. Every one of the Dragons followed them.

The spell broken, Jessa looked around her. A man next to her dropped to his knees and laid his spear at her feet. Another followed suit. Another, and another. Farther away from her, where they could not lay their weapons at her feet, they laid them on the ground in front of their knees. Jessa could not take in the meaning of what they did. Her thoughts were all now with Locheil. He lay beside her, his good hand clutching his bleeding shoulder, eyes closed. "My love," she said, and tore her cloak from her shoulders to wrap his wound. He opened his eyes but seemed to have trouble focusing them on her. "Liandra," he whispered, reaching for her with the bloodied hand that had been holding his wounded shoulder. "My love."

There were clanking armoured footsteps beside her. She looked up to see the kneeling men sidle out of the way as Eldrin and Farrell arrived at her side. Both looked down at her in complete shock. "Liandra?" Eldrin said.

MAiDA

The faint light in the Dragon Cave had come and gone, but Maida lost track of how many times. The torches in the Sacred Marriage Cave had long since burned out. During the night she simply sat in the darkness, grieving beside her lover. Alethilion was there constantly. The others came and went, even Roxtrianatrix. The singing had faded out.

When the light entered the Dragon Cave once more, the Dragon's voices rose again in that weird harmony that must be their music. The Sacred Marriage Cave began to fill with reptilian bodies. Roxtrianatrix stood on the other side of Liandra's body where it lay on the altar, her face covered now. Maida had done this when the bruises and what was obviously a crushed cheekbone began to torment her.

Now Alethilion approached the altar. He gently lifted Liandra into his claws once more and turned to go. "No," Maida cried. "Where are you taking her?"

It was as if she hadn't spoken. With Alethilion in the lead, bearing Liandra's body, Roxtrianatrix beside them, the Dragons filed out of the mountain into the open sky.

Maida ran back through the passageway and the Reception Room, arriving on the high ledge in time to see the singing procession winging its way around the shoulder of the mountain, heading north.

They came back later in the day. Maida had retreated to the kitchen to find something to eat and drink and felt slightly better for it. When she heard them coming into the Dragon Cave, she ran back down to the Sacred Marriage altar and lit a torch, but none of the Dragons entered. Only Roxtrianatrix came to her and laid his head in her lap, sighed and closed his eyes.

As the light began to fade again in the Dragon Cave outside, there was the sound of a great weight landing on the ledge in front of the Sacred Marriage Cave and then the rustle of belly scales scraping on the stone floor. Maida looked up to see the cave filling with the golden bulk of Glenardinaliat. His vast head lowered in front of her, his slowly whirling opal eyes upon her. Roxtrianatrix lifted his head and looked at the Lead Dragon, then rose and sat to one side of Maida, his eyes upon her as well.

Maida became aware of her body, aching everywhere, echoing her sore heart. With effort, she tore her eyes from the steady gaze of the gigantic creature before her and lowered them, studying her own hands lying curled in her lap. They were strong, dark hands, she thought, and between their work-hardened palms, they held the future of two peoples, or perhaps three peoples. Somewhere on the long road of this adventure, she had begun to think of the Dragons as a people too.

INTERLUDE: ALETHILION'S LAMENT

Weep with me, Dragons
Tear out my heart and offer it
Bleeding
To the sun
Grieve with me, Dragons
Tear the cry from my throat and offer it
Wailing
To the wind

My beloved lies limp in my hands
Spirit gone
She flew without wings
And went down

Down, down
Spiraling down
The hope she brought with her
Of Keepers return
Broken on the stone
Of the mountain

The son she bore me
Left alone
Between her kind and mine

Fly eastward, Dragons
Bring me perfect stones
From the sea
To build her cairn

The Little Dragons

I carry her
To the ceiling of earth
To lie among our ancient ones
And hers.

Weep with me, Dragons
Tear out my heart and offer it
Bleeding
To the Sun
Grieve with me, Dragons
Tear the cry from my throat and offer it
Wailing
To the Wind

JESSA

Jessa found herself in charge. Wherever she went, men fell back from her path, bowed to her. She caught the words "Dragon Priestess" whispered at every turn. "I'm not a Dragon Priestess," she confided quietly to Eldrin, as he bent down to examine Locheil.

He frowned at her. "Then what?" he said. "Liandra, we all just witnessed that Little Dragon, the first seen in generations, lay his head in your hand."

"But that's …" She stopped herself. She could hardly say, "That's Liandra's Little Dragon. She is the Dragon Priestess." In fact, there was nothing she could say.

Eldrin scanned the sky. "Do you think they'll come back?"

She considered this. Her hands still tingled from touching those brilliant blue scales. Roxtrianatrix had, for some strange reason, knelt before her. There had been sadness in his gesture, and also some kind of bond, or promise. She didn't think the Dragons would come back, or at least, not to kill them. She went with her intuition. "I don't think so," she said to Eldrin.

The young man sat back on his heels. "You'll have to help me," he said. "I was Heir and now my brother is dead. I'm officially in command, but the one they will truly listen to is you."

"Me? But, Locheil …" she said, looking down at her husband's pale face.

"He needs to be over there," Eldrin gestured toward the grassy area among the trees behind them, "In the temporary infirmary we set up yesterday, where we can care for him. All the others as well. Liandra, please help me."

She looked around her. Injured men groaned and cried out from where they lay among the dead. Their companions were already pulling them out of the tangle, carrying them or helping them hobble toward the infirmary. "Yes," she said to Eldrin. "You're right." She squeezed

Locheil's unresponsive hand. "I'll return, my love, as soon as I can."

She and Eldrin spent the rest of the day together, making decisions which were then relayed to the remaining officers by Farrell. By late afternoon, the wounded were laid out in rows among the trees, expanding the infirmary to three times the size it had been the night before. Pages and fighting men who had escaped serious injury tended to them as best they could. In her time serving the Lady Merrit and during her brief visit to Liandra in the cabin of the old Earth People Healer in the woodlands, Jessa had learned about the almost mythical skills of the Earth People Healers. "Do you suppose there are Earth People Healers anywhere near here?" she asked Eldrin.

"What is that?" he creased his brow.

"You know, witch healers."

Eldrin's brows rose and he made the sign of the Warrior God's Sword in the air. "What would we want with them?"

Jessa sighed. "I heard they can work miracles with Dragon wounds."

"Really? Well, you're the Dragon Priestess. You should know. But I have no idea how or where we would find one of those." Despite his words, he made the Sword sign again.

Men brought the remaining tents, pack animals, food and supplies from their camp further down the valley. Firewood was collected, food cooked, and a camp sprouted up on the meadow behind the battlefield.

The dead were taken to join the ranks of the fallen lying in rows around Torrie's torn body lying under his shield, wrapped in his bloody cloak. Knots of comrades said prayers over a dead man here or there. Many stopped going in or out of the Field of Honour, as they called it, to bow their heads before their dead King. Eldrin and Jessa paused there too, Eldrin for a long, quiet time. Jessa glanced at him at one point, quickly, but long enough to see the splash of tears on what was left of his tabard. She found herself feeling only anger toward Torrie, dead or not.

Eldrin raised his head and blew his nose. "He gave his life to bring his people back into the light of day," he said.

Jessa immediately felt shamed by her anger. His methods were all he was taught by a life spent in the school of war, and Eldrin was right, his goal was the same as everyone else's, Kings People and Earth People alike.

After a few more minutes of respectful silence, she asked him, "What do you usually do with the bodies of fallen soldiers? Carry them back to the Westlands?"

Eldrin shook his head. "If we have enough able-bodied men, we bury them on the field," he said.

Jessa opened her mouth to ask what happened if there were not enough able-bodied men, but closed it again. She knew.

"Before we leave, we'll have the Chaplains say the Prayers for the Dead in Battle. We'll carry Torrie back, though. He was King, if only briefly. He will have a Royal Funeral."

Well into the night, lanterns bobbed around in the woods as the men finished setting up the camp and crews cut and piled saplings to make stretchers to carry the wounded on the long journey back to the Westlands. Later, Eldrin and Jessa decided that everyone should rest. Most of the men congregated around the cooking fires to talk, eat and sleep. Jessa settled beside Locheil. There was heat in him now and he was restless. The Dragon wounds were beginning to fester. The same must be happening to the men all around her. There was a chorus of groaning and tossing, screams and cries for water and other cries from the depths of nighmares. Those caring for the wounded were kept busy comforting, restraining and running with buckets and dippers of water. Jessa prayed to both the Warrior God and the strange Mother Goddess of the Earth People until she could keep herself awake no longer. She curled up at Locheil's side and slept.

She woke at daybreak with someone shouting Liandra's name and title at her. "Princess Liandra, wake up, look!" She sat up. The men working with the wounded had backed away into a large circle a distance from her, staring with wide-open eyes. The wounded that were conscious were staring too. There was a chittering noise behind her. She turned, and found herself looking into the whirling eyes of Liandra's Little Dragon.

He bobbed his head up and down and made that chittering sound again. It seemed he was trying to communicate with her. "What, Roxtrianatrix?" she whispered. "I wish I could hear you in my thoughts the way Liandra can." He chattered, bobbed more quickly. In the end, all she could do was extend her hands. He became quiet, slithered forward a little and laid his head in her palms the way he had on the battlefield the day before. This time he closed his eyes and sighed deeply. Her arms were aching with the need to shift position by the time he lifted his head, touched his nose to her outstretched palm, then unfurled his iridescent wings and flew away. All around her the men were on their knees, their heads bowed to him, to her.

It was tempting to take one more night of rest, but Eldrin and Jessa felt it was urgent to get the wounded men into the hands of healers. Eldrin was thinking of the King's People's healers in the capital city. Jessa had promised herself that she would ask any Earth People they met where she might find one of their Healers.

As soon as the sun set, they ordered the army to pack up. Everyone gathered for the Chaplains' prayers over the dead and left them with sadness, still arrayed in their rows at the edge of the woods. The King's body went with them, tied to a sapling stretcher carried by two men, the same way they transported the men who were seriously wounded. The less seriously wounded hobbled along, supporting themselves with crutches and walking sticks also cut from the woods. By midnight, they were on the road, although traveling slowly.

There were only a few horses going back with them and they decided the best use of their strength would be to pull some of the wagons, loaded with tents, food and supplies. Only one was saddled, to assist Eldrin and Farrell as they alternated in the task of riding up and down the crawling procession, giving encouragement and solving problems. Jessa walked beside Locheil's stretcher. When Eldrin was not working on horseback, he walked beside her.

"What will happen when we get back?" Jessa asked him.

"First thing, we'll commandeer one of the larger halls and set up an infirmary to care for the wounded."

"Of course."

"My Father's Head Bailiff, Ermin, will be very important. He knows everything about running the government, and he oversees Royal ceremonies. He will arrange Torrie's funeral."

"And then a Coronation?"

"A Coronation?"

"For you."

Eldrin abruptly lost his horseman's posture, walking with a bent head. "Oh God," he muttered.

"What? Do you not want to be King?"

"No. Never. You see, after my Father it was always understood that the crown would go to Torrie. I always assumed he would have a long life. So did everyone else. It was him that got whatever training was to be had in statecraft, little as it was. I never, ever thought in terms of mounting the throne of the Westlands." He looked at her, brow creased, almost panic in his eyes. "Oh the poor people of the Westlands," he said.

"I'm not cut out to be a King."

"What are you cut out for?" Jessa asked him.

"I've always assumed I would have a life-time career in the army. I want to expand the cavalry. Not because I like fighting and all that," he gave Jessa a guilty glance, "But I love the horses." His face brightened and his back straightened at the very mention of the animals. "I have some ideas for breeding taller, faster horses, and training them to be athletes, horses that can quickly carry a messenger any distance without effort, dance through a sword fight as quickly and gracefully as any man on foot, fearless horses, horses with heart." He stopped, breathless. Jessa marveled at the light on his face now. It outshone his travel lantern, but as quickly as it had arrived, it faded away. "But now I guess that's not to be," he said.

"Why not? Can't a King breed horses?"

"Well, sure, but do you have any idea how many hours a day it takes to govern a Realm? Kings oversee military matters, but the day to day work is left to the men under them. I will be the one that walks through the stables or watches the training exercises, suggesting this or that, not the one that knows each horse intimately, its strengths and failings, what it could offer to its offspring when paired with the strengths and failings of a mare I know just as well."

Jessa found his passion moving. "Oh Eldrin, I'm sorry about what fate is handing you."

He nodded, watching the ground at his feet again, apparently not trusting himself to speak. Jessa watched him, so much like his father—their father.

"Is your Father dead, then? We had only heard that he was wounded."

Eldrin looked up at her. "Oh I imagine he's dead by now. He was very seriously wounded."

"Would no one have sent a messenger with the news?"

"While we were fighting? I think they would assume a messenger could not get through to us alive."

"Hmmm," Jessa took a few more steps before responding. "But we don't know for sure he's dead."

"Well, no, but surely, by now." Eldrin fell into his own thoughts, his brow once more creased the way it did when he was thinking.

MAIDA

Maida prepared herself as best she could. She filled the stone tub in
the bathing room and built a fire in the stove. In a cupboard she found
some creams and powders that she could identify. Some were relaxants,
others were intended to soften skin and muscle. She sprinkled a generous
amount of both powders into the water. The bath smelled lovely. She lay
in it until she felt a relaxation beyond anything she had ever experienced
before. Roxtrianatrix curled beside her, on the lip of the tub.

When she felt she was as ready as she ever would be, she dried
herself and wrapped herself in the golden cloak from the closet beside the
couch. With Roxtrianatrix accompanying her, she lit the torches, lay down
on the blankets and pillows she had arranged on the altar and waited. She
thought about the chorus of singers and drummers who once would have
filled this ritual space with traditional chants. As Maida lay on the stone
altar, the only sound was the guttering of the torches, her breathing and
that of Liandra's Little Dragon where he sat a few feet away.

Because it was so quiet, there was no mistaking the weight of
Glenardinaliat landing on the platform at the end of the room. Maida's
heart beat faster, but she quelled her fear with deep breaths and closed
her eyes. His claws scratched the stone as he crawled into the room,
accompanied by the softer scrape of scales on the floor.

Even through her closed eyelids, Maida was aware of the light of the
torches blocked out by Glenardinaliat's reptilian head bent over her. She
couldn't resist opening her eyes. He looked straight into them. His were
whirling quickly, a spiral kaleidoscope of brilliant colour. There was no
mistaking his love for her, strange as it seemed.

She lifted and parted her knees, supporting her feet on the rounded
ridge at the bottom of the altar. His front claws scraped lightly on the
stone floor, moving past her on either side, and then his vast golden belly
was arched over her.

He probed her gently once, twice, and then filled her, deep into her belly. There was pain, but he also felt as golden as his colour inside her. A few minutes later, a ripple passed through the golden scales above her and she overflowed with warm liquid, pouring down her buttocks and flooding the blankets under her hips. She could hear it dripping from the altar onto the stone floor. She barely felt him withdraw, except for blinking away the light as his shadow left her.

She lay there for some time, feeling a glow deep in her belly. It was only when she began to feel chilled that she returned to her still-hot bath, Roxtrianatrix close beside her.

INTERLUDE: THE DRAGONS

Mighty wings unfurled
Great Golden One
Flies to the Sun

He has planted his seed
In his beloved's womb
It lies deep within her
Hope curls warm within her
She will be a Keeper
Of Dragons

Fly, fly with him
O Dragons
And rejoice
For hope lies golden
Within the womb of his love
And she will be a Keeper.

MELISANDE

Anglewart walked unevenly to his chair by the fire, leaning heavily on his walking stick. He sat and indicated the chair beside him for Melisande. "So, our oldest son is dead," he said.

She watched the fire. The sadness of this loss weighed heavily upon her. "And Eldrin?" she said. "Will we see him crowned King, so young?"

"He knows his duty." He was watching her. "And this rumour, about Liandra being a Dragon Priestess, what do you make of that?"

"I don't know," she said, and it was the truth. The rumours that were filtering into the capital city in advance of the returning army were extremely muddled. The last she had heard about Liandra, word that she could trust, was Marle's report that the young woman had been snatched by Dragons from the Barrens near the Healer's School, and her Little Dragon had gone with her.

"And why is she with the army?"

"That I don't know either."

Anglewart turned back to the fire. "I guess we will know more when they arrive."

MAIDA

Maida pushed herself forward, barely aware of the dense Northlands forest all around her. She walked until she was too tired to go any farther, paying no attention to whether she traveled by day or night, except to blow out the travel lantern when its circle of light melted into the greater light of the sun. She became warm in the sun, wet in the rain, cold in the wind, and didn't notice. When she couldn't lift her foot one more time, she would lie down wherever she was and curl up under her cloak. Only complete exhaustion allowed her to sleep without seeing Liandra again, twisting and turning through the air, down, down, leaving Maida clutching the cliff's edge, screaming her lover's name in terror, helplessness and loss. Sometimes Maida wished she had jumped too, but then her attention would focus on the little knot of golden, glowing warmth in her belly. It was this that moved her forward. She must carry it to the Healer's School, where the knowledge was.

Before she had departed, her Servant self clicked into an automatic need to leave the Dragon Priestesses' School in good order. She had cleaned, tidied, put things away. Any food that would keep on the road she wrapped and stowed in her travel pack. She had put the goats into the slings Liandra had made to transport them to the mountains and asked Roxtrianatrix to ask the Dragons to take them to Father Mallory and Lynna. She had no idea if Roxtrianatrix understood spoken words or not, but when she was ready, three young Dragons came, picked up the frightened goats and flew away in the right direction. For all she knew they had stopped just out of her sight and eaten them but, if so, it couldn't be helped. At least the Dragons were well fed at that point. She hoped they preferred dead soldiers to live goats. She tried not to think about it.

One night she passed a clearing where the retreating army had laid out some of those who had died along the way. It was obvious the Dragons had feasted. She was glad it was dark. Her lantern gave her only a momentary glimpse at the edge of the scene. If she had had anything in her stomach at that moment, she would have lost it. She hurried on.

When she woke from her troubled sleep, she would nibble some of the food she carried, find a nearby stream for a drink of cold mountain water, light her lantern if it was dark, and continue on. In daylight, Roxtrianatrix was often with her and overhead she sometimes became aware of Alethilion and Glenardinaliat keeping pace with her.

One day she awoke to find herself in a translucent golden tent, warm and dry, although she could hear rain falling. It was Glenardinaliat's wing, arched protectively over her. The warmth came from his side. She had been curled against him. When he realized she was awake, he had lifted his wing, giving her more room to sit up and eat her scanty rations. When she was ready to travel again, he bent before her and cupped his front claws into a basket, his anxious eyes upon her. He was offering to carry her, but where? "You want to take me back to the School in the mountains, don't you?" she said. His eyes whirled slowly. What was he thinking? "It's the Healers' School I'm going to, on the coast, to the east of the Eastlands." His eyes didn't change. In the end she couldn't imagine him wanting to take her anywhere but the place he thought of as home and she couldn't risk losing all the miles she had already walked. She kissed his lowered nose, just that one part of him bigger than she was, thanked him and walked on. He flew overhead for the rest of the day. From then on she chose clearings for her rest when she could, giving him room to shelter her.

JESSA

The journey home had been terrible. They traveled only a few miles each night because of the wounded men struggling to keep up on crutches and walking sticks. Those who were not injured were exhausted from carrying the stretchers. Every evening when they took to the road they arranged another group of dead soldiers in a nearby clearing and said prayers for their rest. Every morning when they stopped, supper was scantier. They had almost run out of food and hay for their few remaining horses.

Jessa did what she could to tend the men and work with Eldrin making decisions while her heart traveled with Locheil. Sometimes he lay deathly still, and at other times he tossed and moaned, burning with fever. Jessa did not know which she feared most. She wanted so badly to find an Earth People Healer, but the Earth People, it seemed, were staying out of their way. Once they reached the villages of the Westlands, the King's People came out with food and comfort for their retreating army. As word spread about the visits from Roxtrianatrix, they would stare at her or bow to her or scowl at her, always from a safe distance.

While they were still in the wilderness of the Northlands, Liandra's Little Dragon came to visit Jessa every day, usually just after dawn. He would sit quietly with her while she sat beside Locheil. After awhile, he would touch his nose to her hand, unfurl his wings and leave. Once they reached the villages of the Westlands, his visits stopped, although she was aware of him flying over occasionally, looking for her.

She had lost track of the number of nights they had been on the road when they finally reached the capital city. It was a huge relief to have many fresh hands helping to settle the wounded in the hall Eldrin commandeered for an infirmary and the able-bodied but exhausted in their own familiar barracks. The King's healers reported to the infirmary and were of great assistance making the wounded men more comfortable. About actually healing the poison of Dragon wounds, they didn't seem to know much.

Travelling beside Eldrin in a large, closed carriage, Jessa leaned her head against the padded seatback. Although Locheil had rested quite well on a cot the day before, and someone had brought a pallet for her to lie on the floor beside him, she had slept little.

"Are you worried about what we'll find?" she asked Eldrin. He turned to her, looking just as exhausted as she felt. He had spent the day walking the barracks, seeing to the comfort of his remaining men, and then had spent some hours in his father's study, reading the Constitution of the Realm. He had changed into fresh clothes but, apart from that, looked as battered and unkempt as he had on the road. She, too, had done nothing to prepare for this visit besides borrowing a dress, the simplest one she could find in the closet in Princess Liandra's unused room.

"Yes," he said. "I'm glad to know he's still alive, but he could be badly injured. I feel confident about our plans, though."

"Me too," Jessa assured him. They had spent many hours of the journey walking side by side, making plans. Their first choice hinged on what they would find at the Men's Retreat House.

As the carriage pulled into the square in front of the Cathedral, Jessa's eyes were riveted to the lighted windows of the Women's Retreat House. How much she wanted to be free to go there, find the Lady Merrit, the real Queen Melisande, who would understand that the Little Dragon everyone was talking about belonged to the real Liandra, find Ev and fall into her arms, tell her everything. However, she was not Jessa now, Servant of the Women's Retreat House, she was Liandra, wife of Prince Locheil, a Dragon Priestess in rumour alone.

"Don't forget not to tell him about the Little Dragon unless he asks, and then in just the vagest terms," Jessa reminded Eldrin.

"I think he long ago decided killing the Dragon Priestesses was a mistake, but for your safety, I will remember."

141 ANGLEWART

The King rose to his feet, leaning heavily on his walking stick, to greet his children. When they entered the chamber, his heart twisted in his chest. They were clearly battered, exhausted and sad beyond what anyone should be asked to bear. He held out his arms. Jessa – no, he reminded himself, Liandra – ran into them and held him hard. He felt a sob or two shake her shoulders before she gulped down a couple of deep breaths and pulled back to look at him. "Father," she said. "We didn't dare hope …"

He looked to Eldrin, held out his other arm. The boy, now made a man by his trials, hesitated. He had never felt his father's touch in affection before. After a minute, however, he came forward for a brief hug, albeit a little stiffly.

Once seated, Jessa looked at Eldrin and said: "First plan."

He nodded agreement. Anglewart looked from one to the other, his eyebrows raised.

"My Lord," Eldrin began.

"I'm no longer your Lord," Anglewart reminded him, and smiled. "In fact, you are mine."

"Not yet. I've just read the Westlands Constitution of the Realm."

"You have?" Anglewart's eyebrows rose again.

"I'm the Heir Designate until there's a Coronation. You, however, are King until death, and you don't look very dead to me."

Anglewart threw back his head and laughed. "My horseman son has become a lawyer." A minute later he returned to seriousness and said, "My dear son, I am not dead, but I came very close to it. I was saved by a brilliant Healer of the Earth People." Eldrin's glance slid over to Jessa, surprise on his face. "But I have injuries that will never heal, and I feel older than the mountains. I have also made some terrible mistakes. The citizens of the Westlands believe me to be in retreat here, a remnant of a man. I think they deserve a vital young King, with a clean page to write on."

"Father, I am, as you just said, your horseman son. Ruling involves more than riding horses. Torrie had little enough preparation for governance; I have had none, and life in the Realms is about to change."

"Oh?" Anglewart interrupted. "Why do you think that?"

Edrin flushed a bright pink shade. "I don't know. I just think so. It's a long story."

The King nodded. "Go on," he prompted.

"If things begin to change, or not, the people of the Westlands need an experienced hand at the helm."

"Where is Ermin?"

"I don't know. I haven't seen him yet."

"Hmmmm." The King nodded thoughtfully.

Eldrin surprised him by shifting forward, out of his chair, settling on his knees on the floor. "My Lord, I mean, Father, if you would come back to rule, I could learn from you, and Ermin, of course, and prepare to take my turn."

"Eldrin, get up. I am not your Lord. All right, perhaps legally I am." He looked into Eldrin's beseeching eyes but also felt the ache of his aging and wounded body. He dropped his head into his hand, rubbed his forehead. "I'll think about it," he said. "Do what you need to do to heal your men. Find Ermin to conduct the day-to-day business of the Realm. Arrange your brother's funeral. We will talk again soon."

It was a dismissal. Eldrin and Jessa got to their feet, but before they could bow and leave, Anglewart addressed Jessa. "My daughter, before you go, is there anything I can do for you?"

She had not planned to say it, but found the words right there on her tongue. "I would like to visit the Lady Merrit," she said. "She lives across the Square, in the Women's Retreat House, but I don't know how to arrange it." She glanced at Eldrin. He looked puzzled.

"Be seated," Anglewart said. "Let's see what I can do."

142 MELISANDE

Melisande had seen the carriage standing in the Square. It did not surprise her to get a message from the Men's Retreat House as soon as it pulled away. When she discovered Jessa in Anglewart's chamber, there were delighted shrieks and a long hug. "My dear," said Melisande, standing back to look her daughter over.

Jessa, in turn, studied her mother, instantly taking in, Melisande saw, her white veil. "Lady Merrit, I mean, what do I call you?"

"How about Mother? At least in private, and yes, I am now Head Mother Merrit. Head Mother Mabonne died the week after Torrie's coronation. She appointed me her successor."

"I didn't hear."

"We didn't hold a large public funeral because the Coronation was so recent and preparations for war had begun.

"Have you taken your full vows as a Sister then?"

I know. It's unusual for a Widow to be Head Mother. I promised Mother Mabonne that I would start the process of preparing to make my full profession."

Jessa smiled. "You will make a good Head Mother."

"Thank you, my dear. I'm so sorry about Locheil. Is he …?"

"He lives, but he is very, very ill. I need to find an Earth People Healer for him, and the others."

"That we can do," said Melisande. "And you, dear Jessa, you look so thin and tired."

Jessa's eyes were on Anglewart. How much did he know about Liandra? Dare she ask? She decided to ask but say as little as possible. "My sister," she said. "Is there any word of her?"

"Not since we had word that she was snatched by Dragons."

Jessa's face paled. "Snatched by Dragons?"

"Did you not get my letter?"

"No, not before we started out to join the army."

Anglewart and Melisande spoke in unison. "We?"

Jessa's face went from white to red. "There's a story to tell."

"Just a minute while I ask for a pot of tea," Melisande said, going to the door.

The story took more than one pot of tea to tell. When Jessa reached the part about Roxtrianatrix's arrival on the battlefield, she paused, questioned Melisande with her eyes.

Melisande glanced at the King. "No, he doesn't know that part," she said.

"What part?" Anglewart asked.

And so Anglewart learned what Melisande knew of their other daughter's story, and learned where Little Dragons come from. He blushed furiously. Melisande turned to Jessa. "Men are such prudes," she said.

Much later, when Jessa had left to return to the Infirmary with Melisande's promise to send Marle, Anglewart let out a deep breath and let his head rest on the back of the chair. "I am so tired," he said, and he certainly looked it. "But we need to make a decision, soon. Eldrin has asked me to return as King."

"Do you want to?"

"No."

"Do you think it would be the best thing for the Realm?"

"I have to admit, I do. He has no training in statecraft. I told him to rely on Ermin, but Ermin betrayed me and now his young King is dead and his old King is still living. If I were Ermin, I'd have left in advance of the returning army. Who, then, does Eldrin have to teach him?"

"And who better than you? You have been a good King, Anglewart."

He turned to her, a look of amazement and gratitude on his face. "Do you really think so?"

She nodded. "The crown will go to Eldrin all in good time."

"I think he would prefer it to be never. You know his passion for horses."

"Kings can breed horses."

"But servants do most of it. I think he would like to manage a stud himself."

Melisande laughed. Anglewart reached for her hand. "But if I become King again," he said, "I will need my Queen by my side."

"You won't marry a Rodolph, now that you have the chance again?"

Anglewart shook his head, his eyes expressing his love for her.

"But my vows to the Women's Retreat House, and my position as Head Mother, I …."

"You are not yet fully professed, and your entry vows were taken under an assumed name. I think we might be able to get around them, perhaps with the promise that if you are ever widowed, you will take your place in the Women's Retreat House again."

She squeezed his hand. "May that not happen for a long, long time, but I am officially dead. You held a huge public funeral for me."

"I'll call all the nobles together and confess the terrible error I made."

Melisande was almost overwhelmed by sadness. "My dearest, I love you, you know that, but stop thinking like a lover and think like a King. You were officially engaged to a Rodolph. Even if she then married your son, she is a widow now. Her family might accept that you do not want to marry your son's widow, but you owe it to them to marry another woman of their family now. They might feel justified in assassinating you if you don't. At least they would break their alliance with you and become powerful enemies once more. Your whole Kingdom would probably split over such an action."

Anglewart's head had dropped into his free hand while she spoke. There was a long silence. She squeezed the hand she held once more and he squeezed back. He turned to her, his eyes filled with his pain. "Such a stupid, arrogant, power-hungry thing I did. It will haunt me to my grave, and perhaps beyond. I guess it will have to be enough that you, at least, have been ready to forgive me and love me again." He gave her a sad smile. She lifted his hand to her lips and kissed it, her tears trickling over his scarred knuckles.

MAiDA

Maida used the stars to keep herself on a southward course. She needed to travel south to the Westlands, then east, but wondered how she would know when she had crossed the border. In the end it was not difficult to tell. She began to encounter villages, mostly those of the King's People. She stayed out of sight, hoping to find an Earth People's village and a Healer. She tried to remember who had a practice near the northern border of the Westlands, but her mind was blank. Her feet were blistered and raw. She wanted some salve and bandages for them.

As night began to fade, she was stumbling with exhaustion. She spotted a clearing ahead and pushed herself to reach it. Breaking out of the woods into the open, she stopped abruptly. There were two woodcutters in the clearing, not as tall as most King's people, but strong-looking. They were tying the wood they had cut into bundles, ready to carry to their village, which must lie ahead on the path, since she had not passed one on the trail behind her for some time.

Maida wished she had been more cautious in her approach. Now it was too late. They were staring at her and one had lifted his lantern to see her better. "Well, well," he said. "And who's this on the trail so close to morning?"

"Sir," she said, and then because they were obviously waiting for her to explain herself, "I'm looking for a Healer, an Earth People Healer."

"Ah, well," said one of the men, slightly taller than the other. "There just might be one nearby, close enough to take you there on our way back to Lipkin." His eyes narrowed. "What's it worth to you?"

Maida could stay on her feet no longer and sank to her knees. The second man jabbed the first in the ribs. "Fool, she's in rags. She ain't got nothing to pay with. She's sick or something, isn't she? Why else's she looking for a witch?"

The first man took a step or two closer to Maida and held his lantern up, examining her, especially her pack, which now hung limp on her back, almost empty of food. "Yeah," he said. "She ain't got nothing." He turned back to heft his load of wood. The other man followed suit. "So follow us, then, but mind you keep up," he said.

Maida wanted so badly to find a Healer that she roused a bit of strength from somewhere to get to her feet and stumble along behind them. They walked quickly. She despaired of losing sight of them. Just when she thought she had, she found them waiting by the meeting point of the trail they were on and a much smaller one that veered away from it. "There," said the slightly taller man. "The witch lives up there. It's not far."

Maida thanked them and turned to take the smaller path, but wavered on her feet. "You should take her there," said the shorter man. "Won't take a minute and she's going to die on the path and the witch'll blame us."

"If I'm going up to the witch's cabin, you're coming too."

They dropped their loads on the main path and took Maida's arms, one on each side. They marched her quickly up the path, traveling crabwise most of the time because it was so narrow. Just a few yards along, they arrived in a small yard containing an even smaller cabin. It was lit and warm looking. A tall woman appeared outlined in the doorway, a lantern in her hand. "Who's there?"

Maida immediately recognized her voice. Sheil, Kendra's Apprentice, although she must be a Sister now to be here in the Westlands practicing on her own. Sheil stepped forward, lantern held high. The two woodcutters dropped Maida and disappeared in a rustle behind her. She staggered and landed once more on her knees.

"Maida! What are you doing here? And what's happened to you?"

With overwhelming relief Maida accepted Sheil's hands to rise and then fell into her firm embrace, tears already pouring down her cheeks and into the bodice of Sheil's dress.

144 ODD AND GiMLiN KiNG'S MEN-AT-ARMS

Odd and Gimlin ran back to where they had left their bundles of wood sitting beside the path. "Did you hear what the witch called her?" Odd said, breathless.

"Maid, or something."

"No, you idiot, Maida."

"So?"

"That's the one we were sent to find."

Gimlin thought for a moment. "The name was something like that."

"So, what are we going to do?" Odd led the way back to the village, speaking over the load of wood on his shoulder.

"What'd'y mean, do?"

"The King wants her, you fool. There's probably a price on her head."

"The King's dead."

"Well the new King then, why wouldn't he want her too?" Gimlin plodded on behind his friend, not responding. Odd turned to face him, walking backwards. "So how well has this worked out, cutting wood for a living?"

"What living?" Gimlin sniffed.

"Exactly. So why don't we turn back into soldiers and take her to the capital? Collect whatever reward there is for her and start collecting army pay again?"

Gimlin frowned. "They might feed us to the Dragons."

"The Dragons beat them, didn't they? They won't be going anywhere near them for awhile."

"So, you want to grab her and take her to the King? The new King?"

"Sure. We'll just say we've been looking for her all this time and finally found her."

Gimlin shrugged, unsure.

After selling their loads of wood to the innkeeper for a few pennies and a mug of ale, however, Gimlin was convinced. After a day on a pile of mouldy hay in the innkeeper's barn, they went to the small cave in the woods where they had hidden their King's livery. Mice had nibbled a hole or two in the leather jerkins, but there was enough left to wear. They hid themselves in the woods all the next night, watching the road south from the witch's cabin. When no one came, they hid under a fallen tree for the day and slept. The next night they resumed their watch.

MAIDA

Maida felt much better leaving Sheil's cabin, her feet salved and bandaged in a new pair of leather shoes, food and fuel in her pack, comforted, well fed and, after sleeping nearly around the clock, rested, although sometimes rest was not a good thing, she reflected. It gave her some spare attention for her broken heart.

She took a side trail that Sheil had told her would avoid the village of Lipkin. She had traveled only a few hundred yards, however, when a very ragged King's Man-at-Arms stepped into her path. In a confusing flash, she thought that he was one of the two woodcutters who had led her to Sheil's cabin. There was a footstep behind her, but before she could turn or cry out, a dirty hand was clapped over her mouth.

146 ANGLEWART

Standing in his study, Anglewart was acutely aware of how bent his body had become, and how lumbering his walk, now that he must lean heavily on a stick. When he last stood here he had been tall, straight, agile and athletic. When last he stood here, Ermin was beside him. Now it was Eldrin.

He had watched his eldest son's funeral from the balcony of the Men's Retreat House, sitting in the third row, so he would not be obvious to the congregation below. Across the cathedral, the Women's Retreat House balcony was curtained, but he knew Melisande was there. He wished so much to be with her, holding her hand. Recent history had faded and he grieved for the young son that was so eager to learn, so eager to do well as Heir and eventually, King. He knew it must be worse for Melisande, who knew the children so much better than he did.

His middle son gave him a look of apology. "I don't know where anything is here," he said. "In fact, what I know about the business of the Kingdom would fit on the hilt of my sword. It never occurred to me to prepare for this."

"Nor me." Anglewart looked at the papers on the desk, lifted the top ones to look beneath. He turned slowly and surveyed the neat piles of documents on the shelf beside him. "It doesn't look to me as if anything has changed since I left, except for the daily business."

"Torrie left it all in Ermin's hands, while he prepared to march on the Dragons."

"Ermin knows the business of this room well. We have done it together for almost thirty years. So, where is Ermin now?" The King had to work to keep a dark tone from creeping into his voice with the question.

"I think he's gone. When we arrived back here, I searched everywhere for him. All I could find was a gatekeeper who said he left the night before, mounted and with a heavily loaded wagon behind him. He gave another name, but the gatekeeper recognized him."

Anglewart nodded. "All right. We'll have to find a capable assistant to take his place. He can learn along with you."

"What about Farrell?"

The King thought for a minute. "That is a good idea, eventually. For now, he's only ten, just starting his soldier's training. No, you need an assistant, a Head Bailiff. I would like you to choose someone of your own age, someone you feel comfortable with, for you will hopefully spend many years working together."

Eldrin nodded agreement, but his face was sad. Anglewart put his hand on his son's shoulder. "I know it is not your calling, even if it is your blood. That is how life works sometimes."

Alone again, Anglewart moved some of the papers on the desk aside, took a fresh sheet of parchment and a quill, and sat down to organize his thoughts. Before he had written a single word, however, there was a light knock on the door. In response to his permission, it opened to admit the Lady Thalassa. Her face was very pale, or perhaps it was the contrast with her black widow's dress. The King noticed that the colour was the only element of mourning in the outfit, for the dress was full, made of expensive fabric, hung with jewels and extremely low cut at the bosom. There was also nothing sad or cowed in the young woman's approach across the study, although, when she reached the King, she knelt in front of him and bowed her head.

His hand was resting on the edge of his chair, and after a few moments, she reached out and took it in her own, a bold thing to do, then raised her eyes to his face. "My Lord?" she said, speaking before he did.

"So, my Lady Thalassa, you are now a widow, so soon after becoming a bride. I am sorry."

"And free to marry again, my Lord," she said.

"Ah, you were always bold, weren't you?" Anglewart suddenly felt crowded by her. He lifted his stick from where it was leaning on the side of the desk and struggled to his feet. He walked over to the window, looked out briefly, then turned back. He caught the surprise and revulsion on her face. "Yes," he said, "I am an old man now, a cripple." As an afterthought, he added, "You may rise." She did and stood there, beautiful and haughty. What did he ever see in her? Did Ermin reach so far into his mind? No, he reminded himself, don't blame Ermin for that. It was you who became hungry for power.

The Little Dragons

He studied her for a moment, took on a light tone. "Perhaps a life in the Women's Retreat House would suit you?"

As he knew it would, this remark brought a dark red flush to her face. She sputtered, but apparently could find no words, because she turned on her fine heel and ran from the room. That was a little more nasty than was called for, he thought, but couldn't resist a brief smile.

JESSA

The night after Jessa's meeting with the King and Lady Merrit, the former Queen arrived at the infirmary, a group of Widows and Sisters with her. "Head Mother," Jessa exclaimed in surprise and, out of long habit, grasped her skirt to curtsey.

Melisande reached out instantly to restrain her hand. "No." She moved close to Jessa's ear and whispered. "Until Eldrin marries, you are the highest lady in the Realm, Dragon Priestess." It took Jessa a minute or two to absorb this. Her mind and heart had been filled utterly with the necessity of organizing the infirmary and caring for Locheil. She had become used to giving commands without thinking about why even men leaped to obey her. "I have sent a message to Marle and heard back," Melisande said, in a more natural voice. "She is at the Healer's School, but says she will come and bring other Earth People Healers with her. For the time being, these Sisters and Widows have volunteered to help care for the wounded men."

Jessa looked at the women standing behind the Head Mother. She recognized all of them and they obviously recognized her, staring at her in frank curiosity. "I explained about the Servant Jessa, who was taken by a Dragon in the Eastlands, being your secret Second Twin." Melisande said.

Jessa nodded, her mind racing to keep up with these developments. She must remember that they believe her to be Liandra, who has never met any of them before.

The expressions on the women's faces also said they were frightened, as of course they would be. Few would have set foot outside the Women's Retreat House since whenever they entered. She addressed them: "This is a courageous thing you are doing. Thank you." The women had begun to look around at the rows of seriously ill soldiers filling the room. Several lifted their sleeves to their noses. Jessa had spent so many hours here she had ceased to notice the smell of rotting flesh as the men's Dragon wounds festered.

The Little Dragons

Best to keep them busy. Jessa called over a King's healer and gave him the responsibility of assigning the women to tasks. Within an hour the aisles between the rows of cots whispered with the swish of grey skirts as the brave volunteers from the Women's Retreat House carried water and bandages, bathed brows and washed wounds, their Head Mother among them, her sleeves rolled up, serving along with her flock.

At one point Melisande came to visit Locheil briefly. She frowned as she touched his flushed face. "Will the men not recognize you?" Jessa whispered very softly.

"Few would have seen me close up," Melisande replied, equally softly. "And belief is strong. The woman I was is dead, not only to them." Jessa puzzled over that comment, while Melisande studied Locheil's face again. "Marle and the Healers will know what to do when they come."

There was not, however, time for Marle and her knowledge to arrive. Later that night Locheil began to struggle for breath. Jessa put her arms around him, raising his head and shoulders a bit higher, in hope that it would make it easier for him. He gasped another breath, and another, and then he sighed and beathed no more. Slowly, gently Jessa laid him back down. In her mind she was wailing: No! No! No! No! No! But she was all too aware of the position she held now, of the many eyes upon her. She laid her head down on Locheil's still chest and quietly sobbed.

Moments later, Melisande was behind her, holding her shoulders. "Go about your business," she heard the Head Mother say to those who had paused to look.

They sat like that for what seemed like a long time, until two men arrived with a stretcher to take Locheil to the room that served as a morgue. It was Jessa's own decision that the dead would be taken elsewhere quickly, but now she had to restrain herself from clutching Locheil's lifeless body and refusing to hand him over.

Melisande took her to Liandra's old room. Waving away the servants, she changed Jessa into one of Liandra's soft nightgowns and put her to bed, where Jessa could only clutch the pillow and sob into it. Melisande lay down beside her, a protective and comforting arm around her daughter's shoulders.

Much later, well into the day, the door opened. Melisande raised her head to snap at whatever servant had disobeyed her order to leave them alone. It was not a servant. It was the King. After a moment, he too lay down on the bed, his long arm wrapped around both of them, the daughter he had saved and the wife he had killed.

JESSA

Locheil's funeral flowed over Jessa in a painful blurr. She hid her tears behind a translucent black veil, and so saw the proceedings as if in a thick fog, before her eyes and in her mind as well. Life without her beloved Locheil stretched ahead of her, on and on and on, barren of joy.

As she left the Cathedral, one of the King's pages approached her with a message. The Healers from the School stayed in Portla the day before, a village less than a night's travel from the capital. They might arrive before daylight. Jessa's heart clenched in bitterness. They were too late.

King Leo and Queen Calanthra stayed for the meal after the service and then prepared to mount their carriage. Jessa rested her head briefly on Locheil's coffin, sitting on an open carriage just ahead of the one that would carry his parents. They were taking him to the Southlands for burial in the family crypt.

Queen Calanthra looked around. "Where is your luggage, Liandra, dear?"

Jessa's mind reeled briefly. "Luggage?"

"You will travel with us, won't you?"

This thought had never crossed Jessa's mind. "Ummm, no. I have responsibilities here."

Queen Calanthra's brow folded into a frown. "Your responsibility is to Locheil. You are, were, his wife."

Jessa took the Queen's hand, unable to restrain yet another tear from trickling down her cheek. "If he were alive, it would take all that is left of the army to pull me from his side, but he is dead now. Others still live and are in my charge. They are mine to save."

Queen Calanthra pulled her hand roughly from Jessa's. "You are a disgrace to your family and mine," she said. As her serving women helped her into the carriage, Jessa realized her in-laws didn't even know she had accompanied the army to the Northlands. They thought "Liandra" had been here all along, dressed in silks, still a lady.

King Leo did take Jessa's hand and squeezed it. "She'll get over it," he said.

As they pulled away, the page appeared again at Jessa's elbow. "Are they here?" she said.

"No Princess, but the King requests your presence in his study.

The King himself let Jessa into the study, closing the door and locking it behind her. A circle of family was gathered there – besides Anglewart there was Eldrin, Farrell, even Head Mother Merrit and Imelda, who gave Jessa a warm, if sad, smile over Head Mother Merrit's shoulder. The former Queen, Jessa saw, had tears on her face.

In the centre of them all sat a small, dark woman of the Earth People, wearing dirty rags. When she saw Jessa, her eyes widened and she clapped both hands, hard, over her own mouth. In a flash, Jessa recognized her. She was Mother Peg's Apprentice, the one she had met when Lady Merrit had taken her to meet her sister.

"Liandra," Anglewart said, "This is Maida." As he spoke, tears lept into Maida's eyes, which showed the reddened evidence of many tears preceding them. "I mean, since we are alone, Jessa, this is Maida." Now Eldrin and Farrell peered at her with shock on their faces. The King looked at them. "There is more than one story needs to be told this night," he said, and Jessa suddenly saw that his face looked years older than it had even earlier in the night. "But first, Jessa, Maida has brought news of Liandra."

So, Liandra too was gone. It was almost too much sadness to bear, loss upon loss. After the stories and the grieving, Jessa felt a powerful need to return to the infirmary, to the men who lay there, needing her help, and the healers and Sisters, needing her direction. Maida looked terrible, but she needed to ask: "Maida, you are a Healer. We have a room full of men dying of Dragon wounds. We need you desperately. Will you stay here awhile?"

Head Mother Merrit frowned at her. "Liand … I mean, Jessa. The girl is exhausted. She …"

Maida interrupted. "Dragon wounds?" she said. "Do you have licorice?"

"Licorice?" Jessa repeated. "It that good for Dragon wounds?" She looked at Eldrin. "Does that grow around here?"

"Oh yes, in the woods. We used to mix it with sugar to make a sort of candy."

"Can you find me some? Lots, actually," said Maida.

"Take a group of men with you," said Jessa.

Eldrin glanced at the window. "Not much night left. I'll get a group of men together for the coming night."

"I could …" Maida hesitated. "I could make it safe for you to go by daylight." Everyone in the room turned to her, jaws dropped in surprise.

"The Dragons told Liandra they prefer cattle to humans, and they prefer the killing to be done for them. Do you have a herd of cattle?" She looked at the King. He nodded. "If we take one into an open field…you probably have an execution field, don't you?" Anglewart nodded again. "If we take an animal there and kill it, and I tell the Dragons it's for them, they'll leave us alone as we hunt for licorice."

"Are you sure?" Eldrin said.

She wasn't, completely, but remembering what Liandra reported of her conversations with the Dragons, she was sure enough. She nodded.

"The Dragon Priestesses used to raise cattle for the Dragons, didn't they?"

Maida nodded.

"So it wasn't magic? Just raising cattle for the Dragons?"

"Well, it takes communication with the Dragons, an agreement."

Eldrin turned to his father, face alight. "I could do that, Father."

Anglewart's face softened from the sadness it had borne all through this night. "And raise a few horses on the side?" he said. Eldrin looked at his own feet, blushing. "Seriously," the King continued. "We will think about this. It cannot be you, you have other duties, but there is no reason we can't organize ourselves to raise cattle in greater numbers if we can find a way to communicate with the Dragons." Eldrin's hopeful expression faded.

"So will you come to the infirmary?" Jessa asked Maida. "We are expecting a group of Healers from the Healers' School. They aren't here yet, but probably tomorrow night."

Maida looked thoughtful for a moment. "Your Highness," she addressed Anglewart, a touch of fear in her voice. "Excuse me for saying it, but there is a possibility that you have a Healer in your prison." He waited for her to go on. "His name is Gleve. The last any of us heard, he was captured by a group of your soldiers at a bridge in the Eastlands."

"Ah yes, I remember," the King said. "I will have someone check."

The Little Dragons

In the presence of row upon row of suffering men, Maida and Jessa were able to set aside their grief and become Healers first. An hour or so into the day, there was a disturbance at the door. A guard stepped in and asked for Princess Liandra. Maida rose and let out a small squeak, for behind the guard stood Gleve. He was dirty, thin and hollow-eyed. Maida, who was dirty, thin and hollow-eyed herself, flew across the room to embrace him. When they were finally able to separate themselves to arm's length, Gleve said, "So, can you forgive me?"

"Oh Gleve," she said, "I forgave you a long time ago, and then, when we all wondered if you were dead, I was so sorry I hadn't had the chance to tell you." He closed his eyes for a moment. "Oh," she said, "And you'll want to know, your friend Keiran is at the Healers School, last I heard, well and waiting there for word of you."

"Keiran," Gleve whispered. "I had no idea. I thought he was lost." He passed his ragged sleeve over his eyes.

When he opened them, Maida introduced him to Jessa, and all three, the call of Healing stronger than grief and exhaustion, turned back to the fearsome work that waited all around them.

149 ANGLEWART

A week later, the King visited the infirmary where the wounded were being attended to by at least twenty of the Earth People's Healers. A group of them had arrived the night after Locheil's funeral and Maida's sudden arrival among them. The day before, Eldrin had overseen the butchering of a steer at the execution field and Maida had invited the Dragons to feast. Eldrin and Gleve had then led a group of soldiers into the woods, where the hunt for the plant they sought was far easier in daylight than it would have been with lanterns.

Jessa had created a well-organized system. The salve was produced and applied, each Healer, assisted by a Sister from the Women's Retreat House, took responsibility for a small group of men. They laid their hands on their patients' heads and feet, saying their strange prayers. Not a man had died since then, and most were recovering quickly. Now the need was for strong soldiers to assist with the healing men's efforts to learn to walk again.

Moving from bed to bed on his own walking stick, the King gave what encouragement he could to the injured men. One man, struggling with a new set of crutches, said, "If you can make it back onto your feet, Your Highness, so can I." This became a theme, until the King realized the best encouragement he could give was his own survival.

He noticed Farrell before his youngest son noticed him. The young man was working with an middle-aged Earth People Healer. He was on his knees and seemed to be bandaging the ankle of a man sitting in a chair, under the Healer's direction, judging by how often he paused and looked up at the man.

When the King approached the little group, the patient saw him first and slid to the front of the chair, obviously about to kneel on the floor. "No, stay there," Anglewart said. "I know what it's like to have trouble moving." After a moment, the man sat back and settled for bowing his head.

Farrell by now had risen. "My Lord," he said, "These Witch Healers are good." He glanced at the old man he was helping. "Earth People Healers, I mean. Father, this is Father Thom. I've been assigned to be his assistant."

"Your Highness," the man said, bowing his head.

"I hope my son is serving you well."

"He is, your Highness, and I am grateful for him."

The King looked at the shining face of his younger son. Perhaps his gifts lay elsewhere than in the military after all. Unheard of that a son of the royal family should not be a soldier but, perhaps, a different kind of soldier. Could there not be healers in the army?

MELISANDE

Melisande knocked on the King's study door. Delight crossed his worried face when he saw her. After checking the hall and closing the door, he bent to kiss her. She blushed. "You shouldn't do that," she said. "I shouldn't do that."

"No one can see."

"You never know."

He grinned at her, a quick flash of the high-spirited young man she had married. He also waved his hand toward a chair by the fire. After ordering two cups of wine, he sat in the opposite one himself. "How are you faring, my dear? I know your grief weighs on you in secret, as it does me."

"That's the hard part, isn't it?" Melisande held her wine cup between her hands, staring down into the ruby liquid it contained. "When Ortrude died I wore mourning and everyone honoured my grief with sympathy and silence. With both Torrie and Leandra …" She paused because her throat had closed. He moved his chair next to hers and laid his hand on her arm. A few minutes later, she looked up at him, smiling slightly, but with glistening eyes. "Thank you," she said.

"With Torrie and Leandra?" he prompted her.

"Yes, with Torrie and Leandra, I must carry my grief around in my heart like a secret."

He sighed. "I know exactly what you mean. Although I can publicly mourn Torrie, I too, carry my sadness for our beautiful Leandra in my inner heart."

She turned her hand upward and grasped his. They sat in quiet sadness for some time. Eventually, she freed her hand and took a sip of her wine. "Have you thought about your re-marriage?" she asked.

"As little as possible," he said.

She clucked her tongue at him.

"I'm not going to remarry, Mel. I can't bear the thought."

"What about the Rodolphs?"

"I'm putting off being definite with them. They seem to accept that I won't marry my son's widow, and they've taken her back into their family castle."

"Thank goodness. She would have been a disaster at the Women's Retreat House."

"Yes, and too young to be entombed there. She will eventually find another husband. Meanwhile, I'm taking every opportunity to display my crippled gait to her father. I'm hoping he just decides I'm too old."

"In fact, I've heard they are turning their attention to Eldrin."

Just then the wine arrived. Anglewart thanked the servant who delivered it and asked him to shut the door again on his way out. He then picked up the conversation where it left off: "Eldrin, poor boy. He's about as keen on marrying as he is on being King."

"How is he doing at learning to govern?"

Anglewart sighed. "Not well. His mind isn't on it. He forgets things. I have to repeat myself over and over."

The former queen looked thoughtful. "Actually, that is what I came to talk to you about, the succession. I have an idea." Anglewart took a sip of wine, waiting for her to continue. "Isn't it time, perhaps, for the Realms to see their first Queen?"

Anglewart choked on his wine. When he had recovered, he said, "Oh no, my dear. The Realms are far from ready to accept that."

"Even one who saved an army from a Dragon attack? And is rumoured to be a Dragon Princess, even though we know she's not?"

"Mel, dear …"

She cut him off. "No. Listen to me. I've been watching her run the infirmary. She is authoritative, efficient and is succeeding at keeping peaceful relations among some very different groups: soldiers, Sisters and Earth People Healers. She is earning a reputation for good listening and fair decisions. Jessa is the one that has inherited the best of your gifts as King."

"Oh for the Warrior God's sake, Mel, my dear, you are mad." Anglewart sounded exasperated, but Melisande knew him well enough to know that the seed had been planted.

151 MAIDA

The infirmary was shrinking. Some of the men had returned to partial duties in the army, or moved to other King's service. Many had gone to their homes to recuperate further. Only the most disabled still remained, receiving care and daily lessons to learn to walk, or at least care for themselves.

Maida was hiding her rounding belly with loose clothing. She had also begun to hear a small, sibilant voice in her head. Her Little Dragon's name was Hermagloxian, and when Maida was figuring out what to do for one of her patients, he would whisper clues to her. He also reported the activities and thoughts of Glenardinaliat, Roxtrianatrix and the other Dragons. Through Hermagloxian, the Dragons had begun to make requests for meat when they were hungry. The King had finally agreed to give Eldrin the job of developing a large cattle farm where he could breed horses as well. His place at the King's side was gradually being filled by Jessa as her duties at the infirmary decreased. Jessa had confessed to Maida one night that Anglewart had talked to her about the possibility of becoming Queen, not a consort Queen, but the actual ruler of the Westlands. He wasn't sure, though, that the people could accept that. Neither was she.

Despite the painful shocks that Maida sometimes felt when she looked at Jessa, or heard her addressed as Princess Liandra, they had become friends, bonded by their commitment to the injured men in their care and their determination to overcome the many conflicts that had come up between their two very different peoples working side by side in the infirmary.

As Maida sat alone in her room, sipping tea in preparation for sleep, Hermagloxian whispered into her thoughts: "Maaaaaida. Maaaaaida. It's time."

She nodded, although he couldn't see her. "To leave for the Healers' School?"

"Yesssss. Time. Harder to hide me. And we need time to learn. Quiet time. Ssecret time."

Maida had instinctively known, when she told Liandra's story to her family, that this part of it must be left out. "I know."

"Roxtrianatrix come too. Learn with usssss."

"He wants to come?" This news gave Maida more pleasure than she had felt in a long time.

"Call Glenardinaliat. Take usssss."

"You'll tell him where we want to go?"

"Yesssss. Or you send him picture, where you want to go. He see your mind."

"Through you?"

"No, just you, him."

"Oh."

"Go tomorrow?"

"There are a few things to finish up here, but we'll go soon. I promise."

"Go sssssssssssoon."

Two weeks later, Glendardiliat carred Maida to the Healing School. Roxtrianatrix and Alethilion flew beside her most of the way. She had the golden Dragon put her down on the Barrens, so as not to frighten everyone, and walked the rest of the way. As soon as she arrived, word spread faster than she could have believed possible. Among the first to arrive was Aymeric. He swept Maida into his arms and turned her in a circle. "Be careful, Rafe, I mean, Aymeric," she squealed with the breath she had left from his hug. "Put me down." He did, but his grin continued to be visible, towering over the mass of bodies that poured from every doorway, greeting and kissing her from all sides. The story of her recent months in the capital city of the Westlands came tumbling out in response to many questions.

Mother Sarah presided over an impromtu celebratory meal in the Dining Hall. Maida searched the benches from her place at the head table. Finally she leaned toward Mother Tess, who sat beside her, to ask over the clatter of pottery and cutlery, "Where is Mother Peg?"

Tess chuckled, "Oh my dear," she said, "Peg is trying to set a new record for the longest snit ever. She has been studying and taking meals in her room for months and associates with the rest of us as little as possible, especially me and Sarah.”

“Why? You’ve been friends forever.”

“We told her off, child. For her arrogance, for turning Keiran and Aymeric away when they arrived …”

“She did?”

“She did, and finally, for belittling your gifts all these years, using you as a servant, never taking you on as a full Apprentice.”

“You said that?”

“Surely after what you have done in the past few months, you cannot say that you don’t know about your considerable gifts as a Healer.”

“No, I guess not.”

“You would have believed in yourself all along if Mother Peg had.”

After the meal, Maida accompanied Sarah, Tess and Nell to Mother Sarah’s room. She told them the rest of the story. They marveled at her descriptions of the Dragon Priestesses’ School, wept with her as she recounted Liandra’s death, and rejoiced at her news that she would be the next to bear a Little Dragon and Liandra’s Roxtrianatrix would come to learn with them. All three of the Old Ones kissed her and hugged her again and again before she succeeded in departing from the room. An Apprentice showed her to her own quarters but, tired as she was, she did not enter.

Maida found Mother Peg sitting in a chair by her fire. She had aged since her hopeful departure for the Healing School with Liandra and Roxtrianatrix. Maida gave the old Healer an abbreviated version of the story she had told Nell, Tess and Sarah. She tried to read the old woman’s eyes, hoping to find regret there but seeing only impatience. “So, you’re to be the second Dragon Priestess,” Peg said.

“Aren’t you glad?” Maida asked.

Reluctantly, Peg turned to face her. “Of course,” she said. “How soon are you due?”

“Four months, I figure.”

“I guess you’ll have Tess or old Sarah for your midwife.”

Ah, so that’s what was bothering the old woman. “I don’t think they’re experienced enough,” Maida said.

Peg pinned her wth those black, raisin eyes in the old way. “What are you talking about? They are the most experienced midwives alive.”

The Little Dragons

"They've never delivered a Little Dragon, have they?" Maida smiled.

Peg looked surprised for a moment, then, at least for someone who knew her as well as Maida did, a little satisfaction crept over her wrinkled face. "Well," she said. "Well then."

ACKNOWLEDGEMENTS

Thank you to Nina and Jan for reading the drafts. Writing can be a lonely craft. Your comments and encouragement are deeply apprecated.

And to Amy, for the cover, frontpiece and the beautiful little dragon that curls around the chapter numbers. It was fun to work with you and a joy to watch your artistic gift unfolding.

I live in Mi'kma'ki, the unceded territory of the Mi'kmaw people. I am grateful to my Mi'kmaw and other Indigenous friends and colleagues for all you have taught me.

The Author

Rowan Starsmith is the fantasy pseudonym of Anne Bishop, author of seven non-fiction books, including *Becoming an Ally*. First published in 1994, *Becoming an Ally* is in its third edition and has sold more than 30,000 copies in five countries. She is also the author of a novel, *Under the Bridge*, published in 2019. She can be found at *annebishop.ca*.

The Illustrator

Amy McDonald is an illustrator and graduate of the Video Game Design program at Fanshawe College in London, Ontario.

"Growing up in the fields of southern Ontario, you find ways to kill the time. One day I picked up a pencil and never put it down. Over the years, I have been lucky enough to study from a variety of masters. Their time and conglomerated knowledge has made me into the artist I am today. I usually work as a mixed media artist, pulling techniques and abilities from multiple art forms. I combine my skills, with a great understanding of colour, to create a truly unique viewer experience."